"Ma'am? I'm asked to speak to a

He walked across the dirt floor of the barn to stand in front of her. The woman gazed up from under a mop of auburn curls, revealing the most amazing gray-green eyes he'd ever seen. All of a sudden missing out on his barista didn't seem like such a big deal. Her feet didn't quite meet the ground from her seat atop the wooden chest, so she had to jump down to stand. All five feet four inches of her slender build reached his chin.

She offered her hand. "Emily Conners," she stammered. "Sorry, this is my first...um, I'm not sure what the protocol is in this sort of circumstance." Trying to ease the tension, he shook her hand. She was trembling. Why wasn't she wearing a jacket?

"Ms. Conners, my condolences. This must have been quite a shock, finding your friend's body."

****

Emily pulled her hand out of his grasp with a weary sigh. She recognized the tall, arrogant type from the moment she saw him. He even draped himself in the same type of designer suit that her ex-husband favored. True, it looked a lot better on the detective than it ever did on Nick, but clearly, the two of them were cut from the same literal and figurative cloth.

"You can save your smarmy charms for someone else. I'm not crazy. There's no way that horse kicked Pamela to death."

Cause For Elimination

by

Marla A. White

Cause For Elimination

Cover Art by *Diana Carlile*

The Wild Rose Press, Inc.
PO Box 708
Adams Basin, NY 14410-0708
Visit us at www.thewildrosepress.com

Publishing History
First Edition, 2022
Trade Paperback ISBN 978-1-5092-4299-3
Digital ISBN 978-1-5092-4300-6

Published in the United States of America

Dedication

To all the horses who taught me so much, you are always in my heart. Thanks especially to Tequila and her other moms Susan and Peggy. Plus, a loving thank you to Peggy Savage, who got us all started.

Acknowledgments

First and foremost, my heartfelt thanks to everyone who made this possible.

My eventing friends, including Nahmi and Carolyn, who introduced me to this crazy sport, as well as Larry, Jen, Stephanie, Suz, Susan, and so many more who encouraged me along the way. Although I had to step away for the moment, I've never lost the love for riding.

My gratitude to the Friday Night Book Club – Carolyn, Bekah and Jo – without whom I would never have made it to "The End." Also to my Beta readers especially Jen, who pushed me to make Dennis and therefore myself a better person.

Chapter One

Alone in the spacious public barn, Emily Conners tried not to think about the body at the end of the aisle. Dust motes swirled around her in the dim, early morning light as she drummed the worn heels of her ankle-high paddock boots on the large wooden tack box she used as a bench. *God, what an awful way to start the day.* Of course, not as awful as it had been for Pamela Yates, whose bits of brain and gore clung to the toe of her weathered leather shoe.

She couldn't remember the last time she'd cleaned her boots, let alone polished them. There had been a time when things like that mattered to her. Now layers of mud and dust collected on the dried, cracked leather, along with whatever she'd stepped on in Feneatha's stall with a nauseating squish.

Good job, Em, step on your boss's brains.

The memory of Pamela, or what was left of her, laying in stall thirty-eight made Emily's vision slide again for a moment. She gripped the edge of the tack trunk, determined not to faint. *Not now.* Not when all that stood between the little gray mare and a syringe of whatever they used to kill horses these days was her.

She folded her arms and huddled against the bite of the January wind. The cold sliced right through her threadbare work shirt and sweater but failed to penetrate the wooly layer around her brain.

1

Who could have killed Pamela?

Did they really mean to frame the horse for the crime? Or was it serendipity that the cops who arrived in response to her 911 call assumed her boss had been kicked to death by the horse, then called Animal Control to have the 'vicious' animal destroyed?

No one who understood anything about horses would have jumped to that conclusion.

No, Emily was certain the only animal capable of the brutality done to Pamela was the two-legged kind.

She glanced up at the collection of uniformed cops who had arranged themselves across the barn aisle wide enough to drive a truck through. In the soft light, the tall, balding one reminded her of the actor who'd starred in the old TV show *ER*. This being LA, maybe it really was him. A giggle escaped, despite her efforts to bite it back. *You are definitely losing it, Conners.*

Possibly, taking the pill she found in Pam's desk hadn't been such a good idea. For Feneatha's sake, she willed herself to keep her shit together until the detective arrived.

****

Justin Butler could have satisfied his need for a tall, strong drip coffee at any of the dozens of designer coffee shops he passed, but he was too irritated to enjoy a cup now. He normally stopped at the Brew House near the station where the tall, blonde barista with the slightly crooked eye tooth worked. But no, he had to go to the Los Angeles Equestrian Center and talk to a drama queen who had demanded an investigation into what was an unfortunate accident. The disturbance to his morning ritual, which also screwed up his plan to ask the blonde out, left him cranky and sullen. Why him? As a member of L.A.'s elite Robbery-Homicide Division, he handled high-profile cases, not freakish mishaps. Why didn't his boss, Lieutenant Placer, give the handholding/shoulder-to-cry-on gig to someone else? Someone who didn't already have the murder of a city commissioner's son on his desk?

He got why RHD caught this 'death by horse' case. Every movie producer, real estate mogul, and reality star who boarded their horses at the large equestrian facility had learned about the death minutes after the police, then woke up the mayor with frantic phone calls. Worried about the safety of their children/spouse/partner who rode at the Center, they demanded police action. Since RHD was the best, the mayor assigned the case to them personally. Justin suspected the lieutenant had passed the task on to him because Placer resented the way rich people got special treatment and considered Justin one of 'those people.' Sticking him with the case must have seemed like poetic justice.

With a couple of half-assed centering breaths, he tried finding his calm, peaceful place his *dojo* master lectured him about as he turned onto the Equestrian Center's tree-lined driveway. Instead of serenity, a growl of frustration rose as he realized he had no idea where in the seventy-five-acre park filled with dozens of barns and arenas he was supposed to go. Then he saw the black-and-whites parked in front of one of three huge wooden barns just off the driveway. *Bingo.* He pulled into a parking spot and stepped out of his car, only to squash a not quite dry pile of horseshit with his favorite pair of Italian loafers. Great, his morning was now complete.

Inside, one of the unis filled him in on the situation. "Sorry to call you in on this, sir, but the lady over there refused to let Animal Control take custody of the horse until she talked to a homicide detective."

The cop shrugged, embarrassed by the whole thing. Justin dialed back his scowl. None of this was their fault. He peered down the dimly lit aisle of the barn and found the current bane of his existence, sitting on a large wooden box. What startled him was that she studied him right back. There was a shaken air about her. Could be the shock of finding a dead body, but her glassy expression struck him as odd.

"Ma'am? I'm Detective Butler. I understand you asked to speak to a homicide detective?"

He walked across the dirt floor of the barn to stand in front of her. The woman gazed up from under a mop of auburn curls, revealing the most amazing gray-green eyes he'd ever seen. All of a sudden, missing out on his barista didn't seem like such a big deal. Her feet didn't quite meet the ground from her seat atop the wooden chest, so she had to jump down to stand. All five feet four inches of her slender build reached his chin.

She offered her hand. "Emily Conners," she stammered. "Sorry, this is my first...um, I'm not sure what the protocol is in this sort of circumstance." Trying to ease the tension, he shook her hand. She was trembling. *Why wasn't she wearing a jacket?*

"Ms. Conners, my condolences. This must have been quite a shock, finding your friend's body."

****

Emily pulled her hand out of his grasp with a weary sigh. She recognized the tall, arrogant type from the moment she saw him. He even draped himself in the same type of designer suit that her ex-husband favored. True, it looked a lot better on the detective than it ever did on Nick, but clearly the two of them were cut from the same literal and figurative cloth.

"You can save your smarmy charms for someone else. I'm not crazy. There's no way that horse kicked Pamela to death."

"No one is saying you're crazy, Ms. Conners," he explained in a tone which implied exactly the opposite. "I understand how difficult this must be for you, but as you must be aware, horses can be unpredictable. Isn't it possible your friend—"

"Her name was Pamela Yates. I'm—was, I guess—her assistant."

"Excuse me, ma'am, of course. Isn't it possible Miss Yates startled the horse, and the animal kicked out as a natural response, injuring her and causing her death?"

Injured? Pamela's brains were on the wall. On three of them, as a matter of fact. "Have you actually *seen* her body, detective?"

"I thought it would be best if we talked first."

The man's soothing voice made her want to scream. Instead, she fought to maintain a reasonable tone of her own. The last thing she needed was to antagonize him, erasing all hope of keeping Feneatha off the endangered species list.

"Why don't we do this," she said, keeping the *you patronizing, pompous ass* comment to herself. "Why don't we take a look at the...at her...at the stall." *If it doesn't put too much of a dent in your morning, detective, sir.*

Emily clenched her fist so hard that her fingernails

bit into her palm. "If after seeing her you decide it was an accident, I'll move aside and let Animal Control do their job."

"Fair enough," the detective agreed and followed her down the barn aisle to an open stall.

"I swapped the mare to another stall so she wouldn't keep stepping in...on..." Her hands fluttered, dreading the scene that awaited them.

Pamela lay sprawled on her back a few feet inside the enclosed space. Afraid to speak for fear the bile rising in her throat would come spewing out, she gestured at the wall. Bits of brain, bone, hair, and blood speckled the polished wood planks. Poor Pamela must have been standing almost exactly where Emily stood now when something hit her face so hard it left nothing recognizable behind.

An icy chill that had nothing to do with the weather caused her to tremble. The detective took off his coat and wrapped it around her shoulders. She'd given up her own jacket to cover the pulpy remains of Pamela's head in a sentimental gesture she'd almost come to regret. Dammit, she really liked that jacket. This time, when the cop gave her shoulder a comforting squeeze, she didn't pull away.

"Sometimes I didn't even like her, you know?" she whispered as unwanted tears rolled down her cheeks. "But no one deserves..."

Unable to finish, she huddled tight against the detective's chest.

****

Justin held her close, hoping to keep her from seeing what his practiced eye recognized immediately. The pattern of gore continued in a graceful, macabre arc onto the ceiling and the opposite wall. The blood splatter was a classic pattern created by a heavy object being swung at a head and bursting it like an over-ripe melon. Even if the horse had kicked her, the motion would have been straight back, splattering the blood in one direction. Unless the horse knew Tae Bo, it didn't kill the woman.

"I'm afraid the good and the bad news is I agree with you, Ms. Conners. Pamela Yates was murdered."

Chapter Two

"Land of eternal sunshine, my ass."

Exiled from his home for four years now, Detective Dennis Ames bitterly resented Los Angeles for not being Philadelphia as he entered the barn, slogging through the chilly January morning. Conveniently forgetting about the snow back home, he peered down with a sneer.

Fantastic, a dirt floor dotted with piles of hay and crap. He'd never been inside a building in Philly that sported a dirt, hay, and crap covered floor. Not while he was sober, anyway.

Juggling two steaming Styrofoam cups of coffee, he wove his way through various technicians swarming the stall, taking pictures and prints of the crime scene. Farther down the barn aisle, he spotted a familiar looking coat hanging off the thin, frail woman leaning against the wall. Just like Jay, giving up his coat to another damsel in distress. He shook his head, grateful he didn't suffer from the same delusions of knighthood as his partner.

Across from where she stood was another open stall door. Figuring Jay wouldn't stray far from his expensive coat, he took a gander inside. The room was a stall like all the others, only instead of a horse, it housed a desk, file cabinet, and couch. A small flat-screen TV was mounted on the wall, and a cheap rug covered the floor. Justin sat at the desk, his latex-glove covered hands resting on the scarred metal surface. It had taken a while, but somewhere in their four-year partnership, Ames came to appreciate Justin's method of communing with the dead, or whatever he called it, at the start of every case. At first, he'd given him a rash of shit over the ritual, getting their partnership off to a rocky start, but since he closed more cases than older, more experienced detectives, Dennis learned to keep his mouth shut. Almost.

"Getting any news flashes?" He handed Justin the spare cup of coffee in his hand. "Because this horse stuff is way out of my comfort zone. The sooner we solve this and move on, the better."

He accepted the coffee with a grateful nod. "Sorry, if the victim is here, she's keeping her opinions to herself. Looks like we're going to have to do the detecting on our own. There's no computer." He picked up a fistful of random, loose papers. "And from this mess, it seems she was definitely old school. There are bills from a veterinarian and receipts from a feed store. Nothing that jumps out as incriminating, but we'll have to go through them to be sure."

Dennis snapped on his own set of gloves and gestured toward the woman standing just outside the stall-cum-office. "Nice coat she's got on. Didn't you used to have one like it?"

"That's Emily Conners. She found the body."

"And so what, it's a new gimmick? Everyone who reports a murder wins a free Blueberry coat?"

"It's a Bu—never mind, you philistine. What was I supposed to do? We took her coat and shoes as evidence."

Dennis wanted to say, *you mind your own business and solve the crime, not take every hard-luck case you see under your wing*. Nobody, not even Justin, had big enough wings to take in all the strays they met in this line of work. Instead, he left it alone. It was a lesson every cop had to learn for themselves.

Justin ignored his unspoken disapproval and took a sip of coffee. Instantly, his face scrunched up in an expression of pure horror.

"Don't blame me. It was the only coffee I could find around here," Dennis said while he checked out the office. "Hey, you take the horse out of the stall, add a ceiling fan, crappy furniture from the local office supply store, and a phone and you've got—a stall minus a horse."

"People who live in glass cubicles," his partner countered. "I kind of like the Feng Shui, it's very grounding, especially with the window—"

"Yeah, yeah, it's facing south and angled toward the moon, whatever," he scoffed. "This place would have to give off enough good karmic vibes to win the freaking lottery for me to work here. Flies, horses shitting right outside your door? I'll take my cubicle any day." He didn't know L.A. had stables until this morning and hadn't felt deprived by the gaping hole in his life experience.

Justin surrendered the debate with a laugh. "All right, Martha Stewart, what about you? Find anything besides this cup of enamel remover?"

Back to business, Ames pulled out his notebook and recited what he'd learned. "A groom confirmed what Ms. Conners told you. Pamela Yates, forty-two, was supposed to be out of town at a place called

Kinsale Downs near Temecula until Monday. No one has any idea why she came back early, and naturally, nobody saw or heard anything."

"Of course not."

"There's a security guy we're tracking down who is here overnight, mostly to keep an eye on the horses. Can you believe some of these nags are worth half a million bucks? His boss says it's unlikely he saw anything, or he would have reported it. I sent a uniform to get a statement, to be sure. I did learn an interesting tidbit about Ms. Conners." He put his notebook away, possessing a perfect memory for gossip. "She took a pretty nasty spill about six months ago while riding one of Ms. Yates's horses. She attempted to jump some big-ass log and the horse fell, crushing Conners underneath it. The grooms mostly speak broken English, but if I remember my high school Spanish, she broke about a dozen bones, including her neck, and only came back to work a couple of months ago."

Justin rested his chin on his fist, seeming to mull over the information. "Wow. So she's gutsy."

"Gutsy enough to bludgeon a person to death?" Ames pondered. "She was riding the horse for Ms. Yates when it squashed her. Maybe she held her responsible?"

"You didn't see the body." Justin shook his head. "Whoever did this got very messy in the process."

"Maybe that's why she put her coat over the body, to hide the fact there was blood on it?"

"I checked—the sleeves of the jacket are clean. I'm telling you, the killer whaled on the victim. Blood would have covered their face, hands, and hair when they finally stopped, and considering the body was still

11

warm when I got here, Ms. Conners didn't have time to clean up before calling it in.

"Besides, to kill like this, you've got to have a lot of rage going on. I don't get the impression Ms. Conners has it in her."

"All right, Obi-Wan, you win. One suspect down, another four million to go." Dennis had worked with him too long not to trust his instincts. "So what do you want to hit first, business contacts or personal?" he asked as he plopped onto the dusty fake leather couch. A mouse dashed out from underneath and ran over his shoe. "Jesus H," he yelped, leaping to his feet.

Reacting to Justin's poorly hidden snigger, he kicked the couch in revenge for housing the little bugger. The piece of furniture skidded enough to reveal a small white box plugged into the outlet hidden behind the couch. "Huh. Look what we got here."

Justin raised a brow. "Find the weapon?"

"We should be so lucky. It's the Wi-Fi bridge for one of those DIY spy cams." He locked his gaze with Justin's. "Which means there should be at least one camera somewhere close by."

"It might have recorded the killer. Bag it and get it to the tech guys to check the video." Justin stalked out of the office door, giving instructions over his shoulder. "Oh and tell them to search the victim's phone for an app or a subscription in her name to store the video. I'll get the unis to comb the area for cameras."

"Yeah, I get how spy cams work," Dennis called after his partner, but he'd already disappeared down the barn aisle. "Sometimes you're such an asshole."

****

After sending the officers searching for cameras

inside and outside the barn, Justin noticed the Conners woman lingering around the scene like a specter. Although the rising sun had brought slightly warmer temperatures, she leaned against the wall, hunched deeper into his coat. Across the way, men and women brushed horses before putting saddles on them.

Each gave Conners a wide berth, keeping their eyes averted as they passed her as though they might be found guilty by association, but she took no notice. He treaded toward her carefully, sensing she was at a breaking point. "Ms. Conners, do you know anything about the security cameras Ms. Yates had set up around the barn?"

"Hidden cameras?" She glanced up, her gray-green eyes dull and unfocused. "Sounds like Pamela, but she never mentioned it to me. Maybe in the tack room? There's a lot of expensive saddles and bridles in there, and three barns nearby have had break-ins."

"Thank you. If you think of anything else, don't hesitate to call." He pulled a business card out of his wallet and handed it to her. "Would you like us to call someone to take you home? Or I can have one of the officers give you a ride if you'd like."

"Yeah, a police car dropping me off at my apartment is exactly what I need," she said with a bitter laugh. "Thank you, detective, but I have to get Pam's horses out." She glanced at her feet, now sporting a pair of clunky leather clogs someone must have loaned her. They were at least one size too big. "I mean, I can't ride at the moment since you took my shoes. But I can at least turn them out and feed them. I'm just waiting for your people to finish up."

"Is there anyone else who could do that for you?

Finding a body would traumatize anyone," he suggested. Judging from the way her jeans sagged off her rail-thin body, she'd been on a slippery slope long before Pamela's murder.

"It's my job, detective, I'm—"

"Sir," a uni called from down the barn aisle near the crime scene, "we've found a camera."

"Excuse me, ma'am." Justin turned away from her and strode to the stall where the uniformed cop waited for him. A familiar face poked out of the open top half of the stall door—the gray horse initially accused of murdering Pamela Yates. He could swear the horse twisted its lips into a wicked sneer.

"That's the problem, sir," the cop explained sheepishly. "We haven't been able to get inside to investigate."

Dennis joined them to survey the situation but made no move to volunteer for camera retrieval duty. With a doomed groan, Justin slid the heavy wooden door open. The little gray horse reacted by pacing back and forth. He took a measured step inside, only to jump back as an enormous set of teeth snapped at him with lightning speed. "Holy hell."

Dennis leaned over the half-door to give him a nudge from behind. "Keep going. You nearly got the camera."

Justin glowered, noticing his partner wasn't setting foot in the stall with the attacking horse.

Ames grinned. "Hey, no need for both of us to get horse crap on our shoes."

On his second attempt, he managed to edge his way to the back of the stall. Stretching to his full height, he removed the tiny remote camera from its hiding place among the pigeon droppings and cobwebs. The small, black cylindrical device was one of those motion-activated wireless cameras anyone could order off the Internet, and depending on where it was focused, it might have caught the murder in the stall across the aisle. The optimist in him hoped the case would be that easy to solve and turned to leave the stall with a bounce in his step until he realized the horse had set him up. It now stood between him and the door, ears pinned flat against its head, snorting and glaring at its prey—him.

"What are you doing to that mare?"

Emily Connors pushed past Dennis to enter the stall. The horse gave Justin one last sneer before turning its innocent, puppy dog eyes toward the woman.

"What am I doing?" he barked back at her. "It's trying to kill me."

She patted the horse. "Feneatha, you naughty girl. You've scared the big, strong policeman half to death."

He found her sarcasm mildly less irritating than the fact that the mare was the picture of sweetness and light in front while cocking a hind leg to kick him. "That thing has got serious issues. Are you sure it isn't dangerous?"

She escorted him out of the stall, but the mare got the last word, giving out a huge, wet snort that flung snot all over his suit and the expensive trench coat Ms. Conners still wore. Giving the horse one more pat, she latched the stall door, then attacked him like a mama bear protecting her cub. "She's scared. What's your excuse? What were you doing in there in the first place?"

"Retrieving this." He held up the small camera.

"You mentioned a hidden camera seemed like something Ms. Yates would do. Why? Is the horse that's normally in that stall worth watching?"

She shook her head. "Pam hasn't kept a horse in there for months. I meant a hidden camera to spy on people wouldn't surprise me."

"The unis didn't find any other cameras in the area," Dennis informed him. "So why have the only security camera focused on an empty stall?"

"Let's hope the tech guys can tell us once they pull the video off it," he said as he handed the camera to his partner.

"We don't need this. All the footage is in the sync module I found in the office or stored on the cloud."

The news, delivered without a hint of a smirk and an expression the very picture of piety, pissed Justin off even more. "Then why did I risk my life retrieving it?"

Ignoring the rhetorical question, Dennis offered Emily his hand. "Detective Ames, ma'am. I'll be working on this case with Detective Butler. Would anyone else have known about the camera? Perhaps one of the horse owners?"

Emily shrugged. "If Pamela had hidden cameras put up, she wouldn't have told anyone. You can't keep a secret in a barn."

"Evidently Ms. Yates could," Justin replied.

****

Emily frowned, wondering if Pamela hid this, what else had she kept from her? The things she did know were bad enough.

"Emily!"

The shrill screech of her name jolted her out of her dark musings. Lord, that woman's voice could carry. A headache and Kate Williams arrived hand in hand.

The fireplug-shaped woman marched down the aisle as if she owned the place, making a beeline for the detectives. Word of fresh blood coming to the barn sure got around fast, particularly if it involved an attractive man. Kate was freshly showered, her bottled blonde hair shellacked into place, and—was she wearing perfume?

She wrapped a strong, pudgy arm around Emily. "Seeing her like that must have been so awful, you poor thing." She broke off the hug to push her away, scrutinizing her at arm's length. "You look dreadful, even more ghostly than usual."

Kate meant well, but the woman had a knack for saying the wrong thing. She put her hand on Emily's back and shoved her to the door. "Now, don't you worry about a thing. I'll take care of poor Pamela's horses and call her clients to let them know what happened. You go home and get some rest."

Slumping in resignation, Emily shuffled toward the parking lot. Kate usually got what she wanted.

****

Wearing a demure smile, Kate introduced herself while scolding the two detectives. "Shame on you, grilling our Emily. As if the poor girl doesn't have enough trouble already. You know her husband, Deputy District Attorney Nick Conners, left her for a younger woman? Things haven't been easy for her since the divorce."

The two cops exchanged pointed glances. Even ex-wives of deputy district attorneys were treated with kid gloves. The dirt, gleefully dished up by the gleaming-eyed Kate Williams, compelled Justin to make sure Ms.

Conners was all right to drive home.

Remembering how his partner set him up with the camera, he plastered on a charming smile. "I'll be right back, ma'am. In the meantime, Detective Ames here will be happy to take your statement." He hurried after Ms. Conners, pretending not to see the finger Dennis flashed him.

Out in the parking lot, he was surprised to see Conners fumbling with the lock of a 1960s pickup. The macho, classic truck, with its white and mint green paint job accented with rust-free chrome, didn't sync with the diminutive woman trying to unlock the door. And who keeps a vintage vehicle like that hidden under layers of dirt? The screech of metal against metal brought his focus back to the woman. Her hands shook so violently, she missed the lock and dropped her keys.

"Ms. Conners, are you sure you're all right?"

Ignoring the keys still on the ground, she stumbled to the front of the truck, sank onto the bumper, and threw up.

Chapter Three

Kate buzzed around the tiny apartment, an annoying whirlwind of helpfulness while Emily lay on her couch, curled in the fetal position and regretting ever letting that cop talk her into this. She liked Kate, but right now, she just wanted to be alone. The noisy ransacking of her kitchen cupboards pulled at her already frayed nerves. If she had the energy, she would have begged her to go home, but another wave of nausea threatened to overwhelm her.

"My God," Kate bellowed, needlessly considering she stood less than six feet away. "No food in your cupboards and nothing but Diet Coke and beer in your refrigerator. How do you live like this? I mean, sweetie, you aren't a kid anymore."

She blew by, tossing a cold gel pack in Emily's general direction before moving on to rummage around in the bathroom. Em slipped the cold pack behind her neck, letting the icy coolness soothe the ever-present ache, a reminder of the screws and rods the doctors had used to fuse her broken vertebrae and stabilize her spine. Drugs helped dull the constant throbbing, but the only time she completely forgot about it was this morning when she saw Pam's body.

A weight suddenly landed next to her curled up legs, and for the first time all day, she smiled. Samwise Gamgee, her tuxedo cat, nestled up against her and

19

offered the soothing comfort of his purrs. She scratched his chin, turning up his volume another notch.

"No ibuprofen?" Kate called from the bathroom. The sound of drawers opening and slamming shut didn't cover her grunt of disgust. "Don't you have any kind of pain killers at all? Not even for cramps?"

Not here, anyway. Back at the barn was another story. "Sorry."

After she called 911, Emily cleaned out the various prescriptions Pam kept stashed in her desk and threw them in her tack trunk before the cops arrived. She'd meant to abscond with a bottle, but the detective's watchful eye prevented a move in that direction.

"I already took something at the barn. I'm fine."

Kate reappeared in the small living room, a can of diet cola in one hand and an odd assortment of tablets in a variety of colors in the other. "Here, I had these in my purse. Take 'em honey. After what you saw today, you'll need it."

"No, really. The pills I took are pretty potent."

"Which you barfed up," Kate scoffed, as if throwing up was a sign of weakness. "Besides, a little vitamin V never killed anyone. And who needs to be relaxed more than you right now? I mean, you're out of a job, your boss got herself murdered, and it's anyone's guess whether the police consider you a suspect."

Was she a suspect? The idea never occurred to her. *Holy shit*. Kate offered the pills and soda again which Emily gratefully accepted.

"Don't worry about your truck, I called Nick, and he's going to take care of it for you." Kate patted her knee on each of the last words for emphasis.

Could this day get any worse? "Why did you call

my ex-husband? This is none of his concern."

"Oh, nonsense. Just because he left you doesn't mean he stopped caring. He sounded very upset when I told him what happened."

Worried about the damn truck is more like it.

On top of everything else, she had another lecture from Nick about getting a regular job to look forward to. The old *at thirty-five it was time she re-joined the world of grownups and stopped playing with ponies* speech. Emily sunk lower onto the couch, vowing never to answer the phone again.

With a satisfied grunt, Kate stood, patted Em on the head, and opened the front door. "You rest now, sweetie. I'll take care of everything back at the barn."

Samwise nestled closer. It wasn't until she made room for him in the rich folds of the detective's trench coat that she realized she still had it on. She should take it off before she got cat hair on the expensive fabric. Well, more cat hair, since a fair amount had already attached itself. Her eyes slid shut when an annoying K-pop song suddenly blared from the apartment upstairs, shattering the silence. She pulled the coat over her head, drifted off into a drug-induced sleep, and enjoyed the lingering outdoorsy scent of Detective Justin Butler's cologne.

****

Upon entering Pamela Yates's residence, Justin got the same eerie sense of expectation he did going into the home of any victim. He firmly believed after death a person's spirit returned to a place where they felt safe, especially when their lives were taken violently. He'd experienced contact with them too often to dismiss the possibility. Pausing for a beat, he waited for her presence to make itself known. Sometimes an idea or thought would occur to him that could only have come from the victim. Other times *nada*. Unfortunately, this was one of the latter. He remained still for a moment longer in case Pamela was a little shy.

"You're like my Irish grandmother with her talk of *banshees* and *sluaghs*," Dennis complained, rubbing the goose bumps on his arms.

"How about this?" he laughed at his jittery partner as he gestured to the blinking red light on her answering machine. "Is it okay if I press play, or does it count as getting a message from beyond the grave?"

"More like from the land time forgot. Who has an answering machine anymore?"

Justin had to admit he had a point, but guessed if you rode horses for a living, it wasn't out of character to be a little old-fashioned. He pressed a latex-gloved finger on the appropriate button. There was only one unheard message, and it was a doozy.

"Listen, Pammy," a male voice spat. *"I got your notice in the mail and you're not screwing me again, you bitch. I'll squash you like the bug you are."* The message clicked off.

"I'm thinking we just found a real live suspect," Ames said.

"He could at least have had the decency to leave his name and number," Justin mused as his partner put in a call to pull Yates's phone records.

Further search of every drawer, nook, and cranny proved fruitless and more than a little depressing. A potentially cute hillside cottage, Pamela had made her home into a mass-manufactured, personality-free zone. There were a few horse-related items like statues, frames, and a couple of mugs clumped together on the bottom shelf of a bookcase that screamed, *these are gifts, I did not pay money for this crap, but I have to display them to appease my clients.*

Otherwise, there wasn't a single personal item throughout the entire house. No pictures of family, friends or pets, no tacky stuffed animals from her childhood, not even a ribbon or trophy from any of the horse shows she'd competed in.

A little while later, Justin sat at a small desk in the bedroom, eyeballing a laptop that appeared to be pretty new for a woman who still used an answering machine when Dennis drifted in. "I came up empty in the bathroom other than prescriptions for painkillers."

"I found her computer," Justin replied. "I opened it up and voila." He gestured to a file on screen marked 'Studs.' "The thing isn't even password protected; it automatically went to the last file she used."

"Is there any chance the file name refers to horses?" Dennis asked in a pained voice, then groaned out loud when double-clicking on the icon brought up dozens of video files with names like 'Steve S.', 'Frank', 'UPS Guy', and 'Doc'.

"You thinking what I'm thinking?"

"A hidden camera and computer files with the names of a bunch of dudes? I'm guessing they feature a different kind of riding altogether. For someone with an old school answering machine, it seems Ms. Yates learned how to use one piece of technology."

"Let's say our vic was blackmailing men with homemade porn." Justin stood to stretch his back. "Is the threat of exposure enough of a motive for murder?"

Dennis shrugged with a joyless smirk. "There's

only one way to tell if there's anything worth blackmailing—or killing—over. Someone's going to have to watch them."

As per their SOP, they prepared to play rock-paper-scissors to decide who would get stuck with the task when the chirp of Justin's cell phone interrupted.

"Butler," he answered brusquely. After a moment, he mouthed to Dennis, "It's the lieutenant," and continued agreeing and "yes sir'ing," every so often. He closed with, "We'll get right on it," before turning to his partner. "There's a new lead in the Robbie Allen killing."

Dennis brightened. "Oh, yeah? Whadda we got?"

"An anonymous tip came in that Commissioner Allen's son was with a hooker the night he was killed. Allegedly, a thousand dollars in cash and a large amount of cocaine went missing from the hotel room where he was found. The tipster claimed the hooker killed Allen and took the goods. The lieutenant wants us to drop everything and go check it out."

"How reliable is this tipster?"

Justin shrugged. "How reliable is any informant?"

"He realizes we're not sitting around eating donuts, right? We're trying to follow up on solid leads of another murder while they're hot, not anonymous rumors."

"You know as well as I do there's no use in trying to reason with the assh—" Justin sighed, changing his word choice mid-sentence. "—boss. Let's just get it done."

The entire department felt the political pressure over the death of any city official's child, but Justin had to admit, Lieutenant Placer got the brunt of it.

On the other hand, if they didn't catch the killer soon, Placer would have no problem dumping the blame on him and Dennis.

Chapter Four

After a fruitless night of following up on their boss's so-called hot tip, Justin was back at the office the next morning in time for Placer to prowl past his desk and glower at Justin's pressed designer suit. The LT smoothed the wrinkles in his rumpled department store attire before slamming his office door shut.

"Jesus, the boss already has a hard-on for you about being rich." With that stunning revelation, Dennis flopped down at his desk. He sported bags under his eyes that matched Justin's. "You could try coming in just once looking less—"

"Let me stop you right there." Justin slid the to-go cup with Dennis's name scrawled so messily it read *Penis* toward his partner. "Experience tells me you're about to say what you think is a clever put-down but is really a homophobic slur you don't mean. You're a better person than that, it's time to own it."

Dennis blinked at him, mouth agape. Justin waited, figuring his mercurial friend would either blow up in a rage or burst out laughing. He blew out a breath of relief when the response was laughter; he wasn't in the mood for a fight today.

"Point taken," Ames said. "Am I allowed to say if you dressed less like James Bond and more like the rest of us working stiffs, he might like you?"

"You dress like you buy your clothes from a thrift

store, and he doesn't like you either."

He ignored Dennis's muttering about not losing any sleep over whether their boss liked him or not and mulled over where else to search for this working girl who allegedly was with Robbie Allen the night he was killed. Was she a witness or a suspect?

Picking up a tiny rake and dragging it across his desktop Zen garden, he wondered who had told the lieutenant about her and what the anonymous tipster was hiding. Then he noticed silence had fallen over the busy squad room. Curious, he glanced up.

Dressed in knee-high, black leather boots and tight-fitting, tan pants, Emily Conners captured the full attention of a room full of mostly male, overworked cops. He'd seen dozens of similarly dressed men and women yesterday, riding horses at the Equestrian Center, but for men who weren't used to the outfit, the effect was startling.

"Ms. Conners." Justin rose, feeling the jealous gazes from other cops in the room burn holes through his back. "What brings you here this morning?"

Extending one arm, she held out his trench coat. "I wanted to return your coat. I got it dry cleaned. No more horse snot on it."

"It wasn't necessary but thank you." He took the coat. "You're looking…um, better this morning."

****

Yeah, yeah, yeah. Why do men fall to pieces over boots and breeches? At the barn, no one gave her a second glance, but go to the grocery store in this outfit and the ogling began. She'd gotten the goofy leer so often, even when she was covered in sweat and grime, she finally realized the sexual attraction had nothing to do with her and everything to do with the clothes. The novelty had worn off, and now she found it downright annoying.

"I've got horses to ride, and you have my only pair of paddock boots, so I'm stuck wearing my tall boots instead. I usually save them for shows but..." She shrugged.

"It's a great look on you." He gave her a dazzling smile, then cocked his head to one side in apparent confusion when she failed to react. Was he expecting her to swoon? "To be fair, the last time I saw you, you were vomiting, so nowhere to go but up."

Thanks to Kate's magic pills, she slept like the dead last night, but *great*? She didn't feel great, and all the unwanted attention right now didn't help.

Uncomfortable, she blurted out the first thing that came to mind. "Thanks, detective. I wish I could say the same for you. Rough night last night?"

Detective Butler blinked at her in surprise while his partner snorted back a laugh. *Was this guy's ego so big he couldn't take a joke?* Trying to recover his smile, he murmured, "My partner and I were out most of the night, following up on a lead."

Emily sagged with relief that the murderer was no longer running around. "You've found Pamela's killer?"

"In fact, no, ma'am. It involved another case. But our job would be a lot easier if the people who knew Ms. Yates best would speak with us. We tried calling friends, clients, and her ex-business partner with no results. I get the distinct impression we're getting stonewalled."

"There's something you need to keep in mind

about horse people." She picked her words carefully. "Most of these folks have grown up together, riding with or competing against one another since they were old enough to sit up on their own. For a lot of them, the equestrian world is a second- or third-generation thing. It's a tight community and outsiders aren't welcome."

"Even to find the person who killed one of their own?"

Especially to find Pamela's killer, since almost all of them had wanted to kill her themselves at one point or another. Emily opted for a more subtle approach. "They don't like interference, no matter how noble the cause."

"You keep saying *they*, Ms. Conners. Aren't you one of *them*?"

A sharp, mirthless laugh burst out before she could stop it. "I've only worked for Pamela for a few years, so they're not sure what to make of me yet, but if I worked for her for another twenty, I still wouldn't be part of the inner sanctum."

Emily frowned. With Pam gone, she'd have to hunt for a new job. Would another trainer hire her? Pam frequently made a point of telling her how lucky she was to have a job. Between the shock of finding the body, then the sedative, unemployment hadn't occurred to her. But what if Pam was right? What would she do?

The detective studied her, and his brown eyes filled with concern. "Ms. Conners, are you okay?"

Icy panic gripped her chest like a vise. Then she remembered the pills she'd stashed in her tack trunk. That's what she needed—two of those always calmed her nerves. "Um, excuse me, detective, I've got to get going," she stammered and hurried out the door.

29

Chapter Five

By two o'clock, Emily had exercised the fourth of Pamela's dwindling number of horses. Heading back to the barn, her arms, legs, and back ached with every stride. Her brain was as fried as her body. A trainer needed to feel how each horse moves, how they react to a jump, and respond correctly in a split second before one or both of them got hurt. It was like putting together a jigsaw puzzle where all the pieces kept moving.

The other day, Pam accused her of overthinking things, berating her for becoming too timid since the accident. But as Emily kicked her feet out of the stirrups and let Mason, a stout Thoroughbred gelding, take them back to the barn, she realized at some point today she'd gotten too busy to be terrified. The fear was still there, but it was mixed with enough of the joy that hooked her on horses in the first place. Dismounting, she patted the big guy on the head and smiled to herself.

Inside at the crossties, she stripped the saddle off the sweaty horse with the energy of a zombie and began to clean him up when she saw Lottie Gray hurrying toward her.

Per her usual style, her friend was immaculately dressed in the latest, most expensive equestrian garb—which didn't stop her from gripping a very dirty, sweaty Emily in a fierce hug. "Darling, I just got back from

Kinsale and heard the news. How awful for you."

Truly relieved to see her friend, Emily returned the gesture as a wave of emotion threatened to overwhelm her. "It wasn't so great for Pamela either."

Releasing her, Lottie scrutinized Emily, concern etched on a face where no lines or wrinkles dared to go. "Don't you dare feel sorry for that bitch. She undoubtedly deserved it. Are you sure you're okay?"

"As well as can be expected, better since you're home."

"Yeah, about that, I don't know how to ask this," Lottie began, staring at the horse as if she'd never seen one before.

Alarm bells clanged in Emily's head. There was only one subject that drove her friend to consider her words before speaking. She saw what was coming before Lottie asked, "How are you *really*?"

Irritated at the inquisition, she lied without hesitation. "No, Lottie, I haven't taken anything stronger than Tylenol since I found her."

The older woman threw her arm around Emily's shoulders and gave her a squeeze. "All right, I'm sorry. I don't mean to harp on the subject. I care about you and don't want to see this cause another…episode."

Eager to get off the topic, Emily jumped right into what had been on her mind since she woke up. "Why was Pamela home early? I thought the two of you were supposed to stay at Kinsale until after the show jump round this afternoon?"

Though Lottie didn't appear to be satisfied they were done talking about her drug issues, she huffed in resignation and launched into the drama of her own story. "Freaking Pamela got herself eliminated before

31

she even got on the cross-country course. I turn my back for one minute and she drapes Reese's cooler over a jump in the warm-up arena."

Emily's blank stare earned a growl of exasperation. "Oh, for Heaven's sake, does no one read the rule book? Draping anything over the warm-up jumps is cause for elimination. Pamela finally broke into the top five after dressage, only to get us chucked out of the event over something stupid."

"I'm sorry," Emily groaned. "That sucks."

"To put it mildly. Then she gets a phone call and pulls a disappearing act. Leaves my horse with no way home. It took me until this morning to find a hauler to bring Reese back. Where's Pablo? I want to make sure he gives him a good turn out tomorrow."

Emily wiped down her sweat lathered tack and shrugged. "Gone. He probably took a better job at another barn. With Pamela dead, no one is afraid of *retribution* for stealing her groom."

"Or he killed her and took off."

Appalled, Emily simply stared at her.

Lottie shrugged. "What? I'm just saying."

Done cleaning the bridle, she crossed the aisle to the tack room. "It doesn't matter. I'd only need him until the end of the month."

"What do you mean?" Lottie asked, following on her heels.

Emily stretched her short frame to hang the bridle on its hook beside the others. A sharp pain shot through her neck, but she gritted her teeth and managed to place the bridle without dropping it. She thought Lottie hadn't noticed until she turned and saw The Look. The suspicious one she'd gotten since the first time she'd refilled her pain medication after her fall. It reminded her there was very little her friend missed. She ignored the pursed-lip-downward-tilt-of-the-nose and went back to cleaning the horse. "I should be able to find new trainers for all the horses by then. The Whittiers already pulled Samson and took him to Tom Davidson's place."

"The Whittiers are idiots," Lottie spat. "My three horses are staying right here. Of course, we'll have to come up with a new name. Yates Motel is too creepy given the circumstances."

Emily chuckled, imagining how horrified Pamela would be if she knew her clients referred to her Twelve Oaks Farms, using the name of the famous horror movie motel instead of the whimsical *Gone With the Wind* reference she'd intended. "Who are you going to get to train them? Contrary to whatever delusions of god-hood Pamela may have held about herself, I don't think she's going to rise up from the dead."

"Why *you* are, my darling," Lottie stammered, dumbfounded. "We all know as Pamela's assistant you did most of the work, not her."

For a moment, Emily froze, then laughed out loud. "Yeah, right. That's very sweet, but no. I'll be lucky to get a job as a groom."

"Actually, this is perfect," Lottie continued on as if she hadn't spoken. "You're already better than most trainers, but I bet I can get you into the next trainer certification program to add some extra clout."

"Lottie, I said no," she snapped louder than she intended. "No," she repeated softly, hoping to put an end to the discussion.

Her friend produced a horse cookie from the never-ending supply in her pocket and gave it to Mason. He

33

sucked the treat down and continued to nuzzle her hand, searching for more.

"All this time I thought Pamela kept you under her thumb. I never suspected you liked it there." Lottie took her by the shoulders. "This is your chance to leave the nest and fly. Take it, they don't come around very often."

Emily shook off her grasp and backed away. "The problem with leaving the nest is if you aren't a damn good flier, you go splat," she shot back, frustrated with Lottie for expecting so much of her.

"But you can't give up, not now when—"

Much to Emily's relief, a woman leading a dappled gray Arab gelding interrupted. "Excuse me." Darian Holt acknowledged Lottie with a curt nod, their mutual annoyance obvious. "I didn't mean to eavesdrop, but I think it's a great idea for you to take over the barn."

Emily raised both hands in a *hold everything* gesture. "I never said I was."

"Let me explain something to you," Darian demanded in the same way she began most of her sentences, as if she were talking to a moron. "I wanted to leave Pamela anyway, so any change is for the best."

"Oh? Are you unhappy with the way Alex is going?" Emily frowned. He was too small, too old, and just too Arab for Pamela to bother with, so she'd been riding him herself. She scowled at Lottie as if to say, *Exhibit A, I'm no trainer.*

"Alex is going better than ever. The problem was, Pamela stopped showing up for my lessons. And the days she did show up, she'd sit on the fence, scream into her cell phone and smoke. That's why I came over, to see if you would give me a lesson."

"Me? But I've never—"

"You'll pay her, of course," Lottie blurted out, cutting off her refusal.

Clearly Darian hadn't intended to pay anyone, but now she was caught with no graceful way out. "Well, obviously," she replied, fooling no one. "Is it fifty dollars per lesson?"

Emily ignored Lottie's scowl at Darian's attempt to lowball the price. Instead, she argued, "But I've got to put Mason away and I still need to ride two more horses."

"Oh, for Pete's sake." Lottie stamped her foot in disgust. "You're ready to fall down now. The last thing you need is to get on another horse."

She opened her mouth to argue, but had to admit, Lottie had a point. The spirit was willing but her back—hell, for that matter her entire body—was just too weak. Fearing she'd failed the first test she'd faced without Pamela, Emily nodded in sullen agreement.

"Excellent," Lottie gloated. "You two go get started and I'll finish up with Mason."

"*You're* going to finish cleaning him up?" She gave the horse, still covered in sweat and dirt, a visual once over.

"Don't be ridiculous." Lottie turned up the wattage on her perfect smile. "I'm rich, I'll pay someone else to do it."

Chapter Six

Dennis Ames tried interrupting the person on the other end of the phone, but there was no stopping the verbal torrent. Sitting four feet away, Justin still caught several heated curses coming through the line.

Finally, his partner held the phone at arm's length and shouted, "Thank you, sir, have a nice day." He dropped the phone back in the cradle and rose to pour himself a fresh cup of coffee. "Scratch another suspect off the list. The UPS driver denies being blackmailed by Ms. Yates. His wife, however, listened to the message I left asking him to call me about the video and is threatening to cut off his *special delivery unit*."

"You left a message on his home machine?" Justin sputtered.

"I'm not a rookie, I called his cell phone," he argued. "Is it my fault his wife copped his password and checks his messages? Now there's a marriage based in trust."

"But she was right. He was screwing around."

"Or her suspicious nature drove him to cheat." Dennis scoffed. "I tell you, Jay, you got the right idea. Date 'em a few times, have some laughs and move on."

This was not the first time they'd had this discussion, and most likely it wouldn't be the last. Sadly, Dennis was still in love with his ex-wife, who had dumped him for a college professor. He talked tough, but you'd be hard-pressed to find a more hopeless romantic than Dennis Ames.

On the other hand, Justin considered himself to be incapable of falling in love. It wasn't a fact he was proud of, but it didn't distress him either. Despite all the women he'd been with, he'd never once fallen in love. Oddly enough, women usually left him once they sensed his lack of emotional commitment, not the other way around. But he never missed any of them once they were gone. Oh sure, he might remember a particular smile or the way they kissed, but there'd be another woman with charms of her own soon enough. The perfect bachelor life, or at least his buddies thought so.

"...think the videos are a dead end. The camera was pointed in the wrong direction to catch the killer, and so far, none of her co-stars admit to being blackmailed. One of them asked if he could get a copy." He hadn't realized he'd tuned Dennis out until he glanced up to see his partner frowning at him, expecting a response. "You're moody today. Is it that time of the month?"

"How about it's time for me to kick your ass?"

The ringing phone cut their banter short. Dennis grabbed the well-worn handset and shifted from bored to energized as he scribbled the information the caller gave him. Sensing the call must be important, Justin grabbed both their coats, ready to leave as soon as Dennis hung up the phone. "Where are we headed?"

"Got a tip on who may have been involved in the Allen kid's shooting."

"Who?"

"Would you believe Jimmy Gillette?"

"Frankie the Pimp's little brother?"

Dennis shrugged as they left the squad room. "Guess he's expanding the family business, using his girlfriend to turn tricks."

****

Emily patiently ignored Darian's whining excuses and worked with her to get her horse to move better. Lottie sat on the fence rail, observing the lesson and after twenty minutes, she remarked, "You know, you're pretty good at this."

Emily laughed. "Why do you sound so surprised?"

Normally, a comment like that would have eroded her meager confidence. However, seeing Darian transform from kicking and pulling her poor horse all over the place to a somewhat respectable rider who could sit quietly on his back—more or less—gave Emily a feeling of empowerment.

"Okay Darian, that's good," she called. "Why don't you take him for a walk around the barns to cool him down."

"So that's it? My lesson's over?" Riding up to where Emily and Lottie sat on the fence, she sounded more annoyed than happy with her progress.

"Alex has worked hard enough for today. Let's give him a break." She placated her student even though it was the woman, and not the horse, dripping with sweat.

Darian sputtered, "But you haven't yelled at me like Pam did."

Uncertain what to say, Emily stared at her.

Lottie had no such issue. "You mean it's not a lesson unless you've been humiliated? Fine, your shirt makes you look fat. Don't forget to leave a check for *eighty-five dollars* in the office."

Biting back a giggle, Emily hopped off the fence to open the gate and let the horse and rider out. As she glanced at the driveway, her smile fled. A distinctive green truck and trailer headed toward the exit.

"Is that Larry's trailer?" Lottie asked, sounding annoyed.

"The third one to leave the barn today," Emily grumbled and studied her ragged fingernails, too afraid to meet Lottie's gaze. "You still convinced I can do this? Take over her clients, I mean?"

"Kid, I think you can do anything you set your mind to."

The moment hung there between them, full of potential and fear, until the chirp of Emily's cell phone rescued her. She glanced at the screen, snorted in disgust, and shoved the device back in her pocket.

"What was that about?" Curiosity outweighed courtesy for Lottie. It was one of her traits Emily both hated and adored.

"It's the cop who's investigating Pam's death. He wants me to introduce him to Ben Sanders."

Her friend nudged Emily with her knee. "I understand the man is quite handsome."

"Trust me, he'd be the first to tell you so."

Lottie raised an eyebrow at her vehement response. "Why not show him around? I can imagine worse ways to spend a day. Or night."

Blushing at the insinuation, Em stammered, "After last week's rains? The muddy, pothole-ridden street to Ben's place will suck the detective's expensive little hybrid up to its windshield wipers."

"Take Ellie May."

"Why should I get my truck dirty? You're

39

welcome to—"

The obnoxious *meep meep* of a sports car horn cut Emily short. She glanced over her shoulder and clenched her jaw at the former beauty queen driving an expensive red convertible. Right behind her rolled Emily's truck, glowing from a wash and fresh coat of wax. Both vehicles parked along the driveway as far from the dust kicked up by the riders in the other rings as possible.

"Oh, crap," she muttered. A middle-aged man with a boy-next-door kind of charm popped out of the truck and moseyed toward them with a smile.

"So this is what you do all day, sit on the fence shooting the breeze?"

Lottie swung herself around and hopped off the fence. "Nicky, darling," she cooed as she gave him air kisses on both cheeks. "How wonderful to see you. Have you heard what our poor girl has been through?"

Emily trudged over to greet him, and not just because she was stiff from riding. Part of the reason they weren't married anymore was Nick's annoying habit of telling her how to run her life. They'd become friends since the divorce, but his need to fix her lingered on.

"Emily, I'm so sorry about Pamela. Kate told me the police took your shoes and coat as evidence. You should have called me right away."

There it was—the scolding tone. "She shouldn't have called you at all. It wasn't a big deal. They took my shoes to sort out which footprints belonged at the scene and which ones didn't. Don't worry, if I need a lawyer, you'll be the first one I call." *Seeing as how I put you through law school.*

With a mischievous smile, Lottie added, "I understand the detective on the case is a hottie. And gallant as well. He even loaned her his coat, then called to ask her out."

Nick frowned, pushing out his lower lip in an unattractive pout. "Oh really? That's inappropriate—what's his name?"

"Nick, let it go. She's exaggerating, as usual." Emily smacked her friend on the arm. "He did not ask me out."

"I'm worried about you, Em," Nick murmured. "You've lost weight again."

"Are you trying to sound like my mother?"

"Who sends her regards and says to call her, collect, if need be, to let her know you're okay."

She knew it. As soon as Kate said she'd called Nick, she figured he'd immediately call her parents. She banged her head on the white wooden fence and growled loud enough to spook a horse turned out in the next ring. After a couple of thwacks, the dramatic gesture lost its appeal, so she just stood there, head resting on the fence.

"How's Ellie May?" Lottie asked.

"Better now," Nick spluttered, his jab aimed at Emily. "Since *someone* refuses to at least try to keep her clean, I guess it's up to me to make sure she gets detailed once in a while."

She pulled her head off the fence to stare at her ex. She spoke slowly, as if addressing a child. "I work at a barn. Look around, what do you see? Dirt. Everywhere. She—it's a truck, it's supposed to get dirty."

His mouth gaped into an O, sucking in air as if she'd kicked him in the solar plexus. "She's not a truck,

41

she's a classic. I'll be by next week to take her for her oil change, so can you please try to not get her splattered with mud between now and then?"

He spun on his heel and left to wedge himself next to the blonde in the cramped sports car. Watching them go, she pulled out her cell phone and stabbed at the screen. "Hello, Detective Butler? Emily Conners. About going out to Ben Sanders's place. Would tomorrow work for you?"

Chapter Seven

Puzzled, Justin put his phone down. He wondered why the Conners woman changed her mind about helping him. At least it gave him something to mull over on their stakeout, besides the odd smell coming from the back of Dennis's car.

"Are you sure your snitch was right about Jimmy being here for a deal?"

His partner jerked his head toward the shadowy figure skulking toward them. "Why don't we ask him?"

It wasn't Jimmy Gillette, but his older brother, Frank. He waited until the scrawny man had his hand on the door of the run-down apartment building before getting out of the car, hoping the element of surprise would buy him the seconds he needed to grab him. Frank must have spotted their city-issued sedan. Fueled by adrenalin and God only knows what drugs, the shady ex-con spun and took off like a jackrabbit.

"Don't run, don't...shit." Justin took off down the deserted, trash-strewn street after him.

A block later, he felt bad for the guy. While Frank's legs churned toward the end of a narrow alley, his own long, rolling strides effortlessly kept him in pace all the way to the chain-link fence. *Why was there always a chain-link fence at the end of alleys?*

He could have reached up and grabbed the slippery man if he wanted, but he hoped if he let him run long enough, he'd lead them to Jimmy. Besides, from the way the man wheezed, Justin wasn't worried about losing him. After clearing the fence, he backed off a bit for fear of giving him a heart attack. Cigarettes, they'll do it to you every time.

Frank turned onto a street congested with traffic. Justin had to laugh when he tried to do the cop show thing of running along the tops of cars. He obviously hadn't considered how leaping from a small compact to a giant-sized SUV is a lot harder than stunt guys and camera cars make it look. He slipped and fell off, his face sliding down the back windshield and tearing off the wiper. Justin thought he might have to go out there and save the little weasel from the owner of the SUV, but Frank managed to struggle to his feet and took off running.

When he headed for the fire escape, Justin put a little steam on. *Not the rooftop.* He hated it when these guys went for the rooftops. Not because of the height, but because of the pigeon shit. As luck would have it, when Frank reached for the first rung, the rusted metal snapped off in his hand. Frantic for an escape, he staggered around the corner and kept running.

Years of sitting in front of the TV, drinking beer, and smoking pack after pack of cigarettes, had taken their toll. Desperately trying to suck air into his lungs, Frank ground to a halt. Justin caught up to him as he crouched against a building and snaked his right hand inside his oversized coat. Every nerve ending on alert, he picked up the metal lid to a nearby trashcan and threw it at the lowlife like a giant flying disc. It crashed into Frank's hand, evoking a howl of pain as the pale, panting man sunk to his knees. A yellow and orange plastic tube clattered to the pavement.

"It was just my inhaler," he panted, cradling his injured hand

Tires screeched behind Justin. Still hyper-alert, he turned toward the sound, ready for a fight, only to see Dennis fly out of his car. Furious, the slight Irishman rushed to Justin and punched his shoulder holster. "Remember this, asshole?" he hissed. "It's called a gun. The next time it looks like a perp's pulling a weapon on you, use it."

"Really? You don't think I can take him?" he pointed to the wheezing, trembling Frankie. "Without a gun?"

They both glanced at Frankie, sucking on his inhaler. Dennis shook off his anger. "Good point."

Justin straightened his already perfect tie. "Glad you could join us, by the way."

"I called it in and found out Frankie's girlfriend lives in the building across the street. I figured he's stupid enough to go there, and ta-da—here we are." Dennis sneered at Frankie. "Hey, moron, all we want to know is where your brother Jimmy is."

Frank clawed his way up the wall to stand, his eyes darting toward every sound. He scuttled deeper into the shadows of a garbage-strewn parking lot, jerking his head to signal the cops to follow. "I swear, for the kid's sake I'd tell you if I knew where Jimmy was, but I don't know nothing."

"Really?" Dennis got in his face. " 'Cause nothing says, 'I'm guilty,' like running from the cops, dumbass."

"No, I swear," he huffed. "A loan shark is gunnin' for him, on account of money he owes. That's why he's got his girl out on the street. On my sainted mother, I hope you find him first to keep his sorry ass from getting killed. I can tell you this, the guy who got offed was no angel."

"Commissioner Allen's son?"

"Such an a-hole. He got off on roughing up working girls. Like bone-breaking rough."

Justin scowled. The kid was supposedly squeaky clean.

Frank gestured wildly. "No man, I'm serious. There's a hooker on Vine who still limps after taking him on as a client. He paid like triple the going rate, but it got to where no one would service him."

"Then why would Jimmy have pimped his girlfriend to him?"

Frank hesitated, visibly twitchy. "Okay, I'm telling you this off the record, understand me?"

"There is no *off the record*," Dennis snapped. "What do you think we are, reporters? Does this look like a pen to you?" He opened his coat to expose his gun, pressing closer to Frank. Justin put a hand on his partner's chest, forcing him to back off a step.

"Okay, okay. She offered to do it, to help Jimmy pay off his debt. But she told Jimmy to stay close in case something happened."

"Like a murder," Justin muttered.

Now all they had to do was find one scared, desperate man in a city of nearly four million people. Great.

Chapter Eight

Sounds of screams jolted Emily awake. She clawed her way out from under the pile of blankets on her bed. Finally free, the terrors of her nightmare loosened their grip, and her erratic breathing returned to normal. It was then she realized the screams were her own.

Drenched in sweat despite the frosty temperature of her apartment, she stripped off her flannel nightshirt. These days, running her heater was a luxury she couldn't afford. The cool air felt good on her skin for a moment before the shivering set in. It was useless to try to go back to sleep, so she wrapped herself in the old bathrobe hanging on her closet door and trudged the twenty-three steps in the pitch dark to the kitchen.

This trip was one she'd done hundreds of times since her accident. Opening the ancient refrigerator, she grabbed the first beverage she found, a lite beer of all things, and limped to her couch. The half-empty bottle of prescription painkillers she'd obtained in Nick's name sat on the end table. She shook out three pills— two more than the amount prescribed on the bottle— washed them down with the weak beer, turned on her TV, and watched the image flicker to life.

She had no memory of the accident at all. The crushing post-surgery pain burned crystal clear in her mind, but the accident itself was a gray, fuzzy blur. So every night, she watched the video Lottie had shot of her attempting to jump the combination of fences, trying to understand what happened.

It took a lot of arm-twisting to convince Lottie to give her the footage, but she finally got it on a flash drive that stayed parked in her TV set. With a click of the remote, the video popped up so she could study the scene at will. There had to be a reason why things went so horribly wrong. If she could figure out what happened, she could make sure never to repeat the same mistake again.

On the screen, a woman on a horse, face beaming, sent a jaunty wave to the camera. She vaguely resembled Emily, although the rider had full cheeks and a radiant expression. Had she ever really been so happy?

And then it happened. The rider approached the first element of the aptly named coffin combination. Technically, the obstacle was composed of three elements—a jump in, a ditch, and a jump out. It's called a *coffin* because many times the rider ended up in the wooden ditch, which ominously resembled a cheap open casket.

The horse refused the first jump. From beyond camera range, Pamela shouted muffled instructions, and the rider re-approached the difficult combination. This time she sat up taller and they made it over the first fence, a massive log. But then...did she give too much leg? Not enough? Why did he stumble in the middle, after the ditch? They seem to have recovered, but at the final fence—another massive natural wood obstacle—something happened. Did the horse catch a leg? Did she not give him the cue to jump soon enough?

No matter how many times Emily watched the

accident unfold, no matter how much she slowed the video, she could never unravel the mystery of what went wrong.

The ending was always the same. The big bay horse flipped over the jump, landing on his neck and the rider's body at the same time. The same icy knot grew in the pit of her stomach as she watched the horse struggle to regain its feet, fall back on top of the rider, then get up and trot off. The rider—it always seemed like someone else—lay deathly still. The video ended with the sound of Lottie's shriek—then went black.

Samwise leaped into her lap, cuddling up to her with what she swore was a concerned frown on his face. Or maybe the fuzzy comfort of painkillers had taken effect, making her see things as she hit replay.

****

Last night's rain left a mass of dark gray clouds squashed flat as though they wanted to press down on the city, but an unseen force kept them at bay. Justin assumed those kinds of clouds had a scientific name, but meteorology was one of the few subjects he had no interest in. He was more curious about the karmic implications of a dark cloud hanging overhead.

It didn't take long for him to spot Emily Conners riding a reddish-colored horse, its hooves making slapping sounds in the damp sand. The horse appeared to be huge, but her diminutive size made any horse seem big. Brightly painted jumps, trees, and a dozen other riders filled the ring she rode in. It was impressive how she wove her way through the obstacles; goddess-like, as if she were born to rule from horseback. There were other riders in the ring, but the easy partnership she shared with her horse made the pair stand out.

Moving as one, they floated over a jump, then circled back to do it again. When they came around to jump the fence a third time, however, the horse reared up on its back legs, front legs striking out angrily in the air. The beast appeared to be close to falling over and taking Ms. Conners with it. Justin ran to the rail, ready to do something, if only he had any idea what to do.

The picture of grim determination, she reached up and lightly slapped the horse between the ears. All four of the animal's hooves slammed back to earth. It shook its head as a raw egg—shell, yolk and all—dripped down its face.

"What was that?" Justin asked no one in particular and was surprised to get a reply.

"It's an old cowboy trick. Breaking an egg between the ears makes the horse think he hit his head and is bleeding." A female voice answered from behind him. "Horses don't like it, so they won't rear up anymore. Hopefully."

He turned to see a slim, older woman approach; her luminous smile matched the carats of her diamond jewelry. Everything from the top of her chic salt and pepper hairstyle to the tip of her polished riding boots rang of elegance. He had to fight the pull to kiss the hand she offered rather than shake it.

"Lottie Gray," she said by way of introduction. "You must be the detective everyone is talking about." She laughed as Justin furrowed his brows. "You don't have to be Sherlock Holmes to figure out the guy strutting around the barn in a suit isn't here to ride. Wonderful, isn't she?" she asked, nodding toward Ms. Conners.

By now, she'd kicked the horse back into a canter

and approached the jump again. This time, and four more times afterward, they flew over the colorful obstacle without a hitch. She gave the horse a pat and pulled up to a walk. With a wave to Lottie, she sauntered out of the ring on a loose, relaxed rein.

"How did she do that?" he asked. "I mean, the timing, not to mention carrying the egg around the entire time waiting to use it, that's—"

"A showboating stunt no professional trainer would do?" Kate Williams marched up to add her two cents' worth, even though no one asked.

Justin's newfound companion stiffened for a moment, then relaxed as she looped her arm through his. "As I recall, Kate, your 'professional' response was to fall off and refuse to ride him ever again." Lottie's tone was so sweet she practically purred, but he'd heard hardened gang members put less hatred in their voices.

The trainer bristled at the not-so-subtle insult and marched off as Ms. Conners rode up. Patting the horse again, she gracefully swung her leg over its back and dismounted as puffs of steam rose off the animal's belly and hind legs. She was a little damp and winded herself. He'd never thought of riding as being much exercise. Undoubtedly, he had a lot to learn.

"What's up with Kate? Is everything okay?" she asked as she loosened the girth of the saddle.

Lottie shrugged her shoulders and winked at Justin, making him part of her conspiracy. "Beats me, she didn't say." She took the reins from Ms. Conners. "Marvelous job, darling."

"Thanks, I kind of hung on and hoped for the best." Her broad grin was a dead giveaway that she felt pretty good about her ride.

"I was talking to Pete, dear," the older woman teased as she took the horse's head in her hands and kissed him, leaving a bright red lipstick imprint on the white snip on his nose. "I'll go walk him a bit to cool him down." In an unsubtle maneuver, she gave Emily a playful shove toward Justin. "He's awfully hot."

If looks could kill, her friend's glare would have maimed Lottie at the very least. She cringed. "Sorry, she just can't help herself."

"Allow me to change the topic," he joked. Why was he as nervous as a high school kid, he wondered, as he handed her the plastic bag he'd been carrying. "Your shoes."

She pulled her paddock boots out of the bag, stunned. "Wow."

"I had my shoe guy give them a little polish. I hope you don't mind."

"Cleaned, polished, and the seam has been re-stitched. Can't wait to see my jacket. The zipper gets a little stuck about half-way up, so if you want to fix that too, be my guest."

Justin remembered the dark brown stain that had soaked through the coat and grimaced. "Um, I know of a crime scene cleaner who might be able to help. Shall I call her and ask?"

"I'm kidding, detective. I don't plan on wearing it again. Ever." Her eyes glistened as she tramped toward the barn. "I just need to return a few phone calls then I'll be ready to take you to Ben Sanders's place."

****

After she put the horse away, Lottie rejoined Justin. "Ms. Conners went to go make some phone calls," he explained. "Do you mind if I ask you a few questions, Ms. Gray?"

The older woman pondered for a moment before smiling. "It's Mrs. Gray, with an 'a' and my husband would have my hide for talking to a detective, no matter how good-looking he is, about a murder investigation without one of his very expensive lawyers present. So instead of dragging this process out with so much legal mumbo jumbo, how about if for every question you ask, I get to ask one of my own? We both have to answer, though how honestly"— she shrugged —"is up to you to decide. Deal?"

Mrs. Gray with an 'a', as in Spaulding Gray Construction, which was owned by one of the wealthiest men in the city. Justin thought he recognized her. She was right, she could make this into a tremendous ordeal, and all he wanted to ask were the standard questions. "All right, Mrs. Gray, you've got yourself a deal. My turn first—when was the last time you saw Pamela Yates?"

"Down to business so soon?" she *tsked,* pouting. "Sometime late on Saturday, after she stupidly got herself eliminated from the horse show at Kinsale Downs. It must have been three or four in the afternoon when I saw her by the food truck, smoking a cigarette and talking on her cell phone. I could tell from her scowl she wasn't in the mood for anything I had to say, and frankly, I wasn't interested in any of her excuses, so I went back to the arena and watched more show jump rounds."

"She got herself eliminated? You must have been pretty angry with her."

Lottie smiled. "Angry enough to smash her face in? Maybe, at the time. Angry enough to skip Jeremy

53

Steele's party to follow her home and kill her? No way. I didn't know she'd left until Kate called me the next day to say she'd been murdered. And yes, I can prove my alibi. There'll be pictures in next month's *Equestrian Outlook* showing a very drunk me dancing on a table."

"And after the party?"

"In my hotel room, alone."

Justin raised his eyebrows. "Your husband wasn't with you?"

"He prefers to stay home and be a horse show widower. And you cheated, that was more than one question."

Cringing in mock horror at being busted, Justin agreed, "You caught me. Okay, give me your best shot."

He had a pretty good idea what the first question would be—why's a nice guy like you still single, or a variation thereof. It was a line of inquiry he got all the time. She leaned in closer. He braced himself, fake smile ready to be plastered on.

"What kind of police officer drives a luxury hybrid convertible and wears four-thousand-dollar suits?" she asked, dusting a smudge of dirt off his sleeve. She peered up at him, the amused twinkle in her eyes hardening to flint. "Are you a crooked cop or a very lucky one? Because I won't tolerate scum bothering Emily."

He hadn't seen that one coming. "You get right to the point." She would have made a hell of a cop. "Well, Mrs. Gray with an 'a,' I got my money the old-fashioned way, I inherited a fortune."

Her jaw dropped in surprise. "You're one of the

Butlers, as in the Butler Music Center, Butler Theatre Foundation, and the Butler Burn Unit at Children's Hospital. Your mother is my hero."

Madeline Butler had been called many things—a barracuda, a gold digger, as well as less complimentary terms since she took over his late father's sizable fortune, then doubled it—but hero wasn't one of them. He'd have to tell her.

"My turn," he declared, turning more serious. "Tell me about Ms. Conner's accident."

"You know about that?" she murmured. Her lips pursed, opening and closing a few times before launching into the story. "Emily had a terrible fall some months back while she was schooling a cross-country fence. It wasn't even a show, just a practice ride. She broke her neck, among other things. Between the surgery to fuse her neck and other complications, she was in the hospital for weeks." Her voice dropped to a whisper. "It was awful."

Her attempt at a casual shrug fell short of the mark as she continued, "Everyone tries to make eventing as safe as possible, but it's a dangerous sport. She should have been wearing an air vest. It might have saved her from the worst, but Pamela insisted she didn't need the extra protection. Emily blames herself. Me? I'll never forgive that bitch Pamela for what happened."

A huge, diesel horse trailer the size of a house roared into the parking lot. Relief washed over Lottie's features, though he suspected she was happier getting out of answering more questions than she was to see the truck. "I'm sorry, you'll have to excuse me, detective, my boy is home."

****

"But Dr. Saraceno, you aren't listening to me. I'm still in a great deal of pain. I can't take off work just now to come in for an exam. Can't you call in another refill for—"

Emily drummed her fingers on the desk while the old prat nattered on about his hands being tied, it was against the rules to give her more painkillers without seeing her in person. "Okay, how about just a few to tide me over until I can come in?"

Her plea was in vain; he'd already hung up. *Shit.* Her other doctors had given her the same run-around, and she was down to just one refill plus whatever she could scrounge up at the barn.

Focused on calling her doctor, she hadn't noticed the envelope in the middle of the desk until now. She skimmed the note inside, then crumpled the paper into a ball and threw it across the office. Another notice from a client who was leaving. So sorry, nothing personal, etc., etc. That's just great. Clearly, no one else shared Lottie's confidence in her abilities.

The prospect of having to drive the detective around for the rest of the day suddenly lost its appeal. All she wanted to do was crawl into bed and pull the covers over her head. Desperate, she rifled through Pam's desk one more time, hoping she'd find something, anything, to take the edge off, but found nothing.

"Of course not," she muttered. She heaved herself up to collect the detective and get this trip over with.

Exiting Pam's office, she ran into Lottie, who stood there with a silly grin on her face and a huge, dark bay horse at her side. "Look who's home," she cooed.

Standing in front of her was the full brother and near twin to the horse that crushed her. Conquering her rising nausea and shaking knees, she reached up to give the animal a perfunctory pat on the neck before sending him off with his beaming owner for a hand walk and a little grass. She saw the detective and her friend exchange glances and knew from his pitying look they'd been talking about her accident.

Biting back the urge to scream in frustration, she told the cop, "Why don't you meet me outside by my truck? I want to make sure Reese's tack trunk got back in one piece."

After he left, she made a beeline for the trunk now sitting in front of Reese's stall. It was an exact copy of the one she'd sat on the morning she found Pam. Meticulous to the point of obsession, everything in Pam's barn matched.

Emily jerked at the lock, hoping to find a stash of pills inside. To her surprise, the lock required a key. *What the hell?* Pamela made sure every lock in her barn was a combination lock and kept the master list. Why the sudden change, and only for this trunk? Giving up the search for now, she glumly headed out to her truck. The sooner she left, the sooner she'd get back home.

Chapter Nine

Lost in her own thoughts, Emily flinched when the detective broke the relative silence of the pickup's cab, having to raise his voice to be heard over the truck's throaty engine as they roared down the road. "You do realize I'm a cop, right?"

She glanced over and saw his white-knuckle grip on the passenger door armrest. "That's the fourth *orange* light you've run," he fussed, relaxing his hold to make air quotes around the word orange. "Not to mention the speeding," he added as they charged up the freeway entrance ramp.

Who knew detectives were such wusses?

"Oh, come on, even traffic cops tell you it's okay to go ten miles over the posted speed limit."

"You're going twenty miles over and that's an urban myth. Besides, I thought all you horse whisperers were the calm, patient type."

He shifted in his seat. When Nick refurbished the truck, he hadn't gotten around to replacing the bench seat. Unruly springs tended to poke people in rude places. She was used to the rough ride but considering the cop's car was so cushy it probably had heated seats, she took pity on him and throttled Ellie May back to a gentle purr, reducing the bouncing to a bare minimum. "You want scary, you should ride with a DQ."

"DQ?"

"Dressage Queen," she answered. "Talk about brutal. Besides, I told you before, I'm still pretty new to the horse world."

"So, Ms. Conners, what made you want to work in a barn?"

She narrowed her eyes at him. "Is knowing that relevant to your investigation?"

"I'm just trying to make polite conversation," he said with a warm smile.

It had been a long time since she'd had any type of conversation, polite or otherwise. Pam had a way of asking questions as if she cared but ended up using the information against you. And Emily had learned through skilled practice to figure out the answers her various doctors wanted to hear in order to prescribe more painkillers, but that's not the same as conversation, is it? Maybe she needed to brush up on her social skills, but the wisdom of starting off with a cop seemed shaky at best.

Casting a glance at his strong, angular profile, she decided to take a leap of faith. "Please, call me Emily. And...are you sure you want to pass the time listening to my life story? It's pretty boring."

"Considering the people I usually talk to, boring is nice."

"Okay," she said with a shrug. "Don't say I didn't warn you. I used to spend two hours a day commuting to an office I hated, selling widgets to people who didn't need them and couldn't afford them. After my husband's career took off, we didn't need my salary anymore, so I tried being the perfect little stay-at-home wife."

"No children?"

She shook her head. "We'd planned to wait a few years. In hindsight, that was the smartest decision we ever made. I got bored without a job and decided to get back into riding which I'd loved as a kid. Pretty soon, I was at the barn more than I was home. Nick needed a hostess to help him further his career, and I needed room to breathe."

"And after the divorce?"

She pushed her hair out of her face, more out of nervous habit than need. Her life sucked and having it scrutinized by a man who smelled faintly of cedar and spice was not what she bargained for when she offered to drive him out to Ben Sanders's place. All she'd wanted to do was get under Nick's skin by getting the truck dirty, not go through therapy.

As she exited the freeway, he kept at her like a dog with a bone. "You have to admit, going from Mrs. Deputy D.A. to horse trainer is a big lane change."

"You're pretty pushy, you know."

"I'm a cop, I'm supposed to be. There must have been a lot of easier jobs you could have gotten. Why the horse thing?"

"God, your persistence must make you a good detective. Fine, if you want the whole sordid story, I had actually been training with Kate. Pamela always seemed to catch me when I rode alone, offering a compliment there, a bit of advice here. One day, she told me how much she admired me as a rider, considering."

"Considering you weren't under her expert tutelage."

"Tutelage? Wow, your parents got their money's worth out of whatever fancy college you went to. But yes, that was her point. I didn't find out until much later she pulled the same line on everyone. So much for being special, huh?"

He'd seen her ride through Pete's nonsense that morning, so deep down she hoped he would assure her she was special. For the first time since she'd met him, Detective Butler remained silent. Shaking off her disappointment, she continued, deciding not to care what he thought. "I switched trainers and was riding with Pamela after my divorce was finalized."

"How did that work out for you?"

"Trying to find a job selling widgets after being out of the game for a few years proved to be next to impossible. Different people, different widgets. I told myself it was karma, a sign I was meant to change my life and find my true calling. The new age crap I was into back then." Emily laughed, shaking her head at her naiveté. "Pamela had become more than a trainer to me by then. At least, I thought she was my friend. She listened to all my whining about not knowing what to do with my life, and ultimately offered me a job. Her assistant had quit, and she needed someone to manage the barn, ride a few horses, teach a few beginners group lessons, lower-level stuff."

"So you did the yeoman's share, and she paid you minimum wage for your troubles," the detective grumbled.

"Yeah, but it didn't matter to me then. I had investments from my widget days. I was doing okay."

"And then?"

"And now we're here." Emily took a right onto a rutted path, splashing through several mud puddles before pulling up to an old rotting wood sign that announced Sleepy Acres—Hunters, Jumpers, and Equitation. An attempt had been made to spiff the place up with a coat of fresh paint, but it only managed to make it depressing.

****

Feeling both shaken and stirred from Emily's hair-raising driving style, Justin eased out of the truck and took in his surroundings. There were three mismatched barns, a patchwork of plywood, pipes, and metal. The only thing they shared was a tilted corrugated tin roof. Weeds and dried brush sprang out of every nook and cranny of the broken concrete walkways.

The main house on the property was a doublewide trailer—no big surprise there. To top off the hillbilly rustic theme, the recent rain had made the gravel scattered over most of the ground a rocky, muddy quagmire. It was a far cry from the posh setting of the Equestrian Center. There was no doubt Ben Sanders had fallen on hard times. "Well, at least it's quiet."

From beyond the barn, a woman's voice boomed, "God damn you to hell." Another woman shrieked something Justin didn't quite catch in response.

"Poor Ben," Emily muttered as they set off in search of him.

They found him in the arena, moving jumps around to set a new course. Justin supposed the man's tall, green rubber boots churning against the wet sand might account for the wobble to his gait, giving the man the appearance of being drunk, but his money was on a hip flask. He waited at the edge of the arena for Sanders to come to him and was surprised when, instead of staying where it was dry-ish, Emily squished into the soggy ring to help the other trainer move the chipped and faded wooden poles around.

"Emily!" Ben exclaimed in a singsong voice. He dropped the wooden pole he was carrying and rushed over to her. To Justin's annoyance, Sanders ignored her protests and scooped her off her feet in a big bear hug.

At first, she laughed, but when he swung her around, she grimaced. "Ben, you're hurting me."

He dropped her to the ground with a plop. "Oh my God, your neck. I totally forgot. Are you okay?"

"No worries, I'm fine." She glanced over at Justin. "Detective Butler would like to ask you some questions about Pamela. Do you have time to talk with him?"

"A cop? To question *moi*?" he whined, then eyeballed Justin and threw his arm around her. "Honey, you didn't say he was cute. Of course I'll talk to him."

Justin stepped forward to meet them, trying to keep his semi-clean shoes out of the biggest puddles. "Good morning, Mr. Sanders, I'm—"

"Available, I hope," Ben teased, taking his hand. "Ben Sanders, President of the Whomever Killed Pamela Yates Fan Club."

"Ben..." Emily chided softly.

"Yes yes, my big mouth is what got me in this Shangri-La—" He made a gesture, indicating the surroundings. "—but it's not like it's a secret how much Pamela and I hated each other."

If Justin hadn't done his research on the man, he would have placed him as much older than the thirty-two years the DMV and social media stated. Like a lot of people in L.A., he'd been an aspiring actor who never quite got his big break. He clung to his movie-star looks by a thread, his face weathering under his battered Aussie hat. But more than the elements, years of hard living had etched their record on his features, and he had the DUIs to prove it. At this rate, he wouldn't be able to get by just by being a pretty face much longer.

"So did you do it?" Justin asked. "Kill Ms. Yates?"

"Would that I had the *cajones* to do the deed, but alas, I don't. Before you ask, I have an alibi."

Justin raised a skeptical eyebrow. He knew the man was single and according to his social media profiles looking for love. "All night? I'll need to verify that."

"His name is Dr. Paul Johnson and yes, we were together all night. You can reach him at his office in Beverly Hills. He's a plastic surgeon, as if you'll ever need one."

Justin wondered if he was supposed to be more shocked at Sanders screwing a man or impressed that he'd landed a plastic surgeon.

While Sanders bragged about his date, a middle-aged woman rode into the ring. From her timid expression and the death grip she had on the reins, Justin guessed she was even less comfortable around horses than he was. But then her shy smile at her instructor betrayed her real motives for being there.

Wow lady, you are so barking up the wrong tree with this one.

"Ah, Alicia, light of my life, aren't you lovely this morning," Ben crooned. The woman fluttered her clumpy, over-mascaraed eyelashes at him. Justin cringed, embarrassed for her. "Why don't you walk around the ring to warm up while I finish here? Remember, roll those shoulders around, loosen up."

The aging ingénue rode off with a nervous giggle. As soon as her back was turned, the charming smile melted off his face as he reached into his pocket, pulled out a silver flask, and knocked back what little was left.

"Ben," Emily scolded, more firmly this time.

"Hello, a little pot calling the kettle black, wouldn't you say?" he retorted.

She froze, her face blooming bright red. "You are such an asshole," she hissed, turning on her heel and slogging back toward the truck.

Not sure what had transpired, Justin blurted out instructions not to leave town and followed on her heels. Sanders called out, "Detective, there is something you should know, a little factoid even Emily isn't privy to."

He stopped and turned back, crossing his arms. He didn't like people who played games, especially drunks, and Sanders was getting on his nerves. "I'm listening."

After regally settling into the plastic lawn chair that served as his ringside throne, he volunteered his information. "One night before we split, Pamela and I went out drinking. Four martinis in, Pamela confessed years ago she'd given up a son for adoption."

"So do a lot of people, Sanders. Most aren't murdered over it."

"Yes, but how many of the little bastards come back to roost? Evidently, he called her out of the blue to say he'd found her and had moved to L.A. to be near her. From the way she was drinking, it didn't seem like she was happy about it."

"Might be relevant if she'd killed him, pretty poor motive for him to kill her."

"Are you kidding? Everyone who got to know Pamela eventually wanted to kill her, but we were all too scared of her to do anything about it. My guess is Junior didn't have as much to lose as the rest of us. Or he inherited Mummy's brass balls."

He had to admit this was interesting information. His problem was that it came from this idiot. "Any idea of the son's name or where I might find him?"

"Not a clue." Sanders settled deeper into his plastic throne, relishing his momentary place in the sun. "Not long after, we had our little falling out and our drinking buddy days were over."

"I can reach you here if I have any more questions?"

"Naturally, detective. It would appear I'm not going anywhere." A bitter expression marred Sanders's face. Justin almost felt sorry for him, except for the strong sense there was more to his downfall than just Pamela Yates.

He caught up with Emily at the edge of the parking lot. "Do you want to talk about that?" He hoped it was clear he asked as a person, not a cop.

"It's nothing, I—"

"Emily? It *is* you." Behind them, a woman called out, "I thought I recognized Ellie May in the lot."

Emily's shoulders slumped for a moment, then turned to face the perky voice. "Sandy, what a pleasant surprise. How's Colonel liking his new home?"

"He's adjusting to life in the country better than I, I'm afraid."

Justin followed Sandy's nervous glance up the hill and saw the women who had been screaming as they drove in. The heated argument still waged on, but another boarder must have made a comment about the noise level because now the combatants spat at each other in whispers.

"Sandy, this is Detective Butler," Emily said.

"He's investigating Pam's murder; we need to go."

She pushed him toward the truck, but Sandy was faster, stepping in the way as she offered Justin her strong, yet wet and clammy hand. He wanted to wipe his palm on his coat after she let go but didn't want to appear rude.

"Sandy Peters, detective. Nice to meet you." The woman turned her attention back to Emily. "I know you all thought I was nuts moving Colonel simply because Libby said he wanted to, but anyone can see how much happier he is."

She gestured toward a white horse who stood in one of the more rustic—or rusty—stalls, munching on hay. He had the same expression every other horse had, no more or less happy as far as Justin could tell.

"Who is Libby?" he asked.

"You don't know who Libby Case is?" Sandy couldn't have been more dumbfounded if he'd asked, *Who is this Spielberg guy everyone's raving about?*

"Libby is the foremost animal communicator in the country. She's got her own YouTube show and everything. We were fortunate enough to have her come out and give a seminar at the Center, so I had her read Colonel for me."

"Read him?" Justin asked. "What do you mean, 'read' your horse?"

"It's when she talks to them." Sandy's passionate belief showed as she got more animated and spoke even faster. "I asked her why he was misbehaving so much, and Libby told me he wanted to live on a farm, but with my work schedule, this was the closest I could come and still be able to ride every day. The drive is a little inconvenient, but as long as he's happy—" She glanced around with thinly veiled disgust. "—that's what counts."

Emily took advantage of the pause and jumped in. "Great seeing you, Sandy, and I'm thrilled you and the big guy love it here, but I've got to get Detective Butler back to town. I'll come visit real soon."

"Oh, we haven't seen you out and about in such a long time. I'm sure the girls would love to say hi." Sandy's face scrunched into a frown.

"Don't worry about me, Ms. Conners," Justin said. "I've got plenty of time."

He told himself he was sticking around for the sake of the investigation. No one thinks to tell a cop the same details they tell each other while dishing on the dead. Spending more time with smart, funny Emily Conners was totally irrelevant.

"Detective, as I said before, please call me Emily. Ms. Conners sounds so...close to my ex-husband's name."

He flashed her his warmest smile. "Only if you'll agree to call me Justin."

She gave a small laugh and shook her head. "This way then, Justin, and don't believe half of what they're going to tell you."

She gestured for him to follow Sandy through the maze of rickety stalls toward a picnic table under a cheap pop-up. Picking his way up the muck covered walkway, he wondered what dark secrets she didn't want him to find out.

****

"And remember that time—was it at the Salinas River Horse Trials?" Samantha asked. Once Sandy introduced Justin to Erin Jeske and Samantha Barger, two of Ben's other clients, as well as longtime friends of Emily's, they were all too happy to humiliate her by revealing her past escapades.

"No, it was Live Oak," Erin jumped in, and the trio burst into giggles, having heard this story a hundred times. All except for Justin, of course. Emily would have preferred to keep him from hearing the humiliating story, but there was no stopping Samantha once she was on a roll.

"There's Emily, riding one of Pamela's horses, and she enters the dressage arena—"

"Dressage is one of the three phases of eventing," Emily explained to him. "You go into a rectangle arena and do the same routine your competitors do." His quizzical expression said it didn't clear up much, but it was the best *Idiot's Guide to Eventing* she could think of on the spur of the moment.

"A rectangular ring with a little tiny fence around it," Samantha added, holding her hand about ankle high. "She goes up center line, but instead of turning, the horse just keeps going. Steps out of the arena and right past the judge."

"The expression on Em's face was priceless." Sandy laughed so hard she had to wipe the tears from her eyes. "Ten seconds into her first event on this horse and she's eliminated."

"All well and good for you guys to laugh it up," Emily lamented, although she laughed despite herself. "I couldn't get that thing to stop until he had his face buried in the feed bucket back at his stall."

"Pamela had choice words to say about that," Samantha reminisced. "I was glad I wasn't the one on the horse."

Sitting around the rickety picnic table and talking over old times, she almost forgot for a moment why the detective—Justin, she reminded herself—was there. He sat there, loose limbed and relaxed, interested in their conversation while most non-riders soon got glassy-eyed with boredom. But he wasn't just chatting, was he? She had to remind herself he was listening for information to help him catch a killer.

"What about you ladies?" he ventured. "Did any of you ever have any problems with Ms. Yates?"

After another fit of laughter, Erin howled, "Like we'd ever ride with Pam. Despite what everyone around here may think, we're not crazy. Well, not that crazy at least."

"Hunters are more our speed," Samantha chimed in. Emily took in her very un-hunter-like, fringed pink half-chaps and raised her eyebrow. "Okay, we don't fit in with that crowd either," Samantha admitted. "Which is why we're here with Ben."

"Since Pamela had Ben blacklisted, he's stuck with us ladies who hack." The three shared another round of titters.

They may not have realized they'd supplied Ben with a motive to kill Pamela, but Emily did. "Hang on, rumors have blown that way out of proportion. Pamela wasn't thrilled after Ben dissolved their partnership and took his clients to Middle Ranch, but—"

"Hah! 'Wasn't thrilled' is putting it mildly," Sandy interrupted. "First chance she got, she had him brought up on abuse charges."

Samantha added her two cents. "They banned Ben from showing for three years, so naturally, his clients who were serious left him and found another trainer."

"Funny, no one told me this before now." Justin's voice lost its light tone, and the heat of his glare rolled over Emily's skin.

"Well, of course they didn't." Erin continued her rant, oblivious to his irritation. "Everyone was afraid of her." The other two nodded in sad agreement.

"Although," Sandy said, hesitated, then continued, "I have to say, Pamela was always nice to me. She's the one who helped me contact Libby to get her to come out and talk to—oh! That's it, detective."

"Oh God," Emily mumbled as she bowed her head. This was what she had feared from the moment Sandy mentioned Libby Case's name.

"Where is my head these days? I should have thought of it sooner," the woman gushed. "The news said there were no witnesses to the murder, but there was. The little gray mare saw the whole thing. All we have to do is get Libby to come and ask her to identify the killer. I'll call her and set up a reading."

****

"So, when were you planning on telling me about Sanders's career being destroyed by Ms. Yates?" Justin demanded as they made their way back to her truck.

"He has an alibi. What difference does it make?"

The low, weary edge to his voice was worse than if he'd shouted at her. She regretted not telling him, but honestly, if she had to spell out all the grudges people had against Pamela, it would take all day.

"One we have yet to check," he ground out.

Exhausted from the long day, Emily pushed back. "It didn't seem important, okay?"

"The name of a person with a grudge against the murder victim didn't seem important? You ride horses for a living, I'm the detective. How about you tell me what you know. I'll decide what's important."

"Oh yeah? How about this? I'm not your fucking chauffeur," Emily hissed, her blood boiling. "Find your own ride next time, 'cause this little partnership is through."

Chapter Ten

The storm front moving in was nothing compared to the rage brewing inside Emily. She jerked the truck to a halt in the Equestrian Center parking lot and jumped out, slamming the door shut with a bang. Stiff from the drive, she stretched and felt a sickening pop in her spine as she tried to twist the misaligned bones into submission.

Her suffering wasn't restricted to the ache from the screws in her neck. Burning sensations shot down both legs as well. She'd pinched a nerve in her lower back again and the only treatment was lots of ice and a visit to her chiropractor. Unfortunately, she didn't have the time for one or the spare cash for the other. She gritted her teeth against the vise-like pain as she limped into the barn to check on the horses. Inside, she was relieved to see they'd all been fed and blanketed.

There, in the middle of the aisle, calling to her like a siren, was Pamela's tack trunk back from the show. Surely, she'd have pain meds in there to take off the raw edges. If nothing else, she usually brought something for the horses in case one of them developed a sore back after a show. It wouldn't be the first time Emily had taken a drug intended for an equine. She rattled the unfamiliar key lock on the hasp of the trunk. Where the hell would Pamela have put the key? She pulled harder, wondering how difficult it would be to break the lock off.

"I can help with that."

She jumped, startled to hear Justin's voice. The sudden movement rocked her with a fresh wave of pain. "What do you mean?"

Her heart hammered in her chest like a kid caught with their hand in the cookie jar. Would he really help her break into Pamela's trunk? She'd worry about getting the pills without him noticing once they got the damn thing open.

"Your back is clearly bothering you. I learned an acupressure technique in China that can ease the pain, at least for a little while."

She snorted derisively. "Just a little trick you picked up in China?"

"Okay, okay, I'm a pretentious jerk," he admitted with a smile. "But I can help."

Emily eyed him with suspicion. There was no end to the number of people with a way to *fix* her back. Nothing ever worked. "It's nothing, I'm fine, detective."

"I swear, I can help you if you are open to trying something a little different. And can we go back to Justin and Emily?"

Poised to refuse his help, another jolt of pain burned down her legs from the pinched nerve. *What the hell, I've got nothing to lose, right?* "Fine. You aren't going to try cracking my neck or anything, are you?"

"Take a seat," he invited, patting the damn wooden trunk she was sure held the real cure she needed.

She hesitated before giving in to his demand and eased herself onto the flat, smooth surface, biting back a groan of pain. Removing his overcoat, he folded it into a pillow and gestured for her to lie on her back. Emily hesitated before obliging, confident this was the dumbest thing she'd done all day.

"Relax," he instructed, easing her legs so her knees were bent, the soles of her boots flat on the tack trunk.

"What are you going to do?" she asked, rigid and unsure.

He answered by leaning over her and tenderly pressing the backs of her knees. A buzz of energy started in her legs but soon tingled through her entire body. She tried to bolt upright, but he gently pushed her shoulders back down.

"All I'm doing is pressing the B 54 acupressure point," he murmured in a soft, bedroom voice that spread a fire inside her. He rocked her legs back and forth in a slow, rhythmic pace, urging her to "just breathe and relax or this won't work."

She tried to stay calm but inhaling the cedar and spice of his aftershave had the opposite effect. His touch brought tingling sensations she suspected had more to do with her G spot than her B whatever spot. *Oh my God, has it been so long since I've had sex that this is all it takes?*

The chirp of the cell phone in her pocket broke the silence. She gasped at the unexpected call, as well as the extra stimulation from the phone's vibration. Tiny fireworks exploded where he'd already aroused her. She answered the phone in a husky voice.

"Emily? It's Darian, why do you sound so weird?" *Of course, it was Darian.* "Anyway," she rushed on without waiting for an answer, "I'm wondering if Alex is getting enough protein in his diet. I read an article in *Eventing Weekly* and…"

Emily let the phone hang in her hand as her client rambled on. *What had Lottie gotten her into?* She put the phone back up to her ear. "Um, Darian, it's after eight. Can we talk about this tomorrow?"

Sounding like her feathers had been ruffled, Darian vowed to call her first thing. Emily had no doubt her phone would ring precisely at seven, remembering Pamela complaining more than once about getting those calls.

Gazing into Justin's espresso-colored eyes, she realized Darian's call came in the nick of time. One more moment of his gentle massaging and she might have done something really foolish.

"I've got to go." She wriggled out from underneath him and was amazed to discover she actually could move more freely. "Holy crap, that does feel better," she admitted, free of the pain from the pinched nerve.

"Let me take you to dinner," he offered as he brushed the dust off his coat. "It's the least I can do for being a jerk earlier."

And then he turned on the million-dollar smile that must work with every woman he targeted. She hated men who thought they could get away with anything simply by being charming. Maybe she owed it to women everywhere not to let him off the hook without at least buying a couple of margaritas.

"All right," she sighed. "I know a place nearby."

****

Emily dragged Justin through Salud's garish faux-southwestern front dining room. Desperate to avoid the *America's Got Talent* wannabe standing on a tiny corner of the stage, nervously waiting for his turn, she wasn't fast enough to avoid his butchered opening of

Lineman for the County. She quickened her pace until she reached the dark comfort of the old bar in the back where the wailing faded into the background. Thank God. In an attempt to attract new customers in addition to the horse people from the Center, the management had opted for Karaoke Thursdays. The sparse crowd should have been proof enough the ploy wasn't working.

She pulled him into a corner booth, sinking into its worn, red vinyl embrace. The dimly lit, dark wood-paneled room felt like home. Not that she'd hang cheesy lanterns and even cheesier scenes of Mexico on her own walls. The warm, friendly atmosphere was what home should feel like and stood in sharp contrast to her Spartan apartment. It probably didn't make for the best impression on the cop, but having the bar staff hug her in welcome made her feel better. Without her uttering a word, a basket of chips and two margaritas appeared on their table.

"*Gracias*, Phillipè," she murmured, taking a long pull on the icy cold drink. She caught Justin watching her, barely touching his glass. *Oh God, he must think I'm a lush.* Embarrassed, she pushed her glass away so she wouldn't finish the rest of the drink in one big gulp.

"Sorry, guess I've been dreaming about that first sip for a while," she explained. Although she wasn't hungry, Emily focused on the chip basket to keep herself from saying or doing anything else humiliating.

He swirled his drink and took a taste. His eyebrows shot upward in response. "You're right, these are fantastic." He took another sip before breaking the uncomfortable silence. "Listen, I really am sorry about being a such a jerk. I appreciate you taking the time to drive me around and introduce me to some of Pamela's contacts."

His hand brushed hers. The gesture was no doubt a *thank you* for her help, but once again his touch sent an electrical current sizzling to places that made her squirm.

Emily cleared her throat, willing that squeaky, throat-closing-from-stress-and-lust quality to go away. "Did the information help your case?"

He shrugged. "It's hard to say where things will lead so early into the—"

A *thunk* from the front room as the karaoke machine hit the floor caught their attention. She glanced over to see what all the commotion was about and bit her lip, trying not to laugh as her ex-husband freed his ankle from the extension cord and stormed into the bar. His current wife hurried after him, her perky, blonde ponytail bobbing with every stride. In their matched set of tennis whites, they stuck out like sore thumbs in the cowboy bar.

"You did that on purpose," Nick bellowed, his face turning a purplish red.

Shit, he'd seen the truck. She'd driven the newly detailed truck through every mud hole she could find to spite him but hadn't planned on him seeing what a mess the truck was so soon. The other patrons, including Justin, stared at her, waiting for her response.

"What are you doing here?" It wasn't her best comeback, but it was the first thing that came to mind.

"Tori and I were on our way to a tennis clinic when I saw…how could you do that to Ellie May?"

How? His obsession with the stupid truck had always irked her. For a moment, she thought the man might burst into tears. "It's a truck, Nick. Get over it."

"You malicious little—"

Tori Conners's face lit up when her glance came to rest on Justin. She pulled on her husband's arm, interrupting his tirade. "Honey, we should let your ex-wife and her date enjoy their dinner."

"What? Don't be ridiculous, they're not together," he snapped, prying his wife's hand off his sleeve. "He's the detective investigating Pamela Yates's death."

His words were a slap in the face. Was the idea of a man being attracted to her so unheard of, so ridiculous, that Nick automatically dismissed it? She downed the rest of her margarita and signaled Phillipè for another.

"Actually, I'm off duty at the moment, Mr. Conners." Justin may have forced a smile, but his words carried a razor edge. "Emily and I were enjoying a quiet dinner before you interrupted. If you don't mind?" Half standing, he gestured at the door, his meaning clear. She thought her heart would burst. Even if he was just pretending, it was the nicest thing anyone had ever done for her.

"This isn't over," Nick growled as his wife pushed him to the exit.

"Wow, awkward," Emily murmured, noticing everyone in Salud's staring at the retreating couple—except for the three drunks listening to a singer strangle a cat on the mini stage.

"Want me to shoot him?"

Justin's deadpan delivery made it hard for her to tell if he meant it. Then she saw the corner of his mouth quirk up into a smile. She laughed and toasted his joke before realizing she had already downed her second margarita. When did that happen? In the blink of an eye, Phillipè replaced the empty glass with a new one, and she vowed to make this one last longer.

"My own fault." She held tight to her glass, the stem slick with condensation. "That damn truck has always meant more to him than me."

"Hence the reason you were so willing to drive me around today through all that mud." He nodded in understanding. "It was a way to get back at your ex."

"He named the truck, for Christ's sake."

"So how come if he loves the truck so much, you have it and not him?"

"Because my divorce attorney was a lot smarter than his," Emily replied, letting an evil grin spread across her face.

He choked on a chip. "Wait a minute. You took his truck—his pride and joy—from him in the divorce settlement?"

"I didn't ask for any alimony, even though I supported him when he was in law school." She winced, realizing how defensive she sounded.

"But why did you want it?"

She swirled her straw in her once again empty glass. They must be making these things smaller. "Because he did."

To her surprise, he laughed out loud. "You may be a bitchy ex-wife, but at least you're upfront about it. Now, what's good on the menu besides margaritas?"

After an hour of small talk over Mexican food, including what foods scare you—his fear of Brussels sprouts puzzled her—and their worst moments on the dance floor, Emily had to keep reminding herself this wasn't a date. He was only being polite. She washed each reminder down with a sip of a margarita. By the end of the meal, she felt a little tipsy.

"Let me drive you home," he offered, his hand on the small of her back as he guided her toward the door.

She shook her head. "No need, I can walk. I just live down the block."

However, more proof that Fate hated her greeted them as they opened the door to discover the rainstorm that threatened all afternoon had arrived.

"Come on, I'll give you a lift," Justin said, laughing at her sour expression. "I'll let you turn on the cherry light."

****

Emily's apartment was literally down the block, a horseshoe-shaped, two-story building decked out in a cutesy fake Tudor finish. Justin ignored her instruction to let her out at the curb, insisting on dashing through the downpour to her door. He even held his coat over their heads to protect them from the rain—and didn't quite succeed. She opened the door to her miniscule apartment and cringed, concerned about what he'd think.

"It's cute," he commented as he stepped inside to get out from under the steady stream caused by the building's broken gutter.

A tuxedo cat jumped from out of nowhere to growl at him. "Behave yourself," she scolded, picking up the cat with an easy swoop. "Sorry. Samwise takes his role as guard cat a little too seriously."

Amused, he scratched the cat under the chin and was rewarded with loud, rumbling purrs. "So if he's Samwise, does that make you Frodo?"

"A cop who reads Tolkien. How unexpected." He bowed his head in acknowledgement as he continued to

81

scratch Sam's greedy, little chin. "Kudos to your grade school English teacher," she continued. "But even if there were noble quests or ring bearers anymore, it certainly wouldn't be me."

His reply was cut short by the sudden blaring of the same, annoying K-pop song from the apartment above. She dropped the now growling Samwise. "Sorry, again. That's my whacko neighbor upstairs. Ever since she moved in six months ago, we've been having this battle. I exist, so she protests my existence by playing the same song, over and over and over again."

"Want me to shoot her?"

"I'm touched at your continuing offer to shoot people for me. It's so sweet." She laughed. "I talked to the manager, but there's not much he can do. I complain about her making noise, she complains about me making noise, and on it goes. Thing is, I can't afford to move."

"I could pay her a formal visit, flash my badge at her if you want?"

"No, God no." She laughed. "Can you imagine what she'd play if I started responding to her little fits?"

"There's something worse than K-pop?"

Emily shuddered. "Ever hear that kid song about a shark?"

He put up his hands in surrender. "Good point. At least Jungkook is cute."

"Detective," she teased, "you're scaring me with your knowledge of K-pop. Best to say goodnight now before you totally erase all the points you gained with the whole *Lord of the Rings* reference."

Justin hesitated, then gave her a chaste kiss on the lips before saying goodbye. She watched him go, frustrated and confused by this man. *A peck on her lips?* The last time that had happened was on her first ever date in junior high while her dad watched. She shut the door with an irritated grunt.

****

He felt her eyes boring into his back, but he refused to turn around. If he did, it would be his downfall. He didn't trust himself.

Reaching his car, he sank wearily into the leather seat. Alone in the dark, he pounded his head on the steering wheel. Every fiber of his being wanted to say goodnight by pressing his mouth hard against hers, tasting her fully. That moment and what came afterward was all he'd thought about since he saw her riding that damn horse this morning. He was pretty sure he could be in her bed if he applied a little of the usual charm, but he also knew she'd regret it. She'd blame him for taking advantage of her being drunk and never trust him again. And in the span of their brief kiss, what this woman thought of him had become vitally important.

Chapter Eleven

The patrolman's face turned a bright red as Lottie whispered a breathy, "Thank you," in his ear for letting her and Emily into Pamela's house. He beat a hasty retreat to his car, asking Emily to let him know when they were done so he could lock up. Brows furrowed, she turned to her friend. "Did you cup his butt?"

Giving a demure smile, Lottie shrugged. "What's the harm in a little flirting?"

"Other than having to face Detective Butler after he was nice enough to let us into Pam's place and admit you sexually harassed his officer? Yeah, no problem."

"Oh, lighten up. Besides, I thought you'd be on more intimate terms with the man by now."

God, Lottie could be annoying, especially when she was right. Last night, Emily would have been happy to become more *intimate*. One kiss is all it would have taken—so what the hell was the brief buss to her lips all about? "Can we just get on with this?"

She recalled the times they'd come here before for Christmas parties, but the place felt different now. Without all the forced holiday cheer, it was empty and silent. The phrase *quiet as a tomb* sprang to mind.

Lottie picked up a photo of a much younger Pam on a big, gray horse going over a jump. "How did we get roped into putting together her memorial service?"

"Was I supposed to say no when Erin called?"

It was bad enough the woman was brutally murdered, but to add insult to injury, no one cared enough to throw her a wake. Which made Em wonder who would be there to memorialize *her* when *she* died. Besides, this little field trip made for a great excuse to avoid getting back on Reese.

Once Lottie proceeded to the kitchen in search of commemorative worthy items, Emily called out, "I'm going to go to the bathroom. I'll be right back."

"Yeah, whatever."

After flicking on the light, she opened the medicine cabinet and rummaged through the various bottles of pills inside. Rather than bothering with reading the labels, she grabbed them all and stuffed them in the pockets of her coat. She jumped as Lottie's voice came toward her.

"Oh hey, don't forget to grab her..." She popped her head in the doorway just as Emily pocketed her stash. *Had she seen her take the pills?* "Grab her skin cream. The woman may have had a black heart, but she had skin as soft as a baby's. These lotions are too expensive to let go to waste."

Emily let out the breath she didn't know she'd been holding, relieved to have escaped her close call as she tossed the tubes and bottles in a grocery bag she'd liberated from the kitchen. She returned to the living room where she found Lottie gazing at the bookshelves with a frown. "Didn't there used to be a small, plastic trophy on that shelf?"

"You're right. It was one of those cheap ones like you get on Hollywood Boulevard," she agreed. "Wasn't there a framed photograph next to it?"

"Yeah, a picture of Pamela with a man I didn't

recognize. I remember because I asked her about it since it's the only photo I'd ever seen of her where she wasn't on a horse."

"What'd she say?"

Lottie gave her a deadpan look. "She confessed all her secrets, and then we did each other's hair. What do you think? She ignored the question completely."

Curious, Emily pulled a chair out of the kitchen and stood on it to inspect the shelf. Sure enough, there was a mark in the dust where the trophy and picture frame had been. "Isn't that weird?" She surveyed the other shelves from her higher vantage point to see if they had been shifted to another spot, but both the trophy and picture were definitely gone.

"Maybe Detective Butler took them as evidence when they searched the house. Why don't you call him and ask?"

She scowled at the suggestion. Her friend was right, but the thought of calling him made her feel sixteen again, waiting for her high school heartthrob to answer the phone. Feeling so jittery annoyed her back then and was downright ridiculous now.

Squashing down the butterflies, she pulled out her phone and punched a button. "Detective Butler, please."

Lottie waggled both eyebrows at her. "You've got his number on speed dial already?"

"Shut up," she muttered, being sure to cover the phone. "I had to call his office this morning to get in the house, remember?"

A warm, masculine voice rumbled in her ear. "Emily, I thought we agreed to drop the formalities and be on a first-name basis. How's your back?"

Heat rose to her cheeks as she blushed at the

memory. "It's fine, thanks. Listen, we're at Pamela's house and we found a couple of things have gone missing. It seems stupid, but you asked me to let you know if anything came up so…I'm letting you know."

****

Justin hung up the phone whistling under his breath, which wouldn't have worried Dennis except the tune sounded like "Camptown Races." Hard to tell, when someone whistled so off-key, but the choice of tunes made him suspicious. He'd walked in at the end of the conversation, but he had a pretty good idea who was on the other end of the line.

He casually picked a jellybean out of the jar on his partner's desk. "Is it a good idea to mess around with a potential witness in an active investigation? Hell, forget smart, I'm not even sure it's legal."

"What are you talking about?" Justin was a good cop, but a lousy liar.

"The waif, what's her name, in the boots?"

"Emily Conners? That phone call was strictly business. She discovered a couple of items are missing at the Yates house and thought the information might be important."

Dennis took another jellybean, scrutinizing his partner. "So there's nothing going on between you?"

"Don't be stupid," Justin asserted, turning his full attention to shuffling through the files on his desk.

And that's how he knew he was right. Nothing was ever out of order on that meticulous desk. Shit, this must be serious. "Right, so yesterday while you were out playing footsy—"

"Also known as interviewing a suspect in a murder."

"Tomato, tomahto. Anyway, I went over to re-interview Robbie Allen's father."

Justin froze. "You did?"

He was stung by his dubious tone. "Yes, me. Believe it or not, I can behave in public without you there as my chaperone."

A face-to-face with a city commissioner typically fell under Justin's purview. Even Dennis admitted he lacked his partner's more subtle social graces, but after the information they got from Frankie Gillette, they needed to talk to him sooner rather than later. "So what did he say?"

"Actually, I got cock-blocked by a guy named Victor Maxwell, the chief of staff for Commissioner Allen and allegedly a mentor to Robbie." His jaw tightened just thinking about the meeting. "Thing is, Maxwell already knew about Robbie's history with hookers."

"What? When we talked to his father the day after the murder, he claimed the kid was a saint, everyone loved him." Justin leaned back in his chair, steepling his fingers in thought. "Did he have anything new?"

"You mean like where he was the night of the murder? Claimed to be at an awards dinner, but there's something off about this Maxwell guy. He's hiding something." He felt Justin's eyes on him but couldn't make himself meet his gaze. "He knows things he shouldn't. Not just about Robbie, but about me and my...issues in Philly."

Without looking at him, he knew his partner had leaned forward, hands clenched in a fist. Jay was one of the few people who knew about Dennis's troubles after his divorce. "Everything?" he asked in a hushed tone.

"About my stay in the loony bin? Yeah, that thing."

The years hadn't dulled the bitterness he felt about that seventy-two-hour psych hold his ex-wife insisted on after a drinking binge led to him looking down the barrel of his own gun. *For my own good, my ass.* At the *suggestion* of the Philadelphia police commissioner that he work elsewhere, he'd taken the first job he was offered, moved to LA, and completed the department required counseling. Justin, their lieutenant, and a few higher-ups were the only ones who knew.

"He didn't come out and say it, but the implication was he'd expose me if we didn't focus on Jimmy Gillette and his girl as the suspects."

"Access to your personnel files is restricted, which tells me Victor Maxwell might have an informant inside the department."

"It gets better," Dennis continued, jaw loosening a little as the topic shifted off him. "I got a call earlier that patrol spotted Jimmy Gillette's car illegally parked in a handicap spot." He forced himself to take another jellybean. They were organic and disgusting, but he needed to create the illusion he was fine.

"Why would Jimmy do that?"

"Why indeed, when it's one of the few parking violations that means your car gets towed to a police lot? And there on the front seat, they found a gun registered to Jimmy."

"Very thoughtful of a guy, who doesn't have a permanent address, to register his gun," Justin commented. "You think Maxwell is pulling strings in City Hall to set him up?"

Unwittingly, Dennis popped a black jellybean in his mouth and then spit it out into the garbage can.

There were things even he wouldn't eat, and licorice was one of them. "My guess is he's connected to someone with a little more juice." He bent his nose to the side, giving the old-fashioned symbol for the Mafia.

Justin nodded his head in agreement. "Jimmy, Jimmy, Jimmy. What have you gotten yourself into?"

Dennis was more concerned with what Gillette had gotten *them* into.

Chapter Twelve

The morning of the animal communicator extravaganza started out peachy as far as Emily was concerned. First, she discovered—surprise, surprise—she'd gotten her period. Next, her shoelace broke, rendering her tall field boots useless. She tried to use her short paddock boots only to have the zipper on her half-chaps break. Feeling bloated and cranky, with one field boot flopping open at the ankle, broken lace dragging, she stomped into the Saddle Shoppe.

Even when she'd been a lawyer's wife with money to burn, Emily rarely shopped there because it was so expensive. The shop counted on the boarders at the Center being a captive audience and thanked them for their devotion by taking the concept of over-pricing to outrageous heights. But, as the shop was located inside the Center, and she was running late, convenience outweighed price. If she showed up late for the horse reading, Lottie would kill her. Besides, she hadn't been in since the new owners had taken over, so maybe things had changed. How much can you possibly charge for a shoelace?

Behind the counter, a scruffily attractive man greeted her with an attempt at a smile. Through red-rimmed eyes, he offered to find whatever she needed. More drama. Just what she wanted right now. "Uh, I need a pair of laces for my field boots."

"Murph, didn't we get a shipment of shoelaces yesterday?" he called out after a few minutes of fussing around under the counter.

A shorter, balding man materialized behind her, causing her to nearly jump out of her floppy boot. "Hi honey, Joey Murphy. How're you doing?" The newcomer offered his hand on his way to join the other man behind the tall glass counter. "This is my partner, Brandon Sinclair."

From the way he put a comforting arm around the other man, she realized *partner* didn't refer only to business. Seeing how much they cared for each other, she felt a stab of jealousy. If she wasn't careful, she might join Brandon in his crying jag. Damn hormones.

"Cleverly hidden, right in front," Murphy joked as he handed over the laces, continuing to give the attractive man's back a soothing rub. "You look familiar—aren't you a trainer at the Center?"

She shifted uncomfortably, unsure herself what she was at this moment. "I'm kind of taking over Pamela Yates's barn for the time being."

Horrified recognition dawned on both men's faces. She backed away, shocked at their reaction. She'd never even met these guys, what on Earth had she done to make them stare at her with such revulsion?

Brandon's lip quivering kicked into overdrive, his eyes glistening. "Oh my, you're the one who found her, aren't you? Who found Pamela I mean after she—" Stealing a quick worried glance at his partner, he finished. "—after she'd passed on."

Great. A new bit of fame she didn't need. Add it to, "oh, you're the one who broke her neck after your horse crushed you," and it would make for a great cocktail party icebreaker. If she was ever invited to a party after all this.

She crossed her arms, assuming the next questions would ask for all the gross, horrific details she never wanted to recall again. Trying to cut the ghoul seekers off at the pass, she kept her answer curt. "Yes, I found the murdered body of my friend and employer. I don't want to talk about it, so if you don't mind, tell me how much I owe for the laces, and I'll be on my way."

Their stunned expressions made Emily feel pretty good about herself, having put two thrill seekers in their places. Then Brandon choked back a sob as tears trailed down his handsome face. *Shit*. Great job, Em, you've made a grown man cry.

Murphy shushed Brandon's mewling and turned his attention back to her. She expected a tongue-lashing but instead, he gave her a smile so intensely kind she understood what hunky Brandon was doing with this less attractive man.

"You poor thing, you've been through enough. Take the laces, they're on us. You see, Pamela was Brandon's—"

"Friend. Very close friend," he interrupted. Murphy shot him a strange glance, but if there was a message there, it was lost on Emily. "If there's anything you need, give us a shout."

Murphy nodded in agreement, handing her the laces and three pieces of chocolate from the bowl on the counter with a conspiratorial wink.

****

Justin strode down the barn aisle at the Equestrian Center, expecting things would be calmer without all the crime scene tape and unis swarming the place. He was wrong. If anything, the group gathered in front of the stall housing the gray mare who had it out for him thrummed with even more excited energy.

Lottie stood in the middle of the melee, checking her watch and offering her excuses with a tight, unapologetic smile. "Emily will be here any minute, and then we can get started." Her expression dared anyone to start before she arrived.

He didn't know Mrs. Gray very well but suspected he wouldn't want to be in Emily's shoes and face her wrath. He hung back for a moment, more interested in learning about his suspect pool than whatever the so-called horse whisperer could tell him.

A short, round woman with a cherubic face gave Lottie a friendly nod, but then Sandy Peters, the woman he'd met the other day at Ben Sanders's place, waved her clipboard in Lottie's face. "Libby has a schedule to keep. There are a lot of other people waiting to have their horses read, too."

"And how many of those were witnesses to a murder?" she countered.

Justin stepped forward before things got ugly. "Excuse me, ladies, am I late?"

Everyone, including the serene woman in the middle of the group, Libby Case, he presumed, turned toward him. Despite the fact he was the only one who was armed, he felt like a chicken strolling into a fox convention. They all sort of lunged, but Sandy was faster on her feet and beat them all to his side. "Detective Butler, how kind of you to come."

"Yes, ma'am. Your four messages convinced me to at least listen to what Ms. Case had to say."

Clipboard clutched to her chest, Sandy beamed as

she introduced the detective to Libby Case.

"Nice to meet you, ma'am. I've read about your work. It's certainly—" He fished around for something polite to say. "—interesting."

He'd read a number of articles about her but remained unconvinced that she would be helpful to his investigation. He believed she thought she could talk to horses, but there wasn't any way of knowing if she got it right, was there? He hadn't tried very hard to hide his disbelief, but to her credit, what he thought didn't seem to throw Libby the tiniest bit.

"All right," Case said. "Let's go talk to Feneatha."

Over Lottie's protests, Libby led the growing group over to the horse's stall. Just as she opened the stall door to introduce herself to the mare, Emily ambled up next to Lottie, a broken shoelace trailing behind her.

"Do you have to work hard to find ways to drive me crazy, or does it come naturally?" Lottie hissed out of the corner of her mouth. He ducked his head to hide his amused grin.

"It's a gift I try to use only for good, not evil."

He raised his gaze to meet Emily's. The corners of her mouth crept up in a slow smile, and for a moment, he flashed back to how soft they were to kiss. She must have been thinking about it too because he saw her cheeks flush. It was either the kiss or embarrassment as the group collectively shushed her. It was unfair to shush such a lovely laugh in a barn of all places—it wasn't a library after all—but the reading had already started.

****

"Hello, sweetie. Aren't you the pretty one," Libby

95

murmured, petting the fine-boned gray mare's face.

Words spilled out to no one in particular, though at least one of many cell phones in the group thrust in her direction was bound to record every word. "Once the horse has given me permission, I do a body scan to see if everything is in working order."

The growing crowd, which added people like an avalanche picked up snow, held its breath. She continued, her head tilted as she apparently listened to a conversation no one else was privy to, like Lieutenant Uhura at the horsey comm link.

Justin was in mid-eye roll when she broke the silence. "Did she suffer a fall of some kind? She'd like a massage and more heat therapy, her back still hurts."

The group let out a collective gasp. He didn't know what she was talking about, but from the reaction of the crowd, they did. He cocked a suspicious eyebrow at her—there had been plenty of time before he got there for someone to slip her the information.

"Boy and wasn't that embarrassing! She's saying geez, I hope everyone understands it wasn't my fault," Libby continued. "After her back is better, she'd like to be in a parade or a costume class, anything where she gets to dress up."

Twitters of laughter and gasps of "Oh my God, that is so Feneatha. How did she know?" rippled through the crowd.

"Ma'am," Justin interrupted, trying to contain his impatience, "is there any way we can jump to the night of the murder?"

She concentrated on Feneatha for a moment and then shook her head. "Sorry, detective, this little mare has a lot to say and has been waiting a long time to say it. Mares can be that way." She shrugged her thick shoulders while her fans nodded in agreement.

Libby was right. Feneatha did have a lot to say. She continued on for a while, demanding, among other things, more orange Popsicles—to which a young woman whined, "I only did it once"—and a party in her honor.

"Ma'am," he asked the horse communicator, clenching his jaw against the unbelievably stupid question he was about to ask. "Did the horse see anything the night of the murder?" He hoped like hell none of his co-workers ever found out about this farce. He'd never hear the end of it. "Can she identify the killer?"

Libby stared at the mare for a while before shaking her head, perplexed. "I'm sorry, detective. I communicate with animals through pictures and when I ask about the killer, all she keeps showing me is a bear riding a rocking horse."

It wasn't the first uncooperative witness he'd dealt with, but he hadn't expected the horse to be so evasive. As if any of this was real in the first place. He fought hard to keep the sarcasm out of his voice when he asked the surrounding women, "Does a bear on a rocking horse mean something to any of you?"

Everyone shook their heads in muttered confusion and started moving on to the next stall when Libby stopped dead in her tracks. "She's worried about you," she said to Emily in an ominous tone. "She's concerned the same thing that happened to Ginger will happen to you. She's begging you to please be careful."

Everyone backed away from Emily as if she'd been pronounced to be a carrier of the deadly bird flu.

Amused by their stunned expressions, Justin smiled until he noticed she'd gone chalk white. Lottie rushed to her side as she sank onto the nearest tack trunk. The group bustled on to hear the next reading. The flurry of excitement in the air had turned into a cloud of odd discomfort.

He came over and squatted in front of Emily. "I assume from your reaction Ginger wasn't a horse."

Staring at her boot, she cracked a feeble smile and shook her head. "Ginger Mills filled in as Pamela's assistant after my fall." She gazed up at him, her eyes brimming with tears. "It's so stupid to get this rattled, right?" She looked to Lottie for affirmation but got nothing. "It's just—" She turned back to him. "—well, Ginger died of an accidental drug overdose."

Lottie *tsked.* "Accidental, my ass."

"Suicide?" Justin asked.

Lottie bit her lip, hesitating for a moment before replying, "There were whispers she was murdered."

Chapter Thirteen

Emily's thoughts spun in circles. On the one hand, Libby's mojo was smoke and mirrors, revealing only vague horoscope-type information. But while the animal communicator had no way of knowing she'd used the rest of Ginger's painkillers after she died, Feneatha did. Ginger had hidden the bottle of pills and a stash of pot in the tack trunk in front of the mare's stall. She and Emily were the only ones who knew about it. Evidently, the mare was a keen observer. But come on, how did she *tell* Libby?

The idea was laughable, but the accuracy of her statement made it hard to dismiss. She fought to regain control of her breathing. Good God, was she really so easily thrown by an ooga booga warning from a horse? Thankfully, Lottie was too caught up in the moment's intrigue to notice, because she rattled on with more than enough glee. "It makes perfect sense. The same person who killed Pamela must have murdered Ginger."

"Why didn't anyone tell me about another murder before now?" Justin's exasperated tone drove her over the edge.

"Aaaah," Emily howled in frustration, rubbing her temples to abate the oncoming headache. "No one murdered Ginger. Twenty years of heavy drug use caught up with her, and her overtaxed, toxic body gave out. Only Lottie and Oliver Stone could possibly see a conspiracy in her death."

Lottie stared at her in wide-eyed horror. "Her years of drug use are all the more reason it's ridiculous to assume she overdosed. She was hardly an amateur. And Feneatha thinks you might be next."

Truthfully, it was a relief that her friend jumped to that conclusion. It was better than assuming, as she had, that the horse was saying she took too many painkillers, just like Ginger did. She shook her head in disgust at both ideas. "Great, now we're listening to warnings from horses via Libby." Casting a glance at Justin for support, it surprised her to find him scrutinizing her. She squirmed beneath his intense gaze.

"What did the coroner list as the official cause of death?" His diplomatic, non-committal tone revealed nothing about how seriously he may or may not be taking all this.

"But that's the thing." Lottie raised a finger victoriously, stopping short of saying *aha*. "The police wouldn't release information to anyone but family. Why hide it if she died of natural causes?"

"Department policy prohibits releasing information to the public. Fortunately—" He pulled out his cell phone. "—I'm not the public."

****

"Oh, come on, you can't be serious?" Emily babbled, her jaw dropped in disbelief.

"I'm not convinced," Justin admitted, "but two deaths in a relatively small community is an enormous coincidence. What was Ginger's last name again?"

"Mills. She died about three months ago, right before Emily came back to work," Lottie eagerly added.

When Dennis answered, Justin explained the

situation and asked him to pull the case file.

"On it, but listen to this. As usual, you were right, you Jedi motherfucker. There have been several lawsuits filed against Ms. Yates in the past, most of which were resolved out of court. However, there was one active lawsuit on the books at the time of her death. A Heather Dane sued her for a shitload of dough after a near-fatal accident caused by one of Yates's horses."

He glanced at Emily. "Seems to happen a lot. I'll work on tracking down the Dane woman and then see you back at the office." Tucking his phone away, he turned back to the women.

"The file is being pulled as we speak. In the meantime, can you tell me where I might find a woman named Heather Dane?"

The two women exchanged puzzled glances. "Heather? Why do you want to talk to her?"

"Some questions have come up in the course of Ms. Yates's murder investigation, and I need to discuss them with her."

Emily burst out laughing. "I'm sorry," she apologized, but her continued mirth showed otherwise. "But if you're considering Heather as a suspect, you're way off-base. It's impossible for her to—"

He interrupted her. "Again, how about you leave the detecting to me? All I need you to do is tell me where I can find Ms. Dane."

"But—" Lottie started to explain until Emily cut her off.

"No, the *detective* is right." She emphasized his rank, making it clear they were no longer on a first-name basis. "He's much more clever than us mere women. If he wants to interview Heather, who are we to stop him? I'm sorry, Detective Butler, I don't have her current address, but more than likely she'll be at the wake. You're welcome to talk to her there. Now if you'll excuse me, I've got horses to ride."

He assumed from the sarcasm dripping off her voice there was more to this story, but she left, pulling Lottie along with her. God, she could be infuriating, he thought, as he stalked out of the barn.

****

Emily's day snowballed into one disaster after another. The horses were feisty, riders taking lessons whined at the least little things, and her cramps rose to epic proportions. She decided the next time she broke a shoelace first thing in the morning, she would take it as a sign from God and go back to bed. By four o'clock, tired, gritty, and ready for a margarita, she was in no mood to have Doc Ridley waiting in her office. But there he was, in his usual spiffy shirt and dry-cleaned jeans, sitting on the edge of her desk.

Crap.

"Emily," he gushed, holding out a hand in greeting.

She took it, and before she could stop him, he pulled her in for a hug. Only instead of patting her on the back, he grabbed her ass. Disgusted, Emily slid out of his grasp. She wanted to tell him that shit might have worked thirty years ago, before the #MeToo movement and when his bushy mustache was actually in style, but he made her skin crawl too much to engage with him. Whatever potential he once had to be considered handsome had gone soft and pasty, not to mention he managed to make a full head of his own hair resemble a cheap toupee. Top it all off with the tarnished gold chain pushing its way out of the vee-neck of his designer polo shirt and you had quite the appealing picture. How Pamela tolerated the man was beyond her.

"What can I do for you, Doc?"

"Is that why you've been avoiding me? You thought I wanted something from you? Sweetheart, the question is what can I do for you?" He exposed his capped teeth in a forced smile, arms open wide in a benevolent gesture of goodwill. "I'm here to help in any way I can during your time of transition. Smooth the way for Pamela's clients who might be on the fence, convince them to stay with you. Especially when they see I'll still be around as their vet."

So there it was, the pitch she'd been waiting for. It would be easy to accept his offer now, and later on, once she was firmly established, fire him. In fact, that's what Lottie had told her to do. But right now, after the day she'd had, she didn't care about playing it smart.

"I'm afraid that won't be possible."

She expected him to fly into the temper she'd seen him demonstrate more than a few times. Instead, he laughed. "Oh, Pumpkin, everybody knows you're an oxy time bomb, and the fuse is almost up. Do you expect any of the other vets out there want to risk getting involved with you?" Though smiling, he took hold of Emily's arm and pulled her to his chest. "Don't even think about terminating the agreement I had with Pamela. Maybe, if you're really nice to me—" He sneered. "—I'll make you as rich as she was."

Emily tried to pull her arm away, but his grip tightened. A thrill of fear fluttered in her stomach. Would he try anything in a busy barn with people right outside her office door? She didn't wait to find out. Instinct and anger took over as she hooked the side of his calf with the heel of her boot, biting through flesh with the spurs she still wore. He roared in pain and flung her back so hard she nearly fell over the desk.

Desperate to rub her arm to ease the sting of his mauling, she refused to give him the satisfaction. Besides, the arm was the least of her wounds. "You're fired, Ridley."

An oxy time bomb? Is that really what everyone thought?

"You can't get rid of me so easily. I was Pamela's partner, God dammit, she owed me." He slammed his fist on the desk. She backed away, intimidated by the vehemence of his words. Had he killed her over a business deal gone wrong?

Being more flight than fight animals, the horses in the stalls closest to the office became unsettled at Doc's shouting and banging. It set off a cacophony of pounding hooves and fearful whinnies that brought a number of the grooms to the area. Like a cockroach scurrying away when a light is turned on, the attention sent Ridley stomping out of her office. He turned to wag one last frustrated fist in her direction, a bubble of spittle caught in his cheesy mustache. "One way or another, I will get what's rightfully mine."

Once he was gone, Emily's legs collapsed. Fortunately, she was close enough to the desk chair to land mostly on the dusty seat. Her hands shook. Fear and alarm charged her with too much adrenalin. All those years, had Pamela stayed in business with Ridley because she was afraid of him? That made a lot more sense than her liking him. The gnawing fear in the pit of her stomach grew. She could easily imagine the vet's rage exploding to the point where he brutally smashed

Pam's face in. Did he murder her over whatever he thought she owed him? A debt he now assumes is hers?

She should call Justin, tell him what happened, but she didn't trust her voice. The last thing she wanted to do was confirm the idea she was a hysterical dimwit. She needed something to calm her nerves first, so she opened the desk drawer and took out one of the pill bottles she'd taken from Pamela's bathroom. Shaking the amber plastic vial, she realized there were only three left. Someone else must be borrowing them as well.

She read the label for the first time, *Take One As Needed For Pain.*

What the hell; she dry-swallowed all three and waited for the fear and trembling to go away.

Chapter Fourteen

Justin had a hard time following any of the conversations about helmets, horse breeds, and new rules that occupied the mixed crowd at Pamela Yates's memorial service. There must have been two hundred people there from every walk of life, mingling at the little hilltop restaurant where the wake was held. The only thing they weren't talking about was Pamela Yates. He felt a little sorry for her. If the only thing worse than being talked about is not being talked about, the ultimate insult must be not being talked about at your own funeral.

In one corner, a rough-looking man held court over a group of women wearing chic dresses by designers he recognized as favorites of his mother's wealthy friends. Horse whisperer obsessed Sandy Peters was there, engaged in lively conversation with two men in matching casual khaki attire, except one had a designer logo and the other was a cheap knockoff. They made him feel over-dressed in his dark suit. At least he hadn't worn a tie. Gruff stories elicited outrageously loud laughs, particularly for a funeral. Justin sauntered into the small chrome-and-glass-walled bar area, searching the crowd for Emily.

He made his way through the throng, accepting a drink offered by the waitress. What the hell, he wasn't on duty. By the time he made it to the door of the patio, he saw a few actors he recognized from television huddled with a woman with a German accent. It was interesting to see Pamela's ex-partner, Ben Sanders, there staring moodily out of the window nursing a can of diet soda. Two men, who were obviously a domestic couple, glared at him from another table. Justin filed their faces away in his memory, making a mental note to find out what that was all about.

Caught up in the drama, he almost missed Kate Williams, the trainer he'd met the morning of the murder, standing over by the bar. Her overblown, over-sprayed hair had been replaced by a wig that sat askew on her head. Fortunately, he saw her before she saw him. Discretion being the better part of valor, he snuck out onto the restaurant's stone patio as snippets of conversation about a horse going suspiciously lame streamed past him.

The views of the valley below were breathtaking, especially at this time of the year when last week's rain had cleared the air to a bright, crystal blue. The gas fire pits were already roaring, guarding the mourners against the dropping temperatures. The clear sky meant another bitterly chilly desert night, but that was a couple of hours away. He swirled the glass of red wine in his hand, not bad for a house brand, and turned away from the view to study the crowd. He might be standing no more than a hundred yards from Pamela's killer. If only he knew who it was.

"I'll give you this much, you've got a set of brass balls on you." He turned to see Lottie, a glass of bubbling clear liquid and a twist of lime in her hand. "And here I thought police only came to funerals in terrible cop shows."

He half-smiled and shook his head. "Remember, Ms. Conners invited me here herself to talk to suspects, but I swear I'm not here on official business. I only came to make sure she was okay."

He sipped the wine in his glass and waited while Lottie observed him. He knew that expression. It was the one Dennis wore when deciding if a suspect was telling the truth or not. When her sculpted eyebrow twitched, he assumed he'd passed her test. "If you're lying, I'll pull your balls off with my bare hands."

Pull? He winced, never doubting for a minute she was fully capable of such a vicious act. He smiled. She reminded him of his mother. Kind of.

"Scout's honor." He held up the required three fingers. "My partner told me she called in yesterday after a little run in with a guy named Ridley. I wanted to make sure he didn't give her any trouble here." No need to tell her he was never a Boy Scout.

She snorted, taking his arm. "That little worm wouldn't dare try anything in public, not with all this potential income floating around. Come on, genius, there's someone I think you should meet."

He followed her across the patio to a woman sitting alone by a fire pit. "Heather, I'd like you to meet Detective Butler. Detective, this is Heather Dane."

The woman rose to her feet in slow, deliberate movements—immediately catching his attention. "Detective Butler."

She spoke in a voice so soft, he had to lean close to understand her. She raised her right arm to shake his hand in the same slow, cautious manner when she stood up. He took her offered hand. She beamed at him, the twinkle in her eyes undiminished by the odd tilt of her partially paralyzed face. "You have no idea how delighted I am to meet the only person in the world who thinks I'm tough enough to take a whack at Pamela."

Now he understood why Emily insisted there was no need to talk to her. A frustrated sigh slipped out without him realizing it. Ms. Dane glanced between him and Lottie, smiling. "You didn't know about my condition?"

Lottie gasped. "Oh shit, Heather, I'm so sorry, I didn't mean to embarrass you, I...shit, shit, shit."

"What she means to say is she wanted to teach me a lesson," Justin explained, feeling almost as horrified as Lottie looked. "I'm afraid you got caught in the cross-fire."

To their surprise, Heather enjoyed a long, airy laugh at their expense. "Oh please, this is nothing," she said between wheezes of laughter. "You want embarrassing? Try having a total stranger wipe your bottom during six months of rehab." The fact she could chuckle over her hellish experience made her Justin's new hero.

"And don't gawk at me with your big brown eyes full of pity." Heather's voice gained an edge that hadn't been there before. "I hate *you poor brave thing* looks. Ask Emily. If anything sends you over the edge, it's that."

As Lottie and Heather continued to chat, Justin shifted to put his glass down and saw Emily enter the patio. Wow. Audrey Hepburn wouldn't have done the simple black dress more justice. In the movies, the crowds always part for the heroine's entrance, but in fact, she had to shoulder her way through the thickening mass to get to the open space of the balcony. Her gaze found his, and for a moment, he could have sworn she was happy to see him.

Then her attention landed on Heather next to him and her grip tightened on the wine glass clutched in her hand as she marched toward them. "Heather, are you okay? Is the detective bothering you?"

"A hunky man seeks my company, and you think I'm bothered?" Heather chortled. "It may happen to you all the time, but for me, this is a first, so back off and let me enjoy my moment." She gave an impish smile as Emily's face turned bright red. "Detective, I'm assuming you know about the lawsuit. Pamela asked me if I'd ride one of her horses for her. She'd been riding all day and was tired, but the horse needed to be shown to a potential buyer. Like a jackass, I agreed. The next thing I remember is waking up in the hospital two months later.

"At first, the doctors were sure I'd never come out of the coma. Then they claimed the brain damage was so severe that I'd never speak or feed myself. Then it was 'okay, but she definitely won't walk again.' When I beat that, the experts said, 'you'll never sit on a horse again.' Last week I finished my first dressage competition. I proved them wrong at every step of the way, and not once, in all that time, did Pamela come by to see how I was doing.

"Did I wish her ill? You betcha. She was fully aware the horse was a maniac, and she didn't want to risk getting hurt, so she had me get on the thing without a word of warning. Would I have killed her if I could?"

Heather hesitated, her face drawn into a dark, serious expression for the first time since she started talking to him. "I'd like to say no, but I'm not sure. The last time I saw her was seven or eight months ago, at the grand opening for the tack store at the Center. She asked me how I'd been. I wanted to slap her."

Breaking into a wheezy laugh, she said, "At the time, I could barely raise my arm high enough to slap her, but she probably would have liked that."

Emily and Lottie both stared at Heather in disbelief, shocked at her bluntness, then burst out laughing. Justin thought the sound of Emily's laughter was as beautiful as her smile.

Out of nowhere, a large, manicured hand planted itself into the middle of his chest. "I should have known you'd be skulking around somewhere." As Nick Conners stepped closer, the smell of cheap bourbon was overwhelming. "Figures the one time Emily puts on a sexy little dress, it's because you're around."

It seemed to Justin the DDA had enjoyed too many trips to the open bar already, and it was only three-thirty in the afternoon.

The three women abruptly stopped laughing and gaped at the boorish man. Emily, cheeks burning bright red, spun on her heel and stormed off. Disgusted, Lottie jabbed a finger in his chest. "When did you become such a jackass?"

"I didn't mean...I just...it's Pam's funeral, for God's sake."

Lottie caught Justin's attention and jerked her chin toward Emily, who stood alone at the edge of the stone patio's railing. "I'll take care of Nick. Why don't you make sure she's okay?"

Like most people who came in her path, he obeyed her without hesitation and joined Emily at the railing. The painfully bright day was fading into a crystal-clear night, but he suspected the dropping temperature wasn't the reason she shook like a leaf. He took his suit coat off and wrapped her in it all the same. "Come on," he offered, "let me take you home."

Her jaw muscle clenched as she crushed the cheap wine glass in her fist. Glass dropped to the stone pavement with a crash. A shard of the stemware must have bitten into her palm because he saw a splash of blood hit the paving stones as well. The raucous crowd fell silent as all eyes turned toward the sound of breaking glass. Only Justin stood close enough to see Emily, her expression glazed, pull a jagged, bloodstained piece of glass out of her hand. Despite having seen some grisly crime scenes, he winced as she pulled the sharp fragment out without so much as a whimper.

"I don't need your help, detective. I don't need anybody." Emily tore Justin's jacket off and shoved it into his arms, leaving a bloody palm print on the expensive material. "Do me a favor and get the fuck out of my way," she snarled and marched past the gathering crowd, out the front door.

****

Emily was five blocks from home before the steering wheel on her truck became too slick to hold. She found it fascinating that the cause was her own blood pumping from the gash in her palm. It should have been agony to grip the wheel, but she felt nothing at all.

Pain is your friend, someone once told her. It forces you to take care of an injury until it heals. At this moment, she forgot who had been dumbass enough to offer that piece of advice, but she had to admit they might have a point. Since she didn't have so much as an adhesive bandage at home, Emily turned toward the barn to use the first aid supplies there to dress the wound.

The place was spooky quiet on Sunday evenings, this one perhaps more so because anyone who might have been there was at the wake. She hadn't been in the barn when it was this deserted since the morning she found Pamela. Roaming the same aisle, an icy knot of fear formed in the pit of her stomach.

"Hopefully, killers are like lightning and don't strike twice in the same place," she told herself, her voice sounding small and unsure in the dark. She turned on the barn lights and forced herself to march as best she could in her tight shift and heels to the tack room where Pamela kept the first aid kit for the horses. She never thought to keep anything on hand for people, but it didn't matter, most of the supplies were the same.

The temperature continued to drop, promising a cold night, so Emily brought what supplies she needed into the office and cranked up the space heater. Tiny black dresses may be great for attracting attention, but they didn't do shit to keep you warm. She regretted giving the cop back his coat.

Because her first horse had been a klutz, she'd become adept at treating wounds. Once she wiped off the blood, she realized the gash wasn't deep; long, but shallow, and mostly in the meaty part of her hand. A quick flex of her fingers confirmed there was no tendon damage, so she doused the wound with iodine and wrapped her hand in gauze. Icing it would have been great, if she'd remembered to put the ice packs back in the freezer instead of on top of a tack box the last time she used them. *Idiot.*

She reached into the drawer to take another pain pill, but all she found was an empty bottle rolling around the drawer. Incredible. Someone had stolen her stash. How low can a person sink? The bottle held a dozen pills yesterday, she was almost certain of it.

Emily sat back for a moment, blaming the oppressive heat from the cheap space heater and its two settings—igloo or sauna—for her lack of energy. She pressed play on Pamela's old school mp3 player she'd left docked to a small speaker in the office. The dust and dampness would have ruined anything more sophisticated. She leaned back to enjoy an old country song and might have even dozed off, except the next song had the singer wailing about being much too young to feel this damn old.

Oh please, you have no idea.

Looking at the mp3 player through a hooded gaze, Emily stabbed the fast-forward button for a song that didn't hit so close to home, only to have the same peppy song her neighbor played over and over belt out over the tinny speaker. Wasn't Pamela a little long in the tooth to be a K-pop fan? Growling in frustration, she turned the mp3 player off. In the sudden quiet, something made a distinct *bang* out in the barn aisle.

Emily's eyes snapped wide open as she sat up, frozen in terror. Images of Pamela's crushed face flashed in her mind. "Holy crap."

She reached for the phone, but hesitated. Maybe the noise was from a horse kicking. She studied her wrapped hand and remembered the shock on Justin's face when she broke the glass. Worries about being killed were replaced with the more likely concern people would think she had come unhinged. She listened for a while longer, but there was nothing but the normal sounds of horses in their stalls.

"Bob, where the hell are you?" she muttered under her breath, wishing the kindly security guard was less kind and more secure. She could close the office door and spend the night there. The only problem was the door locked on the outside, so she had no way to keep any bad guy, if there was a bad guy, from coming in. Barricading the door wouldn't work because it slid open. If she snuck out to her truck and drove home, would the intruder follow her?

Unable to stand the doubt or the scenarios her wild imagination came up with, Emily decided enough was enough. Unless she wanted to be terrified every single freaking time she was in the barn in the dark—and this time of year that was as early as five o'clock in the afternoon—she had to confront this now. Faking as much bravado as possible, she grabbed the only weapon she saw—a thick, sturdy racing whip—and crept out into the aisle.

The frigid dampness hit her, chilling her to the bone. She thought about turning back but realized if she returned to the warmth and questionable safety of the office, she'd never work up the nerve to leave it again. She'd been running scared from a lot of things for far too long. Tonight, here and now, that was going to change. Attempting to appear more confident than she felt, Emily stalked down the aisle, racing crop at the ready.

Finding nothing, she was about to call it a night when a definite *klunk* resounded from the tack room. Shit, she'd left the door open when she went in for the first aid supplies. Thousands of dollars' worth of saddles, bridles, and other gear and she'd basically invited a thief to clean them out. Seriously, where the hell was Bob? Feeling responsible for the property in her care, she crept toward the door, muscles tensed for a confrontation.

"Freeze!" she shouted as she lunged into the room and found the culprit behind the noise. Moo, the brown and white, longhaired barn cat, stood in the middle of the room with a mouse in her mouth so fresh its tail was still wriggling.

"God dammit, Moo, you scared me to death."

Emily entered the room to shoo the cat back outside when something hit her head hard enough to send her staggering. *Moo, what the hell was that for?* she thought as blackness swallowed her.

****

A fountain ran through the middle of Justin's hillside home, and most nights, the water's meditative gurgle lulled him to sleep. Tonight, the sound was an annoying distraction.

Around twelve-thirty, he gave up, kicked off his covers, and got dressed to work out. The advantage of spending the money to build his own private *dojo* in the back of his house was he could do his *kata* anytime he wanted. Not being one of those purists who insisted on wearing a *gi* every time he stepped on the mat, he pulled on a pair of sweats and walked down the hall lit only by the moon.

A cold, misty rain coated the glass sliding door that led out to a courtyard, and the chill penetrated the room. Even so, a half an hour into his *kata,* a sheen of sweat appeared on his shirtless chest. The rhythmic, graceful,

116

but precise moves bore a resemblance to a dance when done slowly, but when put together at speed, it was more like a martial arts movie fight scene.

The meditative cadence usually relaxed him, but tonight his sense of foreboding continued to grow. His gut screamed Emily was in trouble, and although it made no sense, he'd never be able to focus until he made sure she was okay. Hopefully she was asleep in bed and would be around to hate him for waking her up with a crazy-ass phone call in the middle of the night for a long time to come. After trying her home, office, and cell with no luck, his apprehension grew.

He threw on a sweatshirt and his favorite tattered sneakers, feeling stupid, but up to this point, his instincts had never failed him. On the way out of the door, he changed his mind at the last second and grabbed his gun, just in case.

Chapter Fifteen

Emily woke to the acrid smell of cat pee burning her nose. "Samwise Gamgee, I am going to kill you," she moaned, raising her head off the floor.

The cement floor was the first clue this was not her living room, and it was not her cat who'd pissed all over it. The bridles hanging on the wall reminded her she was in the tack room, but why the walls were spinning was a mystery—until the pounding in her head reminded her, she'd been struck by something. Then the dizziness and nausea kicked in and almost overwhelmed her.

Okay, she told herself, you are lying on the rough, cold floor a mere hundred feet away from a belt of Pamela's expensive scotch she kept in her desk drawer and five minutes from...well, a shitty apartment, but home nonetheless. Focus on the scotch. Even if you have to crawl, how bad can it be?

Rising unsteadily to her hands and knees, she got her answer. Her wounded palm throbbed, and the rough floor bit into her bare knees. Bile rose in her throat, and her head pounded like a drum, but, gritting her teeth, she refused to give up. She clawed her way to the top of a tack trunk and slumped to catch her breath, breaking into a sweat despite the damp, frosty night. God, just getting to her feet could take all night. A trickle of warmth sliding down her neck made her release her grip on the trunk to reach a hand up and confirm what she already suspected—blood.

"Aw crap."

Her whole body began to shiver, though whether from shock, the cold, blood loss, or an intense need to hurl, it was hard to say. She scanned the room an inch at a time, finding if she didn't move anything, including her eyes, too fast, the buzzing in her head was tolerable.

"Of course there are no blankets in here," she ground out through still-gritted teeth. "It's January. The blankets are on the horses. Think, Conners." Her cocktail dress was no match for a California winter night.

Like a swimmer about to dive into a cold pool of water, Emily pumped herself up with a few short, quick breaths and pushed to her feet. The door was inches out of reach when she stretched out her arm. Since the idea of picking herself up off the floor again didn't appeal in the least, she crept toward the solid comfort of the wood door in a few uncertain steps. When she got there, she leaned against the coarse surface for a moment, only to have the spinning replaced by lightheadedness.

The sensation wasn't great, but she'd be okay for the brief trip to the office. Blood flowed down her neck the more she moved, but she pushed aside the fear her head wound might be serious. One thing at a time. First, open the door, then get to the office. Eventually, it'll be fine, she told herself.

Emily tugged weakly at the handle of the door. It stuck, but that wasn't unusual. The tack room was like Pamela's office, a converted stall with saddle racks. Frequently, the tracks for the heavy doors got sticky with dirt and hay. She pulled again, this time putting all

119

of her weight behind the move. There was the sharp sound of metal snicking against metal. When the door refused to give one more inch, she realized the latch had been closed and padlocked.

Someone had locked her in.

She smacked the door once and instantly regretted it. The pounding of her sliced palm intensified. Was she stuck in here until tomorrow? Oh no, the little voice in her head warned. Tomorrow is Monday, the day most trainers take off, so no one will be around.

"Yeah, but the guys will be here to clean out the stalls, and the grooms will come to turn horses out. Someone will find you," she reasoned out loud.

Except on Mondays the guys play music at the top of their little radio's setting. The one that rested in the cross ties across from the tack room. Last Monday she'd had to ask them to turn it down because she couldn't hear herself think.

"Okay, worst-case scenario, nobody opens this door until Tuesday. I probably won't die from the cold. Unless, of course, I have a concussion. Or worse. What are the signs of a serious head injury, I wonder?" *Other than babbling to yourself?*

"Shit, I'm babbling, aren't I?" she mumbled, and then, realizing she spoke the words out loud, yelled, "Aargh, I'm going to die in this cat piss, airless room."

Ignoring the pain, she pounded on the door, hollering for help until a terrifying thought gripped her heart: the only person who knew she was here was the one who hit her. What if it was Pamela's killer? Do they figure she's dead, too? If they're still out there and they hear her, will they come back in to finish the job? She slid down the door and landed on the cement floor in a terrified, defeated heap.

*****

Justin's headlights sliced through the inky darkness of the Equestrian Center's deserted parking lot and spotlighted a familiar hulking shape. He breathed a sigh of relief to see Emily's truck parked near Pam's office. At least she hadn't careened off the side of the road on the way home from the memorial service. He'd driven to her apartment first, but when he got no answer other than the plaintive *meows* of her cat, he came to the only other place he could think of.

From the peaceful appearance of things, it would seem his "Spidey sense," as his partner liked to call it, had sent him on a fool's errand. His intuition had never been wrong before, but something about this woman set him off balance. Concern gelled into irritation. It was two in the morning, what the hell was she doing at the barn in the first place? He slammed his car door shut and stomped to her office. He'd come all this way to make sure she was all right, so he might as well walk ten extra feet and be sure. Thank God the rain had let up, at least.

The barn was eerily quiet, the soft tread of his gym shoes on the hard-packed aisle the only sound, save for the occasional stomping from a restless horse. The hair on the back of his neck stood at full attention, but he disregarded the instinctual warning. He'd overreacted by coming here and he wasn't falling for it again, dammit. When he rounded the corner and saw the dim light spilling out of the open office door, he slowed his steps, unsure of what he should say. She'd been pretty angry with him when she'd left the memorial service and probably wouldn't be too happy to see him barging in at this hour. He hesitated, then entered the office in his most practiced casual air. Justin froze, stunned at what he saw.

Pam's desk drawers were torn out and overturned, papers strewn everywhere. The television had been ripped off the wall and smashed. Even the couch cushions were torn and the stuffing pulled out. In the corner, heat blasted out of the red coils of a space heater lying on its side on top of a stack of loose, crumpled papers. It looked as if someone tried to start a fire with the heater when he interrupted them. Justin drew his gun and uprighted the heater. The good news was his intuition was just fine. The bad news—something was definitely wrong, and Emily was in the middle of it.

He pulled his cell phone out of his jacket pocket and speed-dialed his office, but before anyone answered, heavy shuffling footsteps came toward him from the darkened barn.

"Ms. Conners, you sure are keeping late hours tonight. I—oh." A silver-haired man in a blue security guard uniform stopped short, his eyes fixed on Justin's weapon. A vague memory tickled at the back of his brain. Had Dennis mentioned there was a security guard? Lowering his gun, he handed the older man his cell phone.

"Detective Justin Butler, LAPD. Tell whoever answers this to send a squad car to this location. Now."

As Justin hurried out, the older man stopped him. "Is Ms. Conners in trouble?" Concern clouded the guard's eyes. "I'll go turn the barn lights on for you."

"No thanks, uh, mister…?"

"Bob Young," the man answered.

"Let's keep the playing field level, Bob. No lights,"

he ordered softly as he scoped out the barn aisle. He pointed to the phone in the man's slack hand. "Remember, squad car. Now."

He continued up the aisle, pausing long enough to let his eyes adjust to the grayish light the moon cast into the barn, hunting his prey with casual ease.

****

Standing on top of a tack trunk, Emily's fingertips were inches away from the top of the wall dividing the tack room from the stall next door. If she could climb over like she'd seen Moo the cat do a hundred times, she could let herself out of the unlocked stall. It was now or never.

She paused—was someone talking? *Oh great, now I'm hearing voices.*

Sweat and blood ran down her neck as she rose to her tiptoes, using one hand to pull herself up on the metal bridle rack a few feet from the top of the wall. Her other hand brushed the top of the filthy divider when the room spun again. She gritted her teeth against the wave of dizziness as she pulled herself another tantalizing six inches higher before spots danced and her vision tunneled. Her strength gave out, and she crashed down hard onto the tack trunk.

Collapsing in defeat, she bit her lip against the oncoming rush of tears. Shaky, she grabbed a towel from the nearby basket they kept on hand for cleaning tack and pressed it against the back of her head. The pressure hurt like hell, but at least it slowed the blood flow while she thought of Plan C.

Staying put until her head wound stopped bleeding seemed like her best option. A concussion wouldn't kill her. She'd had one before and she'd been fine in a few days. So why was she trembling so hard her teeth rattled? Buck up, Conners, she chided herself, it's probably shock combined with the cold temperature. But just in case, use your head and find a way out. This isn't Alcatraz, it's a barn stall. Emily rested her head against the rough, grainy wall and closed her eyes, readying herself for another attempt at climbing over it when footsteps echoed in the barn aisle.

She held her breath, oscillating between terror and relief. Was it the killer coming back to finish her off, or a potential rescuer? Should she call out, or silently let the intruder pass by? She choked back a sob, certain whatever she did in the next few seconds would mean the difference between life and death. She picked up a couple of stirrup leathers with irons attached in case the door opened and she needed to defend herself. Hefting the weight, she questioned how much strength she had left as she crept to the door.

"Ms. Conners? Are you here? Emily?" a man called out. The voice sounded familiar, but she couldn't place it. *Crap.* Was that good or bad? She shifted around to press her ear to the door when her makeshift weapon slipped out of her hand and clanked to the floor.

****

Out in the barn aisle, Justin discerned the sound of metal crashing on concrete and stood still, his only movement a soft, predatory smile. Playing cat and mouse was always easier when the mouse made a lot of noise. The shavings on the stall floors dulled any sound, so he ruled the horses out as the source of the *clang*. Which left the empty open area to his right, or the closed door to his left. He crept toward the open space, hugging the wall and glancing around to confirm there were no shadowy figures lurking in the pale moonlight. The only sound was his own steady, rhythmic breathing.

He spun into the open area, crouched low and gun drawn. All he found were grooming brushes stacked in a box in the corner. The concrete floor had been swept clean and showed no signs of any fallen metal objects. Satisfied, he turned his attention to the closed door. Much like Pamela's office, the room was a stall that had been fully enclosed instead. He crept to the wooden door and listened. Nothing, not even heavy breathing. He put his hand on the metal handle but saw the door was secured with a padlock. The sound definitely came from this area, but there's no way whoever trashed Pamela's office had padlocked themselves in that room from the outside. Further up the aisle, the glint of moonlight shone off something metal.

Again, he froze, finger tightening around the trigger of his weapon until he realized the shimmer was just a silver, industrial-sized fire extinguisher hanging cockeyed in its rickety wall holder. A rusty stain on the lower edge made it debatable how effective it would be in case of a fire. Then he noticed the stain dripped onto the floor. Closing the distance in a flash, he dabbed the spot and didn't need a lab to tell him it was fresh blood. Inspecting the extinguisher more closely, he saw strands of curly, auburn hair stuck to the metal. Emily. His heart turned to ice as he ran back to the closed door.

"Emily, it's Justin. Stand away from the door. Can you hear me? Stand back."

There was no reply, but his gut screamed for him to open the door now. Without waiting for confirmation, he shot the lock off and yanked the heavy door open as easily as if it were a beaded curtain. The horses in the barn set off a cacophony of panicked calls and kicks that would no doubt bring the wrath of the elderly security guard raining down upon him. He didn't care.

Emily stood in the middle of the pitch-black room, swaying on her feet. Her entire body shook like a quaking aspen. Her pale skin appeared translucent next to the dark stain flowing from her head down her neck.

"Oh shit, of course it's you," she muttered. Which proved his suspicion that he was the last person she wanted to see. "Fuck off, I'm still mad at you." She swayed, squinting at him. "Both of you," she declared as her knees gave out.

Justin caught her before she hit the ground and scooped her up in his arms. She protested weakly, "Let me go, I don't need your help."

"Yeah, yeah, you don't need anybody. So you've said. Tell you what, how about if you get even with me for being a big male jerk by bleeding all over yet another one of my coats?"

From the heavy weight of her head against his shoulder and her soft steady breathing, it appeared he'd won the argument by default.

Chapter Sixteen

Five minutes after leaving the Equestrian Center, Justin screeched to a halt in front of the emergency room doors of the massive Holy Angels Medical Center. Equipped with a cherry light and siren, his car could have made the trip in three, except he feared Emily would throw up if he drove too fast. His leather seats could take it, but he doubted he could, and sympathy puking right now wouldn't help anyone.

He left his car with the light flashing in the tow-away zone and bundled her into his arms. If an idiot towed a cop car, he'd deal with them later. Right now, the most important thing was Emily, who was semi-conscious and deathly pale. He'd called ahead and ignored the attendants waiting for him at the door with a gurney, opting instead to carry her in himself. He marched past the purse-lipped nurse at the desk and headed straight for an exam room.

The nurse huffed after him. "Sir," she protested in a snotty tone, "you'll have to wait in the lobby like—"

He cut her off with a scowl and the flash of his badge. "I don't think so, ma'am."

"Sonny?" The nurse sniffed, her skin tone darkening to match the ruddy color of her permed curls. "I don't care if you're the Chief of Police, you'll have to wait for the next available doctor."

"That's okay, Gail, I got this." Looking exhausted,

Dr. Carolyn Jones pushed past the nurse and guided Justin into the exam room. "As usual, making friends everywhere you go."

Groggy but awake, Emily gave him a loopy smile. "I like her."

"That's the thanks I get for letting you bleed all over my car?" Justin teased before turning to the doctor. "Thanks for taking my call, Jonesy. I know you're swamped but…"

"Nothing but the best for the Butlers, eh?" she said over his protest. "We've known each other for how many years now? You don't usually act like a rich, privileged asshole, just when you're worried. Now put the woman down on the table and go away, I got this."

****

By the time Justin returned from coaxing a coffee with cream out of the stubborn vending machine, the voices of Dr. Carolyn Jones and Emily Connors were arguing at a level usually saved for baseball stadiums. The discussion concerned Emily staying overnight for observation. Even the biker gang gathered around the guy with a meat fork in his thigh in the waiting room looked ready to book. After his conversation with Heather Dane, Justin understood Emily's aversion to staying in the hospital for even one night.

"You horse people are all alike," Dr. Jones ranted. "I hate to break it to you, but even cowboys can die from a concussion."

Justin poked his head into the exam room and noted the crisp, professional bandage on Emily's hand as well as the dark expressions on the faces of both women. "Jonesy, can I borrow you for a second?"

She hesitated, until he added, "Please?" and then

acquiesced. In the doorway, she turned to Emily. "You, don't move. I'll be right back."

****

Alone in the exam room, Emily did as instructed for about two seconds. Being in a hospital again made her tense and anxious, but it had also been a while since she'd taken her last pain pill and she needed another one to calm her nerves. Her doctors were getting more guarded about refilling her prescriptions and she was running out. Would they keep a few painkillers in an ER exam room? Unsure, she stealthily opened cabinets and drawers until she found a prescription pad. The doctor's name on it wasn't familiar, but did it matter? Ashamed but desperate, she stuffed it in the purse Justin had grabbed for her before they left the barn and returned to her seat on the exam table.

****

Leaving Emily alone in the exam room, Justin guided Jonesy out in the hallway to explain the situation. It took all of his powers of persuasion, which were depleted considering he'd been awake for nearly twenty hours, to convince the doctor to release Ms. Conners into his care.

"You and I both know you can't force her to stay," he said, exhaustion making each word sound like a plea. "What if I stay with her and check her vital signs every couple of hours? She lives close by, Jonesy. If anything goes wrong, I can have her back here faster than you could get to her in your elevator."

"You?" She chuckled, her tension breaking.

"Who helped you get through med school? I can handle checking her pupils and pulse for one night."

Her shoulders drooped in hopeless resignation.

"Oh, all right, stop batting those stupid puppy-dog eyes at me. Here are the symptoms to keep an eye out for."

After she went through the signs of trouble, twice to make sure he understood, the two of them went back into the exam room to tell Emily the game plan. To say she wasn't happy with the arrangement was an understatement, but in the end, Justin suspected her desire to shed the little black dress, now stained with blood, and get into something more comfortable, pushed her to agree.

****

Back home at her little apartment, Emily's hope that Justin hadn't been serious when he said he'd stay with her all night vanished as soon as they stepped over her threshold.

"All right, into your pajamas, and let's get you into bed," he insisted. "Doctor's orders."

"I don't wear pajamas," she shot back with a defiant jut of her chin.

"Makes no difference to me." From his wicked smile, she didn't doubt he meant what he said. *Why wouldn't he go away?* She closed her bedroom door in his face.

Samwise came out from whatever place he'd been hiding and jumped up on her bed. Utterly spent, she gave him a scratch behind the ears. He answered with a rumbling purr. *Why couldn't men be as easy to understand as cats?*

Yearning for a hot bath, but far too tired to go through the effort, she shed her bloodstained dress in favor of a set of soft, flannel pajamas. Surely the detective had someone waiting for him in a bed somewhere. Why the pretense that he cared so much?

She'd barely accomplished the monumental task of crawling into bed when there was a soft knock on her door.

"Are you decent?"

She tried ignoring him, but with more good cheer than was tolerable for three in the morning, Justin came in and took her vital signs. As he leaned in to check her pupils, she flashed on how long it had been since she'd had a man in her bedroom, not to mention one so attractive. Heat rose to her cheeks at her inappropriate thought. She closed her eyes to try to forget he was there, but that only made her more aware of his warm touch on the sensitive skin of her wrist.

"Your pulse is racing. Maybe I should take you back to the hospital," he noted, all teasing gone.

She groaned—how is it possible he smelled so good after all they'd been through tonight? *Focus, Emily, focus.* "I'm fine, I swear, just go away."

"No, really, your heartbeat is so elevated, I—" The silence lingered for so long she opened her eyes to see his lips curl into a wicked grin. "Is your pulse racing because I'm holding your hand?"

"Yes, that's exactly it. You caught me." Emily gave him a deadpan look. "My abnormal pulse has nothing to do with someone trying to kill me by smashing my head in, being locked in the tack room and nearly freezing to death, or having a concussion. Nope, as usual, it's all about you. Just put your strong, manly fingers on my wrist and my heart's all a twitter."

She hoped she'd told the lie with enough bravado to convince him it was true. Samwise peered at her skeptically from his post between her and the male intruder. If she couldn't fool her cat, what hope did she have of fooling a cop?

Justin gave Samwise's chin a scratch. "I'll be right outside if you need anything. Next vital sign check is in a couple of hours, so try to get some sleep." He closed the door softly behind him.

****

The weight of the day settled on Justin's shoulders as he closed her bedroom door. The question of who attacked her and why would have to wait until the crime lab processed the evidence. Dennis was on top of things at the scene, so there was nothing for him to do at the moment.

Roaming around her little apartment ate up a minute and a half, but only because he stopped to make himself a cup of instant coffee. The fact that it didn't taste half-bad proved how much he needed the caffeine. Every magazine and newspaper in the place was dedicated to horses, a topic he neither liked nor disliked. Thumbing through them, all the details on how to make your inside leg connect to your outside rein made no sense to him at all. Finally, he gave up and turned on her TV.

Instead of the usual infomercials he expected from occasional sleepless nights he'd spent in front of the television, an image of Emily on a horse lit up the screen. It wasn't until he saw her there, a few pounds heavier and beaming at the camera, that he realized how haunted her eyes looked now. Her laughter after she and the horse flew over a fence bubbled out as she engaged in banter with the videographer—Lottie, if he wasn't mistaken.

With Emily's encouragement, the horse sailed over huge ditches, fences with impossible brush on top, and

132

down steep drops into water. It all seemed bat-shit crazy to him, but she had a sparkle in her eyes, visible even in the shadow of her helmet. In close-ups, her smile was breathtaking.

Then disaster struck. Pamela appeared, much more imposing in life than she had been in death and pointed to a series of jumps. There was a giant log perched on top of a hill with a sharp decline to a wood-lined hole in the ground, then up another small hill to a larger log.

In the video, Emily laughed and shook her head *no*, but Pamela persisted. Emily got to the top of the hill, but the horse stopped in front of the first fence of the three. More instructions from Pamela sent her to try again. This time the horse flew over the log and the ditch, but something happened at the third obstacle and two thousand pounds of horse flipped over the fence, crushing Emily beneath it. The horse struggled to regain its feet, fell back on her body, then lurched upright and stiffly trotted away.

A woman started screaming, the camera whipping toward the grass at a dizzying speed, and then black.

Horrified, Justin couldn't take his eyes off the screen. This explained so much about Emily but brought up more questions as well. Like, how does anyone go through that and still get back on a horse, nonetheless jump? It made no sense, and yet it drove him to want to understand her even more.

Chapter Seventeen

Dennis Ames rubbed a hand over his tired, bleary eyes. He'd left the crime scene at the barn a little after six this morning and went directly to the office. His wrinkled, dusty suit mirrored how he felt. When he glanced up and saw Justin wander in, dressed as always like the cover of GQ, he wanted to throttle him.

"Hey buddy, thanks for thinking of me last night. Gosh, what a pleasure to get called out of my warm bed to go to a horse barn in the middle of the night."

"Last time I checked, you were assigned this case. If you want off, say the word," Justin snarled while rifling through the messages on his desk.

In the four years they'd worked together, Justin's voice had never had such a jagged edge. Then he remembered the old security guard saying the Conners woman was in pretty bad shape when Justin hustled her out to the closest ER. Shit.

"Don't be such a baby," he said, his gruffness a thin veil for an apology. "I'm always an asshole before my fifth cup of coffee. How's she doing?"

Justin ran his hand through his hair and blew out a frustrated breath. "She's doing fine, but it was close. We could just as easily have been investigating another homicide."

He glanced at Dennis with an expression so intense it was clear he was in way over his head, but if he tried to throw his friend a life preserver, Justin would probably shove it up his ass. "I assume you look like hell because you spent the night with her. Did you at least get lucky?"

Crudeness was always effective in at least getting a grin out of his partner, and this time was no exception. The dark brooding lightened up a shade or two as he shook his head. "It was doctor's orders and nothing...oh screw you." He laughed at himself, rubbing the heels of his hands into his weary eyes. "So, what've you got from the scene?"

He was more than happy to ignore the elephant in the room—Justin's involvement with the victim—and get back to the manageable nuts and bolts of the case. "You're not going to like it. We spent most of the night dusting the place for prints, but there are too many for it to be of any use."

Justin's expression darkened; his jaw clenched. "What about the fire extinguisher?"

"Totally wiped clean."

"The bracket? The wall behind it?"

He shook his head, choosing to ignore the fact Justin was second-guessing him, something his partner had never done before. He knew from experience how much a woman could mess a guy up, so he cut Justin a little slack. For now.

"Nada, zip. Even the handle to the saddle room was clean—except for your prints, of course. You blew the lock to smithereens, but chances are it would have been wiped down as well, so I wouldn't sweat it."

Justin raked through his desk Zen garden, something he typically did when he thought out loud. "We've already got one suspect who, from the financial records you pulled, had business ties with Pamela and threatened Emily."

"You think the vet—this Dr. Ridley—is involved?" Dennis asked dubiously.

"The financials show that both the vet and Pamela were getting irregular but sizable payments from a corporation that sounds like a shady tax dodge, but the forensic accountants are still checking it out. That might give him a motive in Pamela's death."

"Yeah, but why attack Emily?" Dennis began to pace. "Technically, the conversation she relayed to me the other day sounded like he was making threats, but the guy seems like a typical schoolyard bully, all hot air and no balls to back it up." He stopped moving, his gaze meeting Justin's. "Truth is, I'm not convinced the killer and Emily's attacker were the same person."

Justin turned his attention back to his garden, raking slow and steady. First in one direction, then a ninety-degree turn, and repeat. "You have a point, the M.O.'s don't match. Why smash one person beyond recognition to make sure they were dead and leave the other with a tap on the head?"

Dennis took a deep breath, hoping a bit of cop house air might help to clear his brain. "What's our next move?"

Justin snapped to his feet and grabbed his car keys. "I say we go pay ol' Doc Ridley a visit."

****

"Everyone's going to think we've been smoking pot in here," Lottie asserted too gleefully to count as a complaint.

Emily rested her chin in her hand and watched Sandy Peters circle Pamela's office with a smoking bunch of sage in her hand to smudge the place, whatever that meant. As her head still throbbed like it contained her own personal tiny mariachi band, she only managed a weak smile.

Her friend was right. By noon tomorrow, the barn would be alive with gossip. *I heard she smoked a joint and blew the smoke up a horse's nose until they were both stoned then jumped it anyway.* Great, first the animal communicator bit, and now this. Her already shaky reputation would soon be thoroughly trashed.

Still, spending time at the barn beat sitting at home staring at the walls of her apartment. All she'd wanted was fresh air, but the pungent smell of smoking sage made her gag.

"Sorry, almost done," the would-be shaman apologized as she waved the burning bunch of weeds around in clockwise and then counterclockwise circles above her head. "I'm smudging the whole barn to get rid of all the dangerous energy."

She then wandered out the door, leaving Lottie and Emily coughing in the smoky haze as they picked up the jumbled mess of paper and knick-knacks off the floor. So far, if anything was missing, she couldn't tell.

"Oh man, this is shredder fodder." Lottie held up a familiar set of papers. It took her a minute to realize the pages were a Hy Poynt application. "The silly cow nominated Kate."

Kate Williams. That figured. Once every two years, the Hy Poynt equestrian apparel company picked one lucky bastard from a list of riders nominated by professionals in good standing and sponsored them for two years. Based on their show performance, personal recommendation, and interviews with Karen Hyler, the owner of Hy Poynt, the chosen rider would ride one of her incredible horses under the coaching of the top riders in whatever discipline they rode. Although the sponsorship didn't include show fees, Karen usually strong-armed a corporation into covering the cost and kicking in a stipend for rent as well. It was the golden ticket behind a half-dozen careers which, to date, included two Olympic riders.

Emily never expected Pamela would put her up for the prestigious program, but she never dreamed she'd nominate Kate, either.

"I'm sorry dear, did you say something?"

She jumped at Lottie's question, not realizing she had verbalized her thought. "Nothing, just give me the papers. I'll make sure Karen Hyler gets them."

Lottie clasped the application to her chest. "You'll do no such thing. What are you, nuts? Besides, you're too late, the cutoff date happens to be today."

She exhaled wearily and held out her hand, refusing to double the ache in her head by debating the topic. Lottie defiantly slapped the application on the desk rather than handing it to her and went back to work on cleaning up the clutter on the floor without another word. Using the phone number on the application, Emily called Karen to let her know what they'd found.

Karen said, "That's odd. I got a message from Pam right before she left for the show at Kinsale Downs about the sponsorship. I assumed she was going to nominate you."

Her well-intended comment cut like a knife. Emily tried her best to breathe through the pain. "Did you ever talk to her, find out what she called about?"

The silence from the other end of the phone went on for so long she thought the line had gone dead until there was a sharp *huff* of air. "When I called her back, she babbled on about having evidence that would disqualify a rider who was trying to win the sponsorship."

"That's all she said?"

There was more dead air on the phone line before Karen continued, "If whatever information she had was all that important, wouldn't she have mentioned it to you? To be honest, I assumed she wanted to spread more of the usual barn gossip and I'm uncomfortable perpetuating a baseless rumor without proof."

That would make her the first horse person Emily had ever met that let a lack of evidence stop them. "I respect your position, Karen, I really do, and I don't want to get anyone in trouble, but it might be important. Did she say anything more specific?"

"Oh, she feigned all kinds of regret about being the one to tell me about whatever it was, but by then she was on the road to the show and her cell phone reception went out."

"Did she call you back?"

"No. I figured she'd call me when she got back from Kinsale, but then…"

Someone killed her. Maybe Emily had gotten hit on the head harder than she thought, but it seemed awfully suspicious Pamela was murdered before she gave Karen Hyler information that might keep one nominee from getting the sponsorship. She'd meant to take away the chance of a lifetime. A chance a lot of people would say was worth killing for.

"Would you mind if I brought the detective

investigating her murder over to you so you can tell him the entire story in person?" She tried to hit the word murder extra hard so Karen wouldn't brush off the whole thing due to inconvenience.

After a great deal of hemming and hawing, she finally agreed to see them tomorrow morning. "You might as well bring Kate's application with you. I guess death is a pretty good excuse for sending it in late."

She hung up, trying to be glad to help Kate out, but irritated all the same. From the way they'd argued, she always assumed Pamela hated Kate.

"Hello? Earth to Emily." Lottie rapped on the desk. "Did you hear me?"

She could try to lie but was too tired to expend the effort. "Honestly? I didn't."

"I said the Dearg McGregor clinic is in two weeks. Since I already sent in the entry for Pamela and Reese to go Prelim, I thought…"

Emily felt her jaw drop. "Are you serious?"

"You don't have to stay in the Preliminary level group. It scared me to death watching you ride over those big ass fences even before your accident. Take a step down to the Training level group with the rest of the mere mortals. The fences are only three-foot-three. You can just take the jumps you're comfortable with."

Emily tried to say something intelligent in reply, but suddenly her throat was dry. It seemed like she'd graduated to the upper levels of eventing a lifetime ago. Now even the lower Training level petrified her. On the other hand, Dearg McGregor was a legend in the sport. Being able to participate in his two-day clinic and getting his input to improve her stadium and cross-country jumping would be the chance of a lifetime.

"Um, I guess, as long as my concussion isn't a problem, I'll give it a try." Torn between fear and desire, her words sounded forced.

Surely Lottie heard the terror in her voice and would relent? Instead, her friend clasped her hands in happy surprise. "You will? That's so great. Don't worry, I'll take care of everything."

Yeah, everything except for riding the horse.

Emily decided to keep a good thought—this is California. It's always possible an earthquake would hit and wipe them all out before the clinic.

****

Justin wound his car through the tiny suburb right off the freeway exit. Nestled amongst numerous stables in various states of repair, he and Dennis found the tan metal building they were searching for. The cold perfection of the prefabricated barn and bare, grassless surroundings couldn't be more different from the Equestrian Center's green fields and classic wooden structures. Right behind the buildings, they found Dr. Ridley.

The Ron Burgundy wannabe standing before a crowd of adoring women wasn't the image Justin had in mind. His helmet of thick, black hair and bushy mustache were comical, but the ridiculousness didn't stop there. Despite the chilly spring weather, Ridley wore a thin, tight, V-neck sweater bursting with a mass of curly chest hair tangled with a cheap gold chain. He flashed the ladies a toothy, capped smile while he stuck a three-foot-long plastic tube up a horse's nose and kept shoving until it disappeared.

"Aw geez," Dennis groused. Justin saw his partner scrunch his face in disgust, looking even less

141

comfortable than the horse who had the tube shoved up its nose.

He was revolted as well. The tube looked like the vet had dragged it behind him on the way to the stall. Yet none of Ridley's adoring fans seemed to notice as he expounded on the dangers of choking and how he saved the horse's life, yada, yada, yada. When he yanked the tube back out of the horse's nose, Justin thought his squeamish partner would faint.

"C'mon, tough guy," he muttered as he pulled Dennis along to the stall. "Ladies, Dr. Ridley, I'm Detective Butler. This is my partner, Detective Ames." Justin plastered on a tight smile after finishing the introduction.

"Ah yes, the detective the equestrian community is agog over." Ridley hammed it up, putting his hand out for him to shake as if it wasn't covered in a gallon of horse snot.

Playing along with his pretentious bonhomie act, Justin took the vet's hand as if he didn't notice. When he thrust his hand in Dennis's direction, the cop suffered a sudden coughing spasm, making him unable to return the gesture.

Gathering his tools and bidding his fans adieu, Ridley led them over to his shiny pickup truck with a fancy vet rig on the back. "I assume you're here about Pammy's murder?" he asked as he tossed the hose that had been up the horse's nose into a metal drawer without bothering to clean it.

"Can you tell us where you were the night of the murder?" Justin continued in his calm, level tone.

"A bit clichéd but that's all right, I understand," the vet replied. Like he gave a damn. "I was at home all night with my wife and didn't leave until after eight the next morning."

"What about last night?"

The vet stumbled a little. "You saw me at Pamela's memorial service yesterday. I left shortly after you and Nick Conners had your little scuffle."

Out of the corner of his eye, Justin caught Dennis's narrowed gaze. His jaw clamped shut and face grew splotchy red, as it always did when he got pissed. Ridley blithely carried on, missing the silent exchange. "Why do you ask?"

"There was an incident at the Equestrian Center last night. Emily Conners was attacked."

Ridley let out a dismissive sniff. "Please. She took a few too many pills with a few margarita chasers is more like it. Detective, you can't take the word of an addict. She probably made the whole thing up just to get another prescription for painkillers."

Justin smiled and nodded his head in agreement. "Yeah, you might be right, sir, but—" He swiveled his head and spotted a small round pen with high solid walls. Gesturing to it, he asked, "Do you mind if we have a word in there, where it's more private?"

"Sure, whatever you say, detective." Ridley patted down his unnaturally smooth hair as they stepped inside. He was still preening when Justin grabbed him by the sweater and swung him into the metal walls. There was a satisfying double *smack* as Ridley's head hit the wall, bounced back, and then hit it again.

****

Fuck. Dennis had never seen his partner lose his shit like this before. He was about to step in, but Justin was too quick.

"Listen, asshole," he growled, pressing his forearm against the vet's windpipe. They were evenly matched size-wise, but the vet looked too surprised to put up a fight. "Answer the Goddamn question. Where were you last night and don't give me that home with the little woman bullshit because we've already checked."

Dennis thought Ridley might pee himself. Hell, the news surprised him, considering no such call had been made. "S-s-s-some of us went to a bar in Hollywood," the vet gasped.

"What bar?" Justin barked.

"The Red Lantern."

"The strip club?" Dennis asked, not realizing how it sounded until the other two temporarily forgot their issues to turn and stare at him. "So they tell me. Did anyone see you there who can corroborate your story?"

"I, I have a receipt."

Judas Priest, anyone so dumb they get a receipt to prove they'd been to a strip club is not exactly a master criminal.

Instead of being mollified, his partner pushed harder on the man's throat until every breath was a rattling gurgle. "You better hope for your sake Ms. Conners stays healthy, because if she so much as chips a fingernail, I am going to rip your nuts off. Am I making myself clear?"

Wide-eyed in terror, Ridley nodded, his capped teeth parted in an effort to breathe. Justin released him, then caught his foot on the back of Ridley's calf. With an easy flick, he brought the vet down, his crisply pressed chino-clad ass landing in the wet sand with a *splat*. Justin marched off without another word.

Dennis waited until they reached the car before

confronting him. "Wanna tell me what that was all about?"

"It got the job done, didn't it?"

He bore down on Justin, pinning him to the car. "Roughing up the suspect did not get the job done unless your goal was to make him shit himself. Because, in your haste to prove you have the bigger dick, did you notice anything that might be a clue?"

"What are you talking about?" Justin snapped, muscling his way out of his grip.

"He called the victim 'Pammy.' Sound familiar?" But his partner stared blankly at him. "For Christ's sake, the message on the victim's antique answering machine? He called her 'Pammy' as well. Imagine Ridley with a few drinks under his belt and the voice is almost a perfect match."

Justin scrubbed his weary face before giving him a sheepish look. "You're right, about all of it. I wasn't even listening. Good catch. The message on the machine was about getting a notice from the victim. They were both getting money from the same account. They must have been in business together and maybe she was cutting him out."

Nodding in agreement, Dennis stepped closer, not about to let his partner off the hook—yet. "That gives him motive and puts him at the top of the suspect list. But did you also miss the part about Ms. Conners having a drug problem? Or were you keeping that little tidbit from me, too, like your fight with DDA Conners? What the hell, man?"

The stormy expression on Justin's face told Dennis he remained intentionally unaware of her drug use. If Ridley was right and she was an addict, he hoped his partner would be able to face the truth before it blew up in his face and possibly cost him his career.

"Next time we lean on someone, just remember, 'good cop' is not in my repertoire. I'm the crazy cop and I got the papers to prove it, okay?" He playfully shoved Justin before climbing in the car. As they drove away, Dennis smirked. "Rip your nuts off?"

"Like it? I got that from Lottie. It's kind of fun to say, you should try it."

Chapter Eighteen

The tires of Justin's oh so silent, eco-friendly sports car crunched up the long, crushed gravel driveway leading to Karen Hyler's massive estate. The white columns of the main house loomed in the distance. Rumor was that she'd built it to replicate the White House on purpose, but Emily found it hard to believe.

"Wow." The sound of his voice snapped her out of her reverie.

Yeah, and you're rich. Think how intimidated I am.

"Listen, before you go in, there's something you should understand about Karen."

"Page one of the *How to be a Detective* manual—research interviewees." She was relieved he said it with a grin instead of taking her advice as an insult. "Successful businesswoman, big in the horse world. Older, wealthy husband, lots of rumors about their relationship."

He was right but didn't have the whole picture. She feared this was going to be a brief and messy interview if she didn't fill in all the blanks. "Right, but it's...Karen doesn't like to waste a lot of time with pleasantries."

"So she's rude?"

The car glided to a stop in front of the house's intricately carved double wood doors. "She's not rude per se, she's just—she doesn't suffer fools lightly. Or at all, really."

Justin grinned as he got out of the car, walked around the front, and opened her door for her. "Then I'll do my best not to be foolish."

He offered his hand and helped her out of the car. She was impressed—the last time anyone not wearing a red valet jacket had opened the door for her was Nick on their honeymoon, and she soon found out it was a one-time deal.

After a brief wait in a foyer big enough to house a family of four, Karen Hyler appeared and showed them into her office. Her crisp, navy silk suit and rose blouse complimented her dark hair, setting off her striking, if not traditionally beautiful, features.

"Please, have a seat," she commanded, gesturing to the over-stuffed, hide-covered chairs across from her large, oak desk. Almost apologetically, Emily handed her Kate's rumpled paperwork for the Hy Poynt nomination. She shook her head. "You're the only person I know who is honest enough to turn in the missing paperwork to enter someone else for consideration."

Or stupid enough.

"That's who Pam wanted to nominate. The least I could do was make sure the paperwork got turned in."

Karen skimmed the crumpled sheet of paper before adding it to the neatly stacked pile of paperwork on the corner of her desk. Peering over her reading glasses at Emily, she added, "Between you, me, and the fence post, it was a waste of paperwork." She took off the glasses and focused on the detective. "As for any insights into what was going on with Pamela, there's not much I can tell you. Like I told Emily, she called me on her way to the show at Kinsale Downs and left me a message, I called her back, but her cell phone reception died before she finished explaining what was on her mind."

"But she claimed to have information about some kind of wrongdoing on the part of a nominee for your sponsorship program?" Justin asked.

"Well, yes, but knowing Pamela, I doubt she had any actual proof."

"You don't put any stock in rumors?" he asked.

Hyler clasped her hands together and leaned forward, her lips tightening to a thin line. "Detective, I married a man twice my age who happens to be extremely wealthy, so I'm familiar with what unchecked rumors and innuendo can do. No, I do not put any stock in gossip, and with Pamela you never could tell fact from malicious fantasy."

"Many of the people who've won your sponsorship have risen to the top of their fields," Justin pointed out. "People have killed over a pair of shoes, so it's entirely possible an ambitious person might murder for a shot at your sponsorship program."

Emily rolled her eyes at the way Karen's smirk showed she was a little too pleased with the idea. "Point well-taken. All I remember of my conversation with Pamela was a vague claim about having information concerning one of the candidates so damaging it would eliminate them from consideration."

"How about the message she left? Did you, by any chance, save it?"

"Sorry detective, I listened to it, hit delete before calling her back."

"Do you remember any of the exact words she used?" he continued to press.

"I've been thinking about it ever since I talked to Emily, and the more I go over it, the less I'm sure about. I can tell you she was excited, really adamant about talking to me. But with Pamela, well, you know how she was, Emily. Everything was high drama and demanded your immediate attention."

"Any idea at all who she might have been talking about?" he asked. "Any rumors floating around about the candidates?"

"I thought you might ask that." Karen reached for a piece of paper on her desk and handed it to him. "So I printed the list of this year's candidates. The nomination process isn't a secret. The entries are closed now, so we'll publish the list in most of the trade magazines as part of the publicity mill."

"Plus Kate as well," Emily added, reading the impressive list of names over his shoulder. As far as she knew, none of them had ever had so much as a whisper of impropriety brought against them.

"True, but since Pam nominated her, I assumed we could rule her out as a suspect. Though God knows why she did, the woman hasn't shown in forever. Why bother?" At his furrowed brow she explained, "Part of the decision-making process is your show record. In years gone by, Kate had a nice run, I'll give her that, but she hasn't been in the ring in so long, it'd be difficult to justify loaning her one of my horses to get back in the game."

"It's not all her fault."

Emily hated having to rise to the woman's defense but couldn't help herself. "She's had a run of bad luck with lameness issues. It sucks, but it happens."

"Yes, when you're a careless horsewoman," Karen sniped. "But enough about Kate Williams." With a dismissive wave of one hand, she leaned toward Emily. "I'd rather talk about the Dearg McGregor clinic. I understand you're taking Reese?"

A cold pit opened in Emily's stomach at the mention of the clinic. "That's the plan, but I haven't had a chance to get on him since he came back from Kinsale Downs so..."

She shrugged, the universal horse sign for *if he's an idiot when I get on him there's no way I'm embarrassing myself in front of all those people.*

"You were terrific in the Lita Dove clinic we rode in together and you'd only been on that horse twice," Karen asserted, then explained to Justin. "I was riding an expensive Warmblood imported from Europe. Then Emily comes along on some gangly Thoroughbred and rides circles around me."

"But your horse was a much flashier mover, and gorgeous to boot," Emily protested. "Lita said you were doing a great job with him, considering his personality quirks, and she's the dressage goddess. How's he coming along?"

Karen leaned back in her chair. "You remember how he was stiff and hollow, refusing to give me a place to sit?"

That was putting it mildly, but she nodded.

"Well, I'm sitting on him now and so are you."

With that, Karen patted the stuffed chairs, a wicked grin on her face. Emily glanced at Justin in time to see his horrified expression as he jerked his hands off the arms of his chair.

"Well, wow, that was, um," she stammered. She didn't doubt for a moment it was true and had no idea how to respond. Where would you even go to get that done? She rose to her feet and pulled a shell-shocked Justin up with her, figuring the interview was over, at least for now.

"Thanks for your time, Karen, you were very helpful." Justin shook her hand and mumbled for her to call him if she thought of anything else.

****

Justin and Dennis sat outside the Pizza Oven Café on the first floor of the frou-frou outdoor mall at Hollywood and Highland. No matter what the weather, there were always tons of tourists taking pictures of the Hollywood sign on the hill in the distance, buying over-priced souvenirs from street vendors, and reading the lines of movie dialogue written on the sidewalk like it was the guide to ultimate wisdom. It was hard deciding what was more surprising: getting the call from Frankie Gillette to set up a meeting between the detectives and his brother Jimmy, or that he'd picked such a tacky tourist trap to do it.

"So she skinned a horse and made it into upholstery?"

"I'm assuming she didn't do it herself but yeah," Justin said with a laugh, "I kid you not."

Sliding his sunglasses down his nose, Dennis squinted at Frankie and Jimmy as they leaned against the railing of an upper level. "Jesus Christ, I'm going to get a sunburn if we sit here much longer. What do you think they're doing up there?"

"Watching you watch them."

Letting out an impatient huff, Dennis tugged at the

collar of his shirt. "What is it with this town? Last week it was raining and forty degrees. Today it's like frickin' eighty-five."

"And Philadelphia is better, piled with snow and hoping to break the zero mark?"

He swirled his straw in his drink, grumbling under his breath. "At least the weather was dependable, not like this up and down crap."

"Admit it, you just can't be happy no matter what the weather, it goes against your nature," Justin countered, amused at his partner's transparent whining.

Before he could argue the point, Ames's lips curled into a sneer. "Well, hallelujah," he grunted as the two Gillette brothers made their way down the stairs.

"Detectives." Frankie nodded as he scraped the metal chair noisily on the sidewalk to sit opposite Justin. "You remember my brother, Jimmy."

The younger, even scragglier man sat next to his brother and flagged down a server to order a beer. The foursome made small talk like executives at a business meeting until the beer arrived. Jimmy downed the frosty pint like a man dying of thirst and immediately ordered another. Dennis scowled, but the kid stuck out his chin. "I ain't going to lock-up without drinking the last beers I'm gonna see for a while."

"We don't mind springing for a few brews," Justin assured him, "but we need some answers before we buy you another."

"You don't want answers, you want a confession so you can beat the hell out of me," he scoffed, stuffing a piece of buttered bread in his mouth. "Only problem is, I didn't kill the guy. Like I told Frankie, I gave that son of a bitch Robbie Allen about half the beating he deserved for smacking around my girl, and then we left. End of story."

Dennis got in the kid's face. "You left out the part where you shot him, asshole, then stole over a thousand dollars and his stash of coke."

Justin put a hand on his partner's arm to rein him in, back to their usual good cop/bad cop routine. Clichéd, but very effective when done well. "Nobody here is going to force you to confess to anything. We just want the truth."

"The truth? The truth is the only reason I'm sitting here is because I'm being set up for something I didn't do." He gulped the last of his beer with lip-smacking satisfaction. "Plus, that Allen kid was an asshole. Gambling, dealing, he was even blackmailing some dude for—"

A loud *pop* interrupted Jimmy's statement. Frankie's head showered the table with brains and blood.

Justin's first thought was *what the hell, Frankie?*

In less than a heartbeat, he realized what had happened and flung the table over, tackling Jimmy to the ground. "Where is he?" he called out to his partner, who was kneeling behind an overturned chair, his gun already drawn and scanning for the shooter.

"Second floor walkway, but I lost him."

Justin tore off his gore-covered sunglasses and took off running across the courtyard and up the stairs. "Stay with him," he shouted over his shoulder, his long legs devouring the steps two at a time as the mall filled with the screams of horror and fear. He caught sight of a man wearing a trench coat far too warm for the day elbowing his way through the crowd. Bingo.

Sweat poured down his back as he turned on the steam, determined not to let this guy get away. He shoved shoppers out of his way as he ran along the walkway, closing in on the shooter. Concerned that he'd lose the man in the crowded restaurant dead ahead—or worse, have the shooter turn this into a hostage situation—Justin launched into a flying tackle, putting his shoulder into the back of the smaller man.

After the two men tumbled to the ground, the suspect continued rolling, using the motion to pop back to his feet. Justin stayed with him, hand wrapped around the man's coat and bracing for a fight. The last thing he expected was for the shooter to run toward the metal railing of the walkway, dragging Justin with him.

He launched himself over the side, suspended for a moment by the jacket Justin refused to let go of. Too off-balance to pull the shooter back up, he was calculating his options when the cheap material gave way, leaving him holding half a coat. He watched helplessly as the sniper landed with an unmistakable *crack*. The man struggled to his feet and limped out to the street where a waiting dark-colored sedan whisked him away.

"Son of a bitch." The vehemence of his tone scared off the tourists who'd wandered over, probably to see what TV show was filming.

A huffing Dennis joined him. "You okay?"

"I'm fine. Where's Jimmy?"

"Some brainiac rental cop charged in, taser drawn to save the day. By the time I got my ID out so he wouldn't shock the crap out of me, the little twerp ran off. Sorry man, he got away."

"We didn't do such a bang-up job of keeping him

safe," Justin growled. "Until we figure out if the shooter found out about this meeting from our side, Jimmy might be safer on his own. Call it in, I want this mall searched and that gun found."

"Way ahead of you," his partner replied, and the faint sound of sirens growing closer confirmed it. "I doubt we'll get much off it even if we find it, guy looked like a pro."

"It's the only lead we've got." Justin labored not to snarl; he was just so damn frustrated.

How did the shooter know where to find them? Frankie Gillette had trusted him. And now his brains were strewn all over the patio of a chain restaurant. He didn't care how long it took or who he upset in the process. He would find the person responsible.

****

Emily fed the last of her dwindling number of horses their evening bucket of food and walked down the aisle to lock the feed room when she saw Justin shambling toward her. Her heart sped up a couple of beats at the way his bespoke suit emphasized his equally well-cut body. Good Lord, what must he think of her? Sweaty, helmet-hair plastered to her head, and hay sticking to her sweater for an extra touch of style. She swiped both hands on her breeches, ensuring no remaining food or slobber stained his suit.

"Hey, um, detective," she stumbled through a greeting and felt like an idiot.

"I like it better when you call me Justin."

His voice sounded strange, a blend of desperation and defeat. Working with horses had taught her a lot about going with what you're feeling, so she ignored his outstretched hand and embraced him in a hug

156

instead. His body language begged for a human connection, and the way his rigid muscles relaxed as he drew her closer proved she'd been right.

"How's your head?" he asked before breaking contact.

Her hand flew to the goose egg on the back of her head from the attack two days ago. She gave him a half smile. "There's only one of you this time, so that's an improvement."

He rewarded her with a laugh as he glanced around. "Place is deserted, where is everybody?"

"All the big hunter-jumper barns are at Thermal for the kickoff of their show season." It occurred to her the question might not be as casual as it sounded. "Why?" She took a step closer, feeling the need to whisper. "Has there been a fresh development in the case?"

As soon as she asked, she felt like an idiot. Any fool could tell from his melancholy mood he wasn't here on business. She mentally kicked herself. She'd spent so much time dodging sympathy she'd lost the knack for giving it.

"No, not really. I ah...do you have plans for tonight?"

Plans? Oh yeah, she had big plans. Stop at the store and grab whatever was on sale to drink. After her two-minute drive home, she'd sit with Samwise on her lap, glass of aforementioned sale item in hand, and drink, probably a lot, in the hopes of falling asleep.

If and when that didn't happen, she'd take a few of the pills she'd managed to steal from Pam's bathroom and play the video of her accident over and over until she fell into a leaden stupor on her lumpy couch, where she'd more than likely wake up the next morning.

Although she loathed the thought of changing her routine, the idea of offering the stalwart detective the comfort he so clearly needed appealed to her. "Nothing I can't change," she answered. "What did you have in mind?"

"Dinner, a little insignificant but entertaining small talk? Somewhere other than your Mexican hang-out," he quickly added.

"In that case, you're buying," she teased. "Come on, follow me home and let me change. I know the perfect place. It's small, cozy, and has ridiculously overpriced wine. You'll love it."

****

Half an hour later, the *maître d'* seated Justin and Emily at a small table on the enclosed front porch of a charming Italian restaurant. She'd showered, corralled her messy hair into a low twist, and threw on a clean pair of jeans and a light sweater she rarely wore because it was too pretty to survive the barn. Both his formal suit and her more casual attire fit right in with the tiny restaurant's eclectic clientele. Most of the tables were occupied despite it being a weeknight. Tucked away in the picturesque corner of upscale Toluca Lake, the place was a favorite among the locals.

"Now don't spoil it for us by telling all your high falutin' friends about this restaurant and make the place so popular none of us poor Valley folk can get a table anymore," she warned him.

When she and Nick lived on the Westside, every once in a while, she'd cajole him into meeting her here for dinner, but it was always an uphill battle. Besides the hideous drive over the Hill, he was convinced the *maître d'* was hitting on him. He should be so lucky.

158

She'd tried to convince him the cute, vivacious man was simply doing his job and paying attention to his customers, but Nick was certain everyone he met, both men and women, wanted to get into his pants.

"What's so funny?"

She snapped out of it, realizing Justin had asked her a question. "I'm sorry, what?"

"You had a very mysterious smile appear on your face just now. What were you thinking about?"

How much of an idiot my ex-husband was? Probably not a good thing to say when you're having dinner with a man, even if you are nothing more than a shoulder to cry on. "Nothing really, something that happened with one of the horses today."

Their waiter arrived with their bottle of wine at that moment, saving her from further embarrassment. As she suspected, Justin had a great time discussing the selections with him and chose a nice bottle from a local winery. She'd expected him to pick the most expensive wine on the menu because he could, but he impressed her with his thoughtful choice. After the usual tasting of the wine business, the waiter disappeared to get their salads, leaving them alone again.

The moment of silence lingered as Emily put a comforting hand on his arm and waited for him to say whatever had driven him to come to her in the first place. "I saw the video of your accident."

Stunned, she yanked her hand away, uncertain what game he was playing. "You watched it?"

He nodded, staring at the wine in his glass as he swirled the ruby-colored liquid backward and forward, studying it as if he could read the tannins like tea leaves.

"Is that the reason for this visit?" she snapped. "So you can ask what everyone else has? How I continue to ride after I nearly killed a horse?"

"No, God no, that's not what I meant at all." His eyes couldn't have grown wider if she'd slapped him. "What I meant…what I'd like to understand is how you put it behind you. Because to tell you the truth, I could really use a little of that myself right now."

After taking a pause for another sip of wine, he told her about the shooting. "Frankie had pulled his fair share of shit, but he was just trying to help his brother. He trusted me, and now he's dead."

He came to her for tips on emotional healing? He had no idea how laughable that was.

"I don't remember much after getting on and taking a few minutes to warm up," she confessed, then followed it with the lie. "Not knowing what happened makes moving on a little easier."

Right, that's why I keep watching the video, hoping to find whatever mistake I'd made. He wants to forget, and I drive myself crazy, trying to remember.

"I envy you," he contended, his voice dropping to a murmur. "I play back the moment when Frankie's head exploded with Technicolor clarity. It was my fault he was killed. My responsibility."

"Hey, copper." She hooked a finger under his chin to raise his downcast eyes. "The guy who killed him is the bad guy, not you. You can't control the world."

"Kind of like you and that jump, I guess, huh?" His eyes shone with emotion he quickly blinked away. "No matter how hard we try, we can't prevent bad shit from happening, and we can't stop blaming ourselves when it does."

After he emptied the wine bottle into their glasses, he raised his in a toast. "Here's to random acts, both good and bad. May we be able to accept them when they come."

Emily clinked her glass to his in agreement. They spent the rest of dinner talking about movies and the weather, skirting anything more important than deciding the worst reality show on television.

After dinner, she ordered coffee and dessert. She wasn't hungry. She'd barely touched her dinner, but it was a way to prolong the night. When he stroked her hand as they waited for their cheesecake to arrive, there was a pleasant tingle in places that hadn't tingled for a long time. The sensation was very nice.

Until the warm glow of the evening disappeared in a wave of dread—the end of the date nightmare. Things hadn't gone quite as she'd hoped the other night at her place when he gave her a passionless kiss on the lips, which left her uncertain about tonight. What if he wanted to come inside to take their relationship to the next level? What if he didn't? It would have been so much easier sitting alone in her tiny little apartment where there were no surprises, and nothing ever happened.

She jumped when the waiter delivered their coffee, nearly knocking the cup and saucer out of his hand. Once he set them down, she clung to the dainty cup like a lifeline and limited her half of the conversation to one-word responses as her mind spun in circles about how to end the evening. No easy answers occurred to her, and panic gripped her like a vise when Justin stiffly asked for the check.

Chapter Nineteen

The evening had grown chilly by the time they left the restaurant and started down the deserted street to his car. Or maybe the temperature seemed colder because of the company. He shook his head, puzzled at Emily's sudden mood change. As a cop, he knew sudden mood swings could be a sign of a drug addiction. Was Ridley right about her drug use? He'd known addicts, even helped a buddy get clean, but couldn't wrap his head around the idea that this warm, caring woman had a drug problem. It had to be something else.

Funny thing was, he thought they had really connected talking about their personal demons. It wasn't until he touched her hand that she drew back. You're the Rhodes Scholar, he told himself, isn't it obvious? She likes you as a friend, nothing more.

He was stumped by the idea of a woman not being sexually attracted to him only because it had never happened before. Not until now, when he finally met a woman who lit his soul on fire. God, no wonder he repelled her. He'd turned into a babbling idiot who writes lyrics for bad country songs. He was brooding over his failure when they passed a scruffy hipster on the curb with a cigarette in his mouth repeatedly flicking his lighter, to no avail.

"Hey man, got a light?" he asked. Justin shrugged *no* in response when a large, hairy arm came out of the alley behind them and wrapped around Emily's throat, lifting her until her toes barely touched the sidewalk. The pressure on her windpipe choked off her cry as the stranger jabbed a knife into her ribs. He could smell the overwhelming stench of sour sweat and beer.

"Everybody do what I say, and no one gets hurt," Hairy Arm rumbled, ending with a wheezy cackle, "at least not so bad they put you in a box."

A sick, angry feeling exploded in the pit of his stomach as Emily looked to him to save them. Problem was, he'd wanted so badly to forget about his job for a little while that he'd left his gun in his car. He nodded to her, putting his hands up in the air, and hoped his calm, steady demeanor would give her confidence.

Hairy Arm half dragged, half prodded her into the pitch-black alley behind them, where a third man waited. The two shoved Justin against the wall while Hairy Arm played the knife blade along her cheekbone, never taking his eyes off him.

"You need to learn to stay out of places where you're not wanted," he commanded as he wrenched her arm behind her and twisted. Her agonized scream burned through him like a flame. He launched at Hairy Arm, but the other two were stronger than they appeared, and their grip held.

"What do you know, boys, we got ourselves an honest-to-God hero," Hairy Arm barked. He threw Emily to the ground with the order, "Don't move, I'll be right back and then we'll have us a real good time."

Then he rammed a meaty paw into Justin's solar plexus. His knees buckled as the wind was knocked out of him, but the other two thugs held him up, laughing like hyenas. As Hairy continued to pummel his ribs and kidneys, he fought to regain his breath and rational thought process. The man was big, but untrained. He kept swinging away but was in no shape to keep it up for long. Letting his head hang to seem more injured than he was, Justin saw Emily rifling through her purse on the ground. He just had to hold on long enough for her to get to her phone and dial 911. The punches weren't anything he couldn't handle, as long as Hairy didn't get bored and start using his knife. Or turn his attention back to Emily. Unwilling to take a chance with her safety hanging in the balance, he decided to make his move.

Hairy was panting, sweat pouring off him, when Justin sprang to life, using all of his strength to swing Right Hand toward Hairy. The sudden change from holding Justin's dead weight to being swung around took the thug by surprise. Hairy put his arm up to fend off the body coming toward him. His elbow rammed into Right's jaw and snapped the man's head back. Justin shook off Right's wobbly hold and spun to Left, delivering quick and precise karate blows that rendered him a semi-conscious heap on the ground.

Turning his attention to Hairy, he made his first mistake. Focused on the absolute pleasure he would get from beating the shit out of him, he didn't notice Right skulking in the shadows behind him. Too late, he saw the blur of motion as Right swung a thick metal pipe at his head. He rocked back enough to lessen the blow, but he still saw stars.

He shook off the pain, blood flowing down his cheek, fueling his fiery rage. Driven by instinct rather than thought, he grabbed the pipe with one hand and the man's wrist with the other. A quick twist, a sickening pop, and Right dropped the pipe with a howl.

"All right hero," Hairy wheezed, "on your knees or I'll cut her throat."

Slowly, Justin turned and saw Hairy had reclaimed his grip on Emily, holding her head back with a fistful of her auburn hair to expose her white throat. The man's hand shook as he held his wickedly long knife there. A tiny drop of her blood already dripped from where he'd nicked her. Defeated, he put his hands in the air and dropped to his knees on the alley's slimy, trash-strewn pavement. It was strange to think a few hundred yards away grocery shoppers were fighting over parking spots, eager to get their organic tofu and sprouts. He saw Left stumble to his feet and pick up the metal pipe Right had dropped. He reared back, swinging it at Justin like a baseball bat.

Plunging a small, serrated blade into Hairy's thigh, Emily screamed, "No!"

His howl of pain and surprise diverted Left's attention long enough for Justin to sweep his feet out from underneath him and grab the pipe. Hairy dropped his own knife as he grabbed her hand to pull the knife out of his leg, but she hung on. The resulting tug of war caused the sharp teeth of the blade to dig deeper and cut a wider swath of muscle and skin.

Letting go of the knife and shoving her with both hands, Hairy sent her tumbling to the pavement toward Justin, the little knife still in her hand. She held it in front of her, ready for another attack. But Hairy took off, limping as fast as he could. Leaderless, the others ran as well, disappearing behind the darkened buildings.

Justin reached out to see if she was all right. She

swung the bloody knife toward him. "Whoa, easy there," he murmured as he gently pried her trembling fingers off the weapon.

As the adrenalin seeped out of her body, she collapsed into his arms. Then the strangest thing happened. Slowly, she chuckled until it grew into a full-blown laugh. He worried she was hysterical until she gasped out between laughs, "Of all the ways I imagined tonight ending, this was definitely not one of them."

He had to admit, she had him there. He wrapped his arms around her as they sat in the filthy alley and laughed along with her.

****

An hour later, Justin impatiently waited for the EMT to finish tending to the cut on his face where the pipe had split the skin over his cheekbone. He watched Emily gulp another cup of coffee the restaurant had provided. She tried to rotate her arm and winced, sounding more pissed than scared as she related her version of the mugging to a uniformed cop. His lip twitched into a small smile, bursting with pride at her fierce will.

"We notified the area hospitals to keep an eye out for a guy with a big ass chunk missing out of his leg," Dennis reported as he sauntered over. "Call me paranoid, but don't they usually take the purse and wallet in your run-of-the-mill mugging?"

Justin shook his head. "The guy said, 'you need to learn to stay out of places you're not wanted.' "

"Message from someone we know? Someone in City Hall whose name rhymes with Maxwell?"

Justin nodded, cautiously surveying the small crowd around them. Until they had the evidence they

166

needed, it would be better, and certainly healthier, to keep their suspicions to themselves.

His partner changed the subject, waving the evidence bag containing Emily's bloody knife. "What the hell was Annie Oakley doing with a frog sticker like this?"

"Frog sticker?" he laughed, which he instantly regretted when the split on his cheek re-opened, forcing the vexed EMT to start all over again with the bandages.

"It's a roper's knife," Emily answered, her voice laced with equal parts exhaustion and exasperation. "Handy for cutting twine or vet wrap." She turned her attention to Justin and made a horrible face. "Aren't they going to stitch that?"

"We tried," grumbled the EMT as he replaced the butterfly bandage on the wound.

He was about to explain his aversion to a needle going through his face when he saw Dennis scowl at Emily. "Lady, let me give you a brief lesson in tactics. Cute horsey knife." He held up the plastic evidence bag with her knife, and then showed her the bag holding the foot-long, carbon steel knife Hairy left behind. "Versus a sword. Not a bright idea. Next time, grab your cell phone and call for help."

She opened her mouth in rebuttal, but evidently changed her mind and snapped it shut. Justin read the narrowed eye glare she shot Dennis as clearly as if she'd spoken the words. Ass. Hole. But he knew caustic trash talk was the way his partner showed he cared and nodded to confirm he understood even if Emily did not.

Dennis cleared his throat and growled, "I'm going to take this back to the station and get them to run the prints on this. You okay getting home?"

He nodded again. "Thanks, partner. And hey," he added before Dennis hurried off, "you be careful." He saw the question written on Emily's face but decided against worrying her by telling her their suspicions about the attack.

"Here, cowboy," the paramedic huffed as he gave Justin an ice pack, "at least put this on your face to keep the swelling down."

He took the pack, but instead of putting it on his cheek, he placed the cold plastic on Emily's shoulder.

"Am I the only one," she murmured, "or have you noticed every time we get together at least one of us ends up requiring medical care?"

"I'm willing to risk it again if you are."

****

"It's too bad you're going to have to cancel that clinic thing you were telling me about," Justin commented as he drove her home.

"The Dearg McGregor clinic? No way, I'm not cancelling because of this." Maybe because the thought of jumping cross-country terrified her, but not because some jerk twisted her arm.

"You're still going to take a lesson with a bum shoulder?"

"We're talking about a clinic with Dearg McGregor. I'd ride if I had a broken leg." He stared at her like she was crazy. "He's won three Olympic medals."

Need she say more? If anyone could help her overcome her fears, it might be McGregor. The least she could do was try.

"In eventing, I assume," he replied.

How could he not be impressed? She was talking about Dearg McGregor, for Pete's sake. "He's like a god, Justin. I'm lucky—"

"What the hell?"

When Justin cut off her explanation, she turned to see what caught his eye. Parked in front of her building was a patrol car, lights on, and two officers standing at her front door with Gary, the manager of her apartment building. She flew out of the car almost before it stopped rolling and ran toward her door.

"Ma'am are you the sole occupant of this apartment?" the female patrol officer asked her.

"Yes, yes, of course," she huffed. "Gary, what's going on?"

The cowering man stammered nonsensically. The female cop, looking to be the more senior of the two, answered for him. "Ma'am, we got a call complaining about the noise. Have you been having a party tonight?"

"Party? What? No, I wasn't even..." she sputtered, then the realization of who must have called to complain kicked in. Rage crept from the pit of her stomach to the roots of her hair. "That bi—"

"Excuse me, officers, is there a problem?" Justin interrupted, flashing his badge and introducing himself. "Ms. Conners has been out with me since a little after six o'clock. The last hour we spent with four officers, another detective, and a paramedic because of a mugging."

Gary let out a little squeaky gasp, but Emily refused to let him make up for being such a tool by acknowledging his apologetic cow eyes.

"You can check the logbooks or—" He flashed his trademark smile and gestured toward his battered face.

"—take my word for it."

The patrol officers exchanged uncertain glances. "Detective," the woman began, "the neighbor upstairs is insistent we issue a citation."

"Oh, really?" Emily snapped. "Well, I'm pretty insistent that she go f—"

This time, Justin put his arm around her waist and drew her close. The heat of his touch left her speechless long enough for realization to dawn on the cops' faces. They were going to back off because they thought they were a couple? She exhaled sharply and was about to rail against the injustice of it all when he squeezed her a little tighter.

"Have any of the other neighbors complained?"

The two patrol officers looked at each other and Gary. The three of them gave a collective, non-committal shrug.

"Officers, the place is certainly quiet now and I can vouch for Ms. Conners." He kept his voice cool and professional, and yet, laced it with subtext when he added, "The neighbor in question has a history of making unfounded complaints. So what do you say we let this one go? One less report for you to fill out and frankly, one less nuisance call marked against the neighbor. It's a no-lose situation and I'll take full responsibility if there're any problems."

Casting one last look around, the officers got in their cruiser and drove off. Gary mumbled a few words of apology before slinking back to his own apartment across the lawn. For the first time in what seemed like hours, Justin and Emily were alone.

"You sure you're okay?" he asked as she got out her keys, rattling in her trembling hand.

She took a deep breath, trying to calm down. Gazing up at him, she stroked the wound on his cheek. "I'm fine. You're the one who's going to have a shiner tomorrow." She screwed her head around to check his watch. "Make that this morning."

A window smacked open above them, and a gravelly voice bellowed, "Some of us are trying to get to sleep." An angry *bam* echoed across the small complex as the window slammed shut.

A dangerous growl rose from her throat as she started toward the stairs. Fast on his feet, Justin blocked her. She pushed against his rock-hard chest with both hands, but the shove that normally moved thirteen-hundred-pound horses out of her way didn't budge him. *Good Lord, this man is built.* She relaxed, but kept her hands on his chest, liking the way his body felt so solid.

He leaned closer, his warm breath caressing her ear. "Back in the alley, you said the evening had taken an unexpected turn." He drew her into his arms until his lips brushed her cheek. "Was this more what you had in mind?"

Tingles of electricity pulsed through her body. In her fantasies, this evening ended with them having wild sex on every surface of her apartment, but she wasn't about to say that, so she mumbled, "Sort of."

She didn't remember parting her lips, but she must have. His tongue met hers, tasting like coffee, sweet cream, and desire. He sucked on her bottom lip, and a soft moan of pleasure escaped her throat.

He circled her waist with one hand and pulled her closer. His other hand glided up her back until he entwined his fingers in the hair curled loosely at the nape of her neck. She rocked her hips against his and

171

his body responded, arousing her even more. Finally, the need for oxygen overrode their desire to continue exploring each other. Gasping, they marveled at each other in a new and kind of scary light. Wow.

She trembled with longing, her need matching his when that damned voice inside her head barked, *this can't be real.* A man as handsome and funny and wealthy as him would soon tire of her, the same way Nick did. Was she ready to be tossed aside after a one-night stand? The cold logic snapped her out of her fog of pure lust. With an almost superhuman effort, she pulled away from his embrace. He seemed stunned, or maybe relieved? She'd lost all ability to read him.

With a soft kiss on the cheek, Justin saw her to her door, mumbled goodbye, and headed toward his car.

Halfway there, he turned around and jogged back. "Hey, my mother is throwing a gala benefit on the fourteenth. It'll be downtown, a whole ballroom full of stuck-up pricks who're overly impressed with themselves. I'd be honored, Ms. Emily Conners, if you would be my date for the night."

Speechless, she grinned and bobbed her head up and down. He kissed her again. It wasn't as long or deep as the first, but if there'd been a seismograph around, it would have proved the Earth moved ever so slightly. As he strode to his car, she wondered if the voice could be wrong. Maybe she wasn't so unlovable after all.

What does one wear to a gala?

Chapter Twenty

Clutching a to-go cup of coffee in one hand, Dennis put down two cheap paper sacks he held in the other and let out an exasperated snort. "Sweet Jesus, it's not even eight o'clock yet. What are you going for, Super Cop of the Year?"

Between the memory of the kiss and the thug holding a knife to Emily's throat, sleep had been elusive. Justin gave up and went into the office instead of staring at the bedroom ceiling. He refused to believe the mugging was a coincidence and needed to figure out what case it was connected to.

Dennis stalked around him as Justin kept turning his head away. "Okay, hotshot, let's see the eye."

Justin sheepishly tilted his head up, knowing from a glance at his mirror that his cheek had a Pollock-esque pattern of purples and green.

His asshole partner whistled in appreciation. "Damn, you should get beaten up more often. It looks good on you."

"All right, all right, enough with the comedy routine," he groused as he helped himself to half of Dennis's bagel when his mouth gaped open in shock. "There's peanut butter on your bagel."

"I happen to like peanut butter and the operative word there is 'my' bagel." He tossed the other bag to Justin. "This one's for you. As is this." He put a piece of paper on Justin's desk as he sat on the edge, sipping his coffee. "It's the preliminary report on the prints we got off the knife. Belongs to a dude named Van Husen, I shit you not, although his buddies call him Pit Bull."

Justin winced in mock pain. "Hard to be worried about some jackass dumb enough to go by the nickname Pit Bull."

"This is the weird part," he mumbled, licking the melting peanut butter off the rim of the still warm bagel. "You'd expect the guy to be local, right? I mean, after the shooting the other day, my money was on the attack being tied in with our investigation into Robbie Allen's death. Thing is, your mugger's got a sheet about a mile long, mostly for receiving stolen goods, assault, nothing too heavy. And all of it out near Palm Springs. Some backwater town called Thermal."

Justin struggled to remember where he'd recently heard that name. He reached over to his computer and searched for the city. Moments later had his answer. "Oh shit. The horse show."

"I take it this means something to you?"

"The mugger, he warned me about not sticking my nose in where it doesn't belong. He didn't mean the murder of the commissioner's kid, he meant the Yates investigation."

"Hey, wait a minute." Dennis circled around the desk to sit in his own chair and flipped through his notes from last night. "Didn't you tell me he said that as he held the knife to Ms. Conner's throat?"

He shrugged in agreement. "And your point is?"

"Are you sure he was talking to you?"

An icy pit of dread opened in Justin's gut. If the mugger was threatening Emily, she could be heading blindly into danger at the clinic she refused to cancel. He grabbed his cell phone and searched for a moment before finding the person he was looking for.

"Ah, Detective Butler," Lottie Gray purred at the other end of the phone. "How nice of you to call. Emily told me about your exploits last night."

He sat in stunned silence—was she talking about the attack or the kiss? "She told you about last night?"

"Come now, no need to be modest. You saved her life, after all."

He let out the breath he was holding. It wasn't that he was ashamed of the kiss or the feelings he was sure they both shared, but he feared sharing those details would complicate an already screwed up situation.

She continued on in a teasing tone. "Although technically, she saved you. Ironically, the knife was last year's Christmas gift from Pamela. Emily's out. Shall I have her call you when she gets in?"

"Actually, you were the one I was looking for. Did Ms. Yates ever have any business dealings with a man named Van Husen at the horse show in Thermal?"

A harsh laugh erupted from the other end of the phone. "Van Husen? You mean like the shirts?"

"Yes ma'am, although he's more commonly known as Pit Bull."

"You're making that up." She sounded incredulous. "No self-respecting person named Van Husen would use a nickname like Pit Bull, and certainly no one showing in Thermal."

"No, ma'am, I hate to say that's the truth. Did Ms. Yates have any business associates there?"

"The hunter-jumpers are the only ones who have business in Thermal, and they're more the stab you in the back kind of people as opposed to the bash your head in type."

"Are you sure no one in Thermal would have any feud with Ms. Yates? Possibly a horse sale gone wrong? Please, Mrs. Gray, this could be important."

There was a long pause on the other end of the line. The ache in his hand made him aware of how tightly it was wrapped around the phone.

"I'm sorry, detective, I was too caught up in being the entertaining smart ass to be helpful. I can't think of anyone who would be so upset about a horse sale they'd kill over it. Besides, it's unlikely Pam would have a reason to get into any kind of business with anyone in the hunter circuit. It's like—" She paused for a moment before finishing her thought. "—it's like one of those noisy motorcycles that deafen you as they pass you on the street versus a dirt bike. They're both perfectly nice motorcycles, but they're different sides of the same coin. You'd never ride a street motorcycle in a motocross race. Do you see my point?"

The comparison didn't ease his mind. "Would she have had any other reason to go there recently?"

"Detective, no one goes to Thermal if they can help it. Why, what's going on?"

He hesitated, uncertain how much to tell the woman. It was pure speculation at this point, but Emily had been attacked twice already. "I don't want to alarm you, Mrs. Gray," he told her, and then shared his suspicions and the concern that Temecula, the location for the clinic, was a relatively short highway drive from Thermal. "I realize Emily's got a lot on her mind right now, so I think we can both agree there's no need to tell her about this."

"Please, detective, now that we're co-conspirators, call me Lottie. And don't worry, I'll never let her out of my sight."

Justin hung up, wishing her words brought him more comfort than they did. He'd assumed the attack in the barn was a case of Emily stumbling in on a thief breaking into the tack room. She told him robberies happened from time to time. But now, after the mugging, a horrifying thought came front and center.

What if the killer hadn't meant to kill Pamela at all, but mistook her for Emily?

Chapter Twenty-One

Hunching her shoulders under her polar fleece jacket, Emily led Reese up the hill to the show barns. She had gotten up early and braved the damp Temecula morning to let the big horse play and kick up his heels on the lunge line to burn off his excitement before the field got too crowded.

Dearg McGregor's clinic was part of the annual Kinsale Downs fundraiser, which meant several trainers would be using the course at the same time. More riders on the field made it more fun than a show. It also meant at least once every hour a horse would dump its rider, then head, hell-bent for leather, back to the barn, upsetting other horses along the way.

Determined not to be the rider left on the ground helplessly watching her horse gallop rider-less across Kinsale Downs's two hundred plus acres, she'd tried everything she could think of to get out all of Reese's silliness. But as a wispy cloud of steam hung over his body, she worried she hadn't done enough.

Lottie entered the barn carrying two venti-sized coffee creations. "Here, I'll trade you."

Emily took the one without the lipstick on the lid, marveling at how her friend could be awake enough in the morning to put on make-up. She switched out the lunge line for a lead rope and handed over the big horse. "Walk him around for—"

Waving off the instructions, Lottie took the line and the horse in hand. "Ten minutes, I know, I know. Chill out, eat a banana."

Alone, Emily pulled Reese's heavy blanket off the saddle rack where she'd draped it and wrapped the earthy-smelling, thick-quilted nylon around her shoulders. The damp chill seeped into her bones in the dark, sunless barn. She leaned back and closed her eyes, trying to relax.

God, what a week it had been, she thought as she sipped the caramel and chocolate coffee drink, appreciating the warmth more than the flavor. First, Reese threw a shoe and Lottie had to employ several unique and colorful threats to get the farrier to come out before they left for Kinsale Downs.

Then, she went to hitch Pam's two-horse trailer up to her truck and discovered one of the two stabilizer bars was missing. Only Pam would own such an expensive piece of equipment and not take proper care of it. After a mad scramble, they were able to borrow a trailer. God, she loved the generosity of the eventing community.

To top it all off, right after they arrived at Kinsale Downs, they discovered the schedule had changed, and she was riding two hours earlier than planned—which meant staying late in order to clean the tack. Adding up all the minor glitches, it felt as if Fate conspired against her attending this particular clinic.

In theory, this was the easiest one of the two days. They'd work on stadium jumping today before moving to cross-country on day two. Stadium jumps weren't easier to ride, but the knowledge that the jumps would fall down rather than the horse if she made an error made it endurable. Almost.

Emily had ridden in her fair share of clinics before, but never with anyone so famous—or notorious for not suffering fools—as Dearg McGregor. She'd spent a sleepless night and now her stomach gurgled in protest, reminding her why, in the past, she'd given up coffee before an important event.

"Ready to get dressed?" Lottie sang as she rounded the corner with a cool and dry Reese in tow.

Suddenly, all she wanted to do was pull the horse blanket over her head and stay there until it was time to go home. "I don't ride until nine."

Lottie tapped the face of her sleek watch that would be more at home around a bridge table than a barn. "It's almost eight; you have to get dressed."

Eight? It was six-thirty about fifteen seconds ago. What happened to the morning? She sunk farther into the blanket for a moment and then dug deep to find the will to stand. Her limbs were leaden, but somehow she struggled into her breeches, tall boots, and clingy turtleneck. The shirt was the latest trend, supposedly keeping you cool in summer and warm in winter. Lottie bought one for her in a smoky shade of green. "To match your eyes," she'd claimed.

Emily thought funereal black would have been more appropriate as she pulled on her medical armband, safety vest, air vest, and helmet before mounting up. Her gloved hands fumbled at the latch of her air vest, but she finally got the safety cord attached to her saddle. The extra precaution was overkill for stadium jumping, but Lottie insisted. At least this time, if she fell off, the air vest would inflate and hopefully prevent her from breaking her neck. Again.

She and Reese arrived at the corner of the barns just as a booming Scots burr resounded all the way from the show arena. "Your legs are flopping like whale fins."

Dearg McGregor was renowned for having a wicked sense of humor and an unerring eye. What the hell had she been thinking, letting Lottie talk her into riding in his clinic?

"No way."

She wheeled Reese around, prepared to return to the barn but Lottie blocked the way. The woman was tiny compared to Reese, but her crossed arms and determined glare were enough. On his own accord, the horse turned and trotted toward the arena as Emily just hung on. Not an auspicious start, but at least she had nowhere to go but up.

****

"My God, woman. Give the half-halt in rhythm with the horse. It's a dance, not a pub brawl."

Lottie did a poor but humorous imitation of a Scots accent over dinner. An older couple across the floor of the Mexican restaurant in Old Town harrumphed in their direction for being boisterous.

Emily didn't care. With a howl of laughter, she added her own poor version that came off sounding more Russian than Scots. "That's the problem with you Americans. Too much thrusting your hips about in discos, not enough waltzes."

The clinic had been exhilarating. She and the rest of the riders got over their nerves as McGregor charmed them into relaxing. Maybe it was the accent, or the panty dampening vision of him in those skintight breeches. Whatever the reason, the man had a way of making everyone laugh at their own mistakes. She calmed down enough to learn new techniques and was pleased to discover she already was doing quite a few things right. So pleased, in fact, she bought another round of margaritas.

The older woman shot her a frown. "Since when did you start having more than one drink during a competition?"

"Who's competing? This is just a clinic."

She gave her a sideways glance but demurred. "It was good to see the old Emily back in the saddle today. Congratulations, I knew you could do it." She lifted her glass and leaned closer. "So what did he say to you at the end of class?"

She avoided Lottie's inquisitive stare by studying the basket of stale chips, sucking on the straw to control the grin threatening to spread across her face. The great Dearg McGregor had stood next to her, put his hand on her thigh and gazed up at her with those smoldering eyes, wind-tossed dark curls, and a crooked grin.

In that sexy Scots accent, he quipped, "You have a wonderful natural seat, but your style is like a monkey fucking a football." She'd blinked, not sure whether to laugh or cry. Then he leaned in closer. "Forget what Pamela taught you. She was an idiot. Think of riding as a tango. Keep a slow and steady rhythm, don't let it get too rushed. Understand?"

That was without a doubt the hottest riding instruction she'd ever been given. Was there the teensiest chance he wasn't talking about riding a horse? "Does he touch everyone's leg when he talks to them?"

"He's a riding instructor," Lottie said. "He's supposed to adjust people's legs into the correct position; he's supposed to move their arms for a better feel. Why?"

So she must have been mistaken. God, one kiss from Justin and suddenly her ego is the size of Texas to imagine a man like Dearg McGregor might come on to her. "Nothing, never mind. All he said was to relax, work in rhythm with the horse, blah, blah, blah. You know, the usual stuff."

Amused, Lottie quirked an eyebrow and casually mentioned, "The rumor mill says he's single again and moving out here in a few weeks."

"Who is?"

"Who do you think? The hottie you've been ogling all day, you nit. I say tomorrow you make your move," she suggested with a waggle of her eyebrows.

Emily took a huge gulp of her drink. "First off, I was not ogling; I was admiring. He's a legend. Besides, I thought you were pushing for Justin. Are you switching horses mid-race?"

Her friend waved her hand airily. "I was pushing for him, but nothing's happened so…" Heat bloomed on her cheeks, making her regret bringing the topic up. Naturally, Lottie, being Lottie, picked up on it right away. "Something did happen, didn't it? You're holding out, you hag." She hooted and threw a stray chip at Emily.

"No, nothing really. It was just a kiss." Emily sighed, savoring the memory of it all week. *Just a kiss. Like Secretariat was just a horse.* "Shouldn't we get going? Tomorrow's another early day and then the drive home." With a great show of nonchalance, she rose and gathered her things to go.

Smirking, Lottie followed. "Fine with me. I've still

got to walk your cross-country course to find the best places to video from."

With that one sentence, all the warmth from the memory of the kiss, the clinic, and the margaritas drained from Emily's body, leaving her feeling cold and empty. Unlike most clinics, McGregor had posted the fences he wanted them to take tomorrow, so everyone had a chance to get prepared. He encouraged them to bring all the emotional baggage they would carry to a show so they could work on getting over those issues as well as the fences.

He had no idea the steamer trunk she carried on her back.

The two women walked the short course, and sure enough, it included a downhill jump. It was just a little ski jump with no obstacle afterward. For Emily, it brought up all the memories of that awful day. Would she be able to fix whatever had gone wrong? Would she keep Reese on his feet, or would he come crashing down like his brother had with a sickening crunch?

****

Nestled in a scooped-out bowl in the middle of the Kinsale cross-country course, a thick morning mist hung like a shroud over the racetrack. Emily watched the exercise riders take their young Thoroughbreds out on the track and put them through their paces. That would be fun.

With a sigh, she turned to study the downhill jump in front of her. Not so fun. The shiver that ran through her body had nothing to do with the chill of the early morning air. Somehow, she had to face her fears today. If she didn't, she doubted she'd ever find the courage to try again.

Now that her doctors were being such a-holes about giving her refills, she'd started out the morning vowing not to take any of her dwindling stock of painkillers. She still had the stolen prescription pad to fall back on but was nervous about trying to get away with forgery.

Well, maybe one pill. She'd need to keep her hip flexors relaxed and moving and the pain in her back made her stiff and tense. Now, as she fingered the plastic bottle in her jacket pocket, confronting the jump up close, one more little white pill seemed like a good idea. Her grip on the bottle tightened as she felt a silent presence behind her.

"You might as well join me," she snapped.

She saw Lottie cringe at her sharp tone but didn't care. She'd been dogging her every footstep all weekend, and it grated on her frayed nerves.

Her friend held the paper cup out apologetically. "I brought you a decaf coffee, lots of sugar and cream."

At first, the attention had been helpful, even a little comforting, but slowly Emily came to resent it. She felt certain Lottie was spying to make sure she didn't raid any of the good drugs out of the horse meds. Dammit, it wasn't a crime to need a little chemical pain relief once in a while, and she was tired of Lottie acting like it was.

"No, thanks." She glared at the coffee and, without another word, marched back toward the barn, stopping at the first port-o-potty they came to.

Spinning, she barked at Lottie, who was hot on her heels. "I'm going inside. Just so you don't have to listen, something nasty is about to come out of one or both ends. No doubt you'll be here when I get out." She stepped inside and slammed the blue plastic door.

Inside her smelly little fortress, Emily's hands trembled as she shook one more pill out of the bottle and dry swallowed it.

****

By the time Emily was mounted, even Reese could tell something was wrong and reacted by jigging and tossing his head. After changing his bit to a harsher one and putting on longer spurs, she rode down to the arena where Dearg was already warming everyone up.

"Thank you for joining us," he greeted her, overtly looking at his watch. Though the words were laced with sarcasm, his smile was filled with warmth.

He took the group through a number of simple warm-up exercises. Through it all, Reese became increasingly irritable and difficult to manage, not at all the cooperative horse he'd been yesterday. Dearg frowned but said nothing.

Finally, the riders hit the cross-country course. The field was more crowded than the day before, with various trainers working around each other, vying for their turn at a particular section of the course. In short, it was chaos. The Scot had his riders warm up over a straightforward, low log fence, but the blood drained from Emily's face as if it was a six-foot drop jump into a pool of fire. Unlike yesterday where she improved, the more he bellowed his usual humorous comments, the more defensive she became, and her ride spiraled downward. As the group proceeded to larger fences, Reese screeched to a surprising stop in front of a jump shaped like a small church.

The grass field swam as spots danced in front of Emily's eyes. Her breath came in quick gasps, but she blamed Lottie for adjusting her damn cross-country vest too tight. It was only by the grace of God she didn't come off when he slammed on the brakes. At least she didn't pop far enough out of the saddle to set off the air vest.

As self-pity washed over her, she clenched her jaw, determined not to give in. It was her fault her horse didn't jump. She'd taken her leg off long before the obstacle. All right, dammit, you know what the problem is, so fix it, she screamed at herself silently. Or not so silently, as the other students backed off as she wheeled the horse around to take the jump again.

Her eyes locked on the jump like lasers as she dug her spurs into her horse's flanks to make sure they got the job done this time. Clenching the reins in one hand with a fistful of mane, she added a solid smack to his butt with the crop to be sure he understood refusing was not an option. If she'd seen one of her students do that, she'd yell at them for overriding, but right now, the only thing that mattered was getting over the fence.

Likely offended by the rough treatment and unhappy with the harsh bit, for the first time in his life, Reese acted out. He gave a half-hearted rear, but Emily remained determined they would make it over the jump. Her vision tunneled as her heart pounded in her throat. They sailed over the fence, but a loud *crack* echoed as the horse's leg met wood. Their tug of war had put the horse at a terrible distance, and he'd caught a hind leg over the pointed roof of the fence. She circled afterward, gripping his mane to cover how badly her hands were shaking.

"Is he off? He feels like he's limping," she asked no one in particular. "Can you tell?"

She glanced over at Dearg, who watched the horse.

Reese had taken a pretty good whack, but the thick boots on his legs took the brunt of the blow, doing their job and protecting his sensitive bone and tendons from the wood obstacle. From the saddle, it felt like the horse favored one leg, but no more than someone who cracked their shin on a coffee table. Or was it more serious and she should dismount? She waited for Dearg's judgement.

"He seems fine to me," he barked, "keep him moving for a few minutes; we'll see if he works it out."

Glumly, she walked and trotted while everyone else took the next few jumps and got ready to do their full course. As the first rider left the start box, Emily took her feet out of her stirrups, ignoring Lottie's frantic arm waving, and jumped down. She remembered seconds too late to detach the air vest from the saddle. *Shit, that's what Lottie was trying to say.*

With a loud *pop,* the vest inflated before her feet hit the ground. Already agitated, the sound spooked Reese, and he skittered off to the side. Caught off guard by both the horse and the vest, it was all she could do to land on her feet rather than her ass.

"God dammit," she growled in frustration as she struggled out of the bulky inflated air vest.

Busy with the other students, Dearg barely glanced at her after the vest's air canister exploded. The bastard didn't even try to hide his smirk.

"There's something wrong," she said to his broad back. "He's been acting funny all morning. Clearly yesterday was too much for him," she blurted out the accusation before leading Reese back to the barn.

****

Because another rig blocked their trailer, they had

to haul all their supplies from the barn back to the trailer by hand rather than driving it down to the barn. The brooding silence broke when Emily tried to toss the buckets used for water and feed into the loft of the trailer's tack room and missed. "Ow, dammit," she cried out as they fell back on her.

Lottie picked the buckets up and put them in the loft herself. "It takes time to get over an injury. Think of Bruce Davidson. The man nearly died and came back to ride again."

"News flash," she lashed out with barely controlled rage as she stormed out of the trailer's tack room. "I'm not Bruce fucking Davidson. I can't even hope to be an eventing god like Bruce fucking Davidson. There are days I doubt even Bruce fucking Davidson can live up to being Bruce fucking Davidson."

A familiar Scots growl came behind her, "Don't ever doubt Bruce fuckin' Davidson." Dearg ticked off his accomplishments on his hand. "He won the US rider of the year title fourteen times, won more medals than you could carry, and holds the record for the most wins at the Kentucky Three-Day. Do I need to continue?" Abashed, she shook her head. "Not a finer man ever sat in a saddle," he said. "Even if he isn't a Scot."

She turned beet red at having anyone except Lottie witness her tantrum, but especially this legendary man. "Sorry, I didn't see you there."

"I came by to see if you wanted me to take a look at your horse's leg. We both know it would be a waste of time, don't we?" He stood in front of her, all six-feet-four-inches of him. "Emily, look me in the eye."

The voice in her head exclaimed, *Oh dear God, not another inspiring freaking lecture on overcoming my fears,* while in her heart something inspiring was exactly what she needed right now.

"Why?" she challenged even as she complied with his command. She didn't realize how tall the man was, only having seen him from horseback. She had to tilt her chin up to meet his storm-colored eyes.

"That's where your eye should be when you jump," Dearg barked. "When you're ready to pull your head out of your arse and really ride, call me. I can make you into a great rider, but you have to want it."

Chapter Twenty-Two

The drive home from the disastrous clinic started in stony silence. Emily had just guided the truck and borrowed trailer onto the freeway when she and Lottie babbled out apologies to each other. In the end, Lottie promised not to push so hard as long as Emily promised to keep her head, as Dearg so colorfully put it, out of her arse.

Once they were back in L.A., Lottie kept her promise and didn't push. Unfortunately, with her confidence shaken to the core, Emily failed to hold up her end of the bargain. Using the excuse that the horses still in training with her needed more flat work and conditioning than they needed to jump, she didn't go over a single fence for days on end.

The noisy inner dialogue in her head, with half of her brain accusing her of being a coward, while the other half argued it was prudent to work on the horses' balance without the wear and tear on their legs from jumping, was the only reason she could think of that she'd let the date of Justin's gala slip her mind. It was only days away and she still had nothing to wear.

Turning to Lottie for help, her friend loaned her a simple but elegant black gown that was perfect for the occasion. With a little help from a tailor to take it in here and there, even Emily had to admit she looked pretty damn good. However, the dress was backless, and she felt self-conscious about the scar on her neck from her surgery after her fall.

Lottie disagreed. "You can hardly see it," she argued as the two of them entered the Saddle Shoppe to get a new bridle for Reese.

"Easy for you to say, you're not the one with a Frankenstein zipper on your neck."

Lottie's left eyebrow shot toward her hairline. "Really, drama queen? I've seen it more often than you, and I'm telling you it's not that bad."

"Regardless, it's going to be cold. I need to find a shawl or pashmina so I don't freeze to death."

She hated to cover up the gorgeous dress, but the weather had turned nippy after the recent heat spike. Even though the event would be held indoors, running from and to Justin's car wasn't going to happen in the ridiculous heels Lottie sent along with the dress.

"Ladies, I couldn't help but overhear," Brandon Sinclair, the co-owner of the shop commented as he restocked the display of bits located next to the bridles. "This might sound a little bizarre, but back in college I belonged to a drag *a cappella* group, The Five Lizas. Part of our costume was this gorgeous, beaded wrap. It might be the perfect solution."

It was easy to picture the good-looking man in front of her transforming into a beautiful woman. Emily appreciated the offer but demurred, worried she'd find a way to ruin his irreplaceable item, but he and Lottie both ganged up on her.

"Nonsense," he insisted, "It's not doing the wrap any good boxed up in my closet. In fact, if you're free now, why don't you come over to our house and I'll dig it out for you? Joey can watch the store by himself for a couple of hours, don't worry."

She was still vainly voicing her objections five-minutes later when Lottie, new bridle in hand, dragged her to her car and followed Brandon out of the Equestrian Center.

****

Having hit a dead end trying to find "Pit Bull" Van Husen or who shot Frankie Gillette, Dennis and Justin decided to take a second look at Robbie Allen's home. Their first sweep, immediately after they landed the case, had been unremarkable. But based on what they'd since learned about him, they wanted to dig deeper.

Unfortunately, Councilman Allen or, more likely, Victor Maxwell, had used their pull at City Hall to deny them permission without a warrant. Getting one wasn't a problem, but the stalling tactic seemed suspicious, so they decided to take an unofficial look instead.

Dennis expertly picked the lock on the front door of Robbie's funky Venice bungalow while Justin scanned the neighborhood. "This kid was screwed from the get-go."

His partner straightened up and glanced around, trying to see what he was talking about. "Oh yeah, this must have been terrible living in the hipster section of town, a couple of miles from the beach. Throw a little misery like that my way."

"No, I mean the way the corners of the other buildings point right at his door and the path to his door is a straight line from the street. Feng Shui poison arrows shooting straight into Robbie's humble abode."

With a twist of his wrist, Dennis popped the door open. "Kinda' blows your hocus pocus out of the water, doesn't it? The kid was shot, not pierced by an arrow."

"It doesn't mean he wasn't stabbed in the back," Justin pointed out as they entered the house.

As soon as they stepped inside, they saw the place had been sanitized since the first time they'd visited. "Somebody didn't want us to find something. Maybe your buddy Maxwell got worried after you two had your little chat?"

Dennis grunted in agreement, but they checked the rest of the place over to be sure. The bedroom was so neat it had to be staged. What little clothing they found in the closet and drawers was new. Even the sheets on the bed still had the creases in them as if they just came out of the package.

"Robbie, you rich prick," Dennis mused, "what were they afraid we might find?"

"The question is, did the cleaning crew find whatever Robbie was hiding or is it still here?" Just to be thorough, Justin rifled through a couple of desk drawers but wasn't surprised to find they were either empty or contained only a few pens and sheets of paper.

He made his way out the bedroom's French doors and inhaled his first breath of air that wasn't tainted by the smell of the chemicals used by the cleaners or Robbie's bad karma. The small back porch led out to a microscopic yard. The lawn wasn't as tidy as the house, with weeds and grass ankle high, and there was an ashtray overflowing with half-smoked joints next to a brightly painted Adirondack chair. Apparently, the cleanup crew hadn't bothered coming out here.

"You know," Justin mused out loud. "If Robbie was trying to hide something from Maxwell, something worth getting himself killed over, he might have been smart enough to put it in this sad little space, where no one would look."

They searched under every floorboard and bush until Dennis spotted a manila envelope tucked into the rafters of the covered porch. The envelope contained a notebook filled with names, numbers, and what might be dates. "Bingo," he crowed. "This must be the dirt the kid had on Vic. Naughty Mr. Maxwell is taking bribes from a lot of very bad people."

"Maybe, but implicating Maxwell in a bribery scheme isn't enough," Justin said. "I want to nail his ass for the murders of Robbie Allen and Frankie Gillette. We need to find Jimmy and his girl to make it stick."

It wasn't until then that he became aware of the background noise of police sirens getting louder. And then they stopped right outside Robbie Allen's home. Dennis dashed to the French doors and peered toward the front of the house. "Oops."

"What do you mean, 'oops'?" he gritted his teeth. "You missed the alarm?"

"Mea culpa. Time to go."

They sprinted through the backyard and climbed over the chain-link fence. As they hunkered down behind the neighbor's bushes to evade the second patrol car on the scene, Justin's cell phone rang. "Shit," he muttered. He answered it without stopping to read who was calling, desperate to silence it as the patrol officers stood a few feet away, surveying the property for the burglar.

"Justin, are you there?" Emily asked.

"Emily?" He saw Dennis roll his eyes, but ignored him as he strained to make out what she was saying. "Why are you whispering?" he whispered back into his own phone. "Hello, are you there? I can't hear you."

Irritated as the police turned in their direction, Dennis took the phone. "He can't talk right now."

****

"No, Justin, wait, we found—" she pleaded to the dead air as the call disconnected. Great. *What the hell am I supposed to do now*?

Trapped in Brandon Sinclair's flamingo-themed bathroom, she slumped onto the fuzzy pink toilet seat cover, wondering if the man was a cold-blooded killer. Calling 911 seemed a bit over the top. And the guy was loaning her a wrap he used to wear as part of a drag group, for cripe's sake. How dangerous could he possibly be?

She and Lottie had followed Brandon to the cozy place he shared with his husband, Joey Murphy. Once inside, he'd dashed into the other room to get the wrap and that's when Lottie spotted it. There, on the mantle of the fireplace, was the plastic trophy they'd discovered was missing from Pamela's house after her murder.

"Serial killers keep trophies from their victims," Lottie whispered, scrutinizing the other knick-knacks lined up on the mantle. "Every cop show says so. Go. Pretend you need to pee and call for backup from the powder room."

Although it seemed like Lottie watched too much TV, Emily had to concede it was possible that Pamela tried to screw over Brandon the same way she had Ben Sanders. While Ben lamented not having the guts to kill her, maybe sweet little Brandon's waters ran deeper than everyone thought.

A knock on the bathroom door startled her. "Are you okay in there?" Brandon asked in a timid voice, sounding very un-killer-like. He probably wondered if she had a serious intestinal illness since she'd been on the toilet this long.

"Fine, thanks, sorry," she answered with a cheerfulness she didn't feel as she opened the door and followed him back to the living room.

"Sorry it took me so long," he said, holding up a beaded wrap in elegant black satin. Emily had to admit he was right; the accessory was stunning. "I wanted to show you the picture of the group, too. We were a crazy bunch."

Faking a gush over the wrap, Lottie chuckled at the photo of five men dressed in glamorous drag while looking over his shoulder at Emily, in a silent demand to know where the hell the cavalry was.

Emily shrugged and shook her head, at a loss as to what to do from here. She glanced back at the tacky gold plastic trophy with a cheap nameplate announcing "World's Best Mom" on the mantle. Did its presence here mean Brandon or his husband Joey was a killer? Since Lottie's plan to have Justin ride to the rescue and arrest Brandon was a bust, she ran through alternative scenarios in her head.

They could mosey out of here without ever mentioning the trophy and he'd be none the wiser. Very few people realized Pamela had kept the trophy. Heck, she hadn't gotten a close enough look until today to see what it said, so there's no reason for Brandon to worry they'd recognize it. If he had, he would have put the cheap plastic cup some place less conspicuous, or never invited them over at all.

On the other hand, he might realize his mistake after they left and get rid of the trophy, destroying any chance of nailing him for the murder. A cold chill dropped on both shoulders. Brandon was at the tack store the day someone attacked her in the barn. Could he have been trying to kill her then? Dammit, if only she'd read more mysteries and fewer bodice rippers, she might know what to do.

Exhausted from too many nightmare-filled sleepless nights since her failure at the clinic, she took the bull by the horns and picked up the trophy. "It's like this, Brandon. Lottie thinks you're a stone-cold killer who bashed Pamela in the face and stole this plastic trophy." She looked him straight in the eye. "So what's the deal? Did you kill her or not?"

"How could you possibly think," he shrieked, "I would kill my own mother?" Tears and snot flowed down his face with equal viscosity.

"Your, um… mother?" Lottie found her voice first.

He nodded, looking too upset to speak. After several high-pitched squawks, he pulled himself together. "She didn't want anyone to know."

"I'll bet," Emily muttered, earning a sharp poke in the side from Lottie.

"It wasn't like that," he said, nostrils flaring. "From the first time we met, she supported my lifestyle. She even bankrolled the purchase of the tack store and helped me get started. But she knew how people around here felt about her and feared it would hurt the business if it came to light that we were related."

Emily hated to admit it, but she was probably right. While there were a few who would have gone out of their way to do business with him if only to suck up to Pamela, there were a lot more who would have found passive-aggressive ways to get back at her through him.

From hogging his parking spots to bad-mouthing his store, she imagined dozens of ways some people might have made his life hell for shits and giggles.

"Brandon, how did you get the trophy?" Lottie asked. "Last I knew, it was in Pamela's house."

"After she was murdered," Brandon blubbered and broke down into sobs.

This was the first time Emily observed a crying jag from the other side and made a mental note never to do it again. After a moment, he retched like a cat coughing up a hairball and continued. "Mother gave me a key when I first moved here with Joey. We stayed with her for a while until we got our own place. When the news of her murder broke, I drove over and grabbed it and the picture of us together before the police got in there and pawed all over everything."

"Why?" Emily asked, trying to keep the dismay out of her voice.

"I bought this for her on Hollywood Boulevard last year for our first...I guess our only Mother's Day together." He ran his fingertips across the rim, as if it were the Holy Grail. Her throat tightened, seeing how much Pamela had meant to this kid.

Wait a minute. If they celebrated last Mother's Day together, Pamela had kept this hidden for almost a year. "I can't believe she didn't tell any of us."

Lottie shook her head. "You know how guarded and cool she was."

Brandon tore his eyes off the trophy to stare at them. "Are you kidding? My mother was one of the warmest people I've ever met."

With a laugh, Emily blurted, "Are we talking about the same Pamela?"

"When I told my parents I was gay, it was the first time they admitted I was adopted. Right before they threw me out of the house. Talk about cold. Afterward, I signed up on one of those chat boards that connects willing birth mothers with their children.

"Six months later, we set a meeting. I go into a coffee shop to get a half decaf—half caf no foam latte and there's this woman ahead of me ordering hers exactly the same way. It was Pamela. We'd been ordering our coffee the same way all these years and yet we just met. Weird, huh?"

No, Emily thought, what's weird is a woman who wouldn't hesitate to cut you off at the knees for wearing your hair incorrectly during a riding lesson would welcome the gay son she gave away with open arms. "Sorry, it's so unlike the Pamela we knew to be so unconditionally supportive."

He gave her a tiny, secret smile, but if he discerned what she meant, he didn't let on. "She cared more than she would ever admit. Especially about you, Emily."

"Me?"

"The responsibility for your accident weighed on her, especially after she saw how hard it was for you to bounce back."

Anger flared. *What the hell was that supposed to mean?* She opened her mouth to protest, but Brandon was on a roll, relieved to speak openly about his mother. "She wasn't as fearless as you all assume, either. Someone in the barn worried her, although I never got the impression she feared for her life as much as she did for the horses."

"Did she suspect a trainer was hurting horses deliberately? Like for insurance or something?"

She understood Pamela's definition of horse abuse depended on the pronoun; *she* didn't beat horses, she disciplined them. But if *they*—as in anyone else—raised a hand to an animal, she was the first to demand punitive action be taken against the abuser. Emily had always suspected her animal rights campaign had more to do with knocking out the competition, but maybe Pam really cared about the horses after all.

Brandon said, "I wish I knew. She kept her horse life separate from our time together. I know she got into a serious argument before she left for the horse show."

"What do you mean by serious?"

"As in, she borrowed my cell phone to call the person because her battery died. Mid conversation with this person, she got so mad she threw my phone against a wall."

Fortunately, Brandon kept the bits and pieces of his phone instead of throwing them away. At Emily's request, he gave them to her, and she slipped them into a baggie, in case Justin could get the phone number off the memory chip. The women left, promising to take good care of the wrap and send him pictures of Emily wearing it.

On the way home, Emily remarked, "Not having a son as manly as her must have been a blow to Pamela."

Lottie shook her head. "Are you kidding? After all he's been through and he's still as sweet as the day is long? That kid is every inch as tough as Pamela."

Chapter Twenty-Three

The next day, Emily was leading Reese back to his stall when she heard someone call her name. She turned and saw Justin plodding toward her, as gorgeous in jeans and a sweatshirt as he was in his tailored suits. Her heart caught in her throat. It had been a week since he'd lit her on fire with a simple kiss. But after humiliating herself at the clinic, she'd not been able to face him. Besides, in hindsight, she was sure he didn't feel the same way about the kiss.

All doubts disappeared when his gaze met hers. He bypassed any pointless greetings by hugging her close, then kissing her.

"What's going on?" she asked after he released her. "You okay?"

"I'm fine. Just wanted to say thanks for telling us about Brandon and sending over the phone."

"Did it help?"

He put his arm around her shoulder as they walked toward her tack room. "The phone was too smashed to be helpful, but we pulled his phone records and found the number. Unfortunately, it's a payphone at a busy bowling alley. Our caller would have had to have had a third eye for anyone to remember them."

"And Brandon?"

"We talked to him, but I think you're right, he's no killer." He shook his head. "Or I'm stereotyping him.

Or—I might be spending too much time with Dennis."

He tried to laugh it off but did a lousy job of hiding his feelings. She stopped them to put a hand to his cheek. "You could have told me all this on the phone. What's really wrong?"

He took her hands, studying them without answering her question. It was clear he was trying to find the right words, and she didn't push. He'd tell her when he was ready.

"They found a girl," he said eventually without looking up. "Someone cut the coke they sold her with rat poison. We'll probably never know who or why."

"Was she the girl you were looking for?"

"No. This one wasn't even thirteen." He dropped her hands and walked over to Pete's stall, raking his fingers through his hair in frustration. "These days it seems like what I do is pointless. At least here, what you do with the horses, there's a sense of accomplishment at the end of the day."

She joined him at the stall, prompting the chestnut horse to nicker, demanding attention. "See? Someone cares if you come into work or not," he pointed out.

The soft muzzle leaned out over the stall door and dug around in Emily's pockets, always hopeful they'd hold a treat. She patted Pete's neck and smiled. After the clinic, she had been certain she had no business even sitting on a horse. After a week of flat work with this one, the improvement in his balance filled her with pride. In fact, it gave her the confidence to try jumping a few fences yesterday for the first time since the clinic and he'd been foot perfect.

An idea popped in her head that was brilliant, and yet so simple, Pete might have thought of himself.

Maybe there was something to this horse communication stuff after all.

Reaching up, she kissed Justin on the cheek. "I know exactly what you need."

****

Justin got out and stretched after the hour-long drive. God, he hated that truck of hers. Had they not invented springs back in the 60s? While Emily unloaded the horses from the trailer and put on their saddles and bridles, he surveyed the little ranch they'd driven to. There was a barn and behind it a meadow with trees and various sized logs on the ground. He had to admit when he saw the gleam in her eye back at the Equestrian Center, he had something completely different in mind.

Once the horses were ready, he struggled into the saddle of a little brown horse and felt a healthy dose of distrust. "Why's this one called Stinky?"

On top of the nutty red one he'd seen her smash an egg on top of his head the other week, she chuckled. "The owner has an odd sense of humor. What can I say?" She rode up close to him and had to lean over to buckle the strap on his borrowed helmet.

"Hey, mine's smaller than yours," he noted.

"You don't get to say that very often, do you?"

"Damn straight," he teased, earning what sounded like a derisive snort from his horse. "What I mean is, if you go running off, how are we going to keep up? This race is rigged."

"It's not a race, and don't worry, she'll keep up. Don't get all macho on me and try to follow me over the jumps. Go around them and enjoy the ride. Okay?"

Without waiting for an answer, she kicked her

horse into a nice easy trot. They warmed up the horses in the field for a few minutes as Emily talked him through the basics. She made it easy for him to feel comfortable on horseback, and in no time, he was actually enjoying himself. All those years of martial arts training gave him a decent sense of balance, enabling him to stand in the stirrups like she showed him. He wasn't as graceful as her, but he felt a bit of pride that he hadn't eaten dirt. When she headed toward the hills where the jumps were located, the little horse underneath him exploded.

He tried to follow her instructions, and go around the jumps, but the horse had other ideas. Emily guided Pete over the larger fences with the elegance of a dancer while Justin battled with Stinky, who ignored him and muscled over the smaller jumps.

"Stop pulling," she called out between peals of laughter while easing her horse to a halt. The mare followed Pete and stopped as well. "I know you think that's how you stop a horse, but with her, it makes her go faster."

"I'm trying to steer around the jumps, but she keeps going over them," he complained.

She shrugged. "She's a mare. Usually, she doesn't want to jump, but today she's in the mood, so just hang on. Don't worry, she won't take anything huge." She urged her horse back into a canter; his horse followed right along.

They took a few more fences, gathering speed as they went, despite his cries of "Whoa." Even he had to admit the question mark at the end didn't make the order sound very commanding, but in truth, he was having a blast. For the first time, he understood why

Emily continued to do this despite the physical and emotional pain being on a horse must cause. The joy on her face as they cantered along did as much for Justin's mood as the riding. Lit by this inner fire, she was more beautiful than ever, helmet and all. They splashed through the pond like a couple of kids, seeing who could get the other one wetter. Thoughts of the job that had been plaguing him before were a million miles away. The quote of Winston Churchill's about the outside of a horse being good for the inside of a man suddenly made a lot of sense.

A fence resembling a miniature fort right out of a western movie sat on top of a small rise in front of them. As with the other fences, Stinky aimed herself right at it, Emily's words lost on the wind as they galloped toward the obstacle. He leaned forward, eager to fly once more. He launched in the air—only the horse wasn't underneath him anymore. He landed on his back on the soft, loamy ground with a thud before he had a clue what happened.

Emily raced up and leaped off her horse before he came to a halt. She knelt over him, checking him over while he removed his helmet and ran a hand through his sweaty hair. "Are you all right?"

"I'm fine, nothing hurt but my pride—ooh, and my butt," he groaned. He was already stiff and sore, laughing despite the aches. "Now I see why they call you Stinky," he mock growled at the horse, who stood nearby munching on grass.

"Idiot." She laughed at him. "Didn't you hear me tell you not to go to that one? She hates the fort."

"That's the sympathy I get?" He grabbed her by the waist and rolled over on top of her. Their bulky safety vests made the maneuver awkward, and she shrieked with laughter. "Think that's funny, do you?" He tickled her, and she wriggled underneath him to get away.

Breathless with laughter, they lay back in the grass. She reached over to pull the leaves out of his hair, near enough for him to drink in the lemony smell of her soap. He pressed closer and kissed her, softly at first, but then more urgently, needing to claim her as his own. She responded, delving deeper into his mouth, matching his ferocious need. Justin longed to touch bare skin, but the solid, padded safety vest was in his way. He racked his brain to remember how the damned thing unfastened, but it was impossible to think with her hand exploring his thigh.

Then she nuzzled his neck, her hot breath—wait a minute, she was kissing his mouth, how was she also breathing on his neck? Justin opened his eyes and saw a horse's muzzle sniffing his head. Heart pounding, he sat bolt upright. Emily convulsed with laughter as she rose to collect Stinky's reins. Once he gathered his wits, and his breath, he stood as well, wishing the vest came down a little lower to mask what his jeans didn't hide.

She handed him his horse's reins and then collected her own. "You've had enough for one day. We'll ride back at a walk to give the horses a chance to cool off if your bruised bottom can handle it."

He shot her a mock sneer and tried to get back on Stinky but found his muscles had tightened so much, he couldn't raise his foot high enough to reach the stirrup. She helped him stand on the fence to get back on his horse and they ambled back over the hill on a long rein, basking in the comfortable silence between them.

Chapter Twenty-Four

The warmth from Justin's hand on the small of her back radiated through the black satin as they made their way onto the dance floor. Miraculously, the delicate beaded wrap stayed in place and kept her scar covered as he took her gloved hand for a waltz. The night was so magical, Emily felt like a princess. The voice in the back of her head warned her the clock would strike midnight eventually, but she ignored it as they waltzed across the floor.

"Not bad for a barn rat," he observed with a seductive smile.

"I'll have you know Walter Smiley and I were runners-up at our seventh-grade cotillion."

"Do they still have cotillions?"

"Seventh grade was a long time ago, but yes, in Grand Rapids, Michigan—only if your mother was determined enough to find a dance studio that held them."

"Walter must have been thrilled."

"Not really. He was three inches shorter than me and couldn't keep up. I led the whole time."

Justin's deep laugh sent a thrill down her spine. She gazed up into his eyes and realized she would have no such problem tonight. Even in heels, she was shorter than him.

The orchestra—and yes, by God there was a full,

live orchestra—switched from the waltz to a sexy Latin beat. He raised an eyebrow at her. "And how did ol' Walt do at the tango?"

"We kicked ass," she whispered, pushing her body against his, ready for a more risqué version of the dance than the Grand Rapids cotillion ever saw. He accepted her challenge, and they made an impressive couple until a strange vibration twitched on her hip.

Justin ignored it and kept dancing, but after the third time, she pulled him off the dance floor. "Answer the phone," she teased. Nothing, not even a ringing cell phone, could ruin her night.

He pulled out his phone and pursed his lips once he read the screen. "You've got to be kidding me," he muttered. "Come on, duty calls." She took hold of the arm he offered and let him lead the way.

They swam through the crowd of celebrities and notables, all arrayed in glittering jewels, precious metals, and Valentine-themed pink, red, and white designer garb. She felt self-conscious in her classic black. Who knew that tonight of all nights, people in L.A. would decide to dress with a splash of color?

People whose faces were familiar halted mid-conversation to wish Justin well. It was like being in a fishbowl, the heat of a hundred eyes on her. She clung a little tighter to his arm, terrified she'd fall off Lottie's perilously high heels. He must have felt her grip tighten because he smiled down at her. It was all the reassurance she needed.

He pointed out his quarry—a tall, lithe woman wearing an off-the-shoulder gown in deep red that showed off a pair of toned arms that likely saw fifty a few years ago. Emily envied the way her dark hair smoothed back into a perfect French twist. It was the same effect Lottie's hairdresser had tried to achieve, but her mane proved too unruly. The woman reached out a jeweled, tastefully manicured hand to Justin.

"Mother," he murmured, kissing her warmly on the cheek. He drew Emily closer to his side. "This, as I'm sure you already know, is Emily Conners. Emily, my mother, Madeline Butler."

She offered a hand to Justin's mother, unnerved when the woman noted the gloves she wore with a smirk. She was certain this woman, who was so perfectly put together she made Lottie seem shlumpy, hated her. Alarmed, she greedily accepted the champagne glass a passing waiter offered and forced herself with all of her willpower not to down it like a shot of tequila.

Justin made a point of turning off his phone in front of his mother before slipping it back into his pocket. "You rang?"

"Yes, dear," she continued breezily, handing him a glass of champagne as well. "Now, I'm no expert, but I remember ordering the top-shelf champagne." He took a sip from the glass as she continued, "Does this taste like it costs a hundred dollars a bottle to you?"

"You are absolutely right," he answered, taking another sip and smacking his lips in great exaggeration. "You are no expert. The champagne is fine. However, I will do my son-ly duty and look into it for you."

He leaned close to Emily and murmured in her ear, "I'll only be a minute. Are you okay?"

She gave him a tight smile and nodded, feeling anything but. With an arched eyebrow and a warning to his mother to be nice, he disappeared. Emily felt wobbly and very much alone.

"You wear those gloves much better than I ever did," Madeline remarked as she held up a regal hand to the bartender, who immediately replaced the champagne flute with a lowball glass of a dark amber fluid. If she noticed Emily's failure to respond, she made no note of it. "My son's right about one thing. I never did like that bubbly crap. Growing up, I worked for my father. My hands were so calloused and weathered, I could never pull on nylon stockings without running them." Her confession came with a wistful smile as she peered at her now perfect hands, brought back to a simpler time.

"Your father owned a ranch?" Emily asked.

Mrs. Butler gave a genuine laugh without a single note of haughtiness. "Worse. A circus. I was his roustabout, trapeze artist, and did a little Roman riding until I left for college."

The idea of this elegant woman standing on the backs of two horses, racing them around an arena was unexpected, to say the least. "Wow. That's...amazing," she stammered.

With an appreciative smile, the older woman lifted her glass in salute. "Almost as amazing as a horse trainer. I tried to hide how unfeminine my hands were when I went out on dates by going retro-cool and wearing gloves, but you, my dear, carry it off with style. Now I understand why my son ditched me at my own party and brought you instead."

The color must have drained out of Emily's face because she quickly added, "Oh no, dear, that's a good thing. I can't remember the last time I saw him so happy. Frankly, he's never shown amazing judgment in women, as evidenced by the fact he's dated half of this crowd. I rather like the idea he's finally dating a woman who works for a living." She leaned in close, like two conspirators sharing a secret. "Remember, I can still swing a sledgehammer. If you break my son's heart, I won't be afraid to use it."

Emily chuckled—until she realized she wasn't kidding. "Um, Mrs. Butler, this is our first official date. Well, second if you count the mugging, so I'm not sure heart-breaking is even on the menu at this point."

Madeline's eye sparkled as much as her tasteful earrings. "Yes, he told me about the attack. Beautiful and scrappy. Ms. Conners, you are my kind of people." She hooked her arm through Emily's and drew her along with her as she paraded the length of the room. "Now, what embarrassing details can I tell you about my son? Did he ever tell you about the time he—"

Right when they were getting to the juicy stuff, a mob of worried people clamored for Mrs. Butler's attention. With a sincere apology, she hurried off to go solve the latest crisis, leaving Emily to wander through the party alone. Somehow, without her noticing, the glass in her hand had been drained. She took another from one of the servers working the room, her legs going rubbery again as soon as her cheerleader left her.

She repeated her silent mantra of *I will not fall off these damn shoes* as she searched for Justin.

She fingered the evening bag that held the last of her prescription pain meds. Still, she'd only taken one. Maybe she should take another one now to calm her nerves. Instead, she forced herself to stand a little straighter. None of these people have wrestled nearly two tons of horse over a fence and won, had they?

"Justin left you already?"

The voice behind her surprised her so much she jumped, champagne sloshing out of her glass. She turned to find a group of sniggering women, all skinny and wearing the same sly, bitchy smiles she'd seen at hunter shows after some poor rider fell and was left sitting in the dirt. At least it was the devil she knew.

The tall platinum blonde with features too perfect to be natural spoke again, leaving her minions to cast shrewish glares as backup. "He usually sticks by the shock value dates at least until dessert."

"Shock value? Sorry, I'm not following."

The group twittered together, batting fake lashes no doubt an endangered insect gave his life to manufacture. "You don't think you're the first S.V. date he's brought to one of these functions to prove how he's not a snob, do you?"

The tall one circled Emily like a hyena, practically sniffing the air for the scent of fear. Satisfied, she pressed in closer. "He loves bringing outlandish dates to make the point he doesn't care about our opinions, but it's only a matter of days before he goes back to one of his own kind. Sooner, God help you, if the old lady likes you, because there's nothing very shocking about dating someone Mummy approves of, is there? It's kind of pathetic, really, but we indulge him because he's so damn cute." Her smile morphed into an ugly sneer. "What was the one at the New Year's party, girls, a stripper?"

"A Laker Girl," one of the others replied with disdain.

"Some kind of dancer, anyway. The week before it was the French volleyball player who didn't shave."

Cheeks burning with rage and shame, Emily peered at the bubbles rising to the top of the champagne flute. In the interest of trying to control both emotions, she drank a third of it in one gulp.

"You're the dog trainer, aren't you?" The blonde didn't bother to hide the contempt in her voice. "It's so hard to keep track, what with Justin's turnover rate being so high."

"Horse trainer, actually, but I know a few things about dogs if you're interested."

"Really?" she taunted before the chill in her voice dropped another fifty degrees. "And what on Earth makes you imagine we have the slightest interest in your doggie wisdom?"

"Because"—she whispered, forcing them to come closer— "when a bitch growls in my face, I give her a smack on the nose to show her who's boss." She smiled at the gaping women as she glided regally past them to the safety of the ladies' room. Just when she thought she had them beat, the wrap slid down her back, exposing the six inches of puckered scar tissue where the screws held her spine together. Was it her imagination, or did the group let out a collective gasp?

She remained poised long enough to lock herself into a stall before collapsing against the cool metal of the wall. She tipped her head forward so her tears fell straight to the floor instead of running down her face. Good old Mom, not much on inspiration, but great with tips on how to save your make-up.

Her hands shook as she opened her bag and reached in to get a pain pill. Two of them slipped through her satin-gloved fingers and bounced onto the tile floor. *Shit, shit, shit.* Those were the only pills she had. After a moment's hesitation, she picked them up and dry swallowed them, trying to block out of her mind what foreign substances might be on the bathroom floor.

Those bitches were right. This shock date thing was the only explanation that made any sense. Hadn't she told Lottie right from the start, a guy like Justin Butler wouldn't be interested in a girl like her?

It was tempting to stay in the sanctuary of the bathroom stall until the calming effect of the pills kicked in, but she recognized their type; those skinny bitches were waiting outside, watching to see if they got to her or not.

Fuck. Them.

Defiant, Emily jerked her chin up and marched back into the party, an escape route already in mind.

****

Justin snaked his way through the crowd in search of Emily. A cadaverously thin blonde whose name he couldn't remember gave him a smug grin. Puzzled, he returned her greeting, recalling her snootiness was why he'd only gone out with her once. He forgot all about her the moment he saw Emily through the French doors, standing on the balcony, staring at the city below. He smiled at the way she didn't seem to notice the breeze playfully freeing a few stray curls from her twist of hair. *God, she's beautiful.*

One step outside reminded him why they were alone. The cool February evening had gained a knife-like edge in the past few hours. "Sorry that took so long. Champagne crises are tricky, but here's hoping we're squared away."

She smiled at him, apparently oblivious to the

chilly night air. "No worries, I was enjoying the stars."

A quick upward glance confirmed the city lights made it impossible to see any stars at all. *Okay, that's not too weird.* He grew more concerned at the odd, glazed expression in her eyes.

He tried a fresh approach. "You've made a huge fan out of my mother. She can't stop singing your praises."

Emily snorted, murmuring, "Naturally." She drained the rest of her champagne from the glass and put it down, leaving it teetering until he steadied it. "I could stop shaving if you like."

"What? No, I…are you okay?" he asked, realizing even as the words left his mouth how stupid they were. There was something else going on here other than a few too many drinks. Whatever it was, she was anything but okay.

"I'm one hundred percent okey-dokey," she replied as she unsteadily hoisted herself up to sit on the stone wall of the balcony. The wall with no safety railing between it and the pavement fifteen stories below.

"Hey, you want to be careful up there," he said, trying to keep his voice light. He tried to edge closer, but she pushed away from him with a laugh.

"You're into all that Zen crap, aren't life and death supposed to be all the same?" She drew her feet up on the wall, making him more nervous, but he didn't dare move too fast for fear of startling her. What the hell happened since he left her fifteen minutes ago that brought all this on?

"That's a lot of deep thinking, and neither one of us has a drink. Why don't we go back inside and finish this discussion over a glass of champagne?" It was lame, but it was the first thing he thought of to keep her talking. Sadly, it didn't work.

With a playful grin, she peeled off one of her gloves and dropped it over the edge. Her gaze snapped to meet his, lit by a new fire as if she'd made a decision. "It would take a person the same amount of time to hit the ground as the glove, wouldn't it? Isn't that what Galileo or somebody discovered? Two rocks of different sizes dropped at the same rate? Or is it the other way around?"

"Um, I...I honestly don't know." All he could think about was how close she was to the edge.

"Fat lot of good all the money your parents spent on education did you."

She peered over the edge one last time, shrugged, then swung her legs over to jump back down to the balcony. Relief washed over him until the ankle that had been giving her trouble all night crumpled. It threw her off balance and sent her closer toward the edge of the building instead of to safety. He lunged to steady her against his chest.

The brief scare over, she gazed up at him, her eyes bright with tears. "I am more than a shock value date," she whispered, then passed out.

Justin gathered her into his arms. The anxiety etched on her face melted away, her mien one of peaceful repose. He worried about what was going on behind those beautiful eyes as he discreetly carried her out through the back service entrance.

Shock value date.

What the hell was that supposed to mean?

****

The morning sun filled Justin's large kitchen with a

217

light far cheerier than what he felt. Impatient for the coffeepot to fill, he tapped his fingers on the counter.

"Screw it," he muttered and poured himself a cup from the still-filling pot, even though the half-brewed coffee always tasted different to him. He needed a shot of brain juice to clear his head so he could figure out what to do about Emily. Had the vet, Ridley, been right about her drug abuse problem, and he'd been too blind to see it?

The soft sound of bare feet padded down the hall and hesitated before entering the kitchen. How was it possible that with no makeup and bed-tousled hair, she looked more stunning now than she had last night? The thick fleece robe he'd left for her came well past her knees and yet she turned away from the heat of his gaze, blushing.

Neither of them spoke for a moment until he mumbled, "Good morning." Almost as a second thought, he offered her a cup of coffee.

She accepted the mug but stared into it rather than drink. He sensed she wanted to ask about last night, but she needed to be the one to bring it up, so he waited, meticulously preparing his own coffee to milk ratio while she worked up her nerve. "Did we, um…you know, you and I, last night, after the party…"

"After the party? You mean you don't remember jumping me in the middle of the dance floor and demanding, I think the phrase was 'ride you like a stallion'?" Her face blanched and her eyes got so wide he couldn't stop from laughing. "I'm kidding. No, we did not have sex."

"You shit." She let out an enormous sigh of relief and laughed at the same time. She took her first sip of coffee and relaxed in its steaming comfort.

"Your modesty is completely intact," he assured her. "I unzipped you, but other than that, you wouldn't let me help. I came in after you were asleep to rescue the dress from the floor, but I didn't peek, I swear. I slept in the guestroom." Barely. He paused for a moment and tried to keep the serious concern he felt out of his voice. "You really don't remember anything about last night?"

"Dancing with you," she purred. "And meeting your mother, having champagne." Then her brows knitted in concern. "But nobody asks a question like that unless you did something pretty freaking memorable. Come on, out with it. What did I break and how much will it cost to fix?"

"No, it's nothing like that. Well, you lost your glove, and you might have broken the heel on Lottie's shoe, but that's not the point." He tried to keep it light, but his voice took a serious, quiet turn. "You don't remember sitting at the balcony railing and talking about jumping off?"

She cringed but reached for the toast he'd made. "Ew, how embarrassing. Please tell me I didn't do this in front of the entire party."

He shook his head, puzzled by her reaction. No histrionics, no denial? He didn't know what he expected, but this felt off. "No, we were alone."

"Thank God. So I only have to apologize to you." She leaned in closer, offering him the toast with a sly smile. "I'm sure we can figure out a way I can make it up to you."

He gently kept her at arm's length, finding it hard to concentrate with only his robe between him and her naked body. "Em, you seemed pretty serious."

Her lips thinned, the playful mood gone. "It was no big deal. My back was bothering me, especially with those shoes, so I took an old painkiller I had left over from a long time ago. It was dumb to mix a painkiller with alcohol, but I never get to have champagne so I thought one little glass wouldn't hurt."

"You had more than one."

"Hence the problem. I like champagne, so sue me." She smiled at him, but he wasn't buying it. Huffing impatiently, she turned her attention back to her toast and coffee. "I'm sorry I embarrassed you. I don't know what else you want me to say."

Justin's resolve melted. He'd gone about this all wrong if she confused concern with embarrassment. He came up behind her and encircled her with his arms. "Say you won't ever do anything like that again."

He pulled her closer and nuzzled her neck. Emily arched her chin back, inviting him to take more of her. His lips traveled from her earlobe down her neck. Pushing the robe aside, he continued to the well of her collarbone when she gasped out loud.

"Ow, shoot," she hissed.

He backed off as if he'd been electrocuted. "Your neck?"

She nodded, rolling her neck and shoulders.

He slid his hands right above her shoulder blades and softly kneaded with his thumbs. "Better?"

Tentative, she stood a little straighter and smiled. "Actually, yes."

"You should get that checked out. It doesn't sound normal to have this much pain so long after an accident."

She stepped away from him and gathered the robe closer. "Justin, I broke my frigging neck, not to mention my collar bone, a few ribs, and, oh yeah, minor issue damage with some internal bleeding. Injuries like that take a toll." Her eyes flashed as she snapped at him. "I'm sure even Bruce Davidson has to take an Advil now and then."

"Who?"

"Bruce—never mind."

Justin closed the gap between them. "I understand how painful it must have been."

"No, you don't." She backed away again. "Everybody says that, but how could you possibly understand? You didn't hear the snapping of your own—" she stopped herself short. "I'm fine, okay? I ache a little, probably arthritis already setting in. When I'm riding, I don't notice it."

"Yeah, but wouldn't you rather—" The ringing of his phone interrupted the rest. A glance at his caller ID told him it wasn't good. "Hey Dennis, what's up?" he asked and walked into another room to talk.

****

Curious, Emily followed until her own cell phone rang. It took a moment to find the tiny purse she'd brought. After unearthing it, she caught the call just in time. "Lottie?"

"Where are you? You've got to get down here right away."

"Here where? What's going on?" The wail of sirens and horses calling carried over the phone. *That can't be good.* "Are you at the barn? Has something happened to one of the horses?"

Her friend took a deep breath before replying.

"There's been another murder."

She glanced over and saw Justin hang up his phone. Their eyes met as she answered, "I'll be right there."

Chapter Twenty-Five

On any day, keeping up with Justin's long strides was hard enough. Trying to do it while holding up a pair of borrowed sweats around her waist was even trickier. But meeting the pointed stares of Lottie and Dennis with any semblance of dignity while jogging after the man defined *impossible*.

Doing her best to ignore the big scarlet A on her forehead, she caught up to Justin just as he joined the crime scene technicians. They were crouched in the three-sided concrete enclosure outside the main barn area examining something on the ground.

Three times a week, a large truck dumped a load of wood shavings, used for bedding the stalls, into this and identical enclosures scattered throughout the Center. This morning, however, the shavings here had been pulled out and left in a pile around the corner.

"I'd estimate time of death to be between midnight and two in the morning," a balding man in a black windbreaker reported. "As far as COD, could be asphyxiation from being buried under this stuff." He picked up a handful of the shavings and let it drift to the ground. "But it's more likely he was already dead when it got dumped over him. As there are no obvious wounds on the body, you'll have to wait until I crack him open to find out for sure."

"So much for our prime suspect," Justin muttered.

Emily peeked around him to look at the body. Doctor Frank Ridley wasn't attractive in life; death only brought out the worst in him. A thick layer of the featherlike shavings clung to his mustache, eyebrows, and helmet of hair like coconut sprinkled on top of a donut. His eyes were open, as if he'd seen himself in a mirror and was aghast at the view.

Someone kept shaking the wall she leaned against. She wished to hell they'd stop. Then Justin put his hand on her shoulder, and she realized the shaking came from her.

"You okay?"

She was speeding down the highway of life with an *okay* sign in her rearview mirror growing smaller with each passing mile. Two dead people in a month might be normal for him; they were the first and last corpses she hoped to see. She opened her mouth to snap but realized how awkward this must be for him. Caught between doing his job and taking care of her had to be a sucky place to be. She pulled herself together and nodded.

Windbreaker man gave him a clear plastic bag containing a piece of leather fringe. "We found this clutched in his hand."

Dennis held up her Western-style, full-length, fringed leather chaps. "Which happens to match these."

"Which he confiscated without a warrant," Lottie sneered as she put a protective arm around Emily. Clearly, she and Justin had interrupted this on-going battle between the two.

Ignoring both, Justin addressed Emily. "Are they yours?"

Confused, she nodded. "I don't understand. Why

would he have pulled a piece of fringe off my old chaps?"

"Are these common around here?"

"No." As always, the thought of them made her smile. A few years ago, when she wasn't hip enough to realize the cowboy style leather leg covering was passé in a barn where everyone rode English style, they were the one thing she wanted most. After Lottie got word of this secret yearning, she took up a collection and got everyone in the barn to donate. It would have been easier for her to simply write a check, but it meant so much more to her that everyone cared enough to contribute to the Emily Connors Relief Fund.

"They were custom made for me by a guy out in Calabasas. One of a kind. Wait a minute." It dawned on her where this was going, "I didn't—"

"Yeah, I know," he noted grimly, confusing her even more.

"I take it from her snazzy attire she was with you last night." Dennis's remark sounded more like an accusation. "All night."

Her cheeks burned at the snide attitude, but he backed down after a glare from his partner. "Yes, I can verify Ms. Conners was nowhere near this barn last night."

Justin's cold, businesslike tone sent a shiver through her as she figured out what it all meant. In a tiny voice she hardly recognized as her own, she asked, "Which means the killer tried to frame me for the murder of Doctor Ridley?"

"Em'ly." The familiar Scots accent came as a welcome sound. To her surprise, Dearg McGregor strode toward her. In polished tall boots, white breeches, and a fitted navy jacket with a red collar as befitting an Olympian, his presence stunned every female in the area and a few of the men as well. "My poor wee *bairn*," he murmured as he enveloped her in a bear hug. "Are ye all right?"

With a last squeeze, he let her go, gazing into her eyes as she mutely nodded. "I came over as soon as I heard." He ran his hand through his thick, dark hair with practiced carelessness, fluffing up where his riding helmet had squashed it flat. When his glorious mane bounced back to its curly, untamed state, a guy in a police windbreaker sighed.

"And they sometimes call Scotland bloody." Dearg kept one arm draped over her shoulder and grinned. "When we're unhappy with a vet, we fire 'em, we don't kill 'em."

Wee bairn? She wondered when they had grown so close but shrugged it off. Right now, his exuberance delighted her as much as his accent.

****

All the years of Zen training sailed out the window as a wave of possessiveness washed over Justin. It took all his self-control not to knock the big ape's arm off Emily's shoulder. He breathed deeply, unclenched his jaw, and fought to keep his voice steady. "I'm Detective Butler. This is Detective Ames. And you are…?"

From the little bit of information he'd gleaned from Emily about the clinic, he knew perfectly well who the man was, but refused to give him the satisfaction of being famous.

"Oh, sorry," he replied jovially, taking his arm off Emily to offer his hand. "Dearg McGregor. Nice to meet you."

He decided that anybody who had an actual, honest to God twinkle in his eye when meeting a cop over a dead body had to be guilty of something, even if his only crime was being an idiot. "How did you learn about Doctor Ridley?"

The Scot jerked a thumb to indicate the bustling riding ring in the distance behind him, "Word about the discovery of a dead body is flying around the warm-up arena."

"I didn't know you were showing here this week," Emily exclaimed, a smile lighting up her face. Justin bristled at the way her gaze fixed on the jerk.

"Yeah, I'm here with three babies, trying to get in some stadium work before I take 'em Training next month at Stormgrove. Hey." He brightened up. "Do you have time to come by and be my eye on the ground?"

"Me?" she stammered, "Help you? But I'm not, I mean, what could I—"

"Oh, come on, you have a sharp eye."

Justin saw her gaze drop to the ground, as if her whole body was shrouded in a cloud of self-doubt. If this man, whom she idolized, recognized she was good at her job, why couldn't she? He wanted to wash away all her insecurities, but right now he had a murder investigation to run.

"How well did you know the victim?" he asked McGregor.

"Me?" He smiled. "Not at all. This is the first year I've given the west coast events a go, but I can tell you no one at the warm-up arena is mourning his passing." The phone at McGregor's belt crackled to life. After a quick check, he said, "Excuse me, detective, I need to go mount up unless there's something else I can help you with?"

"If there is, I'll find you." *And kick your ass.*

The Scot said to Emily, "Come with me and see my new horse. He's wee, but he's a grand mover. You'll love him."

She hitched up her sweatpants. "I'm not dressed."

"Och, come on, nobody's going to care what you're wearing. Watch one round and tell me what you think."

She glanced back at Justin. He could see she wanted to go, but he wondered which held her interest more—the horse or the rider? He wanted to wrap his arms around her and kiss her so hard it would chase all thoughts of the Scot out of her mind. But right now, he had to be a cop, not a boyfriend.

He nodded that she was free to go and frowned as he watched them saunter away, engaged in an animated conversation. She threw her head back and laughed, sending a surge of jealousy through his chest. The fact that the mere prospect of losing her made him so irrational blackened his mood. He focused on more pleasant things, like the dead body behind him, and forced the picture of the other man's arm around Emily from his mind.

****

Back at his desk, Justin stabbed the tiny rake into the Zen garden, far from feeling one with the world. He'd gotten off the phone with Jonesy an hour ago but couldn't get their conversation out of his head.

"Jay," she'd said, reluctantly, "I'm not sure what this means, but a prescription pad went missing the night you brought your friend in with the head trauma."

228

But she knew exactly what it meant, and so did he. Emily had been alone in the room long enough to have taken the missing pad. All too often, people who needed painkillers for legitimate reasons get hooked on them. Drug abuse would certainly explain her erratic behavior last night.

"The knucklehead who reported it stolen claims he locked it in a secured drawer, but he's in a shit ton of trouble over this so he might be lying." She paused, then continued, "On the upside, whoever took the pad won't be able to get any narcotics."

"Why not?"

"Ever since this whole oxycodone epidemic, California and other states require we use a different, tamper-proof pad for narcotics. The minute someone tries to get anything using the stolen pad, they'll get busted."

He'd thanked Jonesy for the call and considered what he should do. If Emily had stolen the pad, should he warn her not to try to forge a prescription?

"Hey, Mary quite contrary. No need to ask how your garden grows." Dennis came in and pointed to Justin's desk. Sand from his Zen garden littered the normally pristine surface, as his stabbing had grown more violent. "No time to clean it up now, I've got something you need to see."

He plugged a thumb drive into Justin's computer and opened a video file on it. "That Scottish guy sounded familiar, but I couldn't place it, so I went back through the video clips from Pamela Yates's hidden camera."

He hit play and a grainy picture blipped to life, albeit difficult to see at first. Eventually, Justin got used to the poor quality and could distinguish the shape of a man and woman ripping off each other's clothes. The man's back was to the camera, but the woman was clearly Pamela Yates. His partner forwarded through fifteen or twenty more minutes and though the couple enjoyed a few unique positions, none of them revealed the man's face.

"Wait, here it is." he slowed the video back to normal speed and cranked up the volume. Pamela's moans and yelps of pleasure were so loud even on the computer's tiny speaker, Justin grew uncomfortable in the busy police bullpen. The man yanked her to her knees and began taking her from behind. He turned his head in disgust. "Is there a reason—"

"Shh, listen."

On screen, the man called out, "Come on, my *wee bairn*, who's your daddy, eh?"

Justin had seen enough. He turned the video off and once more demanded, "What the fetch did you have me watch that for?"

Dennis raised his eyebrows in shock at his response. "Don't you get it? That's the Scottish guy banging our murder victim."

He ground his teeth, willing himself to be patient with his demented partner. "And you couldn't have just told me, you had to show me?"

Like a kid who had shared an amazing treasure only to find his audience unimpressed, Dennis crossed his arms over his chest. "Yeah, but it was relevant to his character and our case, right?"

True, Justin thought as he rubbed the heels of his hands in his eyes in an attempt to erase the pornographic image from his brain. The fact that

McGregor called the woman he cared about by the same pet name meant nothing. Probably.

After all, Emily spent a weekend with the man, and they came back the best of friends.

Shit. Why was everything so complicated?

Chapter Twenty-Six

Everything seemed so simple when Dearg did it.
Up since dawn, he'd taken each of his three horses
through five or six classes, then coached several other
riders, and he still gave the crowd a jaunty smile as he
finished another flawless round.

Having changed from the borrowed sweatpants to
her own breeches and boots, Emily remembered why
she'd started eventing in the first place. In their sport,
the rules were straightforward: either the horse and
rider made it over the jumps, or they didn't. Even in the
stadium jumping phase, either the poles stayed up or
they didn't. Hunters, on the other hand, were more
subjective. A number of horses might make it around
the course without touching a pole, so scoring came
down to the judges deciding which horse looked the
best while doing it.

Winning wasn't *all* about politics, but it didn't hurt
if the rider had a famous last name. Plus, in eventing,
you had exact ride times, at least for the cross-country
phase. None of this standing around and waiting all day
to jump. The torture of these hunter/jumper shows
sucked the life out of her while Dearg seemed to thrive
on the frenzy.

Despite being the interloper, and using this
competition to get his horse ready for the show jump
phase at the next event, the crowd applauded

enthusiastically. He returned the favor by doffing his helmet to them as he left the ring.

The horse was barely out of the ring before he jauntily swung his right leg over the front of the saddle and slid off. With a word of thanks, he handed the horse and helmet over to his groom and made a beeline for Emily.

"You were right," he admitted with an unabashed grin. "I was picking at her too much. Did you see? I took your advice, left the reins alone, and she was perfect."

She blushed, speechless at the compliment he'd paid her. The boyish excitement was contagious as he went over the course with her jump by jump until a voice she'd come to love interrupted. "Mr. McGregor. The show office told us you would be here."

Both Justin and his partner, Detective Ames, stood there, standing out like grim, sore thumbs among the riders and spectators. Justin was cool, controlled, and all business. His demeanor stood out in sharp contrast to Dearg's warm, friendly grin, but she was too excited to notice. High off the compliment he'd paid her, and happy to see Justin, she bounded over to him to kiss him hello, but he stopped her dead in her tracks with a curt nod.

"Ms. Conners," he uttered, void of any emotion, then turned his attention back to the Scot. "May we have a word with you?"

"Och, the Bobbies are onto me, Em," he joked, then shook his head and continued on more soberly. "Certainly, detectives. What can I do for you?"

Justin cast a heated glare in her direction. "We'd like to speak to you in private, if you don't mind."

She met his gaze with a frosty one of her own. "As you wish, detective," she retorted before asking Dearg, "We're still on for dinner, right?"

She was as delighted to see his nod as she was to notice how it made Justin's jaw clench. Good.

****

"Can you describe your relationship with Pamela Yates?" Justin asked after McGregor guided them out of the busy warm-up ring to a space behind the announcer's booth.

"I knew her, but not very well. I just started coming out to the West Coast shows, like I told you this morning. We met here at the Center at some function or another and would catch up from time to time at shows. I wouldn't exactly call it a relationship."

"Really? Because we have a recording of you and Ms. Yates engaged in sexual activities."

A smile crept across his face. "That twisted little cunt..."

"Answer the question, McGregor," he pressed, ignoring Dennis's chortle. "Were you having a sexual relationship with Ms. Yates?"

"I'm a Scot, detective. Of course I had sex with her," the man leered. "But did I have a relationship with her? No."

"Was she unhappy with the state of things?"

His expression grew broader. "I'm a McGregor, of course she was satisfied."

Justin crossed his arms, barely controlling his temper. "Sir, this is a murder investigation, not Comedy Central. Downtown in an interrogation room or standing here, it's all the same to me, but you will answer my questions."

A glint of something dark flashed across McGregor's face. "It wouldn't be the first time I've seen the inside of a police station but ask away."

"Was Ms. Yates using the recording to blackmail you?"

The darkness disappeared altogether as he laughed out loud. "What, did I kill her to keep it quiet that I was, as you Americans put it, 'boning' her? Are ye daft?"

Dennis jumped in. "A rider of your lofty heights getting caught on tape banging a local nobody? Thing like that gets out, a man loses his mojo."

His smile wavered for the first time. "Pamela wasn't a nobody, Detective Ames, but perhaps your attitude is why you haven't caught her killer yet. As to what if people found out, I'd be happy to jump up on this announcer's stand and tell the entire world I screwed Pamela if it will prove I'm innocent."

A wiry man, apparently McGregor's groom, met him with another horse in hand. "Aw, thank ye, Joe. Now, be sure to grab yerself some lunch, eh?" The Scot turned back toward the cops as he put his helmet back on. "Detectives, if there's nothing else, I have more classes to ride today."

Justin stepped into his path. "There is one more thing, Mr. McGregor. What are you playing at with Emily Conners?"

"Are you seriously asking me what my intentions are toward the lady?" A flicker of heat flared in his eyes. "I don't go for the fragile, vulnerable type, detective. A bit like shooting fish in a barrel, don't you think?"

The accusation hung there, the tension mounting before he continued. "I intend to help Ms. Conner's

235

career if I can, to be her friend and perhaps bed her one day when she's in a better emotional place."

****

"Whoa." Dennis stepped between them. "You don't pull any punches," he told the Scotsman, hoping to de-escalate the situation. No such luck.

"That's the key to my success, detective." McGregor turned a flinty gaze from him, then to Justin. "Both horses and women always know where they stand with me. I don't play games like being all cozy one minute and then cold as ice the next. Now if you'll excuse me." He shouldered past them both, got on the waiting horse, and rode off.

"So, how's that Zen thing working out for you?" Dennis asked his partner.

Superman's laser vision had nothing on the glare he shot Dennis. "Shut up."

"I'm just saying the guy has a point. You can't be Galahad and rescue the girl one night and then shut her down the next day because a guy she's friendly with had sex with another woman."

"You're the one who implied there was something to worry about," Justin snarled.

"Yeah, but I'm an a-hole. Ask my ex-wife, she'll be happy to tell you. Good cop," he said, pointing to Justin and then to himself, "bad cop. Remember?"

Instead of decking him, which Dennis was grateful for, Justin turned away and let out a frustrated groan. "I'm trying to keep it professional. I've never been in this situation before."

Dennis wasn't sure if by *this situation* he meant boning a woman involved in a murder investigation versus being in honest to Goddamn love. Either way, his partner was screwed.

"Don't tell me all this shit, go tell someone who cares." He jerked his thumb toward the barn. "She went that away."

****

First, it's 'call me Justin, let me take you dancing.' And the next, it's 'Ms. Conners.' What the actual F?

Still fuming about Detective Butler's on-again off-again attitude, Emily decided to sort through recent bills for horseshoeing, feed, and board. Looking them over, she entertained ninth, then tenth thoughts about Lottie's crazy idea of her taking over the barn.

With the few horses left, she couldn't see how she'd be able to stay in the black. Going over Pam's old books for answers was like reading hieroglyphics. It figured that a woman who still used an answering machine would keep her books on paper ledgers and not a computer spread sheet. From the vague numbers scrawled on the incomplete pages, training and lessons barely kept her head above water. Pam's real profit should have been from selling horses, especially since Ridley always gave them glowing reports about their soundness, but Emily didn't find any record of the money from the sales at all. What kind of secret scheme was she into with the vet?

Or was it something else?

She'd brought along her own aging laptop to try to update the barn's financial records, but nothing made sense. Frustrated, she gave up and shoved the ledgers back in the desk drawer. She started to slam it shut when a thumb drive caught her eye. It was the same one she'd retrieved from Pamela's tack trunk last week after she'd gotten Kate to cut off the lock since the key was

MIA. It irked her that after she had gone to the trouble of forcing the damn thing open, it only held dirty blankets and the stupid thumb drive. The bottles of painkillers, both horse and human, Pam normally kept in it, were gone.

Curious and eager for the distraction, she slipped the thumb drive into her computer to see what was so important to make Pamela lock it in the trunk. A blurry shot of the empty stall wavered on the screen, then one of Kate leading one of her horses into the stall. From the dim quality of the video, it must have been in the middle of the night, which struck Emily as odd but not impossible. She watched as the trainer left the horse in there and closed the door. *Wow, this was riveting. Well worth making a video of.*

Seeing how dark it had already gotten outside, she realized she needed to hurry to get cleaned up before meeting Dearg for dinner. She yanked the thumb drive out of her computer and tossed it back in the drawer to give to Kate the next time she saw her, then packed her computer to take home. She left the office, pulled the sliding door shut, and snapped the lock in place before spinning on her heel and running straight into a man. Startled, she screamed and jumped back into the closed door, which bounced her back into him.

"Hey now." Justin put his hands on her shoulders to steady her. "You scared the shit out of me."

"Me? What's the matter with you?" Her eyes met his, both flashing with emotions before they broke into laughter. Then Emily remembered she was pissed at him, and the smile faded. "Is there something I can do for you, Detective Butler?"

"Okay, I deserved that. Look, I'm sorry if I

was…aloof before."

"Aloof?" She marched toward the exit to the parking lot. "Try, you were a dick. We have a great time last night and then this afternoon you're shaking my hand and calling me Ms. Conners? What the hell, detective?"

He raised both hands in surrender. "I know, you're right. I admit I'm not sure how to handle this."

"*This?* What is that supposed to mean?" she snapped. If this was his way of apologizing, he would end up digging himself to China before he was through.

"You…distract me."

Her heart skipped a beat. Granted, it was a weird compliment, but no one had ever told her she distracted them before. She allowed her glacial façade to melt a little, and he must have sensed it, because he stepped closer, tempting her with a hint of his aftershave.

"Being around you, it makes me feel…" He gave her a brazen smirk. "You must see how it makes me feel, but I am a cop investigating a murder. I don't know if I'm supposed to act differently when I'm 'Justin the cop' versus 'Justin the man' around the woman I'm attracted to. Do we kiss hello? Am I allowed to put my arm around you? I've never had a homicide figure into a relationship before."

She took his hand and gave it a gentle squeeze. "We're both sailing in uncharted waters, but it doesn't help when you act like you walk on them."

That earned her a chuckle. "Point taken. So what do we do from here to avoid this problem?"

"In a perfect world, how would you have greeted me, if you could do anything you wanted?"

"I'm not sure. Let's give it a try. You stand over

there and I'll come in and say hello." She pursed her lips, still a little pissed at him. "Come on, you're the one who asked the question, let's find out the answer."

Complying with his idiotic request, she waited as he walked around the corner and then came back. "Emily, good to see you," he said as he gave her a peck on the cheek. "No, hang on, let me try again."

She blinked in confusion as he exited, came back, and without saying a word, kissed her again, harder this time. She stared at him, dazed and breathless. "Seriously?"

He shook his head. "Yeah, you're right, probably isn't what I would have done either."

She shrugged. "I mean, it's fine with me, if you want to greet me like that."

"No, let me try again." He left for the third time, came back in and put his arm around her, and gave her a gentle, but deep, kiss. "I missed you, Em. Every minute I'm away from you feels like an hour."

Okay, wow, how can a girl stay mad?

"Apology accepted?" he asked, holding her close.

"Since you put it that way. Although if you wanted to apologize again, I wouldn't object." It surprised her when he went rigid, and all humor drained out of his face. "Okay, you get I'm kidding, right?"

He glanced at her with a fleeting smile. "Yes, it's just…We need to talk about last night. I know drunk when I see it and there was more going on than just booze."

The pain in his eyes kept her from growling in frustration. "Don't make a big deal out of this. There's nothing going on."

In a whispered reply, he told her, "I know about the

stolen prescription pad, Emily. Talk to me, please."

Stunned by the accusation, she rocked back. The icy edge crept back into her voice as fear gripped her heart. "I don't know what you're talking about."

"I'm trying to help you."

His body tensed, his frustration clear, but she didn't care. She didn't have a problem. She just needed a little help once in a while to push the pain aside and get through her day. Why didn't anyone understand?

"Right now, I'm dying to make a dramatic exit and slam a door in your face," she said through gritted teeth as she gestured to the large opening at the end of the barn, "but I'm all out of doors. Please leave. Now."

She waited as Justin stormed past her. She was pretty sure this wasn't the way either of them wanted the day to end, but he'd left her with no other options.

****

Later that evening at Salud's, Emily took a gulp of her second margarita when she felt more than saw Dearg enter the small restaurant. The laid-back atmosphere amped up to match his frenetic drive. Every woman in the place except for the lesbian couple in the corner sat taller and fluffed their hair. Imagining how it would drive them crazy when he sat down with her, she took another sip of her drink to hide her smirk.

Like a cat pouncing on a mouse, Kate sprang from her table near the front door and blocked his path. She flipped her frizzy, blonde hair and put her pudgy hand on his chest. He smiled politely and kissed her hand before stepping around her and heading for Emily's table.

"What was all that about with Kate?" she asked once he released her from his bear hug and sat.

He took a sip of her margarita and grimaced. "Yuck. You Americans and your sweet drinks." After having Philippe deliver the darkest beer they had, he grunted. "Is that her name? Evidently your friend got wind of my conversation with the detective and pointed out I hadn't slept with everyone because she and I had never done it, as she so charmingly put it."

"A situation I'm sure she'd be happy to remedy."

He took a long gulp of beer at the thought. "Normally, I find all women attractive, but that one—" He shook his head. "—there's something not right about her." He gazed at Emily and his face brightened as instantly as a switch flipping on. "But she's not what I came here to tell you, *mo chuisle*," he boomed, his trademark grin back in place. "I talked to Karen Hyler about her sponsorship program and told her if it's truly meant to help a talented rider take their game to the next level, I knew just the person."

"What are you saying?" she asked tentatively, half afraid of the answer.

"I've nominated you for the Hy Poynt Award."

Every head in the place, including Kate's, snapped to attention. Emily drained the rest of the glass before she squeaked, "But how? I haven't ridden in months, my show record is non-existent, I...I..." Reeling, her mind blanked on the dozens of other reasons she didn't deserve the nomination. "The deadline for nominations was over a week ago."

"Lass, please." He waved off all her concerns as if they were nothing. "When Dearg McGregor calls to personally recommend a rider, little things like deadlines don't matter. And, not to sound like a braggart, but when I recommend someone for a thing, they usually get it."

Ohshitohshitohshit.

Her thoughts raced. She smiled weakly at him, feeling horrible because she could tell her reaction wasn't what he expected. He probably imagined screaming, jumping up and down in elation like any normal person would respond to such a monumental announcement. Oh well, life's a bitch.

How could he do this to her? There was no way she was even vaguely qualified for this award. From across the room, the dark expression on Kate's face confirmed her fears. Of course she wasn't. She fumbled in her purse and shook out a pain pill, then changed her mind and added a second, then downed both with the icy dregs from the bottom of her glass. His brow furrowed in confusion, adding to her guilt.

"Sorry, I've got a headache," she muttered as an excuse. "Listen, I really appreciate what you've done, but I'm not ready for a step that big."

His eyes blazed with a scary intensity. "Technically, you got some pretty sizeable holes in your training, but you're one of the most naturally gifted riders I've ever seen."

"But for the level of riding, the quality of the horse...you saw what happened at your clinic." She took a deep breath and blurted out a secret so dark she hadn't even told Lottie yet. "I've been considering giving up riding altogether and getting a normal job."

He leaned closer to her, his voice a low, gentle whisper. "You want me to tell you everything will be all right; you're a skilled rider and will be a successful trainer. I can't, no one can. The only thing I know for certain is you've got the right instincts, but whether you've got the heart for it..." He shrugged. "But how are you going to find out if you don't try? And you aren't going to get the answers you're searching for here, hiding away in this bar."

She didn't realize she was crying until he reached over and brushed away her tears with the pad of one thumb. "It's all right, *mo chuisle,* you've got a lot to think about."

"What does that mean? It sounds lovely, but for all I know, you're calling me an old shoe."

"*Mo chuisle?*" He chuckled. "It's nothing, it's a greeting like darling or sweetheart. Scots women roll their eyes, but it works on you Americans every time."

She doubted any woman still breathing would be dismissive of this man no matter what he called them, but she had bigger problems. Their entire conversation left her reeling, her brain functioning at half-speed. Also, the three margaritas on an empty stomach didn't help. Shaky, she gripped the edge of the table to steady herself.

"Let me take you home so you can nurse your headache. We'll talk more tomorrow," he assured her, cupping her elbow with his hand to help her to her feet.

She felt everyone's eyes on them as they left Salud's, giving her disdainful glares, silently accusing her of being a poseur, stealing an opportunity that rightfully belonged to half the people there.

****

After a trek that was both too long and too short, they arrived at her door. Dearg noticed the nosy neighbor and gave her a friendly wave and a smile, muttering a curse under his breath.

"Well, I guess..." Emily turned her face up at him

and then put out her hand. "This is good night then."

He gave a throaty chuckle proven to make women weak at the knees. He took her extended hand and kissed the back of it but didn't push. When he took her—and he had no doubt he would—her policeman friend wouldn't be between them. He was patient, he could wait. Letting go of her hand, he bade her goodnight. Once her door closed, he stood there a moment longer and rested the palm of his hand on the cheap wood surface.

"Good night, *gaol mo chridhe,*" he whispered.

And it was true. Somehow, she'd become the love of his heart. If anyone had been close enough, they might have seen his cocky attitude slip as regret dimmed the perpetual twinkle in his gray eyes. But then, if anyone had been close enough, he'd never have let the veil slip.

He'd honed his acting skills long ago to almost match the level of his riding. He'd had to in order to get out of the crappy little village where he was born. Being where he was today proved how accomplished he'd become at both, but sometimes he longed for...*ach.* It didn't matter what. He shook off the growing melancholy and stalked off in search of mindless entertainment.

Chapter Twenty-Seven

The next morning, the ache in Emily's back arrived as usual, accompanied by a pounding headache. Disheveled and sweaty from her morning rides, she tore through the drawers of Pam's desk desperate to find anything to relieve the pain. She wrenched the last one off its track and turned it over, dumping the contents alongside the growing pile on the floor.

"Looking for anything in particular? Because if it's a knife, there's one you left in my back," Lottie complained from the doorway, making her jump in surprise. "Why did I have to hear about Dearg nominating you for the Hy Poynt from my least favorite person and barn gossip, Darian Holt? Scratch that. Why didn't you call me the minute you got home from having dinner with him? Best friend, my ass."

Emily shook her head and went back to her search. "Can we not do this? My back is killing me, and I don't have the energy to deal with your neediness today."

"Oh really?" She gestured to the assorted papers and office supplies strewn on the floor. "Your bad back hasn't slowed down your tour of destruction."

"You're the one who expects me to tough it out through the pain, remember? Which is pretty big talk for someone who doesn't ride."

For the first time since she could remember, Lottie was speechless. Realizing she'd gone too far, Emily softened her tone. "I'm sorry. I've got three more horses to ride, and right now, I can barely stand up straight. The thought of handling feed buckets tonight is more than I can take."

Putting a light hand on her arm, her friend offered, "I have a few ibuprofens in my car."

"Come on, when you've got oxy in your medicine cabinet, all you carry around is ibuprofen?"

Lottie stopped cold. "How did you know that?"

She stared blankly at her for a moment, searching for an excuse. The truth was, she'd gone through her friend's bathroom in search of any pill to ease her pain and found an old prescription bottle buried in the back. "You told me about it back when you had that tooth thing done," she lied.

Features as cold as ice, Lottie took a deep breath. "You need help."

"Oh Christ, not this again." She threw her hands up in disgust, weary of this argument.

The other woman persisted. "How long has it been since you took your last pill? A day? Twelve hours? This was exactly what I was afraid of when those doctors kept doling out pain meds like penny candy."

"That's it? Even if it were true, the best you've got to offer is 'I told you so'?"

Shoulders squared, her gaze meeting Emily's, she lashed back. "No, what I've got is an ultimatum. I've turned a blind eye for too long, telling myself you wouldn't lie to me, you really were okay, but no more. As of right now, I'm taking my horses out of your care. Get help and I'll bring them back. Keep doing what you're doing, and you'll be out of business in a month."

With that, she walked away.

Emily rushed out the door of the office and shouted at her receding back, "Fine. Screw you. This was all your idea. I never wanted any of this."

She retreated into the office, kicked the garbage can halfway across the room before snatching her car keys off the hook and rushing out of the barn.

****

How was it possible there was so much flippin' traffic in four small blocks? Emily jiggled her leg nervously, afraid she wouldn't get back to Dene's Drugstore before it closed.

Thank God she thought of the little mom and pop place in Beverly Hills she used to go to all the time when she and Nick were married. She rarely needed medication for herself back then, but was constantly picking things up for Nick, the hypochondriac. She'd gotten friendly with the pharmacist, Dene's son Ed. He was a nice guy and a little flirty. If there was one place she had a chance at passing off a forged prescription, it was here in the heart of all those Beverly Hills plastic surgery offices where requests for a few opioids were a dime a dozen. She'd changed into her best bored housewife outfit and gave it a shot.

A wave of relief surged over her when she entered the little store and Ed greeted her like an old friend. When he asked how she'd been, she felt almost no guilt smiling and responding, "Same old, same old. You?"

She got nervous when he took a second, then a third look at the prescription, but once he put his reading glasses on, it all must have been a lot clearer. He smiled at her. "Wouldn't you know, we've been swamped all morning and I've got quite a back log here. Can you come back in an hour?"

"Sure, that'll be fine. I've got errands to do in the meantime," she'd replied through gritted teeth.

What was she going to do for an hour? It would take too long to go to the barn and back. Walking around and grabbing a cup of coffee was also a no go. The last thing she wanted to do was run into someone she used to know and be stuck faking utter joy at seeing them.

Wired and frustrated, Emily did the only thing she could think of—got behind the wheel and drove. With no particular destination in mind, she found herself going past her old house, the café where she and Nick used to have breakfast every Sunday morning, and of course, the hotel where they met once in a while, pretending to be strangers having a one-night stand. Too bad he was stupid enough to meet his actual one-night stands there as well, or she might not have been so gung-ho to leave him.

She finally found a place to park on the street and raced breathlessly into Dene's exactly one hour after she'd left. She stopped short at the door when she saw Ed grimace at something to her right. Fearful of what she might see, Emily gave a sidelong glance and swore. There, in all his official Deputy District Attorney glory, stood Nick Conners.

****

Justin came out of the shower in the police locker room to find Dennis waiting for him, finishing off the largest, greasiest burger he'd ever seen. He'd had a salad and an eight-mile run to keep in shape. His partner could sit around all day, eating crap, and never put a pound on his skinny frame. Life wasn't fair.

"Do you ever consider exercising?" he asked as he

wrapped the towel around his waist.

Dennis snorted, wadding the fast-food wrapper into a ball and tossing it at the trashcan two feet away. It bounced off the rim and landed on the floor. "That's not the kind of six-pack I care about," he retorted as he bent to pick up the paper with a scowl. "Got the report back on the dead vet."

"COD?"

"Enough Ketamine to kill an elephant."

The news didn't surprise him. Although it had become popular as a street drug, Special K was first and foremost a horse tranquilizer. No big shock it was available around a horse barn.

"Three interesting points, however," Dennis added while he scratched and sniffed the mystery spot on his tie. "One, the killer stabbed the needle in Ridley's back hard enough to cause bruising even though the vic was dead in under a minute."

"Just like with Pamela Yates, a lot of anger involved in the murder. Maybe a need for revenge," Justin said as he slipped into a fresh shirt. "But payback for what?"

"Which leads me to point two—the killer brought their own drugs. Our guys checked the vet's truck, nothing's missing."

"So the murder was premeditated." Great. Crimes of passion are usually easier to solve. In the heat of the moment, mistakes are made. But if a killer takes the time to plan a murder, they've put a lot of thought into not getting caught. "You said three points?"

"The guy was dead so fast there was no struggle, confirming the killer planted the piece of fringe torn from your girlfriend's fancy duds to frame her."

He gave up on the spotted tie and turned his attention back to Justin. "You gotta' ask yourself, what's he gonna' do when he finds out it didn't work?"

****

Emily threw open the door to her apartment so hard the knob put a dent in the drywall.

"I get it. You're pissed, but you know what? I'm pissed, too," Nick ground out, lowering his voice to add, "We're going to have to talk about this sooner or later."

"No, we don't. My life is none of your business. Why did he call you, anyway?"

"The man was our pharmacist for seven years. Maybe when he sees my wife trying to pass off a forged prescription, he figures it's something I should know about?"

"Ex-wife," she corrected, as she rifled through her cupboards.

"Would you rather he called the cops?"

Ignoring his question, Emily pulled a tiny airline bottle of Campari out of the back of her cabinet. Dissatisfied, she threw it back and stomped to the refrigerator.

"Do you have any idea how much trouble you'd be in right now if he had called the police instead of me? You'd be facing jail—what are you doing?" He gave an exasperated huff.

"If I'm going to get a lecture from you, I need a drink," she snarled. Finding nothing in the fridge, she turned back to the Campari and poured the dark orange, bitter liquor over a few ice cubes. She grimaced, wondering why anyone drank this stuff on purpose.

"Perfect, a drug addict and an alcoholic."

She slammed the glass down so hard she scared Samwise, who had been trying to get her attention. She bent to pick up the ice that flew out of her glass and noticed his water bowl was bone dry. Something else she'd screwed up. Her hands shook as she filled his bowl at the sink.

"Don't you dare judge me; you have no idea the pressure I'm under."

"Pain pills are for pain, not stress." Nick gently put his arm around her shoulders. "Emily, talk to me. What's going on?"

If he had ranted or thrown something, she could have dealt with it, but the supportive warmth of his arm broke her. She leaned back into his body and let the tears flow. "I'm so scared."

He led her over to the couch and sat down, one arm still around her shoulders, and stayed quiet while she cried it out. After a few minutes, she raised her head but couldn't meet his gaze as she spoke.

"I feel like crap every morning until I take that first pill. Without it, I'm exhausted. Like I'm wading through quicksand and getting nowhere. After one, I'm physically able to ride, but my anxiety is through the roof. I'm terrified of falling again, so I take another to calm down."

"Don't you see that what started off as two pills a couple of times a day is now four or five pills too many times a day?" He chastised her as if she were a disobedient child. "You need help, Em."

She pushed out from under his protective arm. "Jesus, you and Lottie need to get over it. I don't have a drug problem, I have a 'my life sucks' problem."

"And you don't see how the two are related?" he

barked. "Look at you. You're breaking into a sweat already and you've only gone what, six hours without taking a pill? How do you think you're going to feel tomorrow?"

"That's not your problem anymore, is it?" she snapped back. "Go home to your trophy wife, I can take care of myself."

She realized she'd stepped over a line when he stared at her in a mix of fury and disbelief. Before she could sputter out an apology, he stormed out of her apartment, revved the engine of his mid-life crisis vehicle, and was gone.

Miserable, she started reading the latest issue of *Eventing Weekly* to focus on anything else, but a sudden rattling noise from the bathroom beat like a drum in her head. She ran in to find Samwise in the bathtub, batting around a plastic amber bottle he must have dug up from under her bed. He leaped and pounced on it, unaware of her heart pounding at the clatter of a half-dozen pills inside. She watched in horror as he chased the bottle near the open drain.

"No!" she cried and snatched the vial.

The cat cringed, something he'd never done before, and dashed out of the bathroom between her legs. Realizing she'd chased away the last thing on Earth that loved her unconditionally, she had to admit Nick was right. She'd hit rock bottom.

Clutching the small bottle in both hands, she leaned against the cold tile wall and slid to the floor. She held her breath as she opened the bottle and hesitated for a moment before pouring them down the toilet.

The deed done, she bowed her forehead to her knees and wept.

Moments later, Sam's purrs rumbled against her; his sleek fur brushed back and forth across her folded arms. She choked back a sob, feeling a little better now she wasn't completely alone.

Chapter Twenty-Eight

Justin stared off into space until Dennis interrupted his thoughts. "Hey, brooding man, chicks may dig that troubled thing you do, but I've been talking sports here for five minutes and you haven't listened to a word I said. What, are you—"

Justin shot him a glare. "I thought we talked before about the homophobic slurs you're so fond of using."

"Jesus, talk about judgey. I was going to say, 'listening to NPR?' A little touchy these days, Jay?"

He hated to admit it, but he had been touchy since his fight with Emily at the barn. He didn't like the way they'd left things and had been trying to talk to her for days now, but she always had an excuse. Or more to the point, just one excuse—Dearg all fricking mighty McGregor.

The first night, there was the sick horse she had to babysit. He offered to come stay with her, but she assured him it wasn't necessary; Dearg would be there. Today, he called to see how she was doing, and she told him she couldn't talk; she was late for a lesson with Dearg.

"This should perk you up a little," his partner offered. "I was checking out the sports page on my computer instead of the Wall Street Journal, or whatever rich white guy shit you use for your homepage, and who do I see but lover boyo himself."

"You mean McGregor?"

From the smug way he said 'boyo', he had a sinking feeling whatever Dennis was talking about, it was bad. There on the computer screen was captured a moment in time he was sure the Scot would rather not re-live. It hurt just seeing the picture of the spectacular fall where he and the horse had somersaulted over an enormous wall down several feet into a pond of water.

"Here, watch this." Ames chuckled as he made the screen jump to life, showing the fall in slow motion. "Pretty cool, huh?" At Justin's gape of disgust, he tempered his tone. "Oh, right, Mr. Humanitarian. You'll be happy to know, according to the article, the horse walked away uninjured. McGregor, on the other hand, dislocated the few bones that weren't broken." When he said nothing, Dennis added, "Don't you get it? He'll be out of the picture for a while, leaving you a free and open field."

He frowned, reading the text further. The fall happened at a place called Stormgrove in Maryland. *Two days ago.* Which meant Emily had been lying to him all along.

The chirp of Dennis's cell phone jarred him out of his reverie. Whoever the call was from, it sent him flying into motion, on his feet and out the door in seconds, Justin on his heels

"Jimmy brought his girlfriend into the ER down at County," he recounted as they hustled to the car. "Rat poison in her coke, like the other girl. Nurse friend of mine says it's fifty-fifty whether she'll pull through."

****

The pounding was either in Emily's head or at her door. Deciding it must be the door, she shambled her way to answer it. Dressed in the same flannel pants and t-shirt she'd worn for two days straight, and feeling like she'd been hit by a truck, the last thing she wanted was visitors. The knocking persisted like a demented woodpecker, so she swung the door open without bothering with the peephole. Blinking in the glare of the sun, she barked, "What?" At this moment, if it was the world's most polite killer, it would be a relief.

"Oh my God, you look like shit." It wasn't the most cordial greeting she'd ever gotten from Lottie, but she knew it was accurate.

"Thank you, Captain Obvious. I'm not a vampire. I can see myself in the mirror. What are you doing here?" Blocking the doorway, she hugged her arms to her trembling body, freezing, yet at the same time covered in a sheen of sweat.

Lottie held up the plastic grocery store bag. "Kate told me you had the flu. I brought some supplies."

"No, I mean, why are you here? I thought we weren't speaking."

"Oh, shut up and lay down before you fall down."

She put an arm around Emily and guided her to the couch, where she collapsed amid the crumpled tissues and a blanket she'd left strewn there. "What do you want first, flu meds or chicken noodle soup?" She put her hand to Emily's forehead and frowned. "You're cold as ice. It's not the flu, is it?"

Like a balloon with a slow leak, she collapsed against Lottie's shoulder, her body wracked with sobs. After she was cried out, she told her friend the whole sordid story.

****

It wasn't noon yet and the hospital's ER already

overflowed with more patients than their broken plastic chairs could hold. Justin spotted Jimmy slumped in the corner by the broken soda machine, staring at the drinks he couldn't have. His eyes were red and glassy. He and Dennis exchanged glances—did this kid really go out and get high after bringing his girlfriend in?

"Hey, Jimmy," his partner shouted.

The kid glanced up, and Justin saw he wasn't high at all. Grief and guilt had consumed him, leaving him an empty shell. Even if he didn't remember them, he had to know they were cops—anybody wearing a suit down here in the bowels of humanity was bound to be a cop of some kind. Half the people in the cramped room glared at them, but he didn't seem to see them until Dennis put a comforting hand on his shoulder. "How's she doing, kid?"

Surprised at the question, Jimmy stammered, "Not—not too good. I tried, man, I tried to take the junk away from her, but this dude, he kept giving it to her. She just, like, collapsed and stopped breathing."

"This dude, do you have a name?" Justin asked.

"She wouldn't tell me, so last night I followed her, and I saw him. Big, red-haired guy with a messed-up nose. I took the drugs away from her, but she must have hid some."

Dennis shifted his gaze to his partner. "That sounds like a guy I saw in Victor Maxwell's building."

"Are you sure?"

"Are you kidding me?" He pointed to his own mop of red hair, "Kind of easy to remember, and it's way too big of a coincidence for there not to be a connection."

The haggard young man shook as waves of anguish overtook him. "It all started that frigging night. First

Frankie and now…" He didn't finish the sentence, just bent his head and wept.

"Hey," Justin barked, the sharp edge to his voice snapping the kid out of his fog. "We know you didn't kill Robbie Allen, but you must have seen or heard something."

He snuffled and swiped an arm across his runny nose. "We expected trouble. That's why I was down in the bar. We set it up good. All she had to do was hit one button on her cell phone if she needed help, see? But she never did."

"So how did you end up in the room?" Justin pressed.

"You ever get a feeling like something's wrong? I just knew, so I go check on her and I hear lamps crashing and her—" His voice caught at the memory, regret tearing at him. "So I kicked in the door, pounded that bastard in the face a few times to see how he liked it, and then we booked. He was alive when we left, I swear."

"And the money?" Dennis demanded.

"Okay, sure, we took his cash, but we figured he owed us, right? My baby showed him a good time. Then he got a call from some dude and she said he went nuts."

"Did he say who was on the phone?"

"She wasn't sure. It sounded like he called him Uncle Max, but he was all, like angry and drunk and high, so it was hard to tell. Something about this dude wanting a meeting, but Robbie told him to piss off. That's when he started slapping her around." The kid broke down again. Dennis gave his shoulder one more pat before walking a few feet away.

"Victor Maxwell. We finally got the bastard," Dennis muttered, keeping their conversation as private as possible.

"Not yet. We ran his records. There were no calls from Maxwell's phone that night."

"A burner, you think?"

He nodded. "Two upstanding citizens like these assholes, that would be my guess. We don't have any solid proof connecting Maxwell to the crime, just the word of a junkie and her pimp." He continued to stare at the kid as the wheels in his head started turning. "I got an idea. I'll call you from the car."

****

"Detective, I'm afraid there's been some kind of mistake." Victor Maxwell pressed his manicured hands flat on his polished mahogany desk.

"Yes, there has, Vic, and not to be too clichéd, but you're the one who made it when you killed the commissioner's son." Justin sank into an overstuffed chair in Maxwell's office. "Nice leather. I used to have a couple of these, back when furniture like this was in style."

"I'm Commissioner Allen's Chief of Staff. I'm involved in negotiations with international companies to determine who gets the concessions at the airport. I have a hand in deciding what airlines get to fly out of what airport, and a hundred other contracts that keep this city's airports and harbors running. Can you honestly imagine in your wildest dreams any jury in the world that would take the word of a cheap pimp with a criminal history over mine? And what's he going to tell them? His whore claims I was on the phone with Robbie that night? Hardly a smoking gun."

Justin gave Maxwell a special smile he'd been told gave him the appearance of a smug asshole. "Don't be ridiculous Vic, we don't need the pimp. First, we have Robbie's ledger detailing all your sins. But we both know that's not proof enough for the murder. However, once we put the girl on the stand, game over. She can identify your voice as the same one she heard arguing with Robbie over what sounded like a business deal gone bad. A deal that, as you just admitted, could involve international contracts or even top levels of the city government. Now we're talking motive."

The businessman clenched his jaw so hard, the veins on his face popped out in stark relief. "The girl...came forward with this information?"

"After nearly dying from taking tainted drugs she got from your thug, she got very talkative. She's not feeling so hot at the moment, but she's going to be fine. And you, my friend, are going to jail."

Staring at his immaculate nails, Maxwell inhaled sharply. "Quite a nice fairy tale, detective. Shall I tell you one of my own? Have you heard the one about the little girl who rode horses? One day she fell off and all the king's horses and all the king's men couldn't put her back together again."

"Are you making a threat?" Justin forced himself to maintain the casually draped position on the office chair. If Maxwell harmed one hair on Emily's head, no force on Earth would stop him from killing the man.

"Not at all, detective, simply telling a story. And like yours, this one doesn't have a happy ending. You see, the little girl felt so bad she started taking pills to make it all go away. Eventually, none of her doctors would give her more, so she stole a prescription pad and tried to fake it but got caught. Now, the little girl should be in jail, but Prince Deputy District Attorney rescued her, and they rode off together to live happily ever after."

He waited a moment to rein in his anger before giving the asshole across the desk a round of applause. "Interesting story. Imaginative, to say the least. Why tell me?"

"I've got the proof to get your girlfriend into a lot of trouble." Victor reached into his desk drawer and withdrew a small plastic evidence baggie with a crumpled page from a prescription pad inside. He put it on the desk and slid it toward him until it was close enough for him to read. The name of the doctor Jonesy told him about was written in the corner.

A contemptuous grin crawled across the man's face. "What do you say to a little quid pro quo?"

Justin's fist clenched in anger, a pit opening in his stomach. Was Emily in trouble? Someone had written her name on the script, then thrown it away as if they'd changed their mind. Which also meant Maxwell was having her followed. It took all of Justin's discipline to take his time rising to his feet.

"Tell all the stories you want, Maxwell. Whether you pulled the trigger or not, you killed Robbie Allen and I'm going to put you away for it."

Chapter Twenty-Nine

Curled up on her bed, Emily smelled something rank. Much as she'd like to blame it on the litter box, she was pretty sure it was her. It had been four hellish days since she took her last pain killer, and right about now the idea of death held a certain appeal. At least she didn't have to worry about the horses. Lottie had arranged for the trainer in the next barn aisle over to take care of them.

Oscillating between curling up on the couch in the fetal position, curling up on her bed under a load of blankets and afghans, or curling up on the bathroom floor to embrace the porcelain god gave her lots of time to think. About the choices she'd made, about taking the time from now on to clean the bathroom floor better, and a lot about Justin.

Pushing him away before her problems affected him had been the right thing to do. The night he'd called to talk and she blew him off, claiming to be watching over a sick horse, his offer to stay with her made her speechless. In all the years she'd been married to Nick, he'd never once voluntarily come out to the barn. The few times she stayed to take care of a horse, he'd pissed and moaned like a petulant teenager.

"What am I supposed to do for dinner?" he'd complained more than once.

Toward the end of their marriage, she'd stopped

holding her tongue and snapped, "Is pushing the buttons on the microwave really out of the realm of your cooking expertise?" Divorce had been right around the corner.

When Justin offered to come out with her, she was so touched she almost burst into tears. Consumed by guilt for lying to him, she struggled to come up with something to push him away. Like a flash, it hit her. "No, thanks, Dearg is here."

Her ex would have gone crazy, but once again, Justin proved he wasn't Nick. "I can bring coffee or dinner out for the two of you, if you need."

Emily had bit her lip—was this man a saint? Still, there was the tiniest catch in his voice, and she knew she'd found his button. If the horses wouldn't work, pushing Dearg at him would do the trick. She'd felt horrible about hurting Justin, but a little heartache now was better than losing his career over her mistake.

A loud knock at the front door interrupted her reverie. Did Lottie, her constant companion since yesterday, order pizza?

"Where is she?" a male voice asked.

Exhaustion must have gotten the best of her. How weird to hear a voice that sounded like Justin's when she was just thinking about him.

"Back here," Lottie muttered, "and it's not pretty."

Oh crap, he really was here. Squinting through bleary eyes, she saw him standing there in the doorway. Judging her, no doubt, not like she didn't deserve it. And looking so damned good, naturally, while she was in the same flannel pajamas she'd had on for days. He muttered to Lottie which sent her scurrying. A chunk of icy dread formed in the pit of Emily's stomach. After all she'd done, whatever he had to say to her couldn't be good.

"Hey," he whispered, sitting on the bed next to her, "it's going to be okay."

Nice? He was going to be nice to her? Her lip trembled and there was nothing she could do to stop the flood of tears.

"Shh, it's okay," he reassured her, brushing a stray strand of matted hair off her forehead. "We're going to get through this."

Choking back a sob, she sputtered, "I couldn't tell you. I didn't want you to see me like this."

"What, you thought the detox look would be a turn-off?" His smile made something inside her finally let go, relaxing for the first time since Nick picked her up at the drugstore.

Lottie reappeared in the doorway and gave him a nod. He thanked her, then said to Emily, "Lottie's got a nice hot bath waiting for you. It's going to make those aches feel better, I promise. At the very least, you'll smell better."

She groaned at the thought of the effort of getting up to take a bath. Even the smell of the lavender bath salts wafting down the hall made her a little nauseated. Again. But she knew she should at least try to clean up. She pushed her twisted, sweaty sheets aside and swayed unsteadily on her feet.

"Whoa, easy there, cowgirl."

He reached out a hand to steady her, but the room still spun. He swept her up in his arms, the soft material of his overcoat a comforting caress on her cheek. Carrying her into the bathroom, he lowered her into the tub full of warm water, pajamas and all. After he pulled away, she realized it was the same coat he loaned her the first day they met. The one that ended up sprayed with horse snot. This time it was only bath water.

"I'm definitely going to owe you a coat," she murmured, letting the heat from the water seep into aching muscles.

"We'll worry about it later." His voice was soothing and rumbly in the acoustics of her tiny bathroom. He was right. Her all-consuming body-ache melted in the hot water until a horrifying thought occurred to her.

Bolting upright, she asked, "Did this come up at work? Was it Nick? Are you in trouble?"

He massaged her neck with one hand, unconcerned about the water dripping all over him now. "No, it was…it doesn't matter how I found out."

Her cheeks burned with shame. "This is why I didn't tell you. I never wanted this to become your problem."

"Don't worry about work. I'll handle it. Listen to me." He took her face in his hands. "I love you. There's nothing you ever have to hide from me."

After the last four days, Emily thought she was cried out, but she was wrong. Tears flowed, no matter how hard she tried to blink them back. He bent forward to kiss her, but she put a hand against his chest. "I vomited non-stop yesterday and haven't brushed my teeth since. I don't want the first time you tell me you love me to literally leave a bad taste in your mouth."

"You may have a point," he quipped, and kissed her forehead instead.

She blissfully sank back into the tub, unwilling to question her incredible luck at being loved by this man.

Guilt washed over her, and she sheepishly admitted, "I lied to you about Dearg. He wasn't with me; he isn't even in L.A."

The barest glimpse of an evil smile spread across his face that she didn't quite understand. A somber, sympathetic frown took its place. "I know. But I love that you told me." She gazed up at him, getting lost in those brown eyes. He pulled her closer. "What the hell, that's what mouthwash is for, right?" He drew her face to his and kissed her. The heat from his touch melted the very marrow of her bones. They were both a little breathless when he finally pulled away.

A rush of pleasure filled Emily, leaving her uncertain about what should happen next. She fought the urge to pull him into the tub with her and return his kiss until neither one of them could stand. The tub was so small one of them was bound to get hurt. She wriggled to strip off her wet pajamas and come to him when a cell phone chirped.

"Shit," he hissed after he checked the screen. "I've got to go." He rose, giving her another quick kiss. He got to the door and turned back toward her. "We're going to get through this," he repeated with such intensity that for the first time, she believed they just might.

****

The hospital room was cast in shadows, lit only by the dim sunlight sneaking past the closed shades and the eerie blue and green glows from the machines that tracked the patient's vitals. Dennis, disguised in a hospital gown and blonde wig, had been lying in the bed for so long he had to fight the urge to take a nap. Then there was the soft *swoosh* of the door opening and he smiled. It was about damn time.

With his back to the door, he couldn't see who had come in, but the heavy footsteps told him it wasn't a nurse who stepped to his bedside and grabbed hold of the IV hanging there. He waited another moment before he turned over and pointed his weapon at the red-headed thug Maxwell sent to kill the girl.

"Freeze, asshole."

The stunned expression on the big man's face was comical until he saw the syringe in the thug's hand, tiny against his fat, sausage-like fingers, the needle inserted in the IV bag. He understood in a flash what the plan had been. They were going to inject something that would kill the girl, probably meant to make her death appear to be from natural causes.

He laughed when the thug pushed the plunger down, dangling the other end of the IV from his hand. "Hey, dumbass, what'd you think? I'd let them stick a needle in my arm? Detective Ames, hands in the air."

Keeping the gun trained on the would-be assassin, he swung out of bed with perhaps a bit more attitude than a man wearing a hospital gown and no pants ought to have. The big man peered down and barked an ugly laugh. When Dennis glanced to see what he was smiling at, the thug clocked him in the head with an elbow, sending him flying.

The gun skittered under a table and he stumbled, a grin spreading across his face. "So, you want a fight?"

Tearing off the wig, he head-butted the man and then wrapped his arms around him, driving him into the wall behind them. Too stunned to react, the guy's head bounced against the wall with a loud crack. He let go, and the man sagged to his knees. The thug shook his head as if to clear his vision as he looked up. He seemed puzzled to see Dennis gamely bouncing on the balls of his bare feet, ready for round two despite the blood pouring down his face.

"You're under arrest, dumbass. Please resist."

With a roar, the bigger man lurched to his feet, swinging both ham-sized fists with more force than accuracy. Dennis easily ducked one but caught the other in a glancing blow under his eye. He bellowed in rage, grabbed the phone from the nightstand, and slammed it into the thug's face, already disfigured from a lifetime of brawling. His opponent collapsed to the floor again, this time with a sickening crunch as his mangled nose met linoleum.

"Come on, pussy, get up," Dennis sneered. "Or isn't it any fun if you're not pushing around a scared little girl?"

The thug tried to stand but collapsed back down as the door crashed open. A half dozen cops with their guns drawn flooded in, led by Justin.

****

"You can ride a Training course in your sleep," Dearg growled at Emily. From three thousand miles away, disdain dripped off his voice over the phone.

The closing date for the next Kinsale show was at the end of the week, meaning she couldn't put off filling out her entry much longer. The question wasn't whether or not to enter the show. It was time to get back in the saddle, so to speak. She'd been riding for a week now since recovering from "the flu" and getting stronger every day.

In fact, without the muzziness of the painkillers, she used the fear to help her ride smarter, finding a way to control it rather than let it control her. Besides, with Lottie pushing and prodding every day, there was no question she would have to show again soon. But at what level? How far did she dare push herself?

They were split down the middle on that issue. *Down the middle* as in she wanted to ride at the easier Training level while Lottie and Dearg insisted she ride the much more difficult Preliminary course. No matter how much more confident she felt, the thought sent a shiver through her. "Isn't the point to show a level below where you school? Stay within your comfort zone?"

"Oh sure, if you want to be comfortable." Why did such a pleasant word as *comfortable* sound like a curse when he said it? "But if it's comfort you're after, why not stay home and ride a merry-go-round pony? That'll be about as exciting as your somnambulant Training run."

She pulled a face at the speaker phone, but her friend ratted her out. "He can't hear you sticking your tongue out, dear. You'll have to make the raspberry sound."

"I'll be there at the show to work with you. You'll be ready to face that fence, I promise." The scornful edge vanished from Dearg's voice, and he softened his burr to a gentle lull. "If not, we'll bump you down a level, no problem." So he realized they were dealing with the fence that almost killed her. After suffering his recent fall, maybe he understood how she felt. Or was it another way of cajoling her?

Scooping up all the paperwork and cramming it in her desk, Emily put off deciding for another day. "I'll figure it out tomorrow morning, I promise."

Ignoring their groans, she strode back out to the barn to get back to work. Justin was coming over tonight and she wanted to leave early to spend extra time getting ready. After dinner, she'd ask him what he thought. A fresh perspective on things might be just what she needed.

****

Never had Victor Maxwell allowed himself to appear anywhere in public—or private, for that matter—appearing as shabby and careworn as he did right now, standing beside his lawyer in front of a horde of TV cameras ready to speak.

"Wait, here it comes..." Justin muttered as he watched the scene unfold on Emily's small TV. On cue, Maxwell bent his head to wipe a tear from his eye as his lawyer made her statement.

"There, you see that? The old fake tear trick. This guy is unbelievable."

She snuggled in closer to him, catching bits and pieces of the rest of the statement, but not really paying attention. Maxwell's lawyer claimed her client shot Robbie Allen in self-defense, which brought more hoots of derision from Justin.

No matter how subtly she tried to put her clean, non-barn scented hair in his general direction, he remained fixated on the TV. Finally, after Samwise trotted across the remote and accidentally turned the TV off, he snapped out of it.

"Bad kitty," she scolded half-heartedly as she shooed him off the coffee table. "Do you want me to turn it back on?" She batted her lashes and noticed him drinking in her curves, shown off by her soft, clingy sweater. *Finally.* She had started to worry she'd lost all feminine appeal. Her glossed lips slid into a sly smile as Justin pulled her closer.

"If I hear him claim it was self-defense one more time, I'm going to go crazy. I mean, if it was self-defense, why did he leave the scene?"

Okay, so much for hours of primping. His obsession with this case was stronger than any feminine wiles she possessed. In need of consolation, Emily slid out from under his arm to refill their wine glasses. He raised a questioning eyebrow at her, pushing her to defiantly pour a little more into her glass. "What? I'm not driving anywhere tonight."

This time, his scrutiny had nothing to do with her curves. She rolled her eyes. "I'm done with the pills, and wine was never the problem."

He frowned, seeming unconvinced as she handed him his glass of wine, but he accepted it all the same. She snuggled back closer to him, trying to recapture the mood. "What if he got scared?" she offered, hoping to distract him from the wine topic by going back to his favorite one, Victor Maxwell. "Even innocent people get freaked out. Especially when they shoot somebody."

"Sure, it happens, but how did he get away so fast? Freaked out people usually don't just disappear. Hotel security was there in less than a minute and he was nowhere to be found."

"From what you've told me about him, he probably practiced," she said, half-joking.

"What do you mean?"

The wheels began turning inside her head for real now. "When you ride in a show, you walk the jump course ahead of time to make sure you know where you're going and what approach to take to each jump. You make contingency plans in case something goes wrong. If I were your friend Maxwell and I planned on committing murder, I would practice my getaway route ahead of time to make sure I had all my bases covered."

His eyes lit up with enthusiasm for her crazy idea. Justin took her face in his hands and kissed her deeply, but all too quickly. "And if the hotel security cameras caught him casing his exit rout ahead of time, there goes his self-defense claim. You are a genius."

He jumped to his feet to leave. Halfway out the door, he turned around to give her one more kiss. "You look beautiful, by the way."

Yeah, beautiful and a freaking genius. That's why I'm sitting here all by myself. She grabbed her unsuspecting cat to have something to cuddle with.

Chapter Thirty

The morning started with a rush of excitement as the delivery person dropped off a package for Emily at the barn. She tore open the cardboard box and practically gnawed through the cocoon of bubble wrap and packing tape, giddy with anticipation over her new trailer stabilizer bars.

Booked solid with riding and teaching for most of the day, she didn't get the chance to take the bars over to Pamela's trailer to make sure they fit until late afternoon. She wasn't about to have a replay of when she almost didn't make Dearg's clinic because Pam had misplaced one of the two stabilizer bars needed to keep the trailer steady and safe. As she spread the grease on the threaded end of the heavy metal bar, running it in a smooth motion over the palm of her hand, she stewed over how lame it had been for Pamela to lose a tool so essential to providing safe transportation for the animals in her charge.

Then a thought popped in her head that sent chills up her spine. Hadn't Justin described the murder weapon as a heavy metal pipe or a rod with a threaded pattern on the curved end? And didn't he tell her they'd found traces of lubricant in her wounds? Could the killer have used Pamela's own stabilizer bar to smash her face in beyond recognition? Gripping the bar tighter—out of both fear and excitement—she used her free hand to reach for her cell phone.

"There you are."

Surprised by a voice that seemed to come out of nowhere, she fumbled her phone. It clattered to the dirt near her foot. At least she'd squashed the urge to shriek like a child.

Confronting her stalker, relief flooded her when she saw who it was. "Jesus H. Chr—Darian, what the hell?"

"Sorry, I didn't mean to frighten you," the woman shot back, as if it was Emily's fault she'd been scared.

Who sneaks up on someone in a dark, isolated corner of the Equestrian Center and is surprised when they're scared?

"What can I help you with?" she asked, holding the stabilizer bar in a defensive position while she bent to retrieve her phone. Hopefully Darian hadn't noticed she'd dialed 911. She only needed to hit *send*. She thought she knew her inherited student pretty well, but she was tired of people popping up out of nowhere and hitting her on the head. Friend or not, she wasn't about to let it happen again.

"I wanted to talk to you about the show."

Letting out a huge sigh of relief, Emily eased her grip on the metal rod. "What's up?"

Squaring her shoulders, Darian blurted out, "I want to ride in the Kinsale show. On my horse."

"Um, okay. I sent my entry in yesterday, but all we have to do is call and I'm sure we can stable together, no problem." Actually, Lottie had snatched the entry out of her hand as soon as Emily signed off on going Prelim and driven it to the post office before she could change her mind.

"Really?"

She furrowed her eyebrows, trying to figure out if Darian was that naïve. "Yeah, why not?"

"Pamela never let me show, no matter how many times I asked," she stammered, no longer powered by righteous indignation.

Her meek attitude made the idea of Darian being a deranged killer laughable; Emily went to back work attaching the stabilizer bars while she talked. If she was right about it being similar to the murder weapon, Justin was bound to want to take Pam's remaining bar in for testing and she wanted to be sure the new ones fit first in case she needed any information off the original one to order another.

"What do you mean, wouldn't let you? Just sign up and show."

"Easy for you to say, you were her super star." The petulant woman kicked a rock and almost nailed Emily as she twisted around underneath the trailer to attach the bar. "She hated my horse and refused to take us to shows until we *earned it*—whatever that meant."

It probably meant whenever you stopped whining about how much she hated you, Emily thought, but never got a word in. Darian was hard to stop when she was on a roll. "I was so pissed with her. We argued and argued before the last show for her to take me, but oh no. She didn't want to be embarrassed by us. Huh."

Something about the triumphant tone in that last little grunt made Emily stand up and listen. It was ridiculous to consider Darian would have murdered Pamela over not being able to show, wasn't it? That cold, creepy feeling down her spine was back as she gripped her phone.

"Seriously, it's no problem. Fill out the entry, write a check and I'll take care of the rest. Excuse me, I need to call my boyfriend now and tell him where I am." She smiled inwardly at the *boyfriend* bit, even if she might be confronting a killer. "You remember, the police detective, with the gun and the badge? He's back at the barn, waiting on me to go to dinner."

She cringed, knowing she was babbling like an idiot for no good reason. She sagged against her truck in relief when Justin answered his phone.

****

Shirtsleeves rolled to his elbows, collar loosened, and tie draped with cobwebs, Dennis exited yet another room, filled with saddles and gear he didn't recognize, reeking of leather, soap, and dirt. He'd gone through over two dozen such rooms already and found nothing more deadly than rat crap. Hopefully, Jay was ready to call their search of the Equestrian Center for the murder weapon a bust.

"Detective Ames, cobwebs suit you," Lottie greeted as she entered the barn, arms laden with shopping bags. Then she got close enough to see his puffy eye and the lump on his forehead from his encounter with the thug in the hospital. She frowned but refrained from making a smartass remark. "Where's your better half?"

"If you mean my so-called partner," he huffed, running a hand through his unruly hair, "he's off with Ms. Conners, while I'm stuck combing every nook and cranny for the murder weapon."

"Ooh, right, Emily told me your CSI whatchamacallit lab tests confirmed the killer probably used Pam's missing stabilizer bar since the wounds match the bar in her trailer. Why on Earth would they have left it at the scene of the crime? If it was me, I'd have thrown the damn thing in the river and been done with it."

Dennis checked out the matriarch in a new and slightly wary light. "Good to know. Fortunately, most criminals aren't as clever as you. Besides, Detective Butler has one of his *gut feelings*, so here we are."

"Want some help? I watch all those TV shows. I know better than to smudge any evidence or anything. This is so—" She gave a happy shrug. "—exciting."

"Uh, no, thanks," he laughed. "We've got plenty of uniforms out here searching. It's a little like finding a needle in a haystack, but—"

"Lottie, you're back from shopping."

They both turned to see Justin and Emily strolling toward them, hand in hand. The loopy grins on their faces gave Dennis an uncomfortable feeling— somewhere between the irritation on your teeth when you've had too much sugar and the dread of watching the headlight of an oncoming train.

"He's not going to break her heart, is he?" Lottie asked under her breath.

"Lady, I don't know who's going to break what, but I'm pretty sure you and I'll be the ones stuck cleaning up the mess."

****

Two hours later, a drooping and forlorn Dennis argued with Justin. "Jay, the murder weapon is not here. We've searched the place twice and came up empty. Your gut was wrong, get over it."

"Then we're going to search again because I'm telling you, it is here."

Lottie, having sent Emily home long ago, approached with empty feed buckets in her hands. "Still no luck, gentlemen?"

"Oh, we've had luck," Dennis snarled, glaring at his partner, "all bad."

"So far, we've searched the entire place and came up empty," Justin admitted, an unmistakable edge of weariness in his voice. "Thanks to your input we've dredged the river, but no luck."

"Have you searched the kitchens?" she offered helpfully.

"There's a kitchen here? We would never have thought of that," Dennis snarked. She responded with a haughty glower that made him laugh for the first time all day.

"Yes, ma'am," Justin answered more politely. "We even had them unlock the little white house on the lawn to search it, in case it'd been left open at the time of the murder. Nada."

"What about the big storage container behind the house?"

"Locked up tight." He rubbed his hand over his face in frustration. "The guard insists it stays that way unless there's someone from the event staff present to prevent people stealing their equipment."

"Horse hockey," she sneered. "It wasn't locked when Pam and I left for the Kinsale show a couple of days before she was murdered. I know because she went in and borrowed some chairs."

Both cops snapped to attention. While Justin put the call into the Center to get the shed unlocked, Dennis impulsively grabbed her face and planted a kiss on her cheek. "You are my hero."

"Why, thank you, detective," she replied, adding with a wicked grin, "I can't wait to find out what my reward will be if I solved your murder."

Ames found the blatant innuendo unnerving.

****

Emily twirled into her apartment on a cloud. Days hardly ever went better than this one. It had been intoxicating to have Justin so close all day as they searched for the murder weapon. The memory of their stolen kisses sent heat to all the right places.

Being left on her own for dinner, however, was something she was used to. Rooting through the old restaurant takeout boxes and expired yogurts in her refrigerator, the best prospect she could find was one last bottle of beer. "Screw it," she grumbled as she grabbed the beer, took a sip, and grimaced. It was flat, but better than nothing.

Kicking off her freshly polished boots, a habit she'd gotten back into, she plopped on the couch and waited for Samwise to meander across the tiny apartment and take his customary place in her lap. Sitting for the first time all day, the aches and pains from the near disaster with Reese that morning made themselves known. Her confidence had been shaken when the horse came close to tossing her off in front of a fence. On her second attempt, however, she waited for the jump to come to her instead of gunning at it.

It was so simple, she was surprised it worked. So she tried it again, this time at an even scarier jump. Once again, they sailed over it with no problems. It had been a great breakthrough moment. But, as any rider knows, getting almost dumped off can pull, yank and strain more muscles than an actual fall. Better to get up now to take a couple of aspirin before Sam settled on her lap for the night.

The room swam a little as Emily stood. Wow, she'd become a lightweight if a few swallows of beer got her tipsy, but then she had forgotten to eat today. She took two aspirin with one of the last swallows of beer and sat back down on the couch. More out of habit than desire, she reached for the remote for her nightly ritual of watching her fall. Her finger hesitated and then, for the first time since her accident, she chucked the remote aside without turning the TV on. It was time to accept that accidents happen and no amount of analyzing will prevent you from making another mistake. Time to move on with her life.

The thought made her smile. She tried to give Sam a taste of the beer, his favorite beverage, on the tip of her finger, but after a quick sniff, he turned tail and ran. "Okay, you're right," she called after the cat, "we deserve better than this."

She decided to walk to the nearby convenience store for some food, but as soon as she got to her feet, she knew something was wrong. Seriously wrong. Her legs were lead and the room spun before dimming into a tunnel. She felt her pockets, but the damn cell phone was never where she needed it to be. Focusing with all her might, she lunged at the kitchen counter where she'd left it, but her legs collapsed underneath her. She crumpled to the ground, falling into a cold, black pit.

****

The sun having set, the corner of the Equestrian Center where the event staff kept their equipment was now pitch black. Even with cutesy decorative lights twinkling from the trees, the patrol officers needed to use blindingly bright flashlights to see more than two feet in front of them. They'd been searching the unlit storage room, careful of every shadow, in case it hid evidence or a big rat, for nearly an hour before they hit pay dirt. A wave of relief washed over Justin when he saw a metal bar with a rust-colored stain on the curved end hidden under the last stack of chairs.

Dennis rubbed a hand over his face. "Once again, you were right, oh Great Master. Be damned if I know how you do it, but if you're done gloating, can we please go home?"

He allowed himself a hint of a smile. His gut had gone above and beyond the call of duty on this one. He liked to imagine Pamela Yates was helping out from the other side wherever she was. "I told you hours ago to go home. I thought I'd buy everyone a few beers, but if you need your beauty sleep, be my guest."

Happy with the results of the search and ready to spend the rest of the night with Emily, he almost missed it when a patrolman rushed in and murmured something to his partner. His sixth sense kicked in when Dennis made a barely audible response for the uniform, while Lottie, who clearly had eavesdropped, made a gasping sound. Despite the lack of light, he saw the blood drain from her face.

"It's Emily," Dennis said. "She's at Holy Angels. She—"

He was already running toward his car by the time Dennis croaked, "overdosed."

Chapter Thirty-One

Harsh, blurry images shuffled at a dizzying pace: water-stained ceiling tiles, a crowd of faces, the inside of a wailing ambulance, Samwise's fuzzy face. The pictures all changed before Emily could make sense of things. It was like watching TV with Nick in charge of the remote control. The only constant was the horrible taste of charcoal in her mouth and someone assuring her everything would be all right.

Then Justin's voice. Was he shouting at her? About her? She struggled to open her leaden eyelids, desperate for the nightmare to be over.

Gradually, the pain and nausea subsided and a sight she'd come to hate came into focus. The cold, stark hospital room closely resembled the one she'd spent weeks in after her accident. The nightmare was real, but she couldn't remember what she'd done this time to end up here. Something about a show pricked at the back of her mind—had she fallen again?

Moving an inch at a time to keep her head from exploding, she shifted her gaze and saw Justin asleep in a chair close to her bed. He appeared as hellish as she felt. Her knight in rumpled armor. Reaching out, she brushed her fingertips against the back of his hand where it rested on the bed.

"Good morning," she croaked, her throat irritated and sore from...something. Seriously, why did her mouth taste like charcoal?

As the fog lifted from her brain, a layer at a time, Justin roused and blinked at her, his expression dull. He didn't return her weak smile with his usual cocky grin, but she chalked it up to spending the night in a chair. He rose and poured her a cup of water out of the nearby plastic pitcher. It wasn't until he handed it to her that she saw the storm behind his eyes.

Confused, she asked, "Are you angry at me?"

He wearily shook his head. "I'm not angry with you, it's…" He stalked over to the window to stare at the fascinating view of the parking lot rather than finish his sentence.

"It's what?" she demanded, struggling to sit up despite the pounding in her head. Then she discovered the IV in her arm and more of the pieces of last night fell into place.

He turned, that mix of pity and concern she'd learned to loathe marred the contours of his handsome face. "Emily, you need professional help. I was blind to your drug problem before and that's on me, but this latest episode confirms it. I called a place in Malibu; they can take you today."

The half-drunk beer, the dizziness. It was all coming back. "Wait, you think I took something? You, of all people, know what I went through when I stopped before. I'm not about to go down that hole again. I swear I haven't taken anything stronger than an aspirin since—"

"They found the empty bottle of pills in your garbage can." His tired, hollow voice left no room for explanation. "Maybe…it's time to give up riding."

A wave of disappointment slammed against her.

He didn't believe her. "What?"

"For God's sake, Em, you don't have to be a shrink to put together your near accident yesterday with taking a nearly fatal overdose." He paused, clearly trying to select his words carefully. "Riding isn't worth your life."

Suddenly exhausted, she collapsed against the pillow. It took everything she had to stare into those gorgeous brown eyes. "Go to hell."

He reeled back, putting his hands up in the condescending *now, now little lady* gesture she loathed.

"Horses are the reason I get up in the morning, you idiot. And finally, after all this, I have found my purpose. I've been nominated for the Hy Poynt, so why would I want to end it all now?"

"What am I supposed to think? After they found you unconscious, Kate couldn't wait to call and tell me about your near fall. The connection is pretty clear."

Her body shook with rage as competing emotions formed a lump in her throat. "You know what? Fuck Kate and fuck you. You're supposed to take my word for it when I tell you I didn't do it."

"Dammit, Em, they had to give you multiple doses of charcoal to clear out your system. That's how close I came to losing you." He softened his tone. "I understand how hard it was for you to get off the painkillers, anyone is bound to backslide. But with professional—"

He barely had time to duck before she flung the puke-colored water pitcher at his head. "Get out," she rasped. He hesitated, a stunned, uncertain frown creeping across his stupid face. "Get out," she shouted louder now, finding her voice.

She scavenged for something else to throw at him, but by the time she found the bedpan, he was halfway out the door. She flung it anyway, getting little satisfaction as it bounced off the doorframe inches from his head.

****

When Justin parked outside of Emily's apartment, he was surprised to see it had been cordoned off with bright yellow police tape. Despite the way they'd left things at the hospital, he'd come to pick up toiletries and clothes for her and questioned why someone had made so much fuss over a suicide attempt. Her front door was pushed open, most likely left ajar by a paramedic with more important things on his mind than locking up.

"About damn time you showed up."

His hand was on the grip of his gun in the time span it took him to recognize Dennis's voice. He relaxed, slowly letting out his breath, and came all the way inside where the surprises kept coming. There was his partner, sitting on the couch, with Sam the cat curled in his lap. He would have thought he was in the wrong apartment, but when he checked the door, it was the right number.

He scrubbed his face in exhausted confusion. "What are you doing here?"

"Waiting for you. Did you know this cat saved your girlfriend's life?" He gave the little black cat a scratch behind the ears, turning up his purr volume. "The cops came over on a disturbance call from the crazy broad upstairs." He pointed at the TV's remote. "The cat had turned the TV on at full blast."

Sure he did. From his rumpled clothes and

bloodshot eyes, it appeared Dennis's night had been about as restful as his own. Exhaustion was the only explanation for his cat fantasy, so he opted to ignore it. "I appreciate the decorations." He waved a hand toward the police tape around the tiny apartment's front and back doors. "But isn't it a bit much?"

"Not for a crime scene."

He protested, but Dennis dismissed him with a rude grunt. "While you were busy brooding—again—I did some of that detecting thing I've heard so much about from you. Yes, they found an empty bottle of opioids, but doesn't it strike you as wonky?"

"Wonky? Nope, wasn't the word that came to mind."

He put the cat on the couch with a gentleness that continued to surprise Justin's sleep-deprived brain. He paced back and forth, a sign he was on a roll. "Remember when you asked me to check into the death of the other trainer, Ginger Mills, who allegedly overdosed?"

"So?"

"The drug listed in the coroner's report is the same one they pumped out of Emily." He stopped his manic motion to lock gazes with Justin. "Not *something like it*, the identical chemical twin. Taken in exactly the same way—dissolved in a bottle of booze. The other chick used gin, but two people who weren't the type to kill themselves do it using the same M.O.?"

A surge of adrenaline cleared the fog from Justin's brain. How could he have been so stupid? "The horse said it was worried about Emily ending up like Ginger," he muttered.

This time, it was his partner's turn to stare in

confusion. "What the hell are you talking about?"

"It sounds crazy, but the horse whisperer claimed the animal was worried about Emily having the same fate as Ginger. I didn't think anything of it because, well…"

"Because it's completely stupid?"

"Not so crazy now, is it? We should talk to her again, see if there's anything else the horse can tell us."

Justin could tell from the way his partner's eyebrows shot up to disappear under his messy thatch of hair that he thought he was nuts. "Okay, buddy, why don't you go home and catch a few Z's before we interview Mr. Ed."

"First, I've got to go apologize to Emily," he said as he headed toward the door.

"Whoa, wait, what?" Dennis choked out, "What's the point?"

"Because I was wrong. You're right, she didn't take the pills. I accused her of lying, ergo I owe her an apology."

Dennis shook his head in disgust. "Ergo, my ass. My old man taught me the only reason for a man to apologize is to get laid and there's no way in hell you're going to get this one in the sack any time soon. Not after you accused her of trying to off herself."

He stared at his partner for a moment, dumbfounded. "Knowing your father told you that explains so much about you." He ignored the ill-gotten advice and pivoted to the door. Dennis shot out a hand and stopped him with unexpected force. Everyone, even Justin, underestimated his wiry frame as weak or flabby.

"Back off for a bit." His voice was gentle now.

"I've been on both sides of this, remember? They'll release her in a few hours, so wait till she's had time to cool off a little herself before you do the groveling bit—if that's what you really want to do."

"What's that supposed to mean?"

Dennis offered a cheerless, grin. "Hey, I got your back, buddy. But this is the stage where you usually dump them, when the going gets complicated."

He bristled. "That's not true."

"What about the last one, that hot chick you met skiing? You dumped her for giving you a plant."

"Because there was some hidden message there. I mean, why did she think I needed a plant?"

"How the hell should I know? I just shared the stellar lessons I got in relationships." He drew closer, all humor gone now. "God knows how you do it, but you always leave them smiling. But this time it's different. This time, someone could really get hurt. If you're going to ditch her, do it now."

Running his hand through his close-cropped hair, he understood Dennis's message loud and clear. If he was going to break it off with her, better to do it now, while her anger gave her the strength to get over him.

But he didn't want to end things. "Is that what you'd do," he asked the person he recognized as the most unlikely source of romantic advice, "walk away?"

"Me? She'd have to have a lot bigger tits for me to tough it out," he joked, but Justin knew better than anyone, his friend used caustic humor as a defense against feeling too much of anything. "But you? You really like her."

"How can you be so sure?"

"You're here, aren't you?"

Emily's cozy apartment was suddenly closing in, like all the air had been sucked out of it. He struggled to formulate an answer, but the words tumbled around in his head like ping pong balls in a lottery machine. Then his phone rang, and he was literally saved by the bell.

"It's probably another girlfriend already lined up, you lucky SOB."

"Yeah, it's the woman I picked up in a sleazy bar the other night," Justin shot back. "Want me to pass along any messages to your mom while I've got her?" The phone's screen read *Private Number.* He frowned. "Hello?"

"Detective Butler, I hope this isn't a bad time."

His eyes narrowed at the rasp of the familiar voice. "Victor Maxwell," he announced, bringing Dennis's snickering to a confused but sudden halt. "How did you get this number?"

"You may have managed to de-claw me, but this old cat has a few teeth left."

The words were slurred, no doubt soaked in pricey alcohol, but Maxwell's voice maintained an edge of haughtiness. He hit the speaker button on his phone so Dennis could hear.

"I didn't simply de-claw you, Snaggletooth. Your would-be hitman talked and any minute now, a judge is going to issue an arrest warrant for you for ordering a hit on Jimmy Gillette and his girlfriend, not to mention the murder of Frankie Gillette. Plus, we found a video of you at the hotel days before Robbie's murder mapping out your escape plan, so there's another nail in your coffin. You should be enjoying your last breaths as a free man, so why call me?"

"Yes, I heard about my employee using me as a

bargaining chip. That's the reason I'm calling. I want to give myself up, but only to you. No uniforms, not your psycho partner, only you."

Despite the situation, he grinned as Dennis silently mouthed 'asshole' and gave the phone the finger as he made a call on his own phone.

Justin went back to Maxwell. "Now, why would I do that, Vic? When it sounds an awful lot like I'd be walking into an ambush."

His partner showed him a piece of paper with 'running a trace' in block letters.

There was a rumbling sound that was probably supposed to be a chuckle before Maxwell taunted, "How's your girlfriend doing?"

He didn't realize how hard his grip tightened around his phone until the casing creaked. He took a deep, calming breath, needing every ounce of focus and clarity he had to deal with this cold-blooded killer.

Without waiting for a reply, Maxwell continued, a man clearly fond of his own voice. "From what I understand, she met with a little accident. I can give you the person responsible, but only if you come alone."

As coolly as if he were arranging for a business lunch, he asked, "Where and when?" ignoring his partner's frantic signs not to do it.

"Long Beach Marina, slip 16. The *Tranquility*."

"Long Beach? I don't have any authority down there. I can't bring you in without getting their cops involved."

"Detective, come or don't come. I really don't care." The voice on the phone sounded weary, aged beyond Maxwell's years. Silence followed.

He turned his phone off in disgust. The one thing he missed about old-fashioned phones was the satisfaction of slamming the phone down when the conversation was over.

"Dammit," Dennis exploded after hanging up his phone.

He hadn't really expected them to be able to trace the call. "Doesn't matter, we know where he is."

Dennis fumed. "No, we know where he says he is. This asshole could be in Peru and the only thing waiting for you on that boat is a case of C-4."

Glancing at his watch, he swore softly. He really wanted to go talk to Emily, to tell her he was wrong, but Dennis was right about giving her time. If anything happened to him...he pushed the thought out of his mind as he straightened his tie in her tiny hall mirror. "There's only one way to find out."

"Jay, this guy is lying to you. He doesn't know dick about anything and certainly not about Emily."

"We still need to bring him in for Robbie Allen's murder and the attempt on the girl. For Frankie."

Dennis bit back a derisive scoff. "Agreed, but let's deploy a SWAT team. You don't have to do this alone like some asinine superhero."

He knew Dennis was right, but the image of Frankie Gillette's head exploding as they sat at lunch had haunted him every day since then. He owed it to Frankie to try to bring Maxwell in alive. "Fine, call it in, but give me a head start to see if I can prevent this from becoming a shit storm where another innocent person gets killed."

He ran out the door without waiting for his partner's reply.

Chapter Thirty-Two

Justin ducked out of the bright spring sunshine and down the stairs into the dimly lit interior of the *Tranquility.* "Vic, what are we doing here?"

"Come now, detective." Victor Maxwell sneered from the darkness, "Is it so hard to imagine I'd want to spend my last day of freedom enjoying the open sea?"

The slurred speech was a dead giveaway that the bottle in his hand wasn't his first of the day. Stepping cautiously into the mahogany paneled room, he spotted an empty one rolling across the thick carpet with each slap of a wave in the otherwise pristine cabin.

"Except you're sitting down here in the dark. You haven't even left the dock, and oh yeah, those three-hundred-dollar loafers you've got on aren't exactly deck shoes. Christ, you're hammered to the gills."

"Do you remember Michael Burland, the city councilman?"

He poured another drink into a cut crystal lowball glass with remarkably steady hands. His vacant stare sent a chill down Justin's spine. "Sorry, before my time. Why, are you going to try to pin the kid's murder on him now?"

Swirl, sip. Swirl, sip. His movements carried an almost robotic precision. "He failed to deliver the airport concession he'd promised some powerful people. A week later, pieces of him were found up and down the coast." The man was either ignoring Justin's dig or was too lost in his own thoughts to hear it.

The air in the cabin felt heavy, like it was closing in. Tired of Maxwell's games, he snapped, "What does this have to do with who tried to kill Emily?"

A small light sparked in those dead eyes, then vanished. "Oh yes, how is your little girlfriend?"

"I'm not playing with you, Vic. Who did it?"

"I don't know." He chuckled, refilling his glass. "But it was the only carrot I could dangle to ensure you'd come. Really, detective, you're too predictable."

Justin spun to leave and was surprised to find he was lightheaded. "That's it, I'm done. Take your chances turning yourself into the local PD."

"Do you know what boats are, detective?" he continued on unhurriedly, as if Justin never spoke. "They are floating Molotov cocktails. Oh, the fuel itself won't easily ignite, mind you, but there's plenty of propane on a yacht like this to convince it to go 'boom.' Not to mention it produces the carbon monoxide you're probably noticing about now. Anyone who knows their way around an engine can rig up a fuse about as sophisticated as a rag stuffed in a bottle of gasoline."

Sluggishly, Justin recalled Maxwell's bio. His father was a fisherman. Maxwell worked on his boat for a few years before…"Is that what happened on your father's boat? You blew it up?"

He fought his rising panic. Something was definitely wrong, but he couldn't get his head clear enough to figure out what. A step at a time, he forced his feet back toward the open stairway.

"I was so close," Maxwell seethed, ignoring his

question. "Millions of dollars in my pockets and contributions to my bid for mayor. All I had to do was close those airport deals. You want to know the funny part? I told Robbie about the deals, thinking he'd enjoy the joke of how much I would profit off using his idiot father's position."

"What happened? The kid got greedy?" Justin's tongue was thick as he stumbled over the words.

The empty bottle slipped from the older man's grasp. "No, then you happened, detective." Slowly, deliberately, he reached for the cigar on the table next to him and lit it, an expression of grim satisfaction darkening his face as he exhaled the pungent, aromatic smoke. "I had no problem killing the little shit, but you just wouldn't let it go, wouldn't let that whore and her pimp take the fall for his murder."

"Come on, with your money you'll probably get off with a few years at Club Fed."

"And end up like Burland, still alive when the mob cuts me into pieces for not delivering the contracts I promised?" He shook his head. "Better to go this way, quick and painless in one blinding flash of light with the bonus of taking you with me."

And then he laid the cigar back down on the table, where its glowing end met a trail of liquid. He hadn't noticed it when he entered the dimly lit cabin, but now the liquid, obviously some kind of accelerant, flared. The flames made a straight path for the boat's elaborate galley, directly beside him. Willing his leaden limbs to move, he dove for the open stairs and managed to claw halfway up when the roar of an explosion filled the small, confined space.

A heavy chunk of wood struck him hard across the

back, slamming his shoulder onto the cabin stairs with the force of a freight train. He struggled to get out from underneath the debris as another explosion heaved from under the deck. Maxwell had it rigged perfectly. Water rushed in from the gaping hole in the hull. Trapped, Justin's foggy brain noted how weird it was to feel the intense heat from the flames at the same time as the frigid waters pooled around his waist.

A wave rocked the boat, and the weight came off his back. A little more alert thanks to the shock of the cold water, he realized it had lifted whatever had him pinned. He scrambled to climb the ruined stairs, feeling the sucking pull of the ocean threatening to drag him down with the yacht. Shedding his trench coat, he squeezed out of the collapsed cabin doorway to face a wall of flames rising between him and the safety of the dock. As he tried to calculate whether or not he could make the leap, the boat shifted violently, its death throes causing Justin to slip back toward the cabin he'd just escaped. He caught himself, his injured shoulder screaming in pain.

A small gap appeared in the dancing flames, and he knew it was now or never. He lurched through the glowing embers and crossed the slick, wet deck. Dozens of people lined the docks now, shouting and calling out to him, but his ears rang from the explosion. With the last of his strength, he threw himself off the side, hoping like hell he could swim far enough away from the sinking ship to avoid its pull.

Landing on his side like a ton of bricks, the shocking cold of the water took its toll on his battered body. He kicked as hard as he could, but the light of the surface pulled farther and farther away. Exhausted, he stopped kicking, promising himself he'd start swimming again as soon as his muscles stopped shaking.

As the light receded, there was a surge in the water near him, and then a swoosh as something pulled him up to break the surface of the water.

"Hey, dumbass," Dennis shouted in his ear as he struggled, with the help of a couple of cops he brought with him, to heave his body up onto the dock.

Groggy, he felt a slap across his face and then heard his partner's racking smoker's cough. "Don't make me give you that mouth-to-mouth shit." Justin's laugh convulsed into more of a gurgle as saltwater hurled from his lungs.

"Maxwell?" was the first thing he croaked out after getting air back into his lungs.

Dennis collapsed on the dock beside him and shook his head. "An explosion like that?" he panted. "His crispy ass is sitting at the bottom of the harbor."

Struggling to a sitting position, Justin ignored the rivulet of blood coursing down his face. "You dove in to rescue me?"

"More like a belly flop, but yeah, I guess I did." He pulled a damp package of cigarettes and his lighter out of his pocket with nonchalance that puzzled Justin, though admittedly this wasn't his brightest hour.

"I thought you didn't know how to swim?"

It was only then he noticed his partner's hands were shaking so badly he couldn't get the lighter's flame anywhere near the water-logged cancer stick. "Fuck. Now you tell me."

****

Viciously flipping through one of Lottie's vapid

fashion magazines, Emily glanced up as she entered the living room with a freshly brewed pot of tea.

"Easy on the magazines, dear."

Snorting in disgust, she tossed the glossy pages aside. "I wouldn't be so bored if I were in my own apartment. With my cat."

Lottie opened her mouth to argue when the tinny sounds of *Fly Me To The Moon* came from the doorbell. Both women jumped at the unexpected intrusion. "Should we call 911?" Lottie asked in a whisper.

"And report what, a food delivery at the wrong house?"

She pursed her lips, giving Emily a menacing glare. "Don't be an idiot," she hissed. "Someone tried to kill you last night."

"Not according to Detective Butler," she shot back, the rage at his betrayal boiling up anew.

Ignoring her, Lottie picked up the gun she'd retrieved from her bedroom when they first arrived.

"Do you even know how to fire that thing?" Emily asked, shocked that her friend would even own a weapon.

Lottie went through an elaborate check of the gun, making sure it was ready to fire. "The first rule my daddy taught me," she whispered, as if anyone at the front door could hear them through the house's thick stucco walls. "If you shoot 'em, be sure to drag 'em inside."

"Okay, what does that even mean?"

She stared at Emily as if she'd lost her mind. "That way, they're trespassing. It's self-defense." *Duh* was the unspoken ending of her sentence.

Lottie's husband, Spaulding, had insisted on

installing a state-of-the-art security system after a house in their posh neighborhood was broken into last year. It looked like tonight it was finally going to pay off. "Why don't we try seeing who it is first?"

After fumbling with the remote to make the security camera appear on her huge TV, both women were stunned to see Justin waiting patiently at her front door.

"Did you call him?" Emily snapped.

"He's just as much on my shit list as he is on yours. Is that a bandage on his head?"

She studied the image for a few moments, a maelstrom of emotions racing through her. Rage battled concern with the subtlety of Godzilla vs. Mothra, and she wasn't sure which one to root for. Lottie was right. There was a fresh bandage over a good-sized lump on his head. Before she could say anything, the doorbell rang again. He waved at the camera, giving his best winning smile.

"Asshole," Emily muttered. "Ignore him, he'll go away." *Men always do.*

She went back to not reading the magazine pages she was flipping, studiously not watching the security camera when Lottie muttered, "Is that a picture of Sam?"

Sure enough, he held his phone to the security camera, displaying a picture of Dennis Ames, holding her cat and offering him something in a fast-food wrapper. She was out the front door like a shot.

****

Justin was considering the painful option of getting down on his knees in front of the camera when Emily exploded out the front door. She shoved him so hard he had to bite back a yelp as pain sliced through his dislocated shoulder like a dull hatchet.

"Are you seriously holding my cat hostage, you...asshat!"

"What? No." Ignoring the pounding in his head, he amplified the wattage on what he hoped was a charming smile. "I wanted to show you Sam is in excellent hands. Your landlord couldn't keep him because of allergies, but weirdly enough, Dennis and the cat get along great."

"You couldn't have called me to tell me that?"

"I tried calling, sixteen times to be exact, but you wouldn't answer the phone."

Her expression changed from anger to suspicion as she sniffed the air and squinted at him. "Why do you smell like a fish fry?" She felt inside his borrowed puffy winter jacket, frowning. "And why are you all wet?" He saw her eyes shift to the bandage on his head and angled that side of his face away from her.

"It's a long story." He waved dismissively with his right hand, keeping his left one in the pocket of the puffy coat. He felt her scrutiny but plowed on. "The important thing is, I was wrong to assume you took those pills and I'm sorry. Really, really sorry."

"Wow, alert the media. The great Detective Butler admitted to being wrong." Her words were blunt, but her tone softened as she continued to study him.

"Emily," he started, trying to gather his thoughts, but the sight of her rattled him more than the explosion. He bowed his head as he continued, "I was angry because I thought you lied to me." He fumbled for a moment, trying to find the right words. "But I was also pissed off at myself for not being more careful."

"Careful? With what?"

He hesitated before raising his eyes to meet hers. "With you, with my heart, just…everything. I've never felt this unbalanced before, and I feel like I'm doing it all wrong."

"Ah," she said, drawing out the word as she nodded, her curls bobbing with the motion. "By careful, you mean guarded. So what changed your mind?"

"I realized I was being an idiot." He gave her a sheepish half grin, adding, "But I have to admit Dennis got me thinking when he discovered the drugs in your system were the exact match for the ones used to kill Ginger Mills."

Stunned, Emily hugged herself. "So poor Ginger really was murdered. But what's the connection? Why would the same person be after me?"

"I don't know, but I want someone guarding you around the clock until we find them." He halted the objection he saw coming, putting his right hand up like a traffic cop. "I'll make sure they're as subtle as possible; you won't even notice they're around."

"Except for the blue uniforms in the middle of the barn aisle? How's that going to work?"

"I'll hire a private security detail myself if I can't arrange something through the department."

Stepping closer, she gazed up into his eyes. "If I have to have someone around me day and night, I'd rather it was you."

"No way, absolutely not," he protested. "I become a blundering idiot where you're concerned. If it weren't for Dennis, I'd have missed the link to the old murder entirely. The killer could have…"

Could have come back to finish the job, he thought,

but didn't dare say. He'd jumped to the wrong conclusion because his emotions had clouded his judgment, and he was determined not to let it happen again.

"You made a mistake. One I'm going to continue to make you pay for," she noted with a hint of a smile. "But one you're not likely to make again. I trust you with my life unless there's another reason you feel you're not up to it?"

He didn't trust himself to voice a response. All the horrors of the night disappeared as she reached up to stroke his cheek. And then she put her hand on his left shoulder and squeezed. Fireworks of pain exploded, nearly sending him to his knees. "Poor baby," she said, sounding unsympathetic. "Shoulder or collarbone?"

"Separated shoulder," he hissed through gritted teeth. "How did you know?"

"I've been riding horses too long not to recognize someone nursing an arm. Is the sling you're supposed to be wearing in the car?"

Sheepishly, he pulled the sling from his coat pocket. With gentle care, she slid his arm through the black mesh material and put the padded strap around his neck. "And a concussion too, judging from the bump on your head."

"I didn't want to worry you. Or play on your sympathies."

Emily dropped her forehead to his good shoulder. "It wasn't until I saw you at the door that I realized how much I care about you."

He stroked her cheek with his thumb and silently vowed to protect her from whoever was trying to kill her, no matter what the cost.

Chapter Thirty-Three

Thank God Emily agreed to take Lottie's new truck to Temecula for the show at Kinsale Downs. As sweet a ride as it was, with seat heaters *and* coolers, a sunroof, Wi-Fi and every other option in the book, Justin's shoulder was still on fire. The three-hour trip in Ellie May, with her rock-hard suspension and springs in all the wrong places, would have had him crying like a baby.

Now, he sat on a large rectangle of plastic-wrapped wood shavings, propped against the cinderblock barn wall, bored to tears. Emily ordered him to stay there like an errant child while she, Lottie, and Darian sliced open matching rectangles and spread the shavings in the stalls as bedding for the horses.

Nothing made a man feel more useless than watching his girlfriend struggle with bales of hay weighing roughly twice her mass while he sat there and watched. Nothing except searching for the person who tried to kill her and coming up empty-handed. It had been two weeks since the attempt on her life and he still had no suspect. He and Dennis were also no closer to figuring out if Maxwell had help from inside the cop shop to arrange the hit on Frankie Gillette, and that worried him.

It had been a fruitless two weeks in other areas as

well. Between his separated shoulder and her intense focus to prepare for this show, they had yet to consummate their relationship. God knows it's not like they didn't try. Last night, she'd invited him to spend the night at her place to make their ungodly departure at five in the morning a little easier to bear. He'd thought it would be *the* night and prepared a candlelit dinner. Shrugging off the sling, he'd met her at the door with a single, long-stem red rose—a gimmick that always worked with women in the past.

She wearily stumbled to the shower, sweaty, despite the cool March air, from packing the trailer with everything they'd need for the weekend. Trying to be a good sport, she ate half her dinner and was out like a light.

Stuck behind a desk because of his injury, he continued to work the leads on Pam's killer. It had to be the same person who had attacked Emily, the coincidence was too strong. It's too bad the evidence wasn't. Even the murder weapon, the missing stabilizer bar, didn't narrow down the suspects.

Testing the locked trailer door where the bars were stored proved that anyone with a modicum of determination could open it. And trying to identify where the killer got the horse tranquilizer to kill Ridley had so far proven impossible. Which left him here, sitting uselessly on his ass while any of the two hundred competitors or spectators now flooding the show grounds could be the killer planning their next move. And the odds were stacked in their favor. This time, they might finish the job.

****

Arriving at the competition was Emily's favorite

part of any event. Electricity buzzed in the air as folks pulled in with their trailers and unloaded horses and equipment before organizing their little gypsy camps where friends could catch up, exchange news, and gossip over a variety of adult beverages.

The barns at events were nothing like the ones at hunter shows back home at the Equestrian Center. The fun and laughter at events would be frowned on as gauche by the hunter folks, where the aisles were assembled with the precision of a military operation and slightly less sense of humor. It scared her a little to see more and more of the hunter-type show drapes popping up in event barn aisles, but she had to admit the colorful tents and bunting added to the carnival atmosphere.

She glanced over at Justin, who was not so patiently waiting while the three women spread the shavings in the stalls. Thank God Lottie found a groom she trusted to take care of the horses they'd left at home. She didn't know what she'd do without her. And she could see Lottie enjoyed bossing Darian around, commanding her to get hay for the horses and help fill the water buckets. Before she could stop him, Justin sprang to his feet and turned the spigot on.

He answered her glare with a disarming smile. "Come on, I'm not going to hurt myself turning on a faucet."

"All right." She relented, giving him a kiss before leaving to pull the horses out of the trailer. "But we had an agreement, so nothing more physical than that."

Despite the amount of work they needed to get done, she was glad she'd made it a condition of him coming along that he couldn't lift a single solitary finger to help. The last thing she needed was to worry about him. She had enough on her hands between her own show nerves and Darian's.

The chill Emily felt when they realized someone had made an attempt on her life—for possibly the second time—was always at the edge of her thoughts. Having Justin around these past two weeks had been nice, but he'd made her feel guarded, not safe. Here, at the show, she felt protected. Patting Reese as she put him in his stall, it was like she'd come home.

"Hope your lovely smile is meant for me," Dearg McGregor's brogue boomed across the show barn.

Her smile broadened as she saw him limping toward her, one arm restricted by an elaborate brace and his battered face telling the story of his unsuccessful ride at Stormgrove. The reminder of how things can go wrong even for the best of them sent an icy finger of fear down her spine. Instead of caving to it, she took the advice from an old song and shook it off as she made her way toward him. When he wrapped his good arm around her, a rude chortle sounded behind them.

"McGregor." Justin's greeting was curt as he moved to her side.

"Detective," the Scot replied, giving Emily's shoulders a final squeeze before releasing her. "I heard you got hurt a couple of weeks ago. Separated your shoulder, was it?" He clucked sympathetically. "You're right to be careful with those things. I did that once in the first half of a rugby match. Only scored two tries in the second half."

"Guess you heard wrong, I'm fine." Justin put his arm possessively around Emily. His tiny gasp of pain as he raised his arm made her roll her eyes. *Men are idiots.*

"Oh yeah, I can see that." He smirked and gave Justin a light pat on his wounded shoulder. "I envy you. The doc says my broken shoulder will take a few more weeks to heal."

Her dark vision of spending the next four days refereeing these two was shattered by the screech of a familiar voice. "Dear-rag," Kate called out in an annoying singsong patter, "you almost lost me, you naughty boy."

Her quarry hid behind Emily and Justin as Kate's Panama hat with attached blonde wig bobbed into view, weaving through the crowded barn aisle. A small group of giggling Dearg groupies trailed behind her.

"Christ," he muttered, "that crazy bitch has been following me since I left L.A."

"So this is where they put you, Emily." Kate's bright tone contrasted with her pained frown. "I searched all over the main barn where they always stable my horses and here you are, up in the cheap seats." She sneered at the cobweb-strewn, cinderblock tack room Emily had been given. "This is nice too, I guess."

A small geyser of water came from out of nowhere, spraying Kate's feet and dotting her pants with mud. "Oh my gosh, I'm so sorry. I was filling water buckets and didn't see you there," Lottie chirped as she turned off the hose nozzle. Giving Reese a big pat as she left his stall, she added, "So who is in your usual spot since you don't have any horses sound enough to compete?"

Emily gave a silent prayer of thanks for her friend. Barn assignments aren't doled out based on how good you were, but for whatever reason, clearly Kate felt the need to put her down.

Picking a lone piece of hay off her impossibly clean shirt, Lottie kept pushing. "All kidding aside, Kate, what are you doing here?"

Although she tried her best to pull off an innocent expression, it came off more like she was suffering from gas and exclaimed a little too loudly, "I'm here to give my friend moral support, of course." She leaned closer to Emily, lowering her voice to a conspiratorial stage whisper. "I thought you might be a little overwhelmed, seeing as it's your first show since your accident."

In the past, a remark like that would have sent her running to the pill bottle, but today those thoughtless barbs had lost their power. It was nice to have Justin step closer, protectively edging between her and Kate, but she smiled as she realized it wasn't necessary.

She looked at Reese and knew the bond of mutual trust they'd developed since that disastrous day at the clinic had restored her confidence in herself. She was stronger and more capable than she had been in a very long time.

"Thanks, I appreciate the offer, but I'm fine." She saw Kate's eyes narrow a fraction, as if she were trying to see if she was telling the truth, but even Kate's doubts didn't bother her anymore. At least, not enough to spoil her mood.

Turning to Dearg, she bubbled over with a mixture of excitement and nervous anticipation. "What do you say, coach? You ready to give me a lesson before the ring gets too crowded?"

His million-watt smile in response made the groupies practically swoon. Sexy as he was, Emily was pretty sure the butterflies in her stomach had more to do with Reese than him. She grinned, reminding herself these butterflies were the good, thrill-seeker kind of butterflies that made the challenge of riding so damn much fun.

****

"Darlin', you've got a lovely arse, but there's no need to wave it around in the air. Try sitting in the saddle, yeah?"

Justin watched with clenched teeth, wondering who frustrated him more—that arrogant bastard McGregor or Emily. Her fiercely competitive grimace cracked just a smidge as a hint of a smile shone through. A smile. If he'd made a comment like that, she'd have slapped him silly. And rightfully so. It's amazing what you can get away with saying as long as you do it in a Scots brogue.

"There, feel that?" the Scot growled and Emily, clearly exhausted, could only muster a nod. "That's all you need to do to put his tail in the water. Yessssss," he encouraged, "loosen your hips. Now tuck his right hindquarter underneath him more."

A master in multiple martial arts, Justin couldn't imagine how you control one-quarter of a thirteen-hundred-pound animal's body with a slight shift of your own. Especially when you're as tiny as Emily, but damned if something he couldn't quite put his finger on improved about the way the horse moved.

"Okay, let's see a transition to the trot."

The horse switched from the canter to the trot in what seemed to Justin to be a perfectly reasonable manner, but from the way she scowled, the transition was far from perfect.

"Emily, darlin', come over here for a second." Dearg beckoned from his perch on the fence rail. The minions scattered below him twittered until he cocked a menacing eyebrow at them.

Assuming they were simply taking a much-needed break after twenty-minutes of riding in this heat, wind, and dust-filled hell, Justin reached for the bottle of water he brought from the barn for her. He stopped when he noticed the way everyone in the arena turned their heads in any direction other than where she was conferring with her coach.

"Oh dear, Emily must be doing something very bad if she's been called over by the teacher." Lottie clucked as she approached, holding two large, red plastic cups in her hands. She gave one to Justin as she joined him on the rustic wooden bench on the small rise above the arena. "It's gin and tonic," she explained as he sniffed his cup. "Good for the muscles. Don't worry, I figured you for one of those *my body is my temple* types and made yours ridiculously weak."

The juniper smell of the gin hit him hard, but it might be just the lime floating on top. He was about to take a sip when Lottie did a spit take next to him. "*Blyck*." Her face screwed up like she'd taken a bite from a lemon. "Whoops," she said and switched cups. "Too much tonic water. This one's yours."

He glanced at the cup in his hands, sporting a bright red lipstick mark. Turning the cup around, he took a sip from the opposite side and choked. If that was her idea of a weak drink, he'd hate to taste how strong hers was.

"How is she supposed to control just one leg of the horse?" Taking another sip, he understood what she meant about tonic being good for the muscles. His jaws unclenched for the first time since McGregor arrived.

"Honey, if I knew that, I'd be out there riding my own horse. It takes a certain level of rider to have so much control, and she's out there, not sitting here next to you, relaxing with a drink."

Although they were too far away to catch what McGregor said, he caught snippets like, "Wrap your lovely thighs around him," and, "Pull those abs into your spine." When he reached out with his good hand to guide her abs, Justin growled.

"Easy there, tiger, he's simply doing his job."

She was right, of course, but it didn't keep him from feeling powerless and, yes, jealous. "No other trainer seems compelled to maul their students."

"And you wonder why Dearg has all these groupies?" Lottie tsked. "Proof that even handsome detectives can be thick as bricks. It's not only because he's smoking hot, although that certainly helps. He makes you feel special while giving you the tools to be a better rider. A lot of trainers rely on making a person feel like crap. Pamela Yates certainly did."

This morning's brief scene set off alarm bells he couldn't seem to shut off. "Does Kate?"

Snorting rudely, she quipped, "Does a bear poop in the woods? At least Pam had two or three actual pearls of wisdom to throw in the mix once in a while. Kate's just an idiot."

"Does she ever take it beyond mind-screwing other riders?"

"You caught the way she glowered at Emily this morning, too?" She nodded. "There've been rumors about her being aggressive, but I'm sure you've learned by now about barn gossip. Don't worry, I've got plans to keep her away from Emily. If she wants to be helpful, I'll find plenty for her to do."

"There," McGregor boomed. "Now that's a canter you can do anything with."

Emily's head bobbed in agreement, glowing with satisfaction under all that sweat and dirt. Although Justin couldn't say exactly why, she and the horse now exuded elegance, surpassing any of the other horse and rider combinations.

My girlfriend kicks ass, he thought with deep satisfaction.

McGregor apparently agreed as he added, "That's the canter that's going to put you in first place tomorrow after dressage."

All the riders who barely hid their smirks before saw Emily in a new light. Okay, maybe he wouldn't have to beat the crap out of McGregor for embarrassing her after all.

Chapter Thirty-Four

After a long, hot shower, Emily finally felt human. Between setting up the barn, riding Reese, and coaching Darian, topped off with feeding the horses, she had the dust of Kinsale embedded in places it should never go. And her hair had smelled disgusting after baking under her helmet all day. It took three shampoos, rinses, and repeats to feel clean again. Now in her flannel PJ bottoms and tank top emblazoned with *Boss Mare*—a Christmas gift from Lottie—she crawled into bed and turned on the TV. Hopefully, a moronic reality show would put her to sleep before her show nerves set in.

It felt weird not sharing a room with anyone else. Usually at shows, they all bunked together at a cheap hotel to keep everyone's costs down. Clearly from the way she groused about the expense of paying for her own room over dinner, Darian thought they were going to follow their usual routine.

Lottie had been adamant they stay at the swanky Lakeview Resort, insisting Emily get her own room so she could get some proper rest. Justin had been strangely silent on the matter. She was appreciative he understood this wasn't a vacation where they could hook up, but she was a little disappointed he didn't suggest sharing a room. Or a bed.

Ugh. Showing was hard enough. Why was she adding drama on top of it?

A knock at the door interrupted her fretting. She lurched stiffly out of bed, her muscles letting the effects of the day's work be known loud and clear. If this was Darian whining about the room again, she'd kill her. Yanking the door open, she found Justin standing there barefoot in a T-shirt and sweatpants. Grinning like an idiot, he had a small, bright blue bottle in one hand and a candle that exuded a fresh grassy scent in the other. He greeted her with a wordless kiss on the cheek as he sauntered into her room.

How can a man be so hot in expensive suits and even hotter in baggy sweats and a ratty old t-shirt? "What are you doing here?"

"Honey, I came to the show with you, remember? I was the guy who sat on his ass, watching you work all day because you wouldn't let me help. Or do you open your door to every guy who can turn a spigot?" He raised his eyebrows in a failed attempt to imitate Groucho Marx. It was still cute.

"Yes, I get what you're doing in Temecula, idiot." She shoved him playfully, laughing at his lame joke. "I meant, what are you doing in my room? I thought we discussed the whole show nerves thing, my need to focus, et cetera, et cetera?"

"Swear to God, I only came over to give you a massage. This stuff," he held up the blue bottle, "is amazing. It'll loosen those tense muscles in no time. And this," he said, indicating the candle, "is an aroma therapy candle to calm your nerves."

"Massage oil and aroma therapy?" Emily chuckled. "How New Age of you."

"You should see my crystal collection. Look, I saw you were limping when we left the restaurant tonight, and I think I can help."

"What about your separated shoulder?"

"No problem. I studied Swedish massage for three months in—"

"Sweden, of course," she remarked dryly.

"No, from a woman in Tokyo who also taught me Shiatsu. Even with just one hand, I can work wonders with a blend of the two I call Swiatsu." She made a scoffing sound that he ignored. "I helped with your back before, remember?"

"I don't know." Massages never did much for her, but his acupressure had made a real difference.

"It'll help your dressage score."

"Look at you, learning all the lingo."

She was tempted. Especially if a massage really would loosen her up for dressage, where her stiffness would make Reese tense and cost them precious points. Just because his aftershave smelled so damn good she'd enjoy every minute didn't make it less therapeutic, right?

"Oh fine, have it your way," she groaned as she flopped face down on the bed. "Massage away."

"Uh, no," he declared as he lit the candle. "We need less clothing between your wall of muscles and my magic hand."

"I should have known this was a scam to get me naked."

He sat on the bed behind her and started massaging her neck. "Do I really need a scam to get you naked?" His breath played on the back of her neck, making her skin tingle.

She turned toward him, biting her lower lip as if to keep it from crossing the mere inches separating them.

"No funny business, right?"

"Scout's honor."

After a moment of indecision, she nodded her head. "Okay, but you have to go into the bathroom while I undress."

"What are you, ten?" Justin grinned and turned his back. "Promise, I won't peek."

With a huff, she stripped everything off in record time and hopped between the crisp sheets. Lying face down on the bed, she mumbled into the pillow, "Okay, I'm as ready as I'll ever be."

Instead of going to her, Justin turned off most of the lights, the semi-darkness lit by the glow of the candle. "The dimmer lighting will help you relax," he murmured, "and keep me from being blinded by the absurd whiteness of your skin. You horse people need to take a day off once in a while and go to the beach, so the rest of your body matches your arms."

Giggling into her pillow, she had to admit he was right.

True to his word, he took a very businesslike approach to her massage. He pulled the top sheet away to expose her legs, stopping halfway up her thighs. "I'll start with something easy, okay?" Without waiting for her answer, he took her lower leg in his hand and gently kneaded her foot and calf muscles. Carefully, he bent her leg at the knee, working his way down her leg.

"Stop helping me and relax," he growled.

"I am relaxed."

"Oh, really?" He let go of her leg, and the limb stayed rigidly up in the air. "That should have flopped back down on the bed if you were relaxed."

Emily pushed herself to a sitting position,

wrapping the sheet around her. "Okay, this was not a good idea."

"Don't be such a baby," he teased, softly pushing her back on the bed. "Let's get to the heart of the problem, shall we?"

After re-covering her legs, he pulled the sheet down to expose her back, stopping just below the top of her butt cheeks. His caress set off a reaction that both embarrassed and delighted her. Oh, this was such a bad idea, and she was so glad she'd agreed to it.

He knelt on the bed over her, making sure his weight never touched her. Eyes closed, she heard the *splurt* of massage oil being squeezed out and warmed up by his hands briskly rubbing together. When he put his hand on her shoulder blades, she trembled as the oil and the heat of his strong fingers came in contact with her skin. Soon the painful knots melted under his thumb. Then she felt him stop for a moment amid the rustle of cloth.

"What are you doing now?" She opened her eyes and turned her head to see him toss his shirt on the floor. Her mouth gaped open. She'd felt his muscles before, but good Lord, the man had washboard abs.

"Relax," he replied in a calm, soothing tone. "As hard as you worked to build these muscles, I have to work twice as hard to loosen them up. You don't want me dripping sweat all over your back, do you?"

She was naked under a thin sheet and he, half-naked and sweaty, was straddling her. Relax? He had to be joking. She should protest, should call a halt to the massage now, but every nerve ending in her body purred with pleasure. Closing her eyes again, she felt his thumb making circles over the surgical scar on the back of her neck and immediately tensed. Few people had ever seen the ugliness of her scar, and she desperately wished he hadn't been one of them.

Without a word, he leaned over and kissed her scar, starting at the bottom and sensuously working his way to the top. Then he returned to the serious work of massaging his way to her lower back. His powerful hand eased the tensions of the day out of that sensitive, tight area right below her waist. A moan of pleasure escaped her lips.

As he curled his hand around her hips, she instinctively ground into his strong fingers. All the need and desire building since their first kiss was unleashed. It had been too long, and if she'd learned nothing else from Pam's death it was that life could be tragically short. Sliding her hand underneath her body, she put it on top of his and guided him to the place where she really wanted to be touched, gasping as her body responded.

He kissed her scar again, the flicking of his tongue against her skin releasing spontaneous shudders. With a husky purr, she turned over to face him, trapped between his thighs. She stroked his face once before sinking her fingers into his hair and pulling him into a passionate kiss. His body responded, confirming he wanted her as much as she wanted him, but he broke off the kiss, holding her hand in his.

"Are you sure this is what you want?" he asked, his brows furrowed. Unable to speak, she nodded eagerly, sealing the deal by nipping his lower lip between her teeth. He responded by exploring her curves with his hand and mouth, eliciting gasps of pleasure with every touch.

Doing some exploring herself, her belly fluttered in delight as she caressed his back and found his firm ass. Urgently, she tugged at the waistband of his sweatpants and was pleased to discover he had gone commando. Now it was his turn to quiver as she touched him. Quickly shedding his pants along with the tangle of sheets, he removed all barriers between them.

She opened her legs for him, greedy for him to be inside her. But Justin had other plans and tortured her for what seemed like forever, teasing her with touches and kisses, driving her to what she thought was the height of pleasure until he proved her wrong, and took her even higher.

Chapter Thirty-Five

The show nerves Emily chased away last night in Justin's arms reappeared with a vengeance as soon as the morning chores were completed. Muck out stalls, fill water buckets, and run to the bathroom to vomit—what a lovely way to start the day. The only thing that calmed the jittery butterflies was repeating the mantra, *it's only dressage*.

No one ever died during dressage, right?

That particular thought brought little comfort as she changed into her show clothes in the horse trailer's cramped dressing room. Her hands were trembling already, which made buttoning her snowy white shirt next to impossible. Who thought a white shirt and white pants were a good idea? Insecurity about her close resemblance to a giant marshmallow made her empty stomach churn even more.

She forced herself to focus on the long, involved dressage test she would ride in a little over an hour. Remembering a show jump course was a snap compared to visualizing all the circles and transitions a dressage test called for. She'd worked long and hard at memorizing it and spent a good deal of the time this morning tracing the test pattern over and over again on Justin's chest. The error of her method, however, was obvious now. Every time she tried to go over the test in her mind, all she saw was his naked body. Great.

Sexual tension on top of show nerves. What a stellar combination.

A crisp knock rattled the thin, metal door of the dressing room, startling her from her reverie. Assuming it was Justin back from the meaningless errand she'd sent him on to get rid of him, she opened the door without bothering to close her shirt.

"I'd recommend something lacier than a sports bra if you're trying to impress the judges with cleavage," Dearg McGregor said with a grin.

She mumbled an apology, hastily buttoning her shirt and tucking it into her breeches before turning back to face him. He offered her a banana and a power bar with his unfettered hand. The thought of consuming either one made her want to hurl again.

"God, no. Thanks for the thought," she blurted as she wrestled with her stock tie. Trying to re-assemble this Gordian knot of a stupid tie was a task she could usually master. Today, the long cloth flapped in her shaking hands like a demented bird.

"Here, let me help." He set down his offerings and eased behind her in the tiny room with surprising grace for a man with such broad shoulders and one arm lashed tight against his body. He wrapped his good arm around her to take hold of one end of the stock tie and attempted to slip the other out of the restrictive brace, trying to hide his painful grimace behind a smirk. The failure was epic, and he gave up as their eyes met in the minuscule warped mirror on the trailer wall.

"Looks like we're going to have to do this together." Their hands brushed as she took the other end of the stock tie and followed his lead to create a decent knot. She pinned the tie in place, but he stayed where he was, one arm draped casually around her.

"Where's the cop?" He breathed in her ear, his lips brushing her cheek.

"I sent him off to get some tea. It's too hard to focus when he's around."

"But you can with me?" He feigned being wounded. "I must work on that."

At least she thought he was faking it, but for a moment, his pout seemed real. That's when the idea struck her with a giddy clarity that his lips did nothing for her anymore. A few weeks ago, her knees had gone weak at his touch, but now she felt nothing except the warm affection for a friend. Good Lord, she really was in love with Justin.

She wasn't in the habit of sleeping with just anyone, but she wasn't sure until this second how deep her feelings for him really ran. After all, it had been a long time since she'd been with a man. It might have been hormones talking, but it seemed she had fallen hard. Instead of feeling hopeless and terrified, like when she'd fallen in love with Nick as a teenager, she felt like anything was possible.

For another two seconds at least, until the door flew open and there stood Justin with a cup of steaming hot tea in his hand. "Three sugars, stirred, not—oh."

He glowered at Dearg and handed her the Styrofoam cup. Clumsily extricating herself from the Scot's embrace, she gave him the tea and handed Justin her black dressage coat to let him help her put it on.

"You're going to need more than bloody tea before you get on the horse." Dearg again offered the banana and power bar. "Reese is good, but he can't do it alone, and you will be useless without some fuel in the tank."

She choked down the banana to avoid any more conversation, checked her watch, and considered throwing up again but it was too late. Time to go.

****

To paraphrase the old saying about art, Justin didn't know what he was looking for when he watched Emily ride her dressage test, but he knew what he liked. She gave the horse invisible cues, making the whole dance appear to be his idea. The two of them outshone every other horse and rider combination as far as he was concerned, and the huge grins on Team Emily's faces said they agreed. The cheering and celebrating went on all the way back to the barn aisle as Emily, Lottie, McGregor, and Darian kept talking over one another, reliving every tiny detail of the ride.

Bringing up the rear, Kate worked hard to give the appearance of being happy. Justin wasn't sure which came off as less authentic, her forced smile or her wig. Today, she had styled it in a massive ponytail sprouting out of the back of a baseball cap. There was an odd cartoon character on the cap, but he tried to not peer at it too closely for fear she'd misconstrue the attention as him hitting on her.

The crew buzzed around the horse like little worker bees, stripping off his saddle, pad, and bridle. "You've got to warm Darian up in twenty minutes," Lottie reminded Emily.

"I know, I know," she replied. "I'm just going to put this stuff away and change clothes."

"Here, let me help." Justin stepped in front of McGregor and, ignoring the white-hot pain lancing through his shoulder, grabbed her saddle before the Scot could get there.

The scowls the two men exchanged didn't go unnoticed by Lottie. "You," she barked at McGregor in a commanding tone as she grabbed his good arm, "help me hose Reese off." Under her breath, she added, "A good dunk wouldn't hurt you either." Gold medalist or not, she thrust a bucket with a sponge and liniment at him and dragged him off to the wash racks.

"Oh, Kate," Emily exclaimed, "I can't believe I forgot. I've got a thumb drive with a video of you that I found in Pamela's trunk. Here, let me—"

Justin gently but firmly put his hand on her back and guided her into the tack room. "We'll get it for you later," he declared as he closed the tack room door in Kate's puzzled face.

Emily cocked an amused eyebrow at him and smiled as she sat on the trunk, stretching her legs out in front of her. "I'm not sure what you've got in mind, buster, but these boots have gotta come off before anything else does."

"No problem, what do I do?"

"Turn around," she directed with a smirk. With his back to her, she put one booted calf between his legs and the sole of the other boot on his butt. "Pull. But gently," she squealed as he pulled with so much enthusiasm, he nearly yanked her off the trunk.

"These are so tight," he complained. *How on Earth could anyone wear something like this?*

"That's why most people wear boots with zippers, but I'm an old-fashioned kind of girl. Pull a little more while I wiggle my foot."

The boot gave with a sudden slip, and he almost landed on his face once there was no more resistance. He dropped the empty boot as she raised her other leg.

He had this drill down now, no problem. Until she pressed her shoeless foot on his butt. "What the—what are you doing with your foot?" Laughing at the ridiculousness of his position, he found it hard to focus on removing the other boot once she wiggled her toes in increasingly sensitive areas. The whole situation spiraled until they were both collapsed on the tack trunk and laughter became hungry kisses.

****

Yesterday's carnival atmosphere had amped up into a full-blown three-ring circus by the time Darian finished her ride. The smells of hamburgers and chicken from the massive grills permeated the air. The barn aisles were crowded with horses being walked and riders either celebrating or lamenting the day. There were shouts of friendly banter and congratulations as Emily and company hurried to the show office. News had spread fast—the scores were posted, and she was in first place with a solid lead. The scores for Darian's class weren't up yet.

"Oh my God, I don't want to know my scores. No, wait, you can tell me the score, but I don't want to read the judge's comments on the test," the woman babbled on in an unstoppable loop. "I know they're terrible. Why did I even enter?"

"You did great. It doesn't matter what the score is, you had your best ride yet, and that's what counts." Emily's words should have been comforting the first three times she said them. If they didn't work this time, Justin would have no choice but to shoot her. If only he'd brought his gun.

Apparently, Lottie shared his feelings. As the official bartender, once they returned to the barn she poured herself a healthy dollop of gin, adding the tonic as almost an afterthought. The rest she poured with a lighter hand, and Emily's cup contained only tonic. She pulled a disgruntled face, but Lottie stood firm. Her professional supplies didn't end at the lime squeezer and chilled gin. Out of what seemed like thin air, she pulled out a selection of fine cheeses, smoked meats, bread, and all the makings of a gourmet picnic. She was clearly not a woman who settled for roughing it. They all dug in, pouncing on the spread like vultures.

"All right, are you ladies ready for a course walk?" McGregor asked after they'd eaten their fill. His subtle exclusion of Justin in the invitation amused the detective. Let him try to stop him.

Surprisingly, it was Emily who asked him to stay behind. "Remember, I told you about walking the course, so we know how to ride it? It's better if the first time is just with Dearg to help me focus. You'd be super bored with all the talk about shadows and adding extra leg if he doesn't like water—"

"That means make the horse go." Kate's bitchy explanation pleased him. Thankfully, he'd been taken off her hit list, unlike McGregor, who couldn't even reach for a piece of cheese without the woman crowding the rest of them to get it for him. Being a rock star must suck, but he had a hard time feeling sorry for the guy.

"Thanks, I figured that out for myself. And I'm still walking it with you." He wasn't about to let her leave his sight until they caught the killer.

The chirp of his cell phone interrupted Emily's protest and earned him a glare from McGregor. "The first rule is no phones. A rider once missed a jump because they were talking on their phone during their walk and forgot it was part of the course."

"Wasn't that you at Three Pines?" Lottie asked mischievously.

He bellowed a laugh, but Justin missed the rest of the conversation, moving away from the group to take the call.

"So how's it going, stable boy?" Wry amusement dripped from Dennis's greeting.

Clearly, he wasn't getting a break today from any quarter. "Did you call for a reason or just to be an ass?"

"Little of both, actually. I'm calling to pass along an urgent message from the animal psychic."

He groaned. The twitters of laughter from the cops at the other end of the phone came through loud and clear. "You told the whole bull pen, didn't you?"

"Had to, partner. She called to report a threat against an officer. The horse she talked to overheard plans to hurt you as well as Emily at the show."

He hesitated, knowing the rash of shit he was going to get, but he had to ask. "She didn't give you any other information, did she? Like a time and place?"

Guffaws of laughter exploded at the other end. That little shit had him on speakerphone. When he got back, separated shoulder or not, he'd beat the stuffing out of him.

"No, sorry, nothing like that. Although she mentioned a bear on a rocking horse, so we put a BOLO out for Smokey the Bear." His amusement faded, however, as he took the phone off speaker. "Hey, someone wants to kill Emily and you keep screwing them up. They've gotta' be desperate by now, and I doubt all your kung fu shit's going to do you much good with only one working arm."

"Thanks, you're filling me with all kinds of confidence."

"I'm just saying, watch your back since I'm not there to do it for you."

As his partner's warning rang in his ears, Justin worried less about his back—and more about Emily's.

Chapter Thirty-Six

The next morning, the barn aisles buzzed with activity as riders, or their friends, mucked out stalls, fed and walked their horses, or readied their tack and riding attire for the long day ahead. Shouts of encouragement, or advice from those already finished with their course, rang throughout the barn.

From his perch on extra bales of shavings, Justin felt the excitement crackle in the air. Their little group had been there since six that morning getting both horses ready for the day. As he rolled his shoulder, trying to ease the stiffness, McGregor sauntered up, designer coffee in hand, smirk on his face.

"Sleep well, officer?"

If it wasn't for his arrogance, Justin might not have been pushed to answer as he rose. "Yes, *we* did."

The Scot's smile faltered momentarily. "Two nights in a row. Impressive."

"What's that supposed to mean?" He knew his buttons were being pushed, but he couldn't help it.

"I recognize your type," McGregor sniped. "You want what you can't have. Once you've got it, you're on to your next conquest while she's left picking up the pieces." The smirk returned full force. "Fortunately, I'll be there to help."

The words too closely echoed what Dennis had told him, that he moved on once a relationship got

329

serious. "Big talk. If you weren't already in a brace, I'd pop you one right in the—"

"Give it your best shot, princess. Unless your little boo-boo is fashing you too much."

"Enough." Lottie's snarled command took both men by surprise. The vehemence carried the sting of a slap; both men took a step back.

"This is a barn, in case you haven't noticed. Half open doors everywhere and lots of ears around every corner. The last thing Emily needs today is this load of crap from you two dogs in heat." Lottie slammed open the metal door to the cinder block tack room. "And yes, I'm aware it's female dogs that go into heat, but I'm so damn mad, that's the first thing that came to mind."

She yanked out a little step stool they used as another mounting block and pushed it at McGregor. "I can see we're going to have to separate you two. Scotty, take this around the corner to Emily so Darian can get on her horse. Go to the arena with them in case she needs any help." She turned to Justin, exasperation written across her face. "Someone has to get Reese ready for Emily and lead him to the arena so she can get on as soon as Darian's finished."

"Oh, I can help. Let me get him ready," Kate offered with giddy excitement as she rushed over to them. Oddly, she and the cartoon teddy bear on her baseball cap wore matching ridiculous grins. "It's the least I can do for poor Emily."

Justin saw neither of the choices appealed to Lottie, but after mulling it over, she agreed. "At least it'll keep you out of *poor* Emily's way and frees me to give her moral support."

She swung back to Justin. "That leaves you with

the all-important task of documenting Darian's round, so be sure to bring your phone." Wagging her finger, she gave the two men a steely stare. "The two of you behave, or I swear I will beat you myself. Let's go."

****

Darian was already in the crowded warm-up arena by the time Lottie and Justin joined Emily and McGregor at the rail. Riders moved in every direction, turning in front of each other to take one of the three jumps set side-by-side in the middle of the arena. It boggled Justin's mind how they didn't crash into one another.

"Dammit," Emily exclaimed. "Darian isn't wearing her medical armband. How did I forget that?"

"It's her responsibility, dear," Lottie grumped.

"I'll get it," Justin volunteered, eager to take whatever stress he could off Emily.

With a glance at her watch, Lottie shook her head. "It'll take too long to explain what you're looking for. Dearg, be a love and go back to the tack room and get her armband, will you?"

"Oh sure, send the cripple back to the barn," McGregor groused, and jutted his chin at Justin. "He volunteered, let him go get it,"

"First, it's your shoulder that's broken, not your legs," Lottie growled. "Second, he doesn't know what a medical armband looks like or where it is. You do. Third, she can't go in the arena without it, so quit your whining and move."

Throwing his good arm up in surrender, he backed away. "Okay. How many rounds before she goes in?"

"Five, which gives you just enough time to make it if you hurry. Scoot!"

****

Out of breath from having to jog up the hill to their barn, Dearg stumbled into the tack room, swearing for the hundredth time to quit smoking. The small plastic armband was right where he'd seen it last—hiding in plain sight on top of Darian's show kit. The woman must be blind to have missed it. Turning to leave, he noticed Kate bent over Emily's saddle.

He tossed her a casual greeting and was almost out the door when he stopped. "What are you doing there, Kate?"

She had the saddle flipped upside down, diligently working at something hidden deep underneath the flap. It wasn't until she turned toward him that he saw the mutilated billet strap in one hand and a six-inch knife in the other.

"I don't suppose you'd believe me if I told you I was cleaning her saddle?"

The wicked grin on her face should have clued him in as to how dangerous she was, but he figured it out a moment too late. "You crazy bitch." He clumsily pulled out his mobile and punched the buttons with his left hand, "I'm sure the good detective would be happy to know—"

He never got to finish the sentence. He heard more than felt the knife pierce his lung when a curious wheezing sound escaped with every breath. He was sure the stab wound would hurt like a motherfucker once the shock wore off. If he lived that long.

Kate wrapped her stout arm around him. Agonizing pain exploded as his not quite healed broken bones bent to the pressure. She dug the knife in deeper and twisted before ripping it back out.

He'd punctured a lung in a riding accident before and had been able to cope, but his body was still fighting to heal from the recent fall. He wobbled for a moment before collapsing to the cold, concrete floor of the tack room.

Kate bent to his face, her lips brushing his cheek as she whispered, "I really am sorry it was you and not the cop." Pushing him aside, she took his mobile and smashed it under the heel of her boot. She turned and rummaged for a moment in the tack trunk before emerging with a victorious grin, tucking a thumb drive inside her coat pocket. She was halfway to the door before she came back and snatched the armband out of his hand. "Otherwise, they might come searching for this and find you much too soon."

He gritted his jaw in helpless fury. If only he could move, he'd wipe that smug smile off her face.

Casually stepping over him, she grabbed the damaged saddle and a few other pieces of tack before leaving, pulling the metal door closed behind her. Dearg recognized the *click* of a padlock being thrown in place, and icy panic washed over him. Gasping for air, he knew Emily was in danger, and there was nothing he could do to save her.

Chapter Thirty-Seven

"Try calling him again. Maybe he butt dialed you," Lottie snapped. "Where is he with that armband?"

He'd rather eat glass than admit to being worried about Dearg McGregor, but his gut told him something was wrong. "I did. Twice. Nothing happens. It doesn't even go to voice mail, it just rings."

"Try Emily's phone," she suggested. "She left it in the tack room." At that moment, Kate sashayed toward them with Reese fully tacked up, booted up, and ready to go. "Kate, did you see Dearg at the barn?"

Kate handed her the armband. "He gave this to me and then strutted off with two women from the next barn aisle over."

Lottie grunted as she snatched the plastic armband from Kate and marched over to give it to Darian.

Not for a second did Justin believe that McGregor would walk away from their battle over Emily so easily. Stepping a short distance away, he called Emily's cell phone.

****

The trilling of an old-fashioned phone ring confused Dearg, rousing him from his foggy haze. He remembered a saying about bells and angels getting their wings, but this can't be right. It's not even a proper bell. Something in his brain clicked, and he realized it was the ring of Emily's mobile. He crawled across the floor toward the sound, pushing the agony to a separate compartment where he would deal with it later, like he always did. He was halfway there when the phone stopped ringing.

"Shite." The word screamed in his brain but came out as a gurgling wheeze. Frothy blood oozed out of the corner of his mouth.

That can't be good, he thought sardonically. The ringing phone was his and Emily's only hope, so he continued to crawl toward it. Once he retrieved the device, he thanked God she'd opted to leave it unlocked. He scrolled through her call log and tapped on the missed call, almost weeping at Justin's curt greeting.

"Don't let Emily get on the horse," he whispered, the effort costing him more air than he could afford. Black dots swam in front of his eyes, but he gritted his teeth against the dizziness, refusing to pass out. "Kate cut the billets."

"What?" Justin asked. "I can barely hear you, you need to speak louder."

Nae jobby, he thought and coughed up a gob of bloody phlegm. He pulled himself upright, hoping it would make breathing easier, but a cry of agony stole what little air he had left. Ignoring the pain and the wheezing, he breathed in as deeply as possible for one last try.

"Tell Em to check her billets."

Shock was setting in as a blanket of icy chill settled over him. His hand shook, and he dropped the phone. His eyelids drooped as he prayed his message had gotten through.

****

"Right out of stride, perfect," Lottie shouted. "Emily, this time let me see you move him up to it."

She may be a last-minute substitute for the missing McGregor, but Justin thought she was doing pretty well. He came up next to her and asked, "What's a billet?"

"They're what you buckle the girth into, they keep the saddle on." Her brows furrowed, suspicion written all over her face. "Why? What's wrong?"

Before he could answer, there was a sudden outcry from a few feet away. He turned toward the commotion and saw Kate grab a teenager, then toss him off his minibike. She revved the bike and headed toward the barn. Dearg had gasped out a warning about her on the phone, but it wasn't until he remembered the hat she was wearing, it all made sense. The cartoon character on Kate's hat was a bear on a rocking horse, just like the horse described to Libby Case. He hadn't noticed until now. "Son of a bitch, the horse was right all along," he muttered under his breath.

"Here," he called out as he tossed Lottie his badge. "Get Emily off that horse, the billet things have been cut. Then get the EMT to the tack room, tell him it's a police emergency. Now. Go!"

He watched long enough to make sure Lottie followed his orders before taking off after Kate.

****

"What was that about?" Emily asked, dodging traffic in the warm-up arena to make her way to the rail. She'd never seen Lottie flustered as she juggled to catch Justin's badge.

"I'm not sure but get off Reese, check your billets. I've got to get the EMTs to the barn. Dearg's hurt."

"What? How? What's happened?"

"Just get off the damn horse," Lottie yelped as she took off toward the ambulance and crew who were stationed by the side of the jump ring.

More irritated than alarmed, Emily checked her billets while still sitting in the saddle instead of getting off, figuring her girth must be loose. The first billet snapped free in her hand as soon as she tugged on it. A cold jolt of fear exploded in the pit of her stomach as she held the broken piece of leather. If Lottie hadn't warned her, she could have been killed on the course when her saddle came loose and sent her tumbling under her horse's hooves.

Remembering to detach the air vest this time, she jumped off Reese, her knees trembling as she unbuckled the second damaged billet and pulled the saddle off his back. She took unnecessary care putting the now useless piece of tack on the fence rail, using the time to regain her breath.

Angry shouts from spectators caught her attention. She turned to see Kate speeding off on a minibike, its furious owner stumbling to his feet and yelling at her. In a serene moment of perfect clarity, she realized it had been Kate all along. The video of her in the stall wasn't an accident. Pamela's hidden stall camera must have caught her doing something illegal, and Kate murdered her to keep her from telling anyone. That must have been what Pam's phone call with Karen Hyler was all about, to make sure she was ineligible for the High Poynt award.

All the other facts slid into place as easily as calculations before a jump. The distance to the jump, the horse's rhythm, how the shadows will affect the ride…on a good day she processed all the information and reacted in the blink of an eye. She hadn't had a day like that since her accident. During their last lesson, Pamela accused her of thinking too much, but she was wrong.

It wasn't the amount of information she processed. It was that she pondered it all too carefully instead of going with her gut and reacting. A mistake she wasn't about to make now, she decided as she flung herself onto Reese's bare back. Gripping his sides with her legs, she gave him a thumping kick, sending him galloping off after Kate.

The minibike was deceptively fast for its small size. Kate was already at the barn, with Justin trailing far behind on foot. There was no way Emily could catch her on horseback, but that didn't matter. Two fellow competitors, sick of Kate parking where she shouldn't, used their massive trucks to block her in.

Kate's downfall as a rider was her inflexibility. Once she made a plan, she stuck to it even if it wasn't working. Emily headed across the open field, fueled by the certainty Kate would be flummoxed when she saw her car was blocked in. Rather than steal another, she'd stick to her plan, turn the bike around and head straight toward the road. As if on cue, Kate appeared, speeding away from the barns down the driveway toward the road and freedom.

The private drive was a long, swooping curve of asphalt running along the cross-country course. If she rode across the course while Kate predictably stuck to the pavement, she could catch her before the minibike hit the road. The only thing standing between Emily and Kate was the same coffin combination that nearly killed her once before. She slowed Reese's pace for a moment.

Reese answered by wagging his big head and tugging on the reins. Locked on the jump, he wanted to keep going. "Seriously?" She took a deep, calming breath. "Okay big guy, let's do this." The horse picked up the gallop in reply. She willed herself to relax and move with him rather than brace against his enormous stride. Dead ahead was the log, ditch, and larger log of the coffin combination. Panic threatened to overwhelm her. They were moving way too fast, that's what her mistake was before.

Clutching handfuls of mane, she shook off the memory, sat up tall to balance the big horse, and kicked on. Reese sailed over the log, collected himself down the small slope, and easily cleared the ditch. Time seemed to stop as they approached the massive log at the top of the hill. The feel, the sound, even the taste of her fall closed in. Emily fought the urge to close her eyes and sat taller, shoulder blades pressing together. She held her breath as she allowed the horse to go forward. He hesitated as he rocked back on his hind legs and then leaped over the fence in flawless form.

Stunned, Emily let out a "Woo-hoo!" She'd actually cleared it. Riding bareback. The sound of the approaching minibike brought her back to the task at hand. With just a turn of her head and a light touch to his side, she wheeled Reese around to charge at Kate, head on.

The shock on Kate's face turned to hatred as she steered the minibike directly at Reese. Resolute in her purpose, Emily unbuckled her helmet and gripped it by the strap in her right hand. Realizing too late what was about to happen, all Kate could do was stare open-mouthed as Emily moved Reese out of the bike's path and swung her arm, smashing the helmet squarely into her doughy face.

The helmet made a sickening crack as it connected with flesh and bone. Between the speed of the bike and the speed of the horse, the impact was enough to send Kate to the ground. Reese nimbly sidestepped the fallen minibike as Emily brought him to a halt.

Breathing hard through a bleeding nose, Kate staggered to her feet. "You bitch, you've ruined everything." She pulled a bloodstained knife out of her back pocket and lunged.

Emily jumped from the horse to tackle her, trapping the larger woman beneath her. Kate fought back, slashing at her with the knife. The blade sliced through her air vest and found the heavier cross-country vest below, taking a chunk out of both.

She saw her damaged vests and lost it. "Do you know how expensive these are?"

Before Kate could reply, she pummeled her, hitting her in the face over and over until a pair of powerful arms pulled her up and off her feet. She stopped swinging and caught her breath as the two of them stared at Kate's unconscious form.

Justin put Emily down as a crowd of people, including security, clamored toward them. She pushed herself away to face him. "Is this the part where I'm supposed to get weak in the knees and collapse in your arms?" She caught Reese who stood patiently nearby eating grass.

"Right now, all I want to do is kick some ass."

Chapter Thirty-Eight

The velvety darkness out here in the boonies made Dennis uneasy. He didn't trust any place so silent that crickets became the primary source of noise pollution.

"You promised me there'd be drunks dancing on the tables," he accused Justin as they traversed a field toward a huge, brightly lit tent. After an exhausting day trying to wrangle answers out of Kate Williams, he definitely needed a drink.

"Don't worry." Justin gestured with the giant blue bottle of gin in his hand. "The party is just getting started." He led the way past the food line and the dance floor to a table in the back.

"Look who I found prowling around when I went back to the barn to get the gin," he announced to Lottie, Emily, and Darian. It was an awkward moment as Dennis took the empty seat meant for Dearg.

Silence gripped them until Lottie took command. She snatched the bottle out of his hand and stashed it under the table. "Way to keep it on the down-low, copper," she chastised with a wry grimace, subtly swiveling her head to make sure no one else saw the gin. It was the right amount of Lottie to re-start the party mood.

Emily laughed and gave him a quick kiss. "What she means is thank you."

Dennis bowed to Emily. "Remind me never to piss

you off. Kate's face is a fucking mess. Two black eyes, at least one missing tooth, and a nose that doesn't point quite so far up in the air anymore. "

"What did she say, Detective Ames?" Darian slurped the last of what was clearly one too many drinks. "Why did she want to kill Emily?"

Bartending, Lottie *tsked* as she filled a red plastic cup and handed it to the cop. "Cut the poor man some slack. Maybe he needs a break. I know I would after a day of being stuck in a room with that cow."

Dennis accepted the drink gratefully, took a long pull, choked a little, and smiled. "A woman who knows how to make a cocktail." He toasted the older woman. "I think I'm in love."

"I'm glad to finally meet a man who appreciates my skills," she teased, casting an overly dramatic glance at Justin.

"There's not a lot I can tell you, except the suspect can be described in clinical terms as bat-shit crazy. She keeps talking about being rider of the year."

Lottie practically did a spit take. "Rider of the year? In her dreams."

"What can I say? She insists the people were out to get her, blah, blah, blah. But really it all came down to greed. She needed money, so she intentionally injured her horses and collected the insurance when they had to be destroyed. That's what was on the video she was so hot to get her hands on. Pamela's hidden camera caught her cracking the horse in the leg. She figured out Kate's scheme and was about to blow the whistle on her. Ridley found out and tried to blackmail her, so he had to go as well."

"But why Ginger?" Lottie asked.

"She claims Ginger stole the love of her life. We reached out to the boyfriend to check out her story. Turns out he has no idea who Kate is."

Puzzled, Emily chewed on her lower lip. "I'm sorry about poor Ginger, but I still don't get it. I understand why Kate broke into the office that night to search for the thumb drive and plant the forged Hy Poynt nomination. But why come after me? I didn't know anything about her schemes."

He swirled his drink for a moment, pondering how much to tell her. "She pretty much blames you for everything. Claims you stole McGregor and his endorsement for this Hy Poynt thing. She's even miffed you came between her and this hunk of burning love," he said as he jerked his thumb toward Justin. "Like I said, crazy bitch." He took another sip of his drink and let out an appreciative groan. "I'm gonna need food before I get sloshed on one drink."

He started to push to his feet, but Emily sprang up first. "I'll get dinner for you. I need more chicken myself. I'm starved." With a quick peck on Justin's cheek, she all but skipped back to the buffet table.

Dennis shook his head and laughed. "She's sure in a great mood for somebody who almost got killed today."

"Could have something to do with catching a killer single-handedly," Justin boasted. "But probably because she rode a great cross-country round. It took some talking, but they let her run the course after Kate was hauled away, and she had a blast."

"She was amazing," Lottie bragged. "One of only six riders who had a double clear round." Seeing Dennis's brow scrunch in confusion, she explained,

"She took every jump within the time allowed. And did it using borrowed gear."

"But the round didn't count for anything," Darian whined. "She took her horse on the course before her ride time. According to the rules, she was already eliminated."

Emily came back with plates full of food for herself and Dennis, cheerfully oblivious to the conversation as she sat down, leaned against Justin, and smiled. As happy as he was for his friend, Dennis couldn't help but feel a pang of envy.

"You know what the best thing is?" Lottie grinned mischievously. "All those rats who jumped ship to train with Kate are going to have to come crawling back. Won't they be surprised to find their training fees have doubled?"

****

Someone at the front of the tent clinked a fork repeatedly on the side of the cheap glassware. The rowdy bunch of riders and guests quieted like a room full of children waiting for Sunday school to start. Justin raised his head, curious about who commanded such sudden obedience in the unruly crowd.

He recognized Karen Hyler, the sponsor of the Hy Poynt Award, standing beside her wheelchair-bound husband and understood the anticipation-filled silence. "First, I want to thank you all for riding in this as well as all the other Hy Poynt sponsored shows. As you know, money from the shows goes to the Hy Poynt Scholarship to support a local rider who has the talent, but not the financial means, to compete on the international level. In other words, the complete opposite of me."

Her self-deprecating humor earned some twitters and a few guffaws, but to him, they all sounded a bit forced.

"So, on to the business of the evening, announcing the winner of this year's Hy Poynt Scholarship. Dearg McGregor was supposed to be the one making this announcement and, although we miss him, I'm pleased to say he's doing well and will be out of the hospital soon. He's already giving the nurses a hard time and demanding a 'wee dram'." She raised her glass in a toast. "To Dearg, speedy recovery, my friend."

While eventers always seemed eager to drink to anything, Justin noticed this was a solemn toast as the entire crowd raised a glass of whatever they were drinking and murmured, "To Dearg," in agreement. Emily told him earlier they all accept danger as part of the sport, but not at the hands of a fellow rider. This attack hit them hard.

"And now," Karen continued, "on to announcing this year's winner. Because this scholarship is intended to help talented riders with limited resources, it's not unusual for past winners to have a sparse show record. Owning a winner is expensive enough, showing one takes thousands of dollars every year. That's why I rely on you, the professional riders, to nominate people who might otherwise go unnoticed. While some of you continue year after year to nominate yourself— Michael," she muttered under her breath, earning sincere laughter this time as the guilty party stood up and took a bow. "Most of you put serious thought and consideration into this process. For that, I thank you.

"Frankly, this year, there were no dark horse candidates that got me excited. Then, Dearg called me to tell me about the potential he saw in a young lady who he felt deserved the scholarship despite the fact she hasn't ridden, nonetheless showed, in several months. His passion was enough to convince me, and I'm sure you'll all agree after today, no one deserves this scholarship more than Emily Conners."

Emily sat welded to her chair, her mouth pumping open and closed like a guppy gasping for air, until the crowd demanded she stand up and say something. Justin wanted to pull her to her feet and drag her to the microphone, but this was her moment, so he waited like everyone else.

Finally, after an abrupt shove from Lottie, she rose shakily to her feet and made her way to Karen Hyler and the microphone. "This, ah," she stammered, her voice slowly growing from a whisper, "this is unexpected. Thank you, Karen, for this incredible opportunity. I won't let you down."

She stared at the microphone for so long a smattering of applause started before she raised her hand to stave it off. With a gulp of air, she rushed on. "I've struggled with an addiction to painkillers ever since my fall six months ago."

Justin's heart pounded in his chest, grasping how hard this was for her. "I've only recently been able to overcome that addiction thanks to some very special people who were brave enough to tell me what an ass I was. I encourage all of you to follow their lead. If someone you know has a problem, don't stand by and watch them self-destruct. They'll be pissed as hell at first, but in the long run, they'll be grateful you cared enough to speak up."

The stunned crowd answered back with polite

applause at first, but to Justin's surprise, it grew in intensity to an enthusiastic roar. Emily was shocked as several people came up and shook her hand, offering congratulations and support.

He glanced over and saw Lottie wipe a tear from her eye. "Tell anyone you saw that, and you die," she whispered in his ear.

He knew her bark was far worse than her bite. Probably.

****

The DJ must have decided enough was enough and started blaring his music, clearing the dance floor of well-wishers and leaving a few brave souls to bob and weave spastically to the music. When Emily snaked her way through them back to the table, Justin stood and held her close. "Do you have any idea how proud I am of you right now?"

Before she had a chance to answer, the DJ put on an all too familiar K-pop tune. She laughed and dragged him out to the dance floor. "Come on, they're playing our song."

He accepted her challenge, as graceful and sexy in his jeans and t-shirt as he was in a tux. Inspired, more partygoers joined them on the dance floor, and in moments they were surrounded by a forest of flailing elbows and knees. With a lusty gleam in her eye, she beckoned to him, and they waded through the melee to the quiet darkness outside beyond the tent's glow.

Wrapping his arms around her waist, he drew her close. As his lips hovered over their mark, she asked, "Is it true what Dearg said this morning? You only want what you can't have?"

Caught mid-kiss, he blinked. He studied her

expression, but found no clue there as to how much trouble he was in. "Does this mean I'm not getting lucky tonight?"

She laughed. "Oh, there will be sex tonight, don't even try to get out of it. No, I'm not worried. We'll see who has whom." She smiled, running her hand through Justin's thick hair.

"Um, I think who has who is more correct—"

"Justin," she interrupted, pulling him closer, "shut up and kiss me."

Their lips met, but what started out as a tender kiss melted into a hunger neither of them could stop if they wanted to. Finally, he forced himself out of the embrace. "McGregor was right about one thing. I don't have a very good track record when it comes to relationships. I don't want to hurt you."

"Hey," she said as she smiled at him, "there are no guarantees in life. I may turn around tomorrow and break your heart. Who knows? The only thing I'm sure of is I used pills for too long to avoid feeling anything." She grabbed his face with both hands now, running her thumbs along his strong jawline. "I'd rather face a lifetime of heartache than one more moment of being numb. What about you? Are you ready to take that chance?"

Justin pulled her against his body, crushing her to him, and then lowered them down into the rosemary-scented field, giving her his unspoken answer.

A word about the author...

A once and hopefully future eventer, Marla White happily hung out in the lowest levels of the sport drinking gin and tonics.

She started her career as a storyteller by drawing on the TV screen to help Winky Dink get out of mortal danger. It was a thing back then and earned her the spanking of her life. Deterred by the negative feedback, she decided to be a park ranger until a miserable camping trip made her realize it was really a TV show about park rangers she liked and promptly switched majors.

In Los Angeles, her first job was working for the producers of "A League of Their Own" but no, the character of Marla is not named after her. Since then, she's developed and sold several television movies and series. She's also been bossed around by several cats and a few horses.

http://marlaawhiteauthorpage.wordpress.com/

A word from the author

We are facing an opioid epidemic today that last year took over 100,000 lives, shattering the loved ones they left behind. This isn't an issue that only affects people who abuse drugs. Roughly one in twenty adults in the U.S. has taken a prescription opiate that are more dangerous than they know. In 2012, the sport of eventing lost one of its truly great stars to an accidental overdose from a combination of prescribed drugs, including oxycodone. The situation on a nation-wide level has only gotten worse since then.

If you or someone you love is struggling with opioids, you can call the National Council on Alcoholism and Drug Dependence at 1-800-622-2255. It has locations across the country and can refer you to a local facility as well as offer additional resources.